UNDER A RAGING SKY

To camp under a raging sky with a wild moon rising—that was Patrick Sillitoe's dream. An orphaned, raw young Englishman in search of the untamed Africa of the cinema screen and *King Solomon's Mines*, he found himself trapped as a menial clerk in a huge company in Salisbury—his romantic dream abandoned for love of the beautiful, rich Judith. But then he met a drunken, wild-looking, raggedly-dressed old man who hypnotised Patrick into longing for the touch of gold ... and he followed the old man's lead through the wild veld, to the haunted pools of the Ruenya, the River of Gold.

UNDER A RAGING SKY

Daniel Carney

A Lythway Book

CHIVERS PRESS
BATH

First published 1980
by
Corgi Books, a division of
Transworld Publishers Ltd
This Large Print edition published by
Chivers Press
by arrangement with
Transworld Publishers Ltd
and in the U.S.A. with St. Martin's Press Inc
1983

ISBN 0 85119 917 8

British Library Cataloguing in Publication Data

Carney, Daniel
    Under a raging sky.—Large print ed.
    —(A Lythway book)
    I. Title
    823′.914[F]   PR6053.A687

    ISBN 0–85119–917–8

To Norman and Rosemary
and
For Sally

*Beyond these last blue mountains lie
the golden days and dusty sunsets
of one man's dream*

UNDER A RAGING SKY

CHAPTER ONE

'SILLITOE,' a voice called across the vast open-plan office.

'Anybody here called Sillitoe?'

I stood up, the legs of my chair scraping loudly on the floor.

'Telephone,' the man called, waving the receiver in my direction.

I made my way over to him, weaving in between the uniform rows of desks, and took the receiver.

'Sillitoe speaking,' I said formally.

'I love you,' a warm voice said. 'I really love you, Patrick.'

It was Judith and she had a way about her that made me feel as though I'd just swallowed sunshine. I became self-conscious standing there before the sea of grey, faceless people who filled the office and I turned my back on them.

'I love you too,' I answered softly.

'Will you marry me?' she asked, knowing the answer.

'One week from today,' I confirmed.

She chuckled. It was a good sound. 'In that case, I'll pick you up. What time do you finish?'

I glanced at the clock. 'Thirty-four minutes to

go,' I said, and I heard Judith laugh. Once I had been the kind of happy-go-lucky man who took no account of time and it used to infuriate her. But now, after three months of working in this vast, soulless hall, I watched the clock all day and knew time to the minute.

'I'll be waiting for you outside,' Judith said. 'I'm glad that you're marrying me,' she added breathlessly. 'I love you, Patrick. You make me feel happy all over. I wanted you to know.'

'I'll look for you at five o'clock,' I said softly, ending the conversation, and put the receiver down. Then I started the long walk back to my place.

The Head of Buying looked up as I skirted his desk, his narrow face and balding skull glinting in the strip light. 'Sillitoe,' he said, his cold voice of disapproval carrying over the other men in his department. 'Staff are not encouraged to receive personal calls. You should know that by now. Next time kindly inform your caller accordingly.'

I walked over to my seat and pulled up my chair beside an assistant buyer. He was a hunched, ferret-faced man with dandruff on his shoulders, and when he saw the expression on my face he nudged me, marvelling at my courage for even taking the call. 'Don't worry,' he whispered sympathetically. 'It's not so bad when you get used to it. Look at me—been here twenty years. Just five more years to go for my

2

pension—and I've seen some changes.' His lips barely moved as he pretended to work, warming to an old familiar theme. 'I've watched this Company grow from next to nothing,' he said proudly.

Over the next few minutes he traced his working life for me in the path of the desks behind him. In twenty years he had moved eighteen feet across that hall. And if he was promoted before retirement, he could expect to move just another six feet to the next-door desk. Twenty-four feet in twenty-five years of service. Less than a foot a year. He seemed content, but when I worked it out I was filled with panic and sadness and fear for my own future.

Three months ago I had joined this, one of the largest, most powerful companies in Rhodesia, as a trainee assistant in the Marketing Department. And as part of my training I was visiting the various departments. All my colleagues in Marketing were bright young men with university degrees—except me. I had no qualifications in commerce and my position in the Company had been secured by influence. For, as my future mother-in-law had pointed out, a young man only recently arrived from England with two failed, hare-brained ventures already behind him could offer little future for her daughter. Her husband was a prominent industrialist. And when she realised that we were determined to get married and could do

3

nothing to stop us, she had her husband find me this job and blackmailed me into settling for a responsible, secure future. I should have been grateful, but I wasn't. I hadn't come all the way out to Africa to push a pen from behind a desk. If I'd wanted that sort of life I'd have stayed in England.

I was an only child—an orphan, though I didn't see myself as that for I had Aunt Amelia. My father died on the Normandy beaches and my mother died shortly after the War. I was left in holiday homes for a time while people wondered what to do with me. There weren't many of us Sillitoes left—two world wars had seen to that. Then Aunt Amelia, my father's eldest sister, a distant, forbidding figure and a spinster to the core, collected me and took me home.

I was so damn glad that somebody wanted me that I was up and ready at six o'clock that morning waiting for her to arrive, a little boy with a cardboard suitcase hopping up and down with excitement. But Aunt Amelia would allow no unseemly displays of emotion. We, she announced, were the last of the Sillitoes, and as she said it, she set her jaw. She knew nothing about bringing up a child, but she possessed unlimited courage, a Victorian sense of right, and she did her best to make a home for me.

We lived in the manor house at the edge of what had once been the family estate, now owned and farmed by a business combine. There was no money for servants, hardly enough even to feed ourselves. The house was impossible to heat or keep clean and we camped in just a few of the rooms. Even so, Aunt Amelia insisted on maintaining standards. We changed into what passed for formal clothes each evening and ate our frugal supper across a long polished table. A small boy and a ramrod-stiff lady surrounded by shadowy suits of armour and blank gaps on the walls where the more valuable portraits had been sold off.

In the holidays, rather than allow me to get into mischief, Aunt Amelia arranged for me to work in the fields with the farm labourers—but there was a difference. At the age of eight I remember standing blushing bright scarlet in a dung cart dressed from head to foot in white, suffering the hurt and humiliation of taunts flung at me by the other boys. I ran home crying, pleading to be allowed to change. But Aunt Amelia was unmoved. She washed out my clothes and pressed them that night ready for the next day. 'You're a Sillitoe,' she said firmly, her jaw set. 'You are different. You're the last of your breed, the last male in what was once a proud old county family.' I fought my way round the fields the next day and returned home covered in blood, but Aunt Amelia would not relent.

Aunt Amelia trained me to succeed. I was her

hope for the future. Her ambition was that one day I would go forth and re-build the family fortune. To this end she brought me up with an iron hand, allowing me no quarter.

She managed to visit my school only once. It was a long journey and the fees took up nearly all her money. I had been chosen to play rugby for the school and she took her place proudly with the other parents on the touchline. At a late stage in the game the opposing scrum broke through and came pounding down the field in a forward rush. Because my Aunt was watching, and with my heart bursting, I flung myself at the ball in a desperate attempt to save it. The ball was booted out of my arms and the scrum trampled right over me without stopping. I was left a huddled, flattened figure, weakly spitting out blood and mud that had collected in my mouth.

Aunt Amelia understood little about the game of rugby—all she knew was that I had lost the ball and she hated any kind of failure, especially when it concerned me. 'Coward!' she yelled, and the word came whipping clean across the rugby field. 'Get up and fight!' Then she turned on her heel and stalked off towards the tea tent.

The Games Master thought I was hurt, but it was just that my eyes were full of tears as I watched her leave. 'Well done, young Sillitoe,' he said kindly, helping me up. 'That was a very plucky attempt.' But he didn't understand. The only person in the world who I wanted to impress was Aunt Amelia. For all her fierceness, I knew that she loved me—and I loved her too, very much.

Aunt Amelia became ill. She fought off the disease trying to see me through the last of my schooling and she was in bed when I went to say goodbye to her prior to returning for the final term. I think we both knew that we would never see each other again. It was a sad parting and as I walked to the door she put her bony hands in front of her face so that I wouldn't see her cry. I wanted to turn back and put my arms around her frail, wasted figure to comfort her, but she wouldn't let me. Even in dying she was embarrassed by any outward display of emotion. 'Just you see that I'm proud of you,' she demanded fiercely.

I buried Aunt Amelia amongst the other family graves then drifted around London for a while, a restless spirit wondering what to do next. I thought of a career in the City with the banks or business houses, but nothing they offered appealed to me. 'Get out of England,' Aunt Amelia had advised, 'there's nothing for you here.' She had left me with a small inheritance. I decided that my future lay in Africa and, remembering tales of Prester John and King Solomon's mines, I headed for Rhodesia.

CHAPTER TWO

THE late afternoon sunlight slanted on to the steps as I stood searching for Judith. Then I saw her waving to attract my attention. She had parked my battered old Morgan Four-plus-Four in the Directors' car park, an area where privilege was so jealously guarded that the ground was almost holy. The low green car with leather straps to hold down the bonnet looked incongruous among the sleek limousines. I hurried down the steps hoping to get her out of there before we were recognized.

The door did not open and I leapt over it into the passenger seat. Judith had come straight from ballet class. She leaned over and kissed me warmly. As she did so, her coat fell open revealing a black leotard which was all she was wearing underneath. 'Get out of here,' I said nervously. 'Don't you know where you've parked?' She grinned at me and gunned the engine, threw the gear stick into reverse and the car shot backwards, cutting across the smooth gliding path of the Chairman's Rolls-Royce. His black chauffeur braked violently, missing us by inches and ended up sprawled over the steering wheel with his hat over his eyes.

I watched in silent horror, mentally composing my parting speech to Personnel, as

Judith calmly engaged first and negotiated a path around the stranded Rolls. As she passed she waved a cheerful apology to the Chairman, whose startled face was just appearing above the passenger seat window ledge.

'Sorry Uncle Charles,' she called.

'Uncle Charles!' I muttered. 'I didn't know you knew him that well.'

'He's my Godfather,' Judith replied. 'It's a small town and I told you I was well connected. You keep in with me, young man,' she said with a mischievous smile, 'and you'll go far.' With that she let the Morgan go in a cloud of burnt rubber.

We tore through the afternoon traffic, recklessly weaving in and out of the lanes. Judith had her own car, but she preferred to use mine, even though she had to sit on the tool box, and measure the fuel in the petrol tank with a dip stick. She loved the excitement of the wind in her hair, the throb of the engine, and the protesting cry of the tyres as she took the Morgan hard through a corner. But more than that she knew that she was scaring the hell out of me. I sank lower and lower into my seat. My nerves weren't what they used to be. 'Slower,' I said, 'drive slower.' She dropped speed obediently, but I caught her mocking grin. She was a proud, spoilt, wilful woman with a captivating smile, slim-hipped, full-figured, with a sex appeal about her that could curl a

9

man's toes at twenty yards. And I loved her.

We had met less than a year ago, when I was twenty and she was just nineteen. Judith had trained for a career with the ballet in England. She had been talented and dedicated enough to reach the top, but she grew too tall. It took some time for her to master her disappointment. She returned to Rhodesia shortly after I arrived and now she taught others to dance.

I had gone into business in Rhodesia, certain of making my fortune. My first venture involved running a game-viewing boat up the Zambezi River from the Victoria Falls. It was fun but competition from the bigger companies made the venture financially unsuccessful. So a partner and I formed an overland safari company which set out to blaze an adventure trail across Africa. On the third trip across the continent corrupt Congolese officials confiscated our Land-Rovers, stranding the tourists in the bush. The Company folded, wiping out the last of my small inheritance.

During this time I met Judith and right from the start it was a fierce, passionate, burning love. We went everywhere together. We couldn't take our hands off each other, couldn't bear to be parted for a moment. There was a jealousy and hurt and soaring happiness. We consumed each other as though we formed part of a candle and were terrified of the flame dying. In the beginning nothing seemed to matter beyond each one's love for the other. Then we decided to get married. We were both too young and unready, but we were not going to listen to anyone who told us that.

Judith was practical enough to realize that we had, at least, to attempt to settle down and she was ready, for her part, to try to make a home. I was the problem. I wanted to marry her, to be with her, but I still had dreams of trying to make my fortune. And we were to be married a week from today.

The car slowed as we entered Salisbury, the capital city. On the horizon a great red sun was setting, cooling the day, washing the sky with soft, glowing colour. We turned north and headed with the traffic out into the suburbs.

Judith reached out and touched my hand, her eyes showing her concern as she read my face.

'Was your day that bad?' she asked.

I nodded. 'I hate that office,' I said. 'Sometimes when I sit in that bloody great hall with all those people round me I feel as though I'm drowning. Do you know that most of the men in my age group have already worked out their pension and insurance benefits for their date of retirement? And the notice board is full of messages from Personnel. "Company Holiday Cottages available for staff grades four to eight—book early to avoid disappointment!" I don't want to spend my life just trying to sell another bar of soap.'

11

'It's not that bad,' Judith said angrily. 'You know it isn't. You've got to start somewhere. You can't just keep drifting. Give it a chance, Patrick,' she pleaded. 'You'll make it. Don't back out on me now.'

I didn't want to back out on her—nothing was further from my mind. But I was restless. I searched for the words that would make her understand me. Then I kept my peace. I had left it too late now. But my thoughts went back to that office and I wondered which desk I'd fill when I was old and ready to retire. And that thought filled me with desperation.

Judith lived with her family in one of the better suburbs of Salisbury. She skidded through the gates, scattering gravel over the lawns and drew up before a rambling colonial-style house. I looked around at the signs of unspoken wealth that surrounded us—the sweeping gardens and, at the back, the stables and paddocks for Judith's horses. With my present prospects, I decided ruefully, there was little chance of my keeping her in the manner to which she had been accustomed. But Judith did not seem to mind. She had great faith in me.

Her father was a retiring man. But her mother was a vibrant, strong-willed woman who ruthlessly dominated her family with a mixture of charm, low cunning and downright emotional blackmail. She worshipped success and loathed me. I could take that kind of treatment from

12

Aunt Amelia, but I was damned if I was going to start all over again with her. We were at loggerheads from the moment we met. However, Judith was as strong-willed as her mother and she managed to arrange an uneasy truce between us for the duration of the wedding.

Judith got out of the car. 'See you for supper,' she said. 'Please don't be late, you know my mother.' She tried to say it lightly, but the implied warning was clear. We were to discuss the arrangements for the wedding. It was to be held in the evening by candle-light and the guest list ran into hundreds. Judith's mother was ensuring that this was going to be the social occasion of the year and she resented me and each friend that I had invited, claiming they lowered the tone.

Judith saw the look on my face, but she didn't want to fight any more. Her hand reached out and ruffled my hair in a subconscious gesture of ownership. She bent down and kissed me, then stood and watched me drive out of sight.

CHAPTER THREE

I WAS feeling depressed as I drove home to change for supper. I glanced at my watch and decided there was time enough for a quick drink. Near my cottage was a rough, hard-drinking bar. I had never been there before, but it seemed the sort of place to suit my mood and I pulled up outside.

I walked through the doors. The bar was packed, filled with noise and laughter. Cigarette smoke hung like a mist in the air. Most of the men there were farmers, hard-muscled, sunburnt men dressed in open-necked shirts and shorts. They had come to town for the weekend and they were letting off steam as though there was no tomorrow. A general mood of wildness was growing. It only needed one spark and the whole place would erupt.

I elbowed my way through the crowd to the bar and caught the barman's eye. As I did so I stepped over the legs of a man on the floor, his head propped up against the bar rail and his hat down over his eyes.

'Buy you a drink,' I said cautiously to the barman as he took my order. The figure at my feet suddenly came to life and clawed his way up the bar.

'Thank you,' he said, lurching unsteadily

towards me. 'I'll have a double of whatever you're having. Bless you for offering, boy,' he said desperately. 'I was dying of thirst down there.'

As he came into the light I found myself staring into the bloodshot eyes of a wild-looking, raggedly-dressed old man. He was short-legged and barrel-chested and it was difficult to tell his age, but I judged him to be in his early sixties. He clung to the counter for all he was worth and watched the barman fill his glass. Every time the barman hesitated, the old man nodded him impatiently on until the glass was almost full, then he snatched it up and swallowed the contents in one gulp.

His eyes glazed and he staggered slightly as the burning alcohol hit his belly. Then the old man shook himself all over, like a dog coming out of water, and steadied up.

'Thank you, boy,' he said, pretending he had heard me offer another round. 'Mine's the same again'—and he thrust his glass at the barman.

I was stunned. 'Where in the hell did he come from?' I asked the barman.

The barman shrugged. 'Claims he's a prospector come to town to bury his partner. Drifted in here a couple of days ago and he's been on a drunk ever since. When the bar closes we sweep him out with the rest of the rubbish, but then he just sleeps on the steps.' The old man ignored us. He was hungrily watching the

15

barman pour. 'In the good old days of this country,' he said indignantly, 'when a man ordered himself a drink they gave him a bottle and a glass and left him alone. They didn't have some asshole in a white jacket measing his tot.'

'He's got no money left,' the barman warned me. 'You paying for this lot or do I throw him out?'

The old man leaned across the counter and fixed the barman with a bleary eye. 'My old partner Mouldy Duncan came across a barman like you once,' he said menacingly. 'That was down Gwanda way. He came in all hot and dusty from prospecting and the barman poured him a miserable little tot and took the bottle way. Well old Mouldy was so offended that he upped with his gun—like a small cannon it was—and blasted off two shots. The first nicked the barman's ear and the second blew down half the wall behind him. And do you know what the barman did?' The old man paused to give his words effect. 'He rushed back with the bottle, put it down before old Mouldy, then fainted dead away.' The two of them were ready to trade punches and I pushed in between them.

'I'll pay,' I said. 'I'll pay.'

The barman retreated, but I noticed that he left the bottle behind. The old man chuckled, then he turned to me offering the bottle as though he owned the place. 'Pour yourself a drink, boy,' he said.

16

I had come there in a different mood, to drink and think and be alone, but there was something strangely attractive about that wild old man— something in his face that drew me to him like a magnet. Maybe it was because his skin was burnt by the wind and the sun and the expression in his eyes told of all the wild, free living that he'd done. His voice was rough and brandy-flavoured, his long, unkempt hair going white, as was the week-old stubble that showed on his cheeks and chin. And yet etched into that craggy face were crinkled lines of humour—and I had a strong feeling about that old man that, though he was down, he still had something going for him. But watching him cling on to the bar I couldn't for the life of me figure out what it was.

'I'm sorry about your partner,' I said.

'Who?' the old man asked, inclining his head to hear better.

'Your partner,' I said more loudly. 'You said he died. I'm sorry.'

'Don't be. Old Mouldy Duncan was my partner for forty years,' the old man said, working himself up into a fury. 'I knew that bastard so well I could put him together with plasticine. And I'm telling you, he was a rascal and a rogue, and he was so crooked he had to sleep curled up in bed like a cork-screw. He stole our last month's gold smelt and came back to camp all liquored up and then he drank

17

another two bottles. Next morning he had the screaming rats running loose in his head. Serve him right, the bastard! It was the worst attack I'd ever know him have. I tied him to his bed so's he couldn't hurt himself, but it was no good. Mouldy was getting too old for that sort of thing and within three days he died.

'I would have buried him out in the bush like he'd have wanted. But he's got a prissy-faced daughter come out from England and she wants him buried in a proper cemetery. God knows why, as she's not the sort to visit his grave and no one else will. But I'll say this for her: when I brought her Mouldy's possessions—except for his boots, I always did admire his boots—and she saw that all he had was his spectacles and the medals he had won in the war, she cried for him. And I bet she's the only person who ever cried for old Mouldy.

'With him gone and the others going, I'm getting to be the last of my breed,' the old man said, turning back to the bottle, his mood suddenly becoming lonely and sad. He raised his glass to his lips but in the press around the bar someone nudged him and half the liquor got lost in his beard. The old man turned in a fury. 'Bloody farmers!' he said. 'I never could abide drinking near farmers. They're vultures in this country. They even drink on credit. You there,' he said, 'give room to a miner who pays cash for his liquor.'

'Who said that?' asked a giant of a man with a battered fighter's face.

'I did,' the old man replied, bristling. 'I tell you, boy,' he said loudly to me, 'we miners opened up this country. We fought the wars, built the roads and dammed the water. Then when it was nice and safe along came the bloody farmers and scratched at the land. We've even got a government of farmers now and look what a mess they're making, passing laws left, right and centre and buggering up the country.'

Other farmers were gathering menacingly behind the big man with the fighter's face.

'I'll tell you something, old man,' the fighter said. 'If you weren't so old I'd thump the daylights out of you.'

'You and whose army?' the old man jeered.

'Shut up, will you,' I whispered, but the old man took no notice of me.

'You know, I always said you could tell a miner by his smell,' a ferret-faced man at the fighter's side said, wrinkling up his nose. 'I'll bet the old bastard hasn't had his clothes off in a month. What do you say we give him a bath? There's water outside.'

'You with him?' another man asked me, checking on the opposition.

At a quick count I reckoned there were twenty against the two of us and we were about to get our heads beaten in. But I was committed—I couldn't back out on the old man now.

'I'm with him,' I confirmed weakly, cursing the old man under my breath.

The old man put his arm around my neck and bent my head with his over the bar for a hurried conference. 'Now boy,' he said, breathing brandy fumes all over me. 'I enjoy a fight as much as any man, but I reckon in this case we're outnumbered.' I nodded fervently. 'So you just follow me and do as I do,' the old man said.

With that he turned from the bar and raised his hands in a placating gesture. Taking the fighter completely off guard, he kneed him hard in the groin then, moving faster than I would have thought possible for a man half his age, he punched the man who had offered to bath him full in the face. In the confusion that followed I felt the pressure of the old man's hand on my shoulder. We went down on our hands and knees and scuttled through a forest of legs, heading flat-out for the door.

It took a moment for the others to recover and follow us, pushing their way violently through the throng. The old man came up against a beefy leg that wouldn't move for him. He chose a piece of sun-browned flesh between the calf-length socks and the edge of the shorts and sank his teeth into it. There came a howl of pain from above and a series of cracks as the bitten man struck out wildly at those around him.

It needed only that spark to start a riot. Fights

broke out all over the place. Our passage to the door became blocked by a barricade of milling legs as men punched each other and in his frustration the old man took to biting everything in sight, causing panic and confusion above him. The barman moved in to try to break up the fight. But he only lasted a minute before he fought his way over to the telephone and dialled. 'Police,' he said desperately, clutching a bitten thigh. 'Come quickly, there's murder going on here.'

The old man and I made it through the door on our hands and knees. The Morgan was parked just outside. I leapt into the driver's seat and started the engine. The old man jumped in beside me. He looked back to the bar-room from where, by the sounds of it, a small war had broken out and a gleam came into his eye. 'Bloody farmers!' he said triumphantly.

The windscreen was folded down across the bonnet and a warm wind buffeted our faces. The old man leaned back in his seat and let out a howl to a bright African moon that was riding clear of a bank of cloud. I knew just how he felt. His mood was infectious. I was exhilarated, flying high. He passed me the bottle. I took a long swig, then I changed down a gear and let the Morgan go.

'If you've nothing to do tonight,' the old man shouted above the noise of the slip-stream, 'what do you say to our going out and drinking

21

this whole town dry?'

'I'm with you,' I shouted, the alcohol beating in my brain, thinking: to hell with Judith's mother, 'I'm with you!'

The old man settled back in his seat. 'Lead on to the first bar, boy,' he said. 'And all I ask of you is that when I pass out, find me a safe place to sleep. Don't leave me lying in the gutter. I'll do the same for you.'

The Morgan had a souped-up TR3 engine and we were really travelling now. We drifted round a corner with all four wheels screeching in protest, then the old man sat bolt upright in horror. In front of us a row of lights and a barricade of vehicles completely blocked the road. We flashed past the Police Roadblock Ahead sign, but I was going too fast to stop. I thought I saw an opening and headed for it. The old man covered his face with his hands. At the last moment I saw that it, too, was blocked with chains and steel spikes. In desperation I braked and spun the Morgan. We went careering round and round, tyres screaming, lights flashing in a kaleidoscope of shrieking noise and colour. Somehow we ended up without a scratch half way up a steep bank.

I started to shake. There was a chill silence except for the hot engine ticking and the sound of running boots. Then the old man's head popped up from beneath the shelter of the dashboard. 'Boy,' he said hoarsely, as shattered as me, 'I thought we were goners then.' In gratitude he offered me a swig of his bottle.

The arresting officer knew me slightly and he neglected to notice the bottle. At Salisbury Central Police Station we were offered one telephone call each before being put in the cells. But the old man had no one to call and, having missed supper with Judith's mother, I felt it wiser not to try to explain what I was doing in a police station in the middle of the night.

CHAPTER FOUR

THE old man woke me as dawn was breaking, its cold, grey light seeping through the high-barred window of our cell.

'I've been thinking,' he said. 'You don't really want to get married. Not yet, you don't.'

He moved stiffly back to his side of the cell and slid down against the wall, pulling his blanket over him. His face was in shadow, but his eyes were bloodshot and they glowed in the gloom.

'Tell you what I'll do,' he said. 'I'll take you with me. I'm leaving today right after the funeral.'

The old man had been talking half the night and I badly needed to sleep. Already I could feel the steady drum-beat of pain in my mind that foretold a monumental hangover. But I wearily opened my eyes and pulled myself up against the wall. For the old man could tell a tale, all right. He could weave a spell. That man had the power to hypnotize me for as he spoke he could make me feel the warm sun on my shoulders, the smell of the bush in the dawn. More than that, he could make me feel the touch of gold until it itched in the palm of my hand.

'You ever see gold?' the old man asked, his eyes glowing, holding mine. 'You ever touched it? Free, fine gold washed fresh from a river? It's heavy in the palm of your hand and it's got a colour that warms all of you. It's a feeling that every man should have just once in his lifetime—to hold his own, free gold. Not some impure metal cooked up in a jeweller's shop and bent into a ring, but fine, pure, firm, native gold that a man found himself.' I remained silent. I was trying to act wary of him, but the old man was telling me what I wanted to hear. He was offering me the untamed Africa that I'd come all this way to find. Judith, I thought suddenly. Oh God, what about Judith? He was talking so much I'd forgotten all about her.

'It'll take us two months,' the old man said, reading my thoughts, 'maybe three. That's all the time we've got anyway with the rains coming on. Surely she'll wait for you that long— especially if she knows that you're going to make a fortune. And I'm telling you we will—

24

and all in gold, pure, native gold. Come with me, boy,' the old man urged huskily. 'There's more in you than growing old behind a desk. How long is it since you trekked in the wild bush, knowing that where you walk there's a chance that no man, white or black, has ever walked before? Knowing that what you see no man has ever seen before? How long is it since you've camped under a raging sky with a wild moon rising and a river swirling by your side? And you've felt free, really free?'

I thought of the office and my heart hungered to go with him.

'When you're out prospecting, you never feel poor like you do in a city. It costs you little or nothing to live, a bag of mealie meal, some salt, you shoot for the pot. But more than that, always over the next hill there's a chance of a strike, or over the hill beyond that—or the one after that. And you're never lonely because you've got the bush and there's a woman in the town ahead or the one you left in the town behind.'

The old man needed the money I'd saved for my wedding to buy equipment and he was working hard to get it. He could see me weakening. 'This is the last country where a man can go adventuring. Soon they'll pave the bush and there will be no place left for us. Now Mouldy and me had it all figured out,' he said. 'We were all set to go. Leastways that was

25

before the old bastard upped and drank all our money and died. I'll tell you again—here's how it goes.' He knelt on the floor of the cell and traced me a map on the stone. 'We follow the Mazoe River out of Salisbury, panning enough gold from the banks to pay our travelling expenses, heading for the north-east of Rhodesia until we get up beyond Shamva.' He made a mark on the stone. 'Then we cut across through Mtoko and into the Makaha Hills. The Ruenya River runs into the valley through the gold belt and on into Portuguese East Africa. That's how the river got its name—Ruenya, River of Gold. The Portuguese used to tax the Africans on their side of the border in gold. And the Africans used to pan the river for it. Many's the time I've seen them—the women going down weighed by a stone on their backs and a bucket in their hand, breathing through a reed between their teeth, dredging up sand from the bottom of a pool, while their men would sit on the banks and pan it. When a family had panned enough to fill a fair-sized porcupine quill they had enough to pay their taxes for a year—and it didn't take them long.

'While I was up there I met a Portugee—name of Reias. He was a trader buying gold off the tribesmen and he told me, before he died of snake bite, about the haunted pools. These are special pools bewitched by the spirits. The tribesmen won't touch them. Africans are a

26

suspicious bunch, even the best of them. Of course there's nothing wrong with the pools. Most likely what happened was that way back in time a hippo or crocodile took to living in the pools so the tribesmen avoided them. Over the years the stories built into superstitions and the witch-doctors made them forbidden. But think on it—the gold's lain there undisturbed and building each rainy season for all these years.' The old man leaned forward. 'There's a special pool I want to get to. It lies below a waterfall. The Africans call it *Nzimbo ya Dziwaguro*—the home of Dziwaguro. The tribesmen believe that their god lives in the deep water there. Reias saw it once and he reckoned there were patches of gold running pure in places but, of course, they wouldn't let him touch it. But with the trouble brewing there now, the Portuguese have moved the tribesmen away from there back into protected villages. So we can sneak in and out without anyone knowing. I'll recognize that pool anywhere from Reias' description. All we'll need is a few natives to help work the pumps and we're rich. What do you think of that, boy?' the old man asked moving back to his part of the cell.

'What about the Frelimo terrorists?' I asked cautiously. 'And the Portuguese Security Forces? We'll get shot to pieces if we start wandering about up there.'

'Makaha's wild country,' the old man

answered. 'Once I get amongst those hills, no one will ever find me. Besides, from what I hear the war's mostly moved north of the Ruenya again, now that the terrorists can't get into the protected villages and force the tribesmen to feed them. So it's just the odd Portuguese patrol that we'll have to duck.'

'How much do you think is in it for us?' I asked, wondering if I could get Judith to understand.

The old man thought for a moment. 'Most of it will be lying too deep for us to get at, but we should make upwards of thirty thousand each for two months' work. More, if the rains hold off and we can work longer. And all that you need to gamble is that four hundred dollars you've saved. After that,' the old man said expansively, 'well after that, if things work out right between us, I know a way we can turn that money into a fortune.'

'If you're so good at making money,' I asked suspiciously, 'why haven't you done it before?'

The old man looked at me, deeply hurt. 'I've made fortunes before,' he said, 'and lost them. But with me it was never the finding, it was the looking that was important. Money ties you down just like a woman does. You own either of them and you're carrying chains. Me, I'm free. And if you don't want to come, I'll go alone. I don't need you.' He turned away from me, pulling the blankets over his head.

28

'Who are you, anyway?' I asked. 'I don't even know your name.'

'I'm private,' the old man's muffled voice replied. 'That's who I am. I'm private.'

I sat in silence turning the offer over in my mind. Thirty thousand was more money than I could imagine, more money than I could ever hope to hold in cash during the whole of my working life if I stayed on in that office. Even ten thousand would be enough to get Judith and me started. I could build a fortune from that. I struggled with my conscience, but not for long. I was too excited—the old man had set my imagination on fire.

'All right,' I said, promising myself that I'd make it up to Judith. 'I'm coming with you.'

The old man allowed the corner of his blanket to slip a little. 'You sure?' he said. 'Because if I make a bargain with you, I don't want you backing out before we even start and hiding in your woman's skirts.'

'I told you,' I said enthusiastically, 'I'm in. Do we make the bargain now?'

The old man threw off his blanket and leaned forward. 'All right,' he said. 'You provide the capital to grub-stake us and buy the equipment we need. I provide transport, shelter and creature comforts, such as cooking pots and the like. We split whatever we make fifty-fifty. Agreed?'

'Agreed,' I said. And we gravely shook hands

29

in the shadowy light of the cell.

'Just one thing,' the old man warned. 'Boy, do you know what a partner is? What that word means between men out in the bush?' I nodded. 'Partners are bound together, no matter what happens, for the period of the venture. They can rely on each other for their lives—it's a closer state than marriage.' I was very earnest as I said that, very British—Kipling would have been proud of me.

The old man looked at me oddly. 'All right. For the purpose of this venture, we're partners,' he said gruffly. 'Look after me and don't cheat me by so much as one cent, and I'll do the same for you.'

CHAPTER FIVE

THAT morning in court we were charged with malicious injury to property and causing a breach of the peace. The magistrate fined us $50 each—I had to pay the old man's fine.

He collected his suitcase, climbed into the Morgan beside me, and we drove to my place to pack my belongings. At that time I was living in an isolated four-roomed cottage half hidden in the long grass of a mosquito-infested vlei, a little way out of town. Phillimon, my servant, appeared as I drew up. Our relationship, in fact, went deeper than that of master and servant. Phillimon was a year or two older than me, tall, loose-limbed with tribal scars slashed into his cheeks; he had a sleepy-eyed, ready smile that belied a good brain, courage, and a determination born out of poverty to succeed. He was a Matabele from the southern part of the country and he had left his job—herding his father's cattle in a dusty, arid, tribal trust land— to try to make a better life for himself in the city. He came to work as my cook/houseboy only because, as an African with little educational qualifications, he had found it impossible to obtain any other kind of work. But from the time we met and he had thrown in his lot with me, he let me know that he was expecting more than just to remain a house servant for the rest of his life. I could understand that and we got on well together.

'Pack,' I said. 'Take only what's necessary and leave the rest. We're going into the bush.'

I shaved and showered while Phillimon bundled my belongings into a suitcase. He was delighted to be on the move.

The car was loaded up and ready to go when the old man came on to the steps. He had done his best to clean himself up, and he was dressed in a worn, shiny-black, going-to-town suit that must have been cut twenty years ago and brown hob-nailed boots. There was something very sad, very vulnerable about him standing there with his battered suitcase by his side. Because, for all that he'd said about his partner, he had still taken the trouble to dress in his best for Mouldy Duncan's funeral.

I closed the door of the cottage and left the key where the agent could find it.

'You can't take him with you,' the old man said, nodding to the car where my dog had squeezed into the open boot beside Phillimon.

'Why not?' I asked.

'Because no matter how big that dog is, something's going to eat him before we get too far out in the backveld.'

I thought it over. My dog was an enormous lop-eared Rhodesian Ridgeback-cross-Alsatian. I allowed few things to get close to me, but when they did, I cared for them a great deal. I admit he wasn't good-looking, but then I thought he had more character than most people knew. I had brought him up from a puppy and I loved that dog as only a lonely man in a strange country can love and cherish a loyal companion. We stayed together even after I met Judith and it had taken her a while to get used to the idea that she was not only marrying me, but my dog as well. Phillimon had called him Simba after the lion and the courage that animal possessed— and the name stuck. There was no one I could trust to leave Simba with and he would die if I left him in a kennel.

'He comes with us,' I decided. 'I'll take care

of him.'

'All right,' the old man snorted angrily as he followed me down the steps. 'Be ignorant if you want to. But boy, I'm telling you, you are going to have enough trouble stopping *yourself* getting eaten in places where we're going.'

I stopped at a public phone booth and called Judith. Without explanation I asked her if she would meet me in town. I had been dreading the time when I would have to tell her that I was going. I had been putting it off for as long as I could. For a while I had even thought of just leaving her a note.

'You're mad,' the old man argued indignantly as I nosed the car into a bay outside the park and climbed out. 'What in the hell do you want to see her for? By now you should be long gone with no forwarding address.' I ignored him, though there was some truth in what he said. 'Hey!' the old man called after me. 'Could you stake me $5? There's a couple of things I want to buy.' I gave him the money, then made my way into the park. It was cool and green with borders of flowers, the sun screened by giant palm trees.

I kicked my heels for ten agonizing minutes before Judith arrived. She was white with anger, her eyes sparkling and her fists clenched. Any man, I decided, who claims he can admire a woman's beauty when she's truly angry with him must have nerves of steel. I had carefully planned a speech for her, but before I could

33

open my mouth she laid into me.

'Where were you last night?' she yelled. 'Where in the hell have you been? I nearly went out of my mind with worry.' She glanced around. 'What did you want to meet me in this place for?' she asked more quietly. 'Why didn't you just come home?'

'Judith,' I said. 'I want to postpone the wedding.'

She stared at me for a moment, the anger draining out of her, then her shoulders sagged and hurt tears swam in her eyes.

'Oh my God, Patrick,' she said desperately, 'you can't be serious. Not now, not one week before the wedding. You can't do it.'

I reached out to her, raised her face, made her look at me. 'Judith,' I said, 'I love you—you know that. There's never been any other woman but you. I'll marry you—I want to marry you. But there's somewhere I have to go first. I need the wedding to be put back.'

'How long?' Judith asked.

I could feel her getting over the shock, regaining control of herself. 'Three months, that's all. I'll be back here to marry you within three months. Surely we can hold off the wedding that long? People will understand.'

'If it's that important, why don't we get married first, and then you can go?' Judith asked stubbornly.

'I'm having to use the money we saved,' I

34

said. I had the grace to look embarrassed. 'Listen, I've met this old man. He knows where there's gold. Judith, I know I can find it. When I come back we'll have enough money to start something up on our own and I'll be free of that office.'

Judith shook her head. 'Oh no,' she said. 'Oh no, not another one of your schemes. Patrick aren't you *ever* going to grow up? You can't keep chasing dreams all your life. For God's sake, face reality, stop looking for rainbows.'

'Listen,' I said to her. 'That's why I came to this country. Because it's still big enough and empty enough for a man to have dreams. I could have sat in an office in England. I didn't come all this way to sit in an office here. Judith,' I tried to explain, 'I know I've got to find it—or at least try. Give me three months. Give me one last chance to get it out of my system.'

'All right,' Judith said, angry again, a part of her hating me. 'Three months. But I'm tired of waiting for you, Patrick. If you're not back within three months to the day, then don't bother to try contacting me. Don't even look for me. Because I promise you, I really promise you, I won't be there.'

A distant shout turned both our heads. Way across the park the old man was standing on the car, bottle in one hand, waving to us with the other. 'Come on,' he yelled impatiently. 'We'll be late for old Mouldy's funeral.'

I took that as my cue. 'Judith,' I said huskily, 'I have to leave now.'

Judith was staring aghast—it was too far away to see the old man clearly, but she must have gained a pretty good impression of him. 'You're not going with that old drunk,' she said, horrified. 'Patrick, wait,' she called after me, but I was already half way down the path.

I turned before I reached the car. 'Judith, I love you,' I shouted across the grass. 'I'll be back.' She made no response. She just stood there brokenly, tears streaming down her face, watching me out of sight.

The African-operated long distance bus, designed to take bad dirt roads and river crossings, roared out of the city with the old man, Phillimon and me on board. It was crowded to capacity with humans and animals inside and bicycles and baggage on the roof.

I found a seat by the window with my dog at my feet and stared out watching the countryside rolling by. I had sold the Morgan to a used-car dealer. Part of the money went to settle my debts, the rest to buy an old Lee Enfield rifle and a supply of ammunition. I was free now with no possessions to clutter me, nothing left behind other than Judith, and in the excitement of the journey the pain of leaving her had dulled. I thought of a life-time spent in boarding schools, in dormitories with narrow beds each only a regulation twenty-four inches apart from

36

the next. And I looked forward to that night, to sleeping out under the stars, to feeling the freedom, and that special smell of Africa—of camp fires and the empty veld that the old man had talked about.

We crossed a plateau, some five thousand feet above sea level. Rich farmland, stretching to the horizon, lay on either side of the road. Tractors pulling ploughs churned a red dust into the sky and the sun was a great fiery orb overhead. The bus careered down the escarpment, following a series of hair-pin bends past the great dam on the long journey towards the valley floor. Now we began to travel through the real Rhodesian countryside with its stark outline of stunted, tree-lined granite kopjes and rugged hills.

It was August. There had been no rain for five months. The grass was a dry, golden brown. And although it was a full three months before the next rains were due, spring was coming—though the only signs of it lay in the trees. The mahobahobas were heavy with fruit. And the msasas, the most predominant tree on the highveld, were getting their new leaves—starting off a rusty red, changing to yellow and then to bright lime green, so that the outline of the granite kopjes and hills, the whole countryside, was softened for a short season by the differing shades of colour.

We left the bus on the main road and set off across a strip of veld for the village of Mazoe.

37

The old man claimed that his camp was less than two miles from there by the river.

The village nestled against the slopes of a range of hills and had been built to serve some of the first gold mines ever worked in Rhodesia. The old man led the way into the store. He had made out a list of sorts, of the supplies we would need, and he leant across the wide wooden counter and gave his order.

'Salt,' he said. 'Mealie meal. We could use some bread and meat to get us started. We'll not get much chance to shoot for the pot while we're passing through farming land. And brandy. . . .'

The porters loaded up our stores and we set off for the old man's camp at the head of the file. We walked in silence, the old man on one side of the road and me on the other.

It was dark by the time we arrived at the camp which was set a hundred yards off the track in the shade of some msasa trees. His servant came out to greet us holding up a flickering oil lamp to light our way. He was an African even older than the old man, with fuzzy white hair shrouding a sunken, wrinkled face. His shoulders and body were so twisted and bent that he looked like a gnarled old limb off a fever tree. He was called Joseph and, as I came to know him better, I learnt that he had much the same habits as the old man. They seemed to have been together since time began.

38

While the old man paid off the porters, Joseph kicked the embers of the fire to life and set a blackened kettle to cook, watching me all the time with old faded eyes that held both humour and cunning in them, studying me, summing me up, until I had the uncomfortable feeling that he could read me like a book.

We ate a silent supper, then the old man took the lamp and showed me over the camp. There wasn't much to see. His promise of shelter was a filthy old tarpaulin thrown across a rope. His promise of transport turned out to be a moth-eaten old mule called Jezebel and a battered scotch-cart. At first I couldn't believe it. I searched wildly round in the lamp light but that was all. I had been expecting at least a truck of some kind.

'You can't be serious,' I said weakly. 'You're not really suggesting that we walk two hundred miles and more across country to the river. Is this your promise of transport?'

'What did you expect?' the old man asked. 'Boy, you know nothing about the bush,' he said contemptuously. 'All you've seen of it is from a landrover tearing down roads and kicking up dust all over everyone. This mule can carry and a man can walk across country where no vehicle can go. And the time is going to come when we'll have to follow narrow game trails along the banks of the river if we want to find the haunted pools.'

I looked at the mule and she looked back at me. If ever there was an evil animal, it was this one.

'But to walk,' I said. 'It'll take us weeks! A truck would at least have taken us most of the way.'

The old man had had enough of my protesting. He turned and stomped back into the camp with me following. Joseph thrust a mug of strong, dark tea into my hands which tasted like boiled gum leaves, while the old man flung himself down in a battered deck-chair and moodily opened a bottle.

Most of my wedding money was spent and my pride was at stake. I couldn't go crawling back to Judith now.

'You cheated me,' I accused bitterly.

'Maybe I made it sound a little better than it was,' the old man replied uncomfortably. 'But then I was drunk and you shouldn't have believed me when I was drunk. Don't worry, boy,' he said, trying to pacify me, 'the gold's in the pools all right, and we'll get there. It won't take us more than a couple of weeks. As for shelter, well you can share the tent with me.'

I wasn't in the mood to accept the proffered olive branch. My illusions were sadly shattered.

'I'm not sleeping there,' I said, indicating the filthy tarpaulin. I gathered up my sleeping bag. 'I'll make my own camp,' I said, 'separate from yours. And don't drink too much of that brandy,' I warned, 'because I'm not buying you another drop.'

'When I'm in town or visiting another man's camp, I drink heavy and there's no one going to stop me,' the old man growled. 'But when I'm in the bush and there's work to do, I work dry—or nearly dry. And while we're having this discussion,' the old man said, following me down the path, 'seeing as we've got to live together for the next few months, let's get this straight. I don't want you wittering like a woman about my habits. I like myself the way I am and I'm buggered if I'm going to change now. I'll respect your habits the same way. Is that understood between us, boy?'

'All right,' I said, 'as long as nothing interferes with us getting the gold out. I've only got three months. And don't call me "boy".'

'To me you're "boy",' the old man said contemptuously, 'until you can prove yourself otherwise.'

With that we parted. The old man stomped back to the camp fire and I out into the darkness clutching my sleeping bag. I found myself a spot at the base of a tree, hoping that the low-spreading branches would help keep the morning dew from soaking me. I scratched a hole for my hip and crawled into my sleeping bag for the heat of the day was gone and it was now cold. Through the branches I could see a vast night sky clear and full of stars.

CHAPTER SIX

BEFORE dawn the old mule Jezebel, was backed, kicking and protesting, in between the shafts of the cart and we set off in the gathering light. We left the Iron Mask Range behind us, skirting the nickel mines of Bindura, past Paradise Pools, past Shamva, heading north-east.

It grew hotter as we descended from the highveld and trekked across open country. I began to lose what loose flesh I had, growing browner, leaner, harder about the face. And I still remember the creak of the cart wheels, the crunch of boots following in the deep sand tracks; the shimmering, still, sun-scorched days, sweat, flies—then frosty clear nights by a fire beneath a sky full of stars. These should have been good days for me. But there was much in my manner that used to infuriate the old man. Through sheer lack of experience in the bush, I did stupid things and I irritated him so much that there were times when he had only to look at me to fly into a rage. I pretended that it didn't matter, but it used to hurt me, for secretly I wanted his respect and I found myself trying to earn it. But it didn't work. I just used to behave even more awkwardly and that used to infuriate him more.

About two weeks later we passed through the

bottom of the Umfurudzi Wild Life Reserve, following a trail that led through a great forest of mopani trees. The air was laden with the heavy scent of jessie scrub. The temperature stood well over a hundred degrees and Go-Away birds rasped hoarsely. Herds of buffalo, kudu and impala, too hot to move, stood silently, barely noticing our passing.

I was wandering away from the others when I noticed a tiny elephant calf alone in a glade. I knew poachers hunted here and I thought perhaps it had been orphaned. The calf seemed so small and vulnerable that my heart went out to it. I held out a tuft of grass, dusting off the ends as I had seen other elephants do.

'Here, boy,' I said, walking towards it. I was almost near enough to touch it when it turned and trotted off. I followed, concerned for its safety. The calf picked up speed, scampered over the lip and down into a donga. I scrambled down the rocky side after it and held out the grass.

'Here, boy,' I said gently. 'I won't hurt you.'

In front of me loomed a solid wall of dusty grey flesh, lined, scarred and wrinkled into leathery folds. The calf ran between its mother's legs. Her massive head swung towards me and I found myself face to face with a pair of long, curved tusks, up-raised trunk and small angry eyes. I had heard that elephants gave warning, or at least did a mock charge, before they

43

attacked in earnest. But this cow elephant gave one blood-curdling scream of fury and went for me.

I fled up the side of the donga, my feet and hands scrabbling at the loose stone and earth sides for a grip. Then I raced across the bush with the enraged elephant thundering behind me. I must have been running with the speed of an Olympic athelete when I passed the old man.

'Do something!' I yelled, terrified, weaving in and out of the trees in a vain attempt to shake the cow off, but that elephant, for all her size, could turn on a postage stamp. 'For Christ's sake!' I shouted as I passed the old man again. 'Do something, will you!'

But the old man was holding himself up against a tree and beating his hat against his knees.

'Go on, boy,' he shouted through tears of laughter, 'run, she's gaining on you.'

In desperation I leapt for a low-lying branch and swarmed up the tree, hand over hand, hardly using my legs at all. Simba had been following me and now he turned at the base of the tree and faced the great cow elephant, his teeth bared and the hackles of his ridge standing upright along his back.

I tried to call him off, but the fighting madness was in him and he took no notice of me. Instead, he went for the elephant, leaping instinctively for her throat. The elephant's trunk caught Simba in mid air—the force of the blow must have broken his back, for when he hit the ground he could not move. The elephant lifted him high with her trunk again and hurled him to the ground. Then she knelt on him, crushing bone and sinew, mashing his body into a bloody pulp.

And all that time I did not move. I clung terrified to the tree trunk, stunned by the speed and awesome power of that elephant. The dog demolished, she peered short-sightedly about her, lifting her trunk, searching for my scent. But the air was still and eventually she ambled off, followed by her calf.

I climbed shakily down from the tree, bent on revenging my dog. I was going for my rifle when the old man stopped me.

'It was your fault,' he said, 'not hers. That'll teach you to stop interfering when you are in the bush, boy—that's the best lesson you've ever had.'

I buried Simba that afternoon. I did it alone. I dug the grave deep in the heat of the harsh sun, through rock and stone without a break. I needed to sweat, to feel my muscles hurt, my hands to blister, so that I could, in some way, atone for the death of my dog. I piled heavy rocks over the top of the grave and was standing silently, sick at heart, when the old man came up beside me.

'What are you doing here?' I asked angrily.

'Come to pay my respects,' the old man replied. 'I admired your dog, boy,' he explained, 'it's you I can't stand.'

★　　★　　★

Three days later we crossed through Mt. Darwin into the Makaha Hills. The old man had a prospecting crony working one of the few mines left in this remote but magnificently wild part of the country. We sent word on ahead that we wanted his help in recruiting porters and made for his camp. Once these hills had been alive with small workers/prospectors but as the gold gave out, they moved on, and now we passed mine after deserted mine, the familiar mark of their slimes dumps and rusted headgears standing stark and lonely against the skyline.

On the evening of the second day in the hills we laboured up a steep track. Above us the clatter of a stamp mill and the deeper thud of a James table echoed in the stillness all around.

A man came down the track to greet us. Before the years had worn the muscle and flesh away, this man must have had the build of a giant, but now his clothes flapped loosely on his great frame and his bones showed against his skin. His hair was close-cropped, salt and peppery in colour like his beard. But his face was warm, lined and sunburnt, with merry, twinkling eyes. I took to him immediately.

'Salty McDade,' the old man said, introducing us. Salty took my hand into his firm clasp and shook it warmly. 'You're the first white men I've set eyes on in six months,' he said, 'and it's good to see you, good to see you. I was beginning to worry that I'd forget the language, I've been away from my kind so long. How do I sound?' he asked anxiously.

'You sound fine,' I answered.

He seemed reassured and turned to the old man.

'I heard about Mouldy,' he said, 'I'm sorry.' Then his face brightened. 'You took your time coming.' He was so pleased to see us that the words fairly rushed out of him. 'I've organized a party for tonight. The Chief's come—there's plenty of beer and we'll have ourselves a night of it.'

'Did you get us some porters?' the old man asked as we started up the last part of the trail.

'That depends on the Chief,' Salty replied. 'Did you bring him presents?'

'Blankets,' the old man said. 'And brandy,' he added grudgingly, trying to harbour his supply.

'Brandy,' Salty McDade said appreciatively. 'There've been times when I'd worry that I'd never taste real liquor again. I know the Chief feels the same way. For brandy he'd give you an army of men. We'll get him good and drunk

47

tonight—you can bargain with him then.'

★   ★   ★

There were forty men and more—no women—gathered on a flat, sandy stretch of earth which was carved out of the top of the hill by the stamp mill. The Chief sat on a chair made out of old dynamite boxes—a big man with a bald, bullet-shaped skull and angry, bloodshot eyes. In any society he would have been a man of power, but the more so here in the hills amongst his own people.

The night was dark, the moon was late rising, and the men drank thick kaffir beer and brandy. Salty, the old man and the Chief each had their own bottle. Drummers were hesitantly working to one side of us, beating out a sharp rattle like a burst of machine-gun fire or the deeper throb of the bass which cut through the noise and laughter; no form or shape to their rhythm yet—it was as though the musicians were just testing their muscles, preparing themselves for the night ahead.

Wood was piled on the fire in the centre and the glow of the flames was reflected in the faces of the men. I was offered a bottle and I heard the old man's snort of disgust as I refused it and moved away from the circle.

'Give the young 'un a chance,' Salty McDade interceded on my behalf. 'He'll be all right—

48

just take him time to get used to our ways, that's all.'

'It's not that,' the old man replied, a note of desperation creeping into his voice, for he had had enough of me. 'It's just—' he searched for the words to explain, 'that he's so bloody English—he's driving me mad, and he won't take teaching. He's a menace in the bush—I should have shot him for his own good long ago.'

I moved out of earshot, blushing furiously, and sat myself away from them under a tree, feeling a terrible sense of loneliness. I had a strong character—I just couldn't change myself that easily. Besides, I was very conscious of trying to maintain my hold on civilization. Salty and the old man had already gone native. Since that night in the cells, I had not touched another drop of liquor—perhaps because I was afraid of ending up deadbeat like them.

The drummers began to work. A throbbing, rhythmic beat hammered out over the sand— the deep drums, like a heartbeat, sending out hypnotic pulses, the light drums weaving round the main beat, setting up patterns of sound, giving it life, causing the blood to race, the feet to stamp.

Phillimon was the first to rise. He stood in the circle, his body stiff, his arms upstretched, hands clasped above his head. Face sweating, teeth bared, panting and staring-eyed, he rose

on to his heels and his hips began to undulate
with a sensuous, rhythmic power. One by one
the others joined him until the circle was filled
with dancing men. I watched the old man rise.
At first he staggered, moving stiffly,
awkwardly, like a marionette with the strings
being pulled by unaccustomed hands. Then the
rhythm of the drums took hold of him. I saw a
power, like a vital life force, surge through the
old man. His eyes glowing, his head thrown
back, he began to dance in a frenzy. Each man
on that sand danced without restraint in a style
according to his character.

Salty McDade found me in the shadows
under the tree.

'Here, boy,' he said kindly, offering me a
chipped enamel mug, 'drink some of this.'

I shook my head, but he pressed the mug on
me. 'Just a taste,' he urged. 'It'll do you no
harm.'

I took a sip of the liquid—it had a raw,
tongue-curling taste. I took another sip and felt
the liquid burn its way down my throat.

'Drink it, boy,' Salty ordered. 'Don't just wet
your tongue with it.'

I took a gulp. The liquor hit my stomach,
setting it on fire—then the fumes rose and blew
out my brains. I started forward, gasping for
breath, eyes bulging from my head.

'What was that?' I gasped.

'Have some more,' Salty said, and before I

knew what I was doing I had taken another gulp. My blood warmed and my head grew light.

'What is it?' I asked, finishing the mug. I was getting a taste for that liquor.

'Skokian,' Salty replied. 'The very best.'

I dropped the mug as though I had been poisoned—in fact I probably had. Skokian was more than an illicit brew, outlawed throughout the country. It was an alcoholic potion so powerful that it made men blind, drove them mad. Under its influence they committed crimes and ran wild.

I felt terrible—half drunk, half sober. Salty saw all the confusion and uncertainty in my face. He picked up the mug and filled it.

'I wouldn't tell you this if I didn't like you, boy,' he said gently, 'but you're one hell of a pain in the ass. Here,' he said, 'take another drink.' I drained the mug. 'You're not in the city now,' Salty said, steering me on to the sand. 'There's no girl here for you to dance with—so you dance for yourself. Let yourself go loose, boy. Let whatever's in you come out. All you need to do is listen to the drum's beat and find your own patch of sand. That's what it's all about, boy,' Salty urged. 'You're free now. Dance for yourself.'

I stood foolishly by the fire in the circle, weaving hesitantly about, feeling very, very self-conscious. But no one took any notice of me.

51

And after a while it was as though the throb of the drums had invaded my sub-conscious. A pulse began to beat inside me, softly at first then growing louder and louder until my whole body shook and trembled. Sweat broke out on my skin. Throbbing, flashing colours beat time in my brain. Power like an electric storm flooded through me. I raised my arms. Before me the moon was rising above the hill tops, flooding the sand with light.

I danced and I danced—I couldn't stop. I moved completely unselfconsciously. For the first time in my life I felt totally free of all restraint. I felt a passion and a power, a soaring joy in living. Dear God, I had never been so high.

Some time that night I must have passed out on the sand, for I awoke the next morning lying where I had danced with a monumental hangover. My brain felt so fragile that it hammered against my skull at the slightest movement and I was so nearly blind I felt as though my eyes were bleeding.

Bodies were scattered all over the place. The old man was trying to bargain with the Chief but both of them could hardly speak, let alone concentrate. I sat in the shade for a while, nursing my head, then I went in search of Salty. He was sitting outside his shack smoking a pipe. He poured a mug of thick black coffee as he saw me coming. 'Here,' he said, 'drink this—you'll feel better.'

Salty's shack was at the very top of the hill and from where he sat he had a view of fifty miles and more across misty blue hills into Portuguese East Africa. The shack was built against the ruins of what must have once been a substantial house until fire had consumed it and the roof caved in. Signs of civilization still remained in the overgrown garden with moon flower and scarlet bougainvillea now growing wild.

'Why didn't you move back into the main house?' I asked, glancing at the charred rafters. 'The walls are still good.'

'Because I believe it to be haunted,' Salty replied. 'There's a story,' he said. 'I'll tell it to you . . .

'About the turn of the century two Scandinavians came up this way. They had travelled most of the world together, been through a lot—they loved each other. They were partners closer than brothers, some men said. Anyway, they found this mine. It was a good mine and they struck it rich. One of them had a girl back home in Sweden and he sent for her. From then on it's the old story. She married the one and slept with the other. It didn't work and her husband, mad with jealousy, lured her and her lover down into the mine and blew the rock in on top of them, burying them alive. When he realized that he had killed the only two people

53

that he had ever loved, he was filled with remorse. He burned the house and all he could find and then he hung himself from that tree over there.

'When I came here I found the house in ruins, but if you come inside I'll show you something.'

Salty led the way into his shack. Against the wall was a portrait of a woman and you could see where the heat of the fire had charred the frame, but the canvas and the paint were untouched.

'I found her still hanging above the mantelpiece in the house,' Salty said. 'Through fire, wind and rain, nothing's touched it. I keep her in here out of respect. But I believe, and so do the Africans hereabouts, that she walks the house at night. So you see why I don't live there,' Salty said quietly, 'I couldn't—it's still her house.'

The old man came stamping up in a fury and threw himself down in an old car seat that served for furniture.

'Salty,' he said. 'You know that equipment I wanted to buy off you? Well, that Chief's robbed me blind for the porters and we've not enough money left. Will you lend it to us for a share in the profits?'

'Yes,' Salty said. And they made an agreement.

Joseph and Phillimon loaded the porters and organized them into file ready to move out. Salty came to see us off. His men were going underground at the start of a new shift and he looked lonely, sad at our going.

'Salty,' I said, for I cared for him, 'you're old now for this sort of work and being alone in a place so remote. Why don't you go back to town? You must have family somewhere?'

'There comes a time,' Salty replied, 'when you've been away in the bush so long and you've grown so different from your own kind, that you don't know how to go back—even if you wanted to.' He took me to one side. 'Take care, boy,' he warned. 'That's bad country where you're going—full of fever and disease. The old man's salted to it, but you're not—so take care.'

CHAPTER SEVEN

WE came down out of the Makaha Hills entering a land that was largely uninhabited by man but teeming with game. It possessed some of the most spectacular scenery that I had ever seen—a dramatic, haunted land of great rocks eroded by wind and rain into grotesque silhouettes with the twisted, writhing shapes of baobab trees growing in between.

The temperature rose as we entered the low country, often to 90° at midnight. By eight in the morning the whole land shimmered under a heat haze—by midday the thermometer hovered

55

around the 110° mark. All day we marched, slowly dehydrating in the oven-hot temperature. By nightfall our dry stomachs ached for a long drink of cool water, but there was little to spare.

Then one morning, having crossed the border into Portuguese East Africa, we stood amongst the fever trees on the edge of an escarpment overlooking the Ruenya River valley. We had come a long way to see this sight. The travel weariness dropped away and an electric feeling of excitement took its place.

The sandy river-bed was four hundred yards wide in places with banks thirty feet high. Now, in the height of the dry season before the floods, there was just a shallow stream twenty yards wide winding down the middle between massive sand banks and islands of reeds.

The mule made it down the escarpment on her own, following an almost vertical game trail. We lowered the cart and heavier equipment with a block and tackle. As we reached the valley floor an unhealthy, steamy heat hit us and the air grew breathless and stifling with the oncoming night.

The old man was impatient to move on in search of the bewitched pool. At first light he and I set off, leaving Jospeh and Phillimon to bring up the porters. It was slow work for them as the river banks were almost impenetrable with hanging tree ropes and thick coils of undergrowth. And they had to manhandle the cart and equipment through the sand and shallow water.

The old man and I spent that night without a fire to avoid alerting Portuguese patrols. Before dawn we trekked again, leaving a quarter moon dropping behind a great dome-shaped kopje that dominated the distant horizon. Towards full morning the river narrowed and flowed through a series of rapids. We followed it through a high-walled gorge and at the end a waterfall spilled down into a huge, still pool carved out of the rock. The pool was at least three hundred yards long by fifty yards wide, its banks rising up almost sheer on either side, and enormous trees flung shade on the dark water.

The old man stood on the lip of the gorge looking down with water splashing over his boots and falling in a thin veil of spray to the pool below.

'That's it!' he said excitedly. 'Just like Reias described it. That's the bewitched pool.'

We made camp high up on the banks amongst giant creeper-trailing mahogany, cordyla and tamarind trees, some of them hung with gigantic clusters of orchids the size of a man. The air was laden with the steamy scent of the jungle and it was still and sweating-hot, even in the dead of night. Insects chirred incessantly and clouds of mosquitoes swarmed over any exposed piece of flesh.

I could sense a menacing sickness that lay

over this place like a diseased breath. It was white man's grave-type country, every bit as bad as Salty had warned. A weird scream, like a screeching howl, came from the tree ropes that dangled above my head. The sound rose to a shattering crescendo, causing me to start up, the hair rising in warning on the nape of my neck. Then it petered out, like the cry of a lost soul falling into a bottomless pit.

'Fishing owl,' the old man said, sitting across the fire from me unconcernedly cleaning his rifle. 'You'll get used to it.'

A soft beat of wings stirred the flames as the owl passed low and swept out over the moonlit pool.

I stared down into the dark water. All my money was gone—I had gambled everything for this. Dear God, I prayed silently, please let there be gold on the bottom.

*   *   *

Porters arrived shortly after dawn the next morning, and the old man lined them up.

'You know we've come looking for gold,' he said to them without preamble. 'It'll be hard, dangerous work—but if we find it then each man here gets a share.' With that he set them to work clearing a site for the camp.

Guards were posted out in the bush to provide warning in the unlikely event of a Portuguese army patrol stumbling on to us. And, as a further precaution, I set a man on top of the waterfall to watch in case a crocodile decided to make use of the pool.

Phillimon and I worked from the raft sounding the bottom of the pool. We were the only two who claimed we could swim—the old man couldn't.

'Look out for holes,' he advised from the safety of the bank where he was setting up the Long Tom to sluice the silt. 'The gold's most likely to have collected where the water's worn deep in the rock.'

The silt covered the bed fairly evenly and we decided to take our first samples from below the waterfall. Under the old man's direction the porters had stretched a steel cable across the pool and spliced either end around two solid tree trunks. They placed a metal loop over the cable and shackled a pulley below. Then they fed the rope through the pulley and fastened it to a five-gallon oil drum that would serve as a bucket for the silt.

We manoeuvred the raft into position. The old man gave the signal and the men stationed under either tree pulled on their ropes. The loop slid along the cable to the centre of the pool with the bucket dangling below. Then the wooden winch paid out and the bucket came down. As it filled I dropped over the side and went down with it, one hand on the rim to guide it through the dark water. In the other I held a scoop shaped like a small shovel.

The water was about fifteen feet deep. I shovelled silt into the bucket then, with the bucket nearly full and with bursting lungs, I tugged at the rope. The winch turned and the bucket went up, shedding water as it broke free of the surface and slid back along the cable, carrying forty pounds of silt up the steep-sided bank. The porters caught it as it came in and two of them carried the bucket, suspended from a pole across their shoulders, to the Long Tom.

Another bucket was attached to the rope. It swung back across the pool and dropped into the water. I filled my lungs with air and went down again, working in the darkness on the slimy mud bed. The porters soon found their rhythm and after that, whenever I came up, I could hear their voices chanting in harmony from the bank where they worked. We loaded a bucket every eight minutes—that made seventy-seven buckets in an eleven-hour day. I made endless calculations as I dived. At forty pounds a bucket we were going to be able to put one and a half tons a day through the Long Tom. If the gold ran at four, or even five, ounces to the ton, then we could hope to make upwards of seven ounces a day—that was a lot of money.

When I was exhausted I pulled myself over the side and lay panting on the logs.

'All right,' I said to Phillimon, 'your turn.'

He got up, grim-faced, steadied himself, took a deep breath and then leapt awkwardly into the water. The blood was still pounding in my ears and I lowered my head on to my arms. In the distance I heard Phillimon floundering about. I thought he was playing the fool, but the frantic sounds continued and I looked up in time to see him sinking beneath the water. I leapt in, grabbed him and pulled him on to the raft. He was full of water and I held him doubled over so it poured out of his lungs.

'What in the hell do you think you're doing?' I asked angrily when he stopped choking. 'You can't swim.'

Phillimon uncurled his powerful, lanky body. His pride was hurt—he was like a cat with its fur ruffled.

'I can swim a little,' he said, annoyed, 'and I want my big share of the money. If I go back to the bank I'll be nothing—just another porter.' Phillimon looked up at me. His face had been made permanently fierce since puberty by deep tribal scars, but the smoky brown eyes that held mine were pleading with me. 'Will you teach me the strokes?' he asked. 'I'll learn quickly.' My anger subsided. I knew how he felt—how badly he needed this chance—and I nodded. 'You won't have to do all the work,' Phillimon said firmly. 'I can go down with a stone and you can pull me up with a rope until I learn. I'm not afraid.'

He could already dog-paddle after a fashion. I taught him the breast-stroke in the lunch break and in the evenings before we came in from work. He was determined and he learnt quickly.

When I needed to rest from diving I swam to the break in the bank and climbed up past a chain of two hand-operated 'kamina kawena' (from me to you) pumps that drew water from the pool and fed it into forty-four gallon header tanks that stood above the Long Tom. The chanting 'kamina kawena' operators grinned at me as I passed and their excitement was infectious.

The old man was standing by the Long Tom. I went over to him. The water cascaded over the splash plate swirling up the silt, sending small stones rattling down the boards of the flue and racing over the wooden riffles. Joseph worked with a scraper to keep the silt from clogging— for it was here, against these riffles, that most of the gold would be caught. At the end of the Long Tom a special high-riffled corduroy blanket had been laid to catch the fine gold. The waste dropped over the edge and was led away along a channel.

'How's it coming?' I asked.

'Nothing yet,' the old man replied. 'Hardly a colour. Don't worry about the top silt. Move it out of the way and go deeper. You've got to scrape right down against the rock—that's where the gold is.' I went back to work.

That evening Phillimon and I raced up the bank to the Long Tom to see how we had done. The old man was cleaning the sluice and washing the blanket out carefully. There was less than half an ounce of gold. Word went round the camp and you could feel the disappointment.

After we had eaten the old man and I sat across our fire. 'Show you something,' he said, trying to cheer me up. He swirled the gold in his pan, removing as much of the coarse silt as possible, then tipped in a spoonful of mercury and stirred it with his fingers. The gold united with the mercury to form a little silver ball of amalgam. He took a potato, cut it in half, gouged out a piece in the centre and dropped in the amalgam. Then he bound the sides of the potato together with wire and buried it in the hot ashes of the fire. When the potato had baked he opened it up. The mercury was gone and a tiny ball of pure gold shone up at him. 'It's an old trick,' he said, tossing the ball to me.

The gold glinted in the firelight as I caught it. I rolled the ball in the palms of my hands feeling its weight and its warm, smooth texture.

'It's the first gold we've won from the pool,' the old man said. 'You keep it boy, it'll bring you luck.'

He cleaned out his dish and crushed the charred remains of the potato into it. Innumerable little beads of mercury came away and he poured them back into his flask.

'Tomorrow,' he said as we turned in, 'move the raft back twenty feet. We'll try again from there.'

Phillimon and I started work at five a.m. when only the faint glow of dawn was in the sky and the water was coloured slate-grey. In its shadowy light we would swim out to the raft, ready for the first bucket to swing across, the pumps to start up and the soft, sleepy chant of the porters to call out across the pool.

The diving was some of the hardest work I'd known. Whoever's turn it was to rest would throw his waterlogged body down and gulp air into his lungs, certain that he would never have the strength to go down again—but we always did. It was often dangerous and we helped each other to the point where we operated as a team and grew to trust each other completely. Phillimon never did learn to swim as strongly as me and he panicked in the darkness when he went too deep. Many a time I pulled him out half drowned and pumped the water out of his lungs. I thought little of it at the time, but Phillimon never forgot it. He felt that I was responsible for giving him his chance and for saving his life and in return he gave me his loyalty.

We found no gold then, nor the next day nor the next—or at least very little. The sun burned down until my hair was bleached almost blond and my skin turned a deep mahogany colour. At night we burned leaves and evil-smelling tree roots that Joseph found to try to hold the mosquitoes and other insects at bay. Whenever a man could steal a moment from his work he would hover over the Long Tom, hoping to see a colour build up against the riffles that would warn of the rich gold coming through. But in the evenings the old man would clean the sluice and wash the blanket and word would go round the camp—half an ounce today, or, no gold, no gold, no gold.

By the end of the second week we were growing desperate. You no longer heard the men chant, and the work went slowly. The old man hovered between fierce optimism and despair.

'By Christ,' he'd say to me as I dragged myself up the bank and collapsed exhausted at the end of the day, 'I know it's there, I know it! It's just a matter of finding it.'

'There's gold there, all right,' I agreed bitterly. 'It's the amount that has been exaggerated.'

I felt a growing sense of isolation—a need to retain some contact with the life I'd left behind. I owned a battered portable radio and one evening I rigged an aerial high up in the trees and tuned in to Lourenco Marques, a commercial radio station that beamed pop music over the southern part of Africa. I lay out under

65

stars feeling free and lonely, listening to the music that floated waveringly through the static. And then suddenly there came a slow, haunting song that took me straight to Judith—a song that we had danced to, that I identified with her. It was as though her hand reached out and gripped me, as though she called to me through the music. I remembered places, things we did together, and then I felt imprisoned by the empty, echoing vastness of the land that separated us and I missed her badly. When I couldn't reach her and I ached to be near her I moved out of camp and sat with my back against a tree writing to her late into the night by the light of a torch. And the most precious possession that I owned—for it was all that I had won from the pool—was the small ball of gold the old man had given me. If I achieved nothing else, at least I had enough there to make into a wedding ring.

★   ★   ★

Every third week the old man made an eighty-mile round journey to a Catholic Mission to buy supplies. They asked few questions and the old man gave out that we were camped in the Inyanga foothills. The night before he set off I gave him my letters to post and asked him to make sure that Judith got the Mission address to write to. The old man thought I was a fool to contact her and made it clear when he grudgingly took my letters.

'You broke free—what in the hell do you want to go back for? Forget her—you're better off without her. Listen, boy,' he said huskily, his bloodshot eyes fixed on me from across the fire, 'and I'll tell you something that I know is the truth. For a man to be happy he has to be free. And freedom is not what people think it is. There's no easy way to find it. It takes strength and sacrifice—it's something that has to grow from deep inside. A man who's free owes no one and no one owes him. He walks where he wants to and there's no one to stop him. No women or children to tie him down.' The old man leant across to me—I'd never seen him so intense. 'Boy, what I'm trying to teach you is that you have to get used to being lonely, for it's only the lonely who are truly free.'

I was silent for a moment. I thought of the old man's secret fear of dying alone in the bush or drunk in a gutter somewhere. Then I thought of Judith waiting for me.

'Who in the hell wants to die lonely?' I replied. 'Post my letters.'

CHAPTER EIGHT

EACH day we moved the raft back twenty feet and scoured the bottom of the pool. Towards the centre the gold ran a little richer and we were taking an ounce to the ton.

'It's no good,' I said gloomily to the old man. 'It'll take us a year at this rate.'

The old man glanced up anxiously at the sky. 'Just pray the rains don't break early—we're running out of time.'

And he took to spending hours wandering around the banks trying to read the path of the currents when the floods came down.

'Try the far end,' he said to me, pointing to the rock lip where the water ran out. 'Go right down and scrape the bottom.'

Phillimon and I worked that end for three days, holding a stone to take us down deep with the water singing in our ears and our lungs bursting under the pressure. On the third day I lost my sense of direction and came up under the bank. The current had cut the earth away as far back as I could see. And the water level of the pool had dropped, leaving me two feet of head-room. The whole area was protected from sight by the thick tangles of vegetation that reached deep into the water so that the light barely filtered through. Forests of slimy,

68

twisting roots formed tunnels and caverns and barriers, and under water strange unidentified objects stroked my skin. My first thought was to get out of there as fast as possible. But before me lay a tunnel, larger than the rest, that seemed to lead right into the heart of the bank. My curiosity got the better of me and I decided to follow it, pulling myself along by the roots. Within a few feet the roof opened up into a cavern some six feet high by fifteen feet wide. And reaching out from the wall of the bank was a narrow spit of mud, strewn with bones. I realized that I'd found my way into an old croc's lair. I turned and left in a hurry, diving under the wall of vegetation and up to the surface of the pool.

Phillimon surfaced next to me as I neared the raft. 'Where in the hell have you been, Mambo?' he asked furiously, almost beside himself with worry. 'I've been diving for you—I thought you'd drowned.'

I tried to persuade him to return to the crocodile's lair with me, but he would have nothing to do with it and we kept clear of the bank for the rest of the day.

The old man cleaned up the Long Tom at sunset and made his way dejectedly over to the fire. 'I don't understand it,' he said miserably. 'I just don't understand it, Reias couldn't have been that wrong. You sure you're going right down to the bottom?' he challenged me.

'We're working right on the rock,' I answered him tiredly. 'We can't do any better than that.'

The old man could see that I was exhausted. 'We need a break,' he said. 'Everyone's getting short-tempered. Two fights broke out on the bank today. Tell you what we'll do. We'll take tomorrow off. Now get some rest.

But the old man couldn't sleep and he woke me up in the middle of the night. 'What's the bottom like where you're working?' he asked.

'I don't know,' I answered, 'you can't see it. You just hit it in the dark and sink into the mud.'

'There's no channels or anything, no sign of where the currents have scoured the bottom?'

'No, it just feels like one solid mass of silt and mud. I'll tell you something, though,' I said, sitting up stiffly. 'I found an old croc's lair. It's deep under the bank where the flood waters have washed out about twenty feet of earth.'

'Why didn't you tell me that before?' the old man yelled furiously.

'How in the hell could I?' I replied angrily. 'I've been underwater most of the day. Besides, I didn't think it was important.'

'Did you go down?' the old man asked. 'Did you find the bottom?'

I shook my head.

'For Christ's sake, why not?'

'You should see it,' I tried to explain. 'It's a maze of roots and drift-wood. There's a good

70

chance you'll tangle up and drown if you go down there.'

'That's where it is!' the old man said excitedly. 'That's where the gold is, I'm telling you. The current's undermined the bank and the gold's been washed in there. It's heavy, you see, and it'll lie deep in one place while the silt will move all over. Tomorrow you go down and find out—and I'll be there on the raft waiting. Take Phillimon down with you. You can help each other out of trouble.'

'What about my day off?'

'Forget it,' the old man replied, stumbling back to his bed. 'You're working.'

The next morning there was an air of excitement in the camp. The porters stopped work and gathered round to watch as the raft was paddled over to the bank.

Phillimon and I went down together and came up under the bank. 'Mambo,' Phillimon said softly, looking around, fighting off a growing sense of claustrophobia, 'I don't like this place.'

We tried to dive but that meant virtually climbing down through the tangle of roots that formed a mesh below us with the attendant risk of our air giving out before we could find a way back. In any event, it was impossible to go very deep. I went up and told the old man. 'Try following the bank,' he said, 'until you find a clear patch. Then dive. Make for the waterfall end.'

Phillimon and I pulled ourselves along through the roots. It was like wading neck-deep through a swamp at night, the scum on the surface building up and blocking our mouths and nostrils. Then the roof came down and touched the water. We had come to a dead-end. I felt around and found what I thought to be a tunnel below the surface.

'I'm going down,' I said. 'Give me one minute. If I don't come back in that time, start pulling on the rope.'

I filled my lungs with air and dived into the tunnel. It was wider than I thought—a ledge of rock that had resisted the erosion of the current. My back scraped the roof and I could feel no bottom. I was scared to try diving for it in case I came up under the rock again with no air left, and in the pitch dark it would have been easy to lose my bearings. The ledge seemed to go on forever. But I had the sure feeling that I was nearing the end and was about to come up on the other side when the rope started hauling me back.

I came up beside Phillimon with no air left and clung to a root while my vision cleared and my lungs fought to replace the oxygen that had been used in my system.

'I think I nearly made it,' I said and my voice seemed unnaturally loud in the narrow space between the water and the roof. 'I'm going to try again. Give me eighty seconds this time.'

72

I filled my lungs with air and went down, swimming hard under the ledge, trying to cover as much distance as I could. The ledge began to slant down, forcing me deeper. I made the decision to go on, burnt my boats, and followed it. The ledge gave way and I came up fast into a tangle of roots. There was no air, just water and darkness, and I panicked. I was down to the last of my breath. I knew I couldn't make it back. I tried to claw my way through the roots on the chance of finding air. I felt the rope go tight as Phillimon tried to pull me back. Then it snagged and trapped me. My lungs were screaming for air and I felt my vision begin to blur as I fought to free myself. The rope had coiled itself around a root and it wouldn't free. My fingers attacked the knot around my waist but it had swelled with water and it wouldn't come loose. And I knew then that I was drowning.

Phillimon must have realized what had happened. The rope jarred sharply as he fought frantically to free it. The root came away and the rope snaked out, pulling me down. My chest was ridged with bands of fire, my whole body cried out for air. I fought to remain conscious, to keep my mouth from opening and letting the water rush in. I felt myself growing weaker and weaker.

Phillimon dragged me up almost unconscious and held me above the water. 'Mambo, that's enough,' he said firmly and helped me back to the raft. They laid me out in the sun to recover while the old man questioned Phillimon. Then he squatted beside me.

'I've been thinking,' he said, determined not to give up. 'We've been trying the wrong end. The flood, as it comes over the waterfall, must have cut into the bank lower down. This is where it comes out. The gold must have already been dropped farther back. When you're ready we'll go down to the waterfall end and try again from there.'

He could see that I was half drowned and still shaking from shock and exhaustion. He touched my shoulder. 'You're in a bad way, boy,' he said kindly. 'There's no hurry. Take all the time you want.' He moved away, then his impatience got the better of him and he came back to me. 'I'll give you thirty minutes,' he said. 'You should be strong enough to go down again by then.'

We anchored the raft in the spray of the waterfall and Phillimon and I went down through the slimy green water, flattening out and swimming hard along the bottom, the mud sucking where it scraped our bellies. This time we knew what we were looking for. And after several dives we found it. Buried in silt that would have been washed away in the next floods was the path of a deep-water channel. It had been carved in the rock by the currents so that it directed the main flow of water

74

towards the bank.

We came up, filled our lungs with air, and then went down again to follow it. The channel cut into the bank through a wide arch of solid rock, the roof of which was above water level. But, as before, the gap was protected from sight by a dense wall of tangled vegetation so that from even a couple of feet away you would never have known it was there. We trod water in the gloomy half-light, trying to see what lay beyond the arch. 'Stay here,' I panted to Phillimon. 'Pay the rope out as I go.'

The light gave out after a few feet and I swam on in the dark sending water lapping against the rock. Then the sound died and I found myself in what felt like a great underground cavern. The water below me seemed bottomless and I couldn't find the sides. I turned and swam back through the arch to the glimmer of light at the end. 'We're going to need torches,' I said.

The old man had the porters cut dried reeds and bind them into torch brands.

'Is it wide enough to get the raft through?' he asked, almost beside himself with curiosity.

'I think so,' I replied.

We moved up to the bank and cut away the vegetation until the raft was able to slip under the sill. Once through, there was enough head room to enable us to sit up and paddle the raft along. It was an eerie, silent journey through the low tunnel-like passage. And the light thrown by the flickering fire brands sent shadows writhing on the smooth, water-worn walls. At the end the arched roof rose into the darkness and the walls fell away.

The old man stood up and held out his torch to throw more light. 'Jesus Christ!' he exclaimed softly in awe at what he saw. The light picked out the massive stalactites that hung down like icicles from the roof. His whispered voice echoed and re-echoed from all around us as the raft glided out towards the centre of a great underground pool.

The pool was almost completely circular, about one hundred feet wide in diameter. And evidence of water on the rock showed that when the floods came surging down the channel, this whole area must have become one great whirlpool of water. At the far side was the gap that we'd been trying to find from the other end, where the water spun out through the old crocodile's lair.

We gingerly propelled the raft on through a silence so still that even the sound of the water dripping from the paddles echoed. In the middle we tried to sound the bottom, but it was so deep that the leads man ran out of rope. We worked our way across from the centre and found a bottom shelving steeply upwards like a funnel with sloping ledges at regular intervals, each about twelve feet wide. At the extreme sides of the pool the ledge was less than fifteen feet deep.

'Go down and get me a sample,' the old man said, handing me a tin. I dug deep into the silt and brought it up. We panned it there and then in the light of the torches. And the flames picked out the bright colour of gold forming a tail right round the pan. After all we had been through the old man doubted his luck. 'Go down again and take a sample from another place,' he said. 'This might just be a rich pocket.'

We panned the second sample and it left a weight of gold in the bottom of the pan. The old man's caution gave way to enthusiasm and the raft rocked dangerously as he moved about.

'I think we've found it,' he said hoarsely. 'I think we've found it, boy. This is the bewitched pool. Reias, the bastard, only told me half the story.'

The trouble was going to be in getting the gold out of there, but the old man was a born engineer. He rigged up an ingenious system for moving the silt. Two extra logs were floated through and lashed on to the raft to make a more stable platform. Then a primitive wooden winch was added to hoist the bucket laden with silt from the bottom. The bucket was placed on a smaller raft and floated along a guide-line through the tunnel and out into the main pool. A wooden ledge had been built into the sheer side of the bank over the entrance for the porters to stand on, and the cable stretched above. As the buckets floated out they fastened it to the pulley and swung it up to the Long Tom—and an empty bucket was put back in its place. It was the best we could do with our very limited resources and we gave it a trial run. 'I think it's going to work,' I said to the old man.

We were up before dawn the next morning and sat drinking our tea waiting impatiently for the sun to rise. As soon as it was light enough for the porters to work we went down through the tunnel. The torch brands flared and the light flickered over the walls. I was the first to dive. I went down and filled my bucket. The silt was about two feet deep on the ledge and we scraped it carefully right down to the rock, anxious not to lose any gold. One after another the full buckets floated out and the empty ones came back to replace them.

It was worse working in the underground pool than in the main one. At least there you came up into the sunlight. Here it was always dark, the water felt colder. We seemed to get tired more quickly, and we would come up waterlogged, exhausted and shivering, and lie on the raft panting in the dark air, while the winch squealed and the buckets came up.

When it was my turn to rest I went back through the tunnel. I paused, blinking in the blinding hot glare of the sunlight before climbing the bank. I heard the reassuring sound of the porters chanting once more as they worked. The old man met me by the Long Tom. 'The gold's coming through,' he said, almost dancing with excitement 'Rich gold's coming through!'

I watched the water rushing over the riffles. Joseph caught a glint of colour, reached in and pulled out a rounded, water-worn nugget and handed it to me. I washed it in the running water and held it up to the sunlight. The warm colour of pure gold—I turned it in my hands. 'There's plenty more,' the old man said. 'Here.'

He blocked the passage of silt for a moment and, as the water cleared, I saw the colour banking up behind the riffles. Dear God, I'd never seen so much gold! When the Long Tom was cleaned word went round the camp. Ten ounces today, ten ounces. That night the drums beat and the porters danced.

I took myself off into the bush. The solitude, the loneliness and the fear of failure over the past few months had played havoc with my emotions.

The old man found me with my back against a tree. 'I've my last three bottles of brandy set aside,' he announced, 'which I've been saving for a proper occasion.' His battered, lined face cracked into a broad smile that showed, when he chose, all the charismatic warmth of the man. 'Boy,' he growled, 'let's get drunk!'

CHAPTER NINE

I WROTE to Judith, trying to weave words on a barren piece of paper—words that would bind her to me, cause her to keep faith with me. I told her of the gold we were bringing up. I told her of the long hours of diving, the aching muscles, the dangers encountered each day. And that through it all I was growing up—becoming more sure of myself. I knew I wouldn't fail her again.

I told her of my hopes and dreams. She'd heard them before, but this time I had the money to bring them to reality. No more living in a city, crammed into a tight collar behind a desk. Instead we'd go farming. I had it all planned. And I wrote to her in heartfelt, halting words that tried to hold her until I could get back.

The old man made two more trips to the Mission. He returned on each occasion with no reply to my letters. I grew so anxious that on the second trip I went way out to meet him.

'She's gone,' the old man said, 'run off with another man. It happens all the time.'

'How do you know?' I asked.

'I know women,' the old man replied darkly. He shrugged his shoulders. 'Forget her, boy. It's finished now. No woman's worth the pain.'

'Since when were you such an expert on women?' I challenged him furiously, trying to hide the hurt that was burning inside me. 'You know nothing about them.'

A moment of sheer, naked loneliness showed in the old man's face. It was as though I'd caught a glimpse of his soul. And then he retreated into his shell.

'I could tell you, but that's private,' he muttered as he moved away. 'That's private.'

We didn't speak to each other for the next two days. Then I went to him. 'Look,' I said desperately, 'she could be sick or hurt in an accident. There's bound to be some form of radio communication at the Mission. I'll leave at first light tomorrow.'

'You can't,' the old man said. 'I was meaning to tell you. I left the Mission just in time. There've been Frelimo crossings. The Portuguese are pouring troops in and they've frozen the whole area. They'll be on to anything that moves. If they trace you back here they'll take our gold and throw us in gaol—then all we've done will have been for nothing. I'm sorry, boy, but that was my last journey to the Mission. The next time we leave here it will have to be for good.'

The days passed. November came and I lay on my bed in a pool of sweat waiting for the dawn to break with the mosquitoes' high-pitched whine all around me. I counted the notches that I had carved into the tree trunk above my head. We had been at the pool for fifty-seven days.

November is the worst month in Portuguese East Africa—a time when everything is dry and dying, burning up in the harsh glare of the sun. I found myself praying for the life-giving rains to break and cool the sweating air. Everything through the long, dry months leads up to this— the waiting for the rains.

It was as though a clock somewhere deep inside me had started ticking away the seconds—faster and faster as the days passed and the heat built up until my nerves were stretched tight and screaming for relief. It was bad enough on the highveld, but down here on the valley floor the heat was unbearable. Red dust hung trapped in a breathless sky and the sunrises and sunsets were violent with colour. It was a time of year in an untamed place that made me very conscious of living in Africa with all its sadness and passion, its stark, haunting beauty.

The old man was up before Joseph that morning. I watched his shadowy figure kick the embers of the fire to life and set the smoky kettle to boil. No matter how great the heat we drank hot, black tea, infused with the bark of the red mahogany tree, morning and night. Our medical supplies were low. We had run out of malaria tablets and the bark of the red mahogany tree was supposed to have properties that resembled quinine.

He brought my tea over to me and waited while I drank it. Ours was a strange relationship with no in-betweens. There were times when we ignored each other for days on end. Times when I hated him—times when I loved him. Out here in the aching loneliness of the backveld we needed each other badly. We both knew it, though neither of us would have admitted it to the other. And yet by that, and by the battle of getting through each day, we were being bound closer and closer together.

'The rains are coming,' the old man said. 'I've seen clouds building up these last few days.'

'Shouldn't we be packing up and getting out of here?' I asked—for I was anxious to be gone.

'There's no hurry,' the old man replied. 'We'll get plenty of warning before the river floods. Besides, we'll need rain on the low ground to wash out our tracks or the Portuguese or Frelimo will jump us before we can make it back across the border.'

Phillimon and I swam through the tunnel into the underground pool. The winch squealed as the bucket went down at the start of another day. We had tried everything we knew to speed up the work—from make-shift air hoses that leaked and filled our lungs with water—to mechanical scoops that spilled out the silt so that the gold was lost forever in the funnel beneath

83

our reach. In the end we found that for the limited resources at our disposal there was no method as efficient as the sheer hard work of diving. It was slow, but we rarely made less than seven ounces—some days much more.

I emerged that afternoon from the tunnel to see, after months of completely clear skies, a thin layer of cloud on the distant horizon. From then on, with each passing day, the cloud cover grew quickly. The mornings broke clear, but by late afternoon vast regiments of sullen black cloud had built up against the horizon until the sun was obliterated and the days grew dark. In the night storm after storm swept overhead. But in the river valley, apart from the increasing tension and electrical storms of furious intensity, no rain fell on the parched earth.

'It's time we were moving,' I said anxiously to the old man one night as I watched the dark clouds scudding across the moon.

But the old man was still in no hurry to leave. It wasn't the gold that was keeping him—it was something else. 'We'll give it a few more days,' he said.

Neither the old man nor I had experienced a rainy season in this low-lying region of Portuguese East Africa. The only comparison the old man could draw was that of Matabeleland in Rhodesia. And there the effect of the rains had nothing like the intensity they had on the Ruenya River valley.

84

The storms which were passing overhead lashed against a range of mountains two hundred miles away. There the rain fell in a solid incessant roar so loud that you couldn't hear yourself speak—the great fat droplets of life-giving water bouncing in the dust. The parched earth was unable to absorb it all and the rain formed rivulets, then streams, then flooded down in muddy, rushing torrents to feed the tributaries of the Ruenya River.

We had no warning of this on the valley floor. The waterfall changed its note slightly as more water came over from a storm that must have broken while still over the lowlands. And the water level of the pool rose a few inches. But this didn't concern us unduly, for there was still plenty of room to breathe within the tunnel and the overflow at the other end of the pool seemed to be coping. Only when we dived deep into the black water of the underground pool did we feel the first stirrings of the current that would later whip the water there into a frenzied whirlpool.

I walked down to the pool with Phillimon on that last morning. The air was still and hot and charged with tension. The light of the dawn breaking raged up through the dusty sky like a bush fire at the edge of the world.

We swam into the pool and sat on the raft in the darkness amid the echoing sounds of water dripping. I lit the torch brands and shards of reflected light turned the stalactites into blazing

85

crystals.

'I'll dive first,' Phillimon said, and slipped into the water.

I lowered the bucket down to him and we worked solidly for an hour. 'How's the current?' I asked when it was my turn to dive.

'It's all right—but there's something happening,' he replied. 'I can feel a vibration humming in my ears when I'm working on the shelf.'

When I came up from my fourth or fifth dive, Phillimon caught my hand, 'Listen,' he said. As my ears cleared I could hear the drumming sound above water now—a tiny whisper of warning that started in the rock and was amplified to an audible level by the stalactites.

We went through the tunnel and up the bank to find the old man who was working by the Long Tom. I told him what we had heard.

'It's nothing,' the old man said irritably. 'You're imagining things. Go back to work.'

Just then there came a shout from the guard on top of the waterfall. He stood up and cupped his ear showing that he had heard the sound too. The old man was forced to listen.

From far away came the sound, a low, menacing rumble like a storm breaking in the distance—though the sky was clear for fifty miles around. 'It's a flash flood,' the old man said quietly after a while. Both of us could imagine the wall of water sweeping down on us along the river-bed. 'You're right boy—it's time to move.'

I turned to dash away and shout instructions for the packing up of the camp, but the old man grabbed my arm. 'There's plenty of time,' he said 'Take it slow or the porters will panic.'

'How long do you think we've got?'

'I don't know,' the old man answered. 'But I've heard that in this sort of flat country you can hear a flood as much as half a day away before it reaches you.'

'On second thoughts,' the old man said, trying to appear calm, 'it won't do any harm to hurry. The porters are going to hear the flood coming anyway.' He glanced round the site quickly and made his decision. 'There's no time to climb up and over the gorge,' he said. 'You get the raft and start ferrying people across the pool. I'll break camp.'

We were trapped. We'd never get the men and equipment across there in time. 'Why did you leave it so late, you drunken old bastard,' I wanted to shout at him. But the old man had already turned away and was giving orders to the porters.

I followed Phillimon down to the water and we swam into the underground pool. The noise within the cavern was now a furious drumming sound that set the stalactites rattling. The thought of being caught in there when the water flooded in and the whirlpool sucked down spurred us on. We worked feverishly in the darkness to cut away the moorings and manoeuvre the raft back through the tunnel.

We loaded passengers until the logs were awash under the weight, and then, with everyone paddling with whatever they could find, we set off for the opposite bank. Once there I left Phillimon to organize the porters to cutting steps and fastening rope-ways up the sheer side of the bank and hurried back.

Old Joseph was waiting with the mule.

'What about Salty McDade's equipment?' I shouted to the old man as he hurried past.

'I'm burying it,' he replied. 'It might be useful if we ever come back.'

'We promised to return it—what's Salty going to say?'

The old man's head re-appeared momentarily above the ledge. 'Bugger Salty,' he yelled. 'Take the mule and hurry, damn it!'

The sound of the flood was now a distant roar, the noise increasing as though the water was picking up speed as it drew nearer and nearer. Jezebel chose that time to be stubborn. I pushed and Joseph pulled but we couldn't move her an inch. It was no use. We had no more time. I ran up the bank and returned with my rifle. Joseph flung his wizened arms around the mule's neck and tried to protect her body with his own.

'No,' he pleaded, when he saw what I was

going to do. 'Don't shoot her.'

'I've got to, Joseph,' I said desperately. 'We can't move her and I can't leave her to the flood.'

The old man saw the rifle in my hands and came bellowing and stumbling down the bank to join Joseph in protecting the mule. He tried to kick her into the water, but she just kicked back.

'All right,' the old man said breathlessly. 'Take another load across. We'll have figured out something by the time you get back.'

The cart had been broken down into parts. I loaded it on to the raft together with our camping equipment and crossed the pool cursing the time that had been wasted. When I turned Joseph leapt on to the raft carrying a long rope which was attached at the other end to the mule's harness. As the raft filled with porters and was pushed off, the old man took a detonator from his explosive box and tossed it on to the rock. It went off with a sharp crack almost under Jezebel's tail and she leapt into the water and swam beside the wildly rocking raft. The porters were waiting on the other bank. They slung ropes under the mule and with old Joseph almost sobbing with relief, hauled her up the sheer side to safety.

There were still two more trips to make and the sound of the oncoming flood was now so loud that I had to shout to make myself heard. I

89

was beginning to panic. I'd never make it. In my mind's eye I could see, beyond the gorge, the solid wall of water advancing on me—and my paddling became frenzied.

I had sent the guard on the waterfall up on to high ground on the other side to warn me when he saw the flood. As I went back across the pool for the second time I saw him frantically waving his arms to attract my attention. 'It's coming!' he shouted. 'It's coming! I can see it!' The flood must have been less than a mile away.

There were two porters left waiting for me. 'Where's the old man?' I shouted as the raft touched.

'He's still up there,' one of them replied.

I dashed up the bank, through the remains of the camp and found the old man marking the spot where he had buried the equipment. 'Come on!' I yelled and grabbed his arm.

We turned and ran back through the camp. I was scrambling down the bank when the old man stopped dead in his tracks.

'The gold!' he shouted. 'Did you take it across?'

I shook my head. Dear God! In the panic of the moment we each thought the other had taken care of the gold.

We raced back to where we had hidden it. There were twenty bags of gold. The old man had already cut two ropes and tied ten bags equally spaced to each. He hung my rope around my neck and fastened the two dangling sides to my waist with my belt. Then he did the same with his. We climbed down the bank almost bow-legged under the extra weight. If either of us fell in, I thought, we'd sink like a stone. The old man grabbed a paddle and set off across the pool, the sound of the flood roaring in our ears. It had to be almost on us now.

We neared the other side. I held the raft steady. The porters dropped their paddles and jumped for the bank. They scrambled up to safety using the rope-ways provided. But the old man missed his hold and fell back with a strangled shout. I tried to catch him, but the extra weight unbalanced us. He twisted out of my grip and plummeted down to the bottom of the pool.

I cut the rope around my neck, opened my belt and let the bags of gold fall onto the raft. Then I went down after the old man. I found him half buried in the silt and struggling furiously. There was no way that I could save the gold and him and I cut his rope. As the gold fell away he broke free of the mud. I pulled him up to the surface and left him clinging to the root creepers that hung over the side.

The raft with my gold on it had drifted a little way from the bank. I swam a few strokes towards it, then the flood hit the gorge with a booming roar like a cannon shot. Phillimon was screaming at me from the top. Despairingly I let my gold go and swam back for the bank. A rope snaked down by the old man, another rope came down for me.

A wall of water burst through the gorge behind us in a seething, mud-brown torrent that carried full-grown trees and boulders bouncing before it. I tied the old man's rope tightly under his arms and we began desperately to climb. The flood thundered over the falls. The water, with a million tons of pressure behind it, seemed to hang suspended in the air for a moment then, in slow motion, it fell into the pool below. The air was filled with noise and spray and the sudden build-up of air pressure blasted in our ears. A boiling tidal wave rose up below the falls and crossed the pool towards us. We were climbing too slowly. Even with the help of the ropes there was no hope of getting out of its reach.

I put my arms around the old man and tried to press him against the bank with my body. But I knew that nothing could withstand the sheer elemental force of that water bearing down on us. Then spray blinded my eyes—I couldn't see. All I was conscious of was the weight of the old man sagging against me and the fury and the violence and the shattering noise.

The wave enveloped us with a tremendous crushing force. The roots broke away in our hands and we were picked up and dashed against the bank as though we were matchwood, then we were sucked under and swept away.

The ropes took up the strain with a jolt that crushed my ribs. We swung out into the pool, spinning in the raging force of the water. I opened my mouth, gasping for air, and the water poured into my lungs. The old man's grip was weakening and blindly I clung on to him. I felt the ropes pulling us up. Our heads broke the surface. Through a maelstrom of spray I saw the porters above us hauling with all their might while Phillimon and Joseph frantically urged them on.

It was a tug-of-war against the suction of the flood. The ropes vibrated under the strain and I prayed that they would hold as I struggled with the last of my strength to keep the old man's head above water. Then we broke clear of the flood and dangled above the water on the ends of our ropes. The porters pulled us up and laid us on the bank. My body was one mass of pain. Even so, I staggered up and flung the old man, none too gently, over the wheel of the cart and pumped the water from his lungs. When I thought that I'd got most of it out, I let him drop.

He came to with me standing over him. He opened his eyes and shook himself all over like a half-drowned rat.

'Damn me,' he said in an aggrieved tone. 'That pool's near drowned me.'

'What about our gold?' I said bitterly, half out

of my mind with sorrow. 'If it hadn't been for the time spent with that bloody mule we'd never have lost our gold.'

The old man levered himself up and rested his back against the wheel. 'I've known that mule a long time,' he said. 'And the way I see it, boy, it wasn't a bad exchange. She's family—gold we can find any time.'

If that was the way he felt about it, then there was nothing more to be said. For a moment I bitterly regretted saving the old man's life and I thought seriously of tossing him back into the flood. But it wouldn't have served any purpose. The raft was match-wood now and my gold was scattered over a hundred miles of sand.

The river rose all through that day covering the beds of reeds and sand banks in a swirling, mud-brown sea. The game gave way before the rising water, climbing with us to the high ground. And as we made camp we could see herds of wildebeeste, zebra and kudu moving in the bush all round us.

I lay that night under a vast and lonely African sky, staring sightlessly at the stars, my stomach churning with despair, my hands clenched by my sides. I had lost everything, everything. And Judith . . . what in the hell was I going to tell Judith?

CHAPTER TEN

EARLY the next morning we set off on our homeward journey. It took us three times the effort hacking our way through the dense jungle of the valley to cover the same distance that we had made in one day following the river-bed. And to add to our misery the rains broke over the lowlands. Black thunderstorms came sweeping up the mouth of the river valley towards us, bringing first the wind, bending trees, flattening grass, and flapping our sweat-soaked clothes against our bodies. Then the rain, a drenching downpour that turned the parched ground underfoot into a churning sea of mud, drumming painfully against an exposed piece of flesh.

The sun burned down between storms. Steam rose as our clothes dried on our bodies. And the humidity rose to such a degree that everything was dripping and the sweat poured off us. The only things that seemed to prosper during the rainy season in this area were the insects and the snakes, and they multiplied. It was a terrible journey back.

At last we climbed the escarpment on to higher ground. Before us lay two trails. One lay westward, back the way we had come through the Makaha Hills. The other went in much the same direction, but took a slightly different route—more to the north.

The old man lined the porters up. 'You've lost your bonuses through no fault of your own,' he said. 'And I'm sorry about that. Because you did your job well. No man could have asked for better. But at least your Chief's still holding your wages, so you'll have made something out of all this. Now I know each one of you, and if we pass this way again—coming back for the gold we've lost—and you want to take the risk with me,' he grinned at them, a warm reckless grin that erased all the memories of the hardships we'd been through, 'you're on...' And damn me if the porters didn't love him. It showed—ragged-clothed, empty-bellied and all.

We had a party that night. In the morning they took the western trail. It was sad to see them go. We chose the northern route.

'Salty McDade—that's why,' the old man explained. 'I don't want to have to tell him where his equipment's buried in case we can go back there.'

I shook my head in disbelief at the old man's optimism. He couldn't be serious. For as far as I was concerned, I was never going back to that pool again; I was cured of prospecting for life. All I wanted to do now was to get back to the city and find out what had happened to Judith. The three months she had given me were nearly up.

On the second or third day out on that trail I awoke with my head thick and my joints stiff as though I had 'flu coming on. In the late afternoon an intense feeling of cold crept over my body and I began to shiver. It grew so suddenly that at first I thought I had caught a severe chill or my nerves were protesting again. I wrapped a blanket around my shoulders and huddled close to the fire. But the flames didn't warm me. And soon my teeth were chattering and I was shivering so hard I could hardly remain upright.

The old man and I had avoided each other as best we could since that day of the flood, for I had been unable to forgive him for losing my gold. He watched me curiously now as I huddled in my blanket. He called and when I didn't answer him he stamped over to me and pulled back my head. It took him only a moment to understand my deathly pallor and the creases of pain in my face from the rigors that shook my whole body. He snatched one of my hands and held it to the light of the fire. My fingers were white and the flesh beneath the nails had gone blue. 'You've got the fever,' he said to me, and shouted for Joseph.

They helped me into the shelter of the old man's bucksail. There they laid me out on his bed and heaped blankets on top of me. But there was no way that I could protect myself from the cold. It was as though a freezer was at work deep inside me chilling the blood that crept up through my veins. The shivering used up my strength and my teeth were chattering so hard that I couldn't talk. Then the cold eased and I lay for a moment in blessed relief.

Within a few minutes I felt a dry heat steal over my body. All the saliva left my mouth and my eyes felt dry and rusted through. The heat built up and up until I felt as though I was being burnt in a furnace and my skin was flaking off. Whimpering with pain I threw myself around the bed trying to find a cool spot.

The old man and Joseph held me down and kept the blankets on me. Then the sweating started. By that time I was delirious and raving, and the sweat poured off me, drenching the bed and blankets. The fever broke after nearly eight hours and I slept for a while.

When I regained consciousness it was morning and the blankets were hanging in the sun to dry. The cramped space inside the bucksail was filthy. It reeked of the old man, of his brandy fumes and stale tobacco, and of my sweat. I badly needed fresh, clean air, and I staggered outside into the sunlight.

Joseph was stirring a pot on the cooking fire and the old man was bending over him. 'Get back to bed,' the old man said harshly when he saw me.

'I'm feeling better,' I replied. 'The fever's gone. I'll be strong enough to travel by this afternoon.'

'You've got malaria fever,' the old man said again harshly, trying to hide his concern. 'It'll come up again. Now get back to bed.'

I crawled back under the bucksail and within an hour the coldness returned. My teeth began to chatter and I clutched at the blankets drawing them tightly around me. We had run out of medicines but the old man and Joseph did the best they could with native remedies. Joseph boiled up the bark of the red mahogany in water from the roots of the bloodwood tree. Together they sat me up and forced the stringent liquid down my throat. I promptly vomited and no matter how hard they tried they could not keep anything down me.

I didn't have the strength to get out of bed again. For after that the attacks came rapidly, one after another, and I sweated off pounds in weight. The old man and Phillimon took it in turns to sit by my bed and watch over me, while Joseph went in search of different roots and barks for his herbal remedies.

Within forty-eight hours I was vomiting continuously and passing dark urine. The old man stood up from my bed, his ravaged, bearded face drawn with fatigue and worry.

'The malaria's turned to black-water fever,' I heard him say to Joseph. 'Damn me, Joseph,' he said brokenly, 'but I think the boy's dying.' His gnarled hand reached out with a cloth and wiped

99

the sweat from my eyes.

Black-water fever is the disease that became the scourge of the backveld in the early days of Rhodesia. Few men lived through it. There is a rapid breakdown of the red blood cells and when the kidneys collapse the patient dies.

The old man and Joseph fought for my life. When their quinine substitutes didn't work, they kept me alive by forcing me to drink thick, seven-day kaffir beer mixed with water from the boiled roots of the Rhodesian rubber tree. It was the only food I could keep down. They didn't dare move me in search of help in case the jolting of the cart caused my kidneys to collapse completely. But somehow they kept me alive while Phillimon ran to the Mission with a note from the old man demanding medicines. The rains had come to the highveld and the swollen rivers blocked the trails. It must have been a terrible, body-breaking journey—but he made it in five days.

By the time he returned I was close to dying. My periods of consciousness were short and confused and I can remember nothing but brief moments of fear and pain. What I thought were shouts, they told me afterwards, were barely audible whispers that made no sense as I tossed in the sweat-drenched, vomit-stained blankets.

In the middle of the third week the old man and Joseph broke the black-water fever. And I had a strange dream. I dreamt that I was dead, drifting face down just below the surface of the pool and the sunlight filtered down in shafts of light that warmed me. On the surface the water rippled and flowed. But down where I was all was still and silent and peaceful. After all the pain and turmoil I'd been through I felt that if this was death then I was content just to let myself drift. But the current carried me to the bank and left me on the beach. I opened my eyes. There was sunlight streaming through the opening of the bucksail and the old man was standing by my bed.

'You've slept two days solid,' he said indignantly. His eyes were red-rimmed and sunken into a hollow face. He had obviously had little sleep for weeks and he looked a good deal worse off than I did. Then he couldn't hide his pleasure any longer. 'You've made it,' he beamed in response to my questioning glance. 'The fever's gone.'

Joseph and Phillimon crowded into the bucksail, delight at my recovery showing in their grinning faces. But the worry and strain had told on the old man. As he let Joseph fuss over me unaccustomed tears welled in his eyes and he tried to brush them away with the back of his hand. 'You near died on me, boy,' he said huskily. 'We thought we'd lost you many times.' Embarrassed by his emotion he pushed his way through the others and stamped angrily out of the tent.

It was another two weeks before I was well enough to travel. The old man was not anxious to move me and he wasted a day where he could. But I'd heard of a store some fifty miles away that had a telephone. I had to threaten the old man before he'd make the journey, but eventually he loaded me on to the scotch-cart and we set off.

Fifty miles on a good road is nothing. But on a sand track in the rains with a mule and cart it's a long journey. I had plenty of time whilst swaying in the back under the bucksail to think of what I was going to say to Judith. And I'd built myself up into a fever of fear and anticipation by the time we reached there.

The others waited outside while I went into the store. It consisted of nothing more than a long, single-storeyed tin-roofed room built of mud brick. But this was the meeting point for the kraals for miles around, and it was crowded with African women, all chattering excitedly as they haggled over their purchases with the Greek store-keeper. I was half deafened by them and by the jangling notes of an African marimba band that played at full blast from Radio Harare.

The telephone was kept in a battered, unsound-proofed box against one of the mud-brick walls. It took the operator twenty minutes to put the call through to Judith's home. I faced the wall with my hand over my ear to block out the noise and I prayed as I heard her phone ring.

I had been listening for Judith's voice and I was disappointed when her mother answered.

'Hello,' I shouted, desperate to make myself heard. 'Hello, it's Patrick here. Can I speak to Judith?' The static crackled and through the telephone lines that spanned the empty miles of bush, I heard her mother's voice grow cold as she recognized my name.

'She's not here,' she said.

'Where can I reach her?'

'You can't.' Her voice was angry now. 'Don't bother to try. She waited for you long enough— and you were never any good anyway.' Her voice faded into the static. I could hardly hear her, the line was so bad, and I was afraid she was going to put the phone down.

'Don't hang up,' I shouted. 'Please don't hang up.' But she did.

I walked out of the store into the sunlight, feeling weak and empty inside, and I sank down on to the step. The others gathered silently round me.

'What are you going to do now, boy?' the old man asked quietly.

I looked up. 'I'm going to town,' I said. 'I'll need to borrow some money. I've none.' They turned their pockets out for me. Between them

103

they had seventeen dollars and some change. They gave me the seventeen dollars.

I waited at the side of the road for an African-operated long-distance bus to pass. The old man insisted on waiting with me.

'You've been away nearly five months due to that fever,' he warned, 'and things change, boy. You can't expect it to be the same when you get back.'

'I've got to see her,' I answered with quiet desperation. 'That's all I know—I've got to see her.'

The old man shook his head in exasperation. 'Boy,' he said, 'I'm not trying to argue with you, but you're rushing headlong into trouble. If things go wrong for you, Phillimon, Joseph and I will meet you in ten days to two weeks at that camp site we set out from by the Mazoe River. Can you remember how to find it?' he asked anxiously.

I nodded and we were silent for a moment.

The sound came of the bus grinding over the pot-holes towards us and the old man began to fidget. 'Tell you what, boy,' he said, his bloodshot eyes burning with the almost hypnotic enthusiasm that he used when he wanted to talk me into something. 'Damn that woman. There's still time for you to change your mind. Let her go, boy, and come with me. I'll take you places. I'll show you things you'd never believe. It's a good, free life...' The bus stopped and I boarded it, squeezing in among the already crowded passengers.

'Damn you, boy!' the old man yelled after me in fury. 'I tried to help you. I did it for your own good. If you won't listen to me and you get yourself hurt, then it's not my fault.'

The bus pulled away leaving him standing alone on the road.

*   *   *

The bus drove into Mtoko late that night. I slept by the side of the road and early next morning I thumbed a lift to Salisbury in an Internal Affairs Land-Rover. We arrived in the city in the afternoon and they dropped me off near First Street. After being so long in the bush I felt strange at first. The wide pavements were filled with well-dressed people who brushed past me, or stared curiously at my sweat-stained, filthy bush clothes.

The stares had made me ashamed of my appearance. I sneaked past the doorman into a hotel washroom and tried to tidy myself up. I looked at my face in the big mirror above the tiled basin. My hair was like a thick unruly mane curling down over my neck and ears. My eyes and cheeks were hollow and sunken from the fever. I had lost so much weight that my khaki shirt and trousers hung baggily on my body. But for all the ravages of the fever, my face, which had been young-looking and pink-cheeked English, had now grown harder and taken on lines of strength and character. And there was a steely glint of purpose glowing in my dark eyes.

I had decided against 'phoning Judith. I felt that with her mother behind her she might have tried to brush me off. Instead I would go and see her. If I could only talk to her I was sure that I could win her back.

I hitched a lift on the Enterprise Road in the rush of the evening traffic and arrived at Judith's gate. In the soft light of dusk I walked through the lawns up the long drive. I pressed the bell, heard it echo through the house and beat upon the door. I had pushed myself hard over the last twenty-four hours, and the fever was still in me. My hands were cold and I found myself shaking.

A servant answered the door and Judith's mother appeared a moment later. 'Where is she?' I demanded in no mood for an argument. If necessary I was prepared to walk right over that woman to get to Judith. 'I want to see her.'

Her mother looked me up and down—at the wild, dishevelled tramp who had appeared on her doorstep. She couldn't slam the door on me because I had my foot in the way.

'You can't,' she said. 'I told you, she's married.'

Those must have been the words on the

telephone that I'd lost in the static. My mind reeled and I didn't believe her.

'Didn't she get my letters?' I asked hoarsely.

'You never wrote,' the woman answered me viciously. 'The poor girl made herself sick with worry waiting to hear from you. She didn't know where you were. She couldn't reach you. In the end she gave up trying. Leave her alone. You've hurt her enough—she's happy now.'

'She must have got my letters!' I said desperately, my mind crying with pain. 'She must have! Who did she marry?'

'John Churchur.'

I knew him slightly. He had been hanging around Judith for some time. A thought crossed my mind—it wasn't too late. I'd go after them and take her away from him. But her mother read my mind. She knew that she had won and she looked at me triumphantly.

'They're in Europe,' she said. 'On honeymoon. They left two weeks ago. Now get off my property,' she said coldly dismissing me. 'You've caused enough trouble.'

My mind was completely numbed. I turned to go but she remembered something and called me back.

'Judith left a letter with me to give you if you ever showed up. Do you want it?' she asked.

There was still some pride left in me and I shook my head. She should have waited, I kept telling myself. She should have waited. In

Rhodesia even a letter dropped carelessly in the bush has a good chance of reaching its address. She must have received mine.

'You might as well have it,' her mother said. She returned a moment later and thrust the letter into my hands. 'Leave them alone,' she called after me as I walked down the drive. 'They're happy now. Unlike you, he'll make her a good husband. It's the best thing she could have done.'

I was going to throw the letter away, but instead I read it under a street lamp outside her gate. It was a letter from a woman who had got over all the hurt and pain of waiting. The anger in her had died. She didn't love me anymore. And in going to Europe she was letting me know that she had put herself beyond my reach.

The words were sad for she gave me no hope. And as I read them tears burned in my eyes. I'd built her up in my mind all that time in the bush. Now I couldn't believe she was gone. I pulled myself together and went into town. I had no place else to go. I was hurting too much to stay still and I walked the streets. I tried to keep my hurt from the casual glances of the passers-by. But deep inside I was crying, sobbing like a lost child.

I was cold, even though it was a warm night; and the fever was building and swirling in my mind. I saw her there beside me. And though it was too late, all the words I had wanted to say came echoing through my mind. I remembered all the sadness, all the laughter—all the things we'd done together. I'd never felt so lonely or so down. I kept moving, my footsteps following me endlessly up and down the city streets. My body was burning up with fever but I wanted the pain to blank out my mind. I tried through sheer exhaustion to leave the memories behind.

My legs grew too weak to carry me farther and I decided to drink—to fill myself with alcohol and maybe look for a fight and let all the hurt in me crowd out with the spilt blood.

I found my way back to the bar where I'd first met the old man. The barman set up a row of glasses and filled them on my orders. I was shaking so much with the fever that I could hardly lift the first glass to my lips. Anxiously the barman made a move to stop me. But my eyes challenged him to try. And he could see that I was looking for an excuse to fight, so he left me. I hadn't eaten in twenty-four hours and my body was finished and broken. As I drained the third glass I fell off my stool and went crashing to the floor. I tried to get up from the broken glass and spilt beer but I couldn't find the strength. I willed myself with all I had to get up off that floor—but I couldn't move. Something in my mind, when it cleared for a moment, warned me that this was how I'd seen the old man when I first met him. Sad, drunk, and lonely in a bar, with no home to go to and no one waiting for him if he went there. I was no different from him now. I passed out, crying inside to myself.

I regained consciousness in the intensive care unit of the hospital. A doctor was bending over me. 'You've had a relapse,' he said cheerfully. 'But you've got a strong body—you'll be all right.' They kept me there for another twenty-four hours, pumping new blood into me. Then they moved me up to one of the general wards.

I had friends but I felt separated from them now and I made no effort to contact them. A small, dark-haired nurse took a liking to me. When she could find the time she'd come and talk to me. 'Have you got a place to go to when you leave?' she asked. I shook my head. 'Come and stay with me until you're strong again. I've got a small flat quite close to here.'

The day I left hospital she was waiting for me and she took me to her flat. That night some of her friends were giving a party in the next-door block and we looked in on it. The music blared in a darkened room crowded with people. And she and I were two of the loneliest people there. We swayed in the corner of the dance floor, our feet hardly moving, just our bodies rubbing against each other. I kissed her, brushed my lips over her neck, inhaled her perfume, touched her hair. She wasn't Judith, but I told myself it didn't matter. I needed her. 'Let's get out of here,' I whispered. We left the party.

I woke up later in her bed. My head was throbbing and the stale taste of cigarette smoke was in my mouth. I climbed quietly out from beside her and went searching for my clothes. She woke up and sat up naked in the bed.

'Why are you going?' she asked.

And in the pale light of the dawn that was filtering through the window I could see all the hurt in her face, for she must have thought that I had cared for her. She looked ugly to me then, with her hair awry and her make-up smeared. I tried to think of something kind to say but my words would have sounded hollow in the musty quiet of the room and we both knew they would have been false. She looked so small and pathetic, anxiously holding the sheet above her breasts. It made me forget my own hurt and remember that she'd been kind to me, picking me up when I was down and trying to give me back my pride and strength.

I had never bothered to get to know her. I'd thought that I was too dead inside to care. But suddenly I felt a great tenderness towards her. I crossed the room, sat on her bed. I couldn't promise that I'd stay with her, or that I'd see her again. Words were useless so I took her in my arms and held her tightly as she sobbed against my shoulder. And she was crying not just for herself but for me as well—for the loneliness and emptiness that she saw in us both. And all I wanted to do was to shake the dust of the city off my feet and go back into the bush.

The sun was up by the time I reached the Mazoe Road and I thumbed a lift on a passing lorry. During the time I'd lain in the hospital I'd figured out that it must have been the old man who destroyed my letters instead of posting them. It made sense when I thought back to all that he had said and done. A cold anger burned in me.

CHAPTER ELEVEN

I FOUND the camp in the clearing beneath the shade of the msasa trees. The old man had obviously sold off some of our equipment for he had brought new tents for the rainy season. One of the tents was empty and set apart from the others as though he'd known I'd be coming back.

I walked into the camp and found him sitting in his deck-chair by the fire with the kettle brewing for tea. He rose to greet me. But I was ready to murder him.

'You bastard,' I said furiously. 'You never posted my letters, did you?' He saw the wild anger in my eyes and backed away. 'I tried to warn you,' he explained. 'I tried to stop you. With Mouldy gone you're all I've got left, boy. I'm getting old now and ready to die. And I'm scared of dying alone.' He shrugged his shoulders in a pathetic gesture. 'I've got no one else.'

I should have beaten him to a pulp then and there. But as the old man watched me, tears of loneliness squeezed out from under his eyelids, rolled down his craggy face and lost themselves in his beard.

'I'm sorry,' he said, shaking his head. 'I'm sorry, boy. I wouldn't have hurt you. But she'd have done you no good. I thought you'd be better off with me.'

He looked old and broken and very frail. He had a way of playing on my feelings—of making me feel responsible for him. He tied me to him that way.

A storm that had been building up all morning now broke overhead. Heavy drops of warm rain beat on our shoulders and matted our hair as we stood there confronting one another. Wordlessly I left him and stalked off to my tent. As soon as the rain lifted, I promised myself, I'd leave. Joseph would look after the old man—and if not, the vultures could have him.

The storm built up over the peaks of the Iron Mask hills and we were rained in for three days. The ground was awash and the raindrops hammered incessantly on the canvas walls of the tents. We never spoke—the old man and I. We lived and took our meals alone. He was drunk most of the time, but I didn't touch a drop.

Instead I just sat there in the semi-darkness of my tent with the lightning jagging across the sky and the thunder booming and growling all around.

Hour after hour, day into night, I sat there listening to the rain beat on the canvas—scarcely moving in the darkness with nothing to do but think. The wind cried in the guy ropes and overhead the trees swayed and rattled their branches. The melancholy with the damp crept into my bones until I began to lose my mind.

I could see the old man's shadow, thrown by an oil lamp through the walls of his tent. I watched him hatefully as he sat in his deck-chair staring into space and occasionally lifting his bottle to his lips. At first I tried to ignore him but all the anger and resentment in me built up until I could resist it no longer.

I had been cleaning my rifle. I swung it up and aimed at his head. I could see him clearly silhouetted in my sights—and there was murder in me then. My finger squeezed the trigger but at the last split second I moved the sights an inch to the side. The rifle kicked against my shoulder and the bottle, upraised against the old man's lips, exploded and showered him with liquor and shards of glass.

The old man yelled, jumped from his deck-chair and came running from his tent, scared half to death. He saw me at the entrance to my tent with my rifle in my hands and his fear turned to rage. 'So it's a fight you want to clear the air, is it?' he shouted. 'Well you've got it, boy. Damned if I don't shoot you.'

I worked the bolt and put two more bullets into the mud beneath the old man's feet. He leapt into the air cursing and swearing and then he dived into his tent for his rifle. I darted back into mine and filled my pockets with ammunition. He was waiting for me as I came out with his .400 Express at his shoulder. I heard it go off with a boom like a small cannon and the bullet broke the branch above my head clean off.

I ran into the bush for cover and the old man came after me. I turned, catching him in the open, and sent a bullet singing over his shoulder, causing him to throw himself face down flat in the mud. Then we started to hunt each other through the bush—slipping and sliding in the mud, drenched by the grey wall of rain, blasting off with our rifles as we caught sight of each other in the lightning flashes.

The excitement released all the tension and melancholy in me. I was still a little mad with anger, but I was also laughing now—a crazy mixture of pain and pleasure. I slipped down the side of the donga, fell into the stream and came up half drowned and covered from head to foot in mud. I scrambled up the bank as the old man came over the rise and sent a bullet after me.

We aimed to miss each other, but as time

wore on it grew more serious. Our bullets passed closer and closer until I crept up on the old man and put one into a tree trunk an inch from his nose. We would have killed each other then if we had been allowed to go on. But I felt a gun barrel nudge the small of my back and I rolled over. Phillimon was standing above me with the rain dripping down his scarred, black face.

'It's finished, Mambo,' he said. And he leaned down and took the rifle out of my hands. Joseph was doing the same to the old man. They walked us back to the camp at gun point and separated us to our tents.

I slept well that night, deeply and at peace with myself. In the morning I awoke to find the old man standing outside my tent.

'What day is it?' he asked.

'I don't know,' I replied. 'I've lost track of the days.'

'So have I,' the old man said, 'but I think it's nearly Christmas. Would you come and have a drink with me?' he asked shyly, 'to celebrate. I've saved a bottle specially for you.'

I was silent for a moment remembering the madness of the previous day with the rain and the bullets cracking by. And I thanked God that we were both still alive. The old man must have felt the same way. A smile warmed his eyes then his whole battered face. 'Happy Christmas, boy,' he said softly. And I found myself grinning back.

Phillimon, Joseph and I crowded into his tent and at some time on that day we called Christmas, the old man reached into the bottom of his tin trunk and drew out a yellow, much-fingered map that had been drawn on the back of a letter. He spread it out on an up-turned box that served him as a table and looked up at us, his eyes glowing with prospecting fever. 'You ever heard the stories of the lost German mines?' he asked. I shook my head and the old man launched into his tale.

'Well, way back before the 1914–18 War,' he said, 'there was a gold rush in this country. It got so bad that parts near Gwanda were close pegged and a man couldn't move for workings. In those days we produced upwards of nine hundred thousand ounces of gold a year; and much of that was produced by small workers going down their mines with a candle in one hand and one foot in a bucket.

'There were all sorts working the gold fields in those days. Americans, Dutch, Swedes and Germans—a lot of Germans and they made bloody good small workers. Some of them found rich claims way out in the backveld. When the War came they knew that they'd be interned so they buried their mines. You see, under the mining laws you've got to do so much actual development work each year or you'll lose your mine and it'll go to forfeit—then anyone can

117

claim it.

'So a lot of Germans hid their equipment down their mines and filled in the shafts with sand, hoping that when the War was over they could come back and claim them. The records weren't that accurate in those days—you marked your claim with the Mining Commissioner as being so many yards due west of a big tree and north of a kopje and south of an anthill. That was good enough seeing that most of the men could hardly read or write. Some of the Germans didn't make it back and their mines were never found. That's how the stories of the lost German mines got around.

'A lot of it was just stories that became exaggerated over the years. But there was one old man they called Bismarck. He was a wily old devil and he was supposed to have found one of the richest gold mines that this country's ever known. Everyone knew about it because they'd seen him come to town with great nuggets of gold taken straight from the reef that he hadn't even bothered to smelt. But no one ever found his claim, though by Christ they looked. He was old and he died in an internment camp. But before he died old Bismarck got lonely for the family he'd left behind in Germany. He sent them a letter asking that, when the War was over, if they came out to Africa they should visit his wife's grave and bury him beside her. And he sent them a map drawn on the back of the letter showing them where to find her.

'Everyone had been watching old Bismarck—but that was the clue,' the old man said excitedly. 'See, Mouldy Duncan had worked that area in those days—and he was one of the few people who knew that Bismarck had buried his wife down his mine, just before he filled it in. Well, Mouldy joined up like everyone else. But after the War he traced the family to Germany and bought the map off them. They didn't understand what Bismarck was trying to tell them and, anyway, times were hard and they needed the money.

'Mouldy passed the map on to me when he died. We were going to try and find the capital to open up the mine from the bewitched pool. But I know a man we can trust to back us once I tell him the story like I told it to you.'

'There's lots of stories like that in this country,' I said dubiously. 'What makes you think he'll believe you?'

'The story of the lost Bismarck mine has been told many times and in many different ways,' the old man agreed quietly. 'And there's many faked maps about. But this one's real. Mouldy swore it to me and I believed him.'

I glanced down at the faded copperplate script, written with a shaky spidery hand that could have been Bismarck's. And such was the old man's ability to tell a tale that it was hard not to believe.

119

'I'm going looking for it,' he said. 'I'll be leaving as soon as the rain lets up. Are you coming with me?'

I caught Phillimon's eye. He nodded and I shrugged my shoulders. 'Why not?' I said. 'I've no place else to go.'

'We'll be full partners,' the old man said magnanimously. 'Everything split right down the middle.'

We shook hands on it with the rain drumming on the walls of the tent. 'You won't regret it, boy,' the old man promised me. 'I've heard the reef of that mine's so rich it's going to be like finding a jeweller's shop under the ground.'

★　　★　　★

We trekked slowly southwards across the country, through the midlands, over the desolate Somabula flats and into the lowveld of Matabeleland. There we detoured north again, at the old man's insistence, to the Turk and Lonely mine area above Inyati. This had been his favourite stamping ground when Mouldy Duncan was alive—and he went to visit his memories.

We camped when the summer storms broke around four o'clock in the afternoon and then trekked on again by the light of the dawn in the crystal-clear, rain-washed air . . . or sometimes, when the day was very hot, we rested up in the shade and then, if there was a bright moon, we trekked on at night. The old man and the trekking moon. He loved a night sky and a cool wind in his face, following a sandy road that stretched like a pale ribbon across the bush to distant misty moon-drenched hills.

'I'm tired of wandering,' I said to him one night. 'It's time we went looking for the mine—that's if it's there and you weren't lying to me about it,' I added suspiciously.

'It's there all right,' the old man reassured me. 'Give me a few more days here and we'll go.'

Through the old man's eyes I learnt to appreciate the stark beauty of the African veld, the shades of brown that formed a backdrop for the searing bright colours of flowers that faded and died so quickly in the burning glare of the sun. I loved the emptiness of the bush now, the limitless horizons, the haunting sunsets. The veld was much like the sea in that the wind could make the tall stems of elephant grass surge like waves rolling down towards me.

One afternoon we came over a rise and I saw the headgear of a mine against the skyline. From then on, all along the road for the last few miles into the village, there were signs of mines or prospecting shafts being sunk. I grew worried by all this activity, certain that someone would have found the Bismarck mine, but the old man assured me that it was still safely hidden away in the hills. The mines in this district had

wonderful names that excited the imagination—
like the Last Chance and Good Luck, Smiler,
Lone Hand, Long John and Big Ben.

As we walked along those last few miles the
old man told me stories of the mines and the
men who made them. Some of the men were still
around. And for all their age, they were big
men, larger than life.

It was told how one of them, who now owned
half the district, had lost his reef and was so
broke that his pockets were turned out by his
creditors. He went down his mine to place the
last charge before he cleared out of the area and
when the dust settled he found that he had
broken through the barren rock into the reef
again and he was staring at a bank vault of gold
in the quartz.

One last charge, one last blast. I was to hear
those words many times. Every small worker
was a born optimist and a gambler. When his
reef ran rich he made a fortune. But when it
gave out to a barren stringer of quartz he would
follow it through hundreds of feet of waste rock,
using up all his money, until he was down to his
last blast and still hoping. The men who could
walk away from their mines knowing that they
had seen the bottom of the reef and with their
money still in their pockets were the tycoons of
the business. But they were few and far between
and the old man wasn't one of them. Once he
found a reef he believed in he'd follow it to

122

China. It wasn't so much the money with him—he just hated giving in.

We passed through the village and came upon Chinaman Lee's store on a railway line that came out of one horizon and disappeared into the other, in a place so lonely that it was an occasion when a train went by. The store was big and dirty with mealie meal spilt on the floor and the windows grimy so that it was gloomy inside. Goods were stacked from floor to ceiling and it sold everything from bicycles to tins of beans, from prams to prospecting equipment.

We arrived in the heat of the day. There were few people around, just a couple of Chinaman Lee's children working at their lessons behind the broad counter. At first they couldn't recognize the figure standing in the doorway with his face shadowed by the bright light behind. Then they threw down their books and ran yelling and laughing straight at the old man. Other children, alerted by the excitement, tumbled through from the living quarters at the back of the store and launched themselves at the old man. In a moment he was covered by children climbing all over him. He cursed and swore at them indignantly and made as if to throw them off. But the children took no notice for they could see his eyes shining at the warmth of his welcome and his hands searching his pockets to find sweets for them.

A door leading from the back of the store

creaked open and a small white-haired man shuffled forward. His eyes lit with pleasure when he saw the old man and the children dropped away obediently at his signal. 'I am glad you are back,' he said softly, with just a trace of a sing-song lilt in his voice. 'I heard you were dead and it worried me greatly—you and Mouldy Duncan still owe me money.'

Chinaman Lee ushered us into the back of the store and sat us across a table from him.

'It was Mouldy who died,' the old man said.

'I am sorry,' the Chinaman answered in a voice so soft that he was hard to hear. 'For all his faults Mouldy was a good man. I liked him. Who is this?' he asked turning to me.

'My new partner,' the old man answered and introduced us.

Then the old man told Lee the story. He told it so well that he had me convinced all over again. But at the end Chinaman Lee just nodded. He didn't seem impressed.

'I will think about it,' was all he said.

We camped behind the store. 'Don't worry,' the old man told me confidently, 'Chinaman Lee will go for it. He backs miners as his father did before him. They're better than any bank— and don't be fooled by the way he lives. That family's got enough money stashed away to buy half this country.'

Chinaman Lee kept his family to themselves. They didn't mix with the other people in the

124

district. Their only relaxation was on Sunday afternoons after work, when, dressed in their best, the whole family walked down the railway line towards the horizon and back. It was no life for a child and the old man, with his bright-eyed, bearded buccaneer's face and his stories of gold and fires and floods was heaven sent.

On the third day, when I was ready to give up hope, Chinaman Lee called us into his small office. On the table he had placed brandy for the old man and me and a clear, weak tea for himself.

'It is a great risk,' he said as soon as we were seated, 'but I believe in you and I will back you.'

'Bless you, Lee,' the old man said, leaping up from his seat and trying to seize the little Chinaman by the hand. 'I knew we could count on you.'

But Chinaman Lee waved him back. 'I will give you no money,' he said. 'Instead, I will back you with rations and equipment from the store—enough for a six-month search for the mine. I realize that you have little or no security to offer me for this loan, and it is important that you should stand to lose as well as me. So I have a condition: if you fail to find the mine in that time, then you will hand over everything—by that I mean everything you possess—to me.'

I caught the look of anguish in the old man's eyes. He knew how much I wanted that mine and he would have agreed to anything for my

125

sake. But I couldn't put him in a position where he might have to part with the mule and see her sold. 'We'll agree to everything 'We'll agree to everything but the mule—and the cart,' I added.

Somehow I always identified the old man with the mule and cart—so long as he kept those he was complete and could start again. But they were the one portion of security that Chinaman Lee had been aiming for and he refused to give them up.

'Everything,' he repeated quietly, 'everything you possess.' And the way he said it sent a chill through me. 'If, however, you do find the mine,' the Chinaman continued, 'then I will loan you all the development costs to clear the shafts and drives ready to start production again. Once the mine becomes self-financing all loans I have made will be repaid at an interest of three per cent above bank lending rate and thereafter I will take a third share in all profits. This is not a matter between friends,' he warned us. 'This is a business venture and I will expect you to honour your side of the bargain—as I will mine. Think on it carefully before you give me your reply.'

The old man and I argued half the night. 'I told you I'd find the bewitched pool,' the old man said stubbornly, forgetting the large part luck had played, 'and I'll find that bloody mine.'

In the morning we gave our agreement and Chinaman Lee helped us load up the cart with supplies.

CHAPTER TWELVE

WE trekked up into the Gwanda Hills and camped in the shade of some trees near the supposed site of the Bismarck mine. It was desolate, lonely ranching country—almost a desert compared with the highveld.

The directions, according to the map we held, were simple. You lined up a big baobab tree with the brow of a nearby hill. From the centre of that line you then walked due south three hundred yards. All that we found was a flat bladed rock half buried in the grass, and as we trenched we came across the scratchings of other miners who had searched this area without result.

We had only been at this site a few days when a Land-Rover came bumping across the veld towards us and a man got out. His big bush hat was pulled down over his ears and his hands hung like steam shovels by his sides. His name was van Tonder and he was the section manager for the part of the ranch we were on.

'Get off this land,' he said in a heavy Afrikaans accent.

As if to add force to his words his two sons climbed out of the Land-Rover and stood beside him, both of them built like small giants—all muscle and bone and burnt to a mahogany colour from working all day in the sun.

'We're here legally,' the old man said. 'And we're not moving.'

'McLeod doesn't want miners on his land,' van Tonder shouted. 'Now get off, vermin, or we'll run you off.'

The old man didn't like being threatened—it brought out the stubborn streak in him. He raised his .400 Express and van Tonder found himself looking down the barrel of a small cannon. 'Try it,' the old man advised quietly.

Van Tonder turned to one of his sons. 'Go fetch McLeod,' he ordered. 'And you,' he turned ominously to the old man, 'you wait here with me.'

Later in the day the Land-Rover returned. A lean, gaunt-faced old fashionedly-dressed man well into his sixties with a clipped, military moustache and close-cropped grey hair climbed out. Van Tonder and his sons towered above him but the man possessed such immense authority that there was no doubt whose land this was. He was king in this district and something in his face, in his piercing blue eyes, warned me to take him seriously.

'Is that McLeod?' I asked quietly.

'Yes,' the old man answered.

I'd heard of him—almost as soon as we entered Matabeleland. Though old now, Murray McLeod still rose at four o'clock every morning and ruled his empire with an iron hand. The youngest and the last survivor of a group of brothers who had come to this country from Scotland in the pioneer days, his hospitality was famous. When a visitor called at his house he was given a bottle of whisky and a glass. The cap was thrown away and he was not expected to leave until the bottle was empty. On the other hand he was also known to make a ferocious enemy.

According to the mining laws of Rhodesia, a man can prospect over any land provided he does not peg a claim within four hundred and fifty yards of a homestead or within fifteen yards of a ploughed field.

'I don't give a damn what the law says,' McLeod told us. 'I won't have miners on my land. Go before I find a way to run you off.'

'What harm have we done you?' I asked.

'Look around you,' McLeod answered, indicating the rolling hills so bare that only a Matabele could love them. 'My land as far as the eye can see. It's empty but for cattle and the game I've managed to save from being slaughtered by poachers. And I like it that way. Once I let you miners in you'll rape the earth and poison the streams with your slimes dumps. When you're finished here the land will be fit for neither man nor beast. I made this ranch from bush. I cherish each part of it. And I'll protect what's mine—rely on that.' He was silent for a moment and I felt him watching me with eyes that looked down the sights of a rifle and gently squeezed the trigger. 'Be off with you,' he said quietly,'and save yourself some trouble.'

I shook my head.

'All right,' McLeod answered, 'then I'm warning both of you in front of witnesses. Don't cut down my fences. If you use any wood, you pay for it. And don't let your labour go after my cattle or poach my game. You'll be watching them,' he said to van Tonder.

'I will,' van Tonder replied angrily, hating us. 'I will watch them.'

McLeod climbed into the Land-Rover. 'You'll not be on my land long,' he said. 'I'll find a way to move you that's good and legal.'

'Hell!' I swore softly, still badly shaken after they had gone. 'I don't want to cross that McLeod any further than I can help. Didn't you tell me that it was he and his brothers who made their money out of mining?'

The old man nodded. 'That's him,' he said gloomily, sensing trouble ahead. 'And I tell you, boy, there's no one more fanatical than a converted miner when it comes to protecting land.'

The next day we got down to work in earnest.

We dug trenches, expecting to find the shaft or at least strike the sands buried below the grass. For no matter how the bush had grown over there had to be some trace left of the old mine—the concrete base of the suction gas engine, the mark of the stamps, the hollow where the sands had subsided in the shaft. The weeks passed and though we burrowed and trenched and dug like moles and cut down the grass for hundreds of yards around we found nothing. But Bismarck had been in a hurry—he couldn't have hidden his mine that well.

The old man and I studied the map every night by the fire. I was beginning to despair that either Bismarck had been fooling his family, or Mouldy Duncan had bought the wrong map. I went back and re-paced the co-ordinates, figuring out that maybe the baobab tree that Bismarck used for a reference had been struck by lightning and burnt out. But I could find no sign of another one and anyway by this time its roots would have rotted. The search seemed hopeless.

'If you had to hide a mine in a hurry,' I asked the old man, 'What would you have done?'

The old man thought it over. 'I'd lower my machinery and then my headgear down to the bottom of the shaft. Then I'd block it off above the first level—say at about eighty feet—and fill it up with slimes. The top I'd cover with rock and soil. The rest of the slimes I'd spread over

131

the ground as thin as possible, hoping that the rains would leech out the poisons and the grass would grow through.'

The slimes the old man spoke of were the sand residues from the rock that had been crushed in the mill. After being treated with cyanide to remove as much of the remaining gold as possible, they usually formed a small hill beside each mine. To spread thousands of tons of slimes would be an impossible job to do in a hurry.

'He must have pumped it down the shaft,' I said, 'otherwise we'd find the dumps if nothing else.'

The old man shook his head. 'Bismarck wouldn't have done that. Not if he wanted to come back and open up his mine again. To clear a shaft of slimes is one of the most dangerous jobs I know. The outside forms a hard crust like cement, but inside there's pockets that are still wet. You can break through the crust and all of a sudden you've got a mud rush sliding down on you. In a confined space there's no way out ... it makes a terrible way to die.'

'Well then,' I said tiredly, 'we're searching in the wrong place. The Bismarck mine's not here.'

I think the old man must have known that too but we kept looking. And all the time we were watched from a Land-Rover parked on the skyline, and we'd catch the flash of the sun glinting on a pair of binoculars.

Word got around that we were looking for the lost Bismarck mine. A couple of prospectors came to our camp on the pretext of trading supplies. In fact they had really come to check up on how we were doing and see if they could move in on our claim. Their names were Abraham and Samuel, known affectionately as Ace and Sam. Ace was a smaller version of the old man, built like a grubby cock-sparrow, all fiery-eyed with a seven-day beard stubble on his face and a breath which contained so much alcohol that only a fool would have lit a match within ten feet of him. Sam was bigger with a battered boxer's face framed under a floppy hat and a wide grin that showed his broken front teeth. He was very much the younger brother being still in his forties, and he was content to let Ace do the thinking and the talking for them both. Ace, with his ready laugh and quick line of chatter, entered the despondent gloom of our camp like a breath of fresh air. And when he wanted to return our hospitality by inviting us to their camp the old man was tempted. 'It wouldn't do us any harm to rest for a couple of days,' he said.

Ace and Sam were the real gipsy small workers of the Rhodesian mining industry. They made a living by scratching at the small reefs that no one else was interested in, both of them hopelessly convinced that one day the small reefs they happened to be working would miraculously blossom underground into a big reef loaded with gold. In the meantime, when their debts mounted to intolerable levels and the bailiffs came after them trying to collect, they hid in the hills and worked their tiny two stamp mill by night, if necessary, for the couple of ounces of gold it could deliver.

Their camp was a grass-roofed hut with its mud walls proudly white-washed. The living area beyond that was a patch of carefully swept earth in the shade of a tree with old car seats tidily arranged about a wooden dynamite box that served as a table. The equipment put crudely together for crushing the rock and separating the gold was mostly borrowed. By the door of the hut, within easy reach of anyone passing, was a forty-four gallon drum filled with seven-day brewed mealie meal beer. The thick grey porridge stood placidly in the shade with the flies settling on it—until either Ace or Sam felt the need to drink something more active— and then they tossed in a handful of carbide to ginger it up. The heavy brew came to life and heaved and spat and bubbled.

The reef they were mining had first been worked by the ancients, but those people had given up when they found that the values had dropped as they went deeper. The ancients, with their primitive tools, had only worked the rich gold. Ace and Sam were less fussy.

That night we sat on the motor car seats under the stars and passed a bottle around. From the distance came the clatter of the little stamp mill. And every so often Ace would get up with a torch to see if any gold was building up on the plate. Then he'd settle back to swopping yarns with the old man about the mines they had won and lost.

'Who were the ancients?' I asked.

It was Ace who first answered me. 'No one rightly knows,' he said. 'But I can tell you they were a very fine race of prospectors. There's few mines in Rhodesia that weren't first discovered by them and it's been estimated that they took out over nine hundred thousand ounces of gold from the Mount Darwin area alone.'

'Much of what is now this country formed part of the old kingdom of Monomatapa,' the old man said. 'That was in the time when the civilization around Zimbabwe flourished. But even before then—some say back in the days of King Solomon and the Queen of Sheba—the ancients were here. And the gold they took was supposed to have formed much of King Solomon's treasure. For myself I believe in the theory that the ancients came from India in the 4th century BC. But though we've found the bones of their slaves buried under rock slides fifty feet down, no one really knows who they were.'

'I once worked with an old prospector who

had a theory,' Ace said. 'You know those strange bladed rocks you sometimes find in the bush when you're in gold country? Well, his theory was that when the ancients came through here they sent their prospectors ahead of the main body of men, and when they found a likely-looking reef, they set up one of those bladed rocks to show the others the way. The blade is supposed to point the direction and the width gives the distance—say an inch for every two hundred yards. That's how we discovered this reef—we found a bladed rock and followed it. So I figured there might be something in the theory after all.'

The old man choked on his brandy and I had to pound his back before he could breathe again. Both of us remembered the bladed rock on our claim. He caught my eye, imploring me to shut up, and nervously I changed the subject.

Early the next morning we made some excuse and left Ace scratching his head at our sudden departure. 'God damn it,' the old man swore excitedly as we hurried back to our camp. 'I'm a bloody fool. I should have known there was something strange about that rock being there and nothing else. Look at it this way. Imagine old Bismarck locked up in an internment camp knowing that every son of a bitch's looking for his mine, and that all his letters are going to be censored and word must reach his rivals. So what does he do? He makes out a map claiming

136

it's only the site of his wife's grave—and if that doesn't fool you, it'll only lead you to the first clue.'

We cleared the ground around the bladed rock, took a compass bearing on the direction it pointed and measured the width. We followed the bearing for close on six hundred yards and found another bladed rock. A bearing on this one took us in the direction of a steep flat-topped hill, taller than the others around. After that there were no more bladed rocks to be found.

The old man looked up at the hill and shook his head. 'It would be an almost impossible freak of nature for a reef to outcrop up there without showing on the sides,' he said.

We were going to go around it, but instead we climbed the hill to get a better view of the area, hoping that the height would help us to pick out where the slimes dumps had raised the level of the surrounding ground. And there it was. On top of the hill. The crumbling foundations for the machinery and the stamps half buried by the grass—and the hollow where the blocking sands had subsided into the shaft. It was ingenious—and all Bismarck had to do to hide the slimes was to pump them over the sides and they'd form part of the hill.

The old man sat down unsteadily on a concrete slab by the side of the shaft. 'The old bastard's fooled everyone for over fifty years,' he said breathlessly. 'And to tell you the truth, I only half believed the story. But we found it, boy. We bloody found it. We've found ourselves the Bismarck mine!'

CHAPTER THIRTEEN

THE Bismarck mine was situated right on the border of McLeod's land just across a valley from Ace and Sam's claims. I raced back to our camp for a peg. We made out our prospecting notice, placed it in a plastic bag, drove the peg in on the top of the hill, and attached the notice to it. A copy of the same notice had to be sent to the Mining Commissioner and to McLeod as the owner of the land. But it gave us thirty-one days' exclusive prospecting rights within three hundred yards of our peg before we had to register our completed block of claims with the Mining Commissioner's office.

'I've only ever seen one mine like this before,' the old man said as he watched Joseph bringing up the mule and the equipment. 'And that was in the Fort Victoria district. A man went down on a tiny strike like this one and his reef blossomed out good and rich, deep in the bowels of the earth.'

I was for completing the pegging of our claims immediately and heading off for the Mining

Commissioner's office to register it. But the old man wouldn't let me. We were only allowed to block off ten claims and he wanted to see how the reef ran to make sure that we included it all within our pegs before we registered. The old man drove a spike through the slimes and struck solid bottom at twenty-five feet. He was pleased. 'That's not bad,' he said. 'It'll take us less than a couple of weeks to clear it.' He rigged a winch over the shaft and we set to work.

Phillimon and I had to work on the bottom shovelling the slimes into the bucket, while the old man and Joseph winched it up and threw it over the side. The slimes seemed solid enough, but after the old man's warning, I had the unnerving feeling that it was wet inside. At any moment the crust could give way and I'd drown in the quicksand—that, or the supports would go and I'd find myself falling down the shaft into the darkness that lay God knows how deep below. They say that when a man falls a great distance he's dead from shock before he hits the bottom. I believed them. I tried to keep close to the bucket and I hated to see it go up out of reach.

We struck the platform without incident. It made a hollow sound as we cleared away the sand and drilled a hole in the concrete. The old man placed a small charge of explosives and blew it in. We stood on the lip of the shaft, staring down, watching the yellow fumes from the explosion drift upwards carrying with it the sulphurous smell of the underground air. The old man tossed a stone into the darkness. It rattled briefly against the sides and then it was gone, plunging down through space. We never heard it hit the bottom.

The old man shone his light around the rotting timber shoring that held up the sides of the shaft. 'They'll hold,' he said.

I didn't like that dark gaping hole below me one bit. I was suffering from vertigo and I stepped back from the edge.

'What are we going to do now?' I asked.

'You and I,' the old man replied, 'we're going down. Joseph, how much rope have we got?'

'Three hundred feet,' Joseph answered.

'That'll do. Wrap it round the winch. The bucket'll take one of us at a time.'

The rope seemed very thin to me. I remembered a story Ace told me of the time he worked as a timber man on one of the big mines. Those hoists had big steel cables and cages that could take twenty men at once. The night shift was coming up when Ace was called out of bed. The hoist operator had reported that the pressure had gone off the cable. Ace went down in a small skip to investigate. It was a deep mine and he dropped down level after level, checking on the cable with his light, until at about a thousand feet he came across the broken end with the strands of metal frayed where they'd parted.

He stopped off at the next level. Like most big mines, the stations were painted with white-wash and lit by an electric light. The bell-boy who operated the doors was sitting on the stool fast asleep. At his feet was a severed head, and the walls were splashed with blood where a desperate man had tried to jump from the plummeting cage.

Ace shook the bell-boy awake. The African took one look at the gory head at his feet and the blood and flesh on the walls and went screaming down the drive into the darkness.

Ace went on down. At the very bottom of the mine, two thousand two hundred feet below the earth's surface, he found the cage. The metal had compacted like a squashed cardboard box and the bodies inside were mashed into an unrecognizable pulp.

They learned afterwards that thirty-two men had climbed into a cage built to take twenty. And they had to bring the remains up in canvas bags for burial. The bell-boy was found twenty-four hours later hiding in the darkness. He had gone raving mad.

The old man was ready to go down the shaft and I had to help to keep the winch handles from spinning. 'Remember,' he said, as his head dropped below the surface, 'if you don't hear me shout, use the string. One pull for stop. Two pulls for lower slowly. Three pulls, raise slowly.

141

And seven pulls, get me out of there. Got it?' Joseph nodded and let the string pay out with the rope.

We had just about paid out to the end of the rope when we got the signal to stop. Another signal and we raised the bucket ten feet, then we felt the pressure go off the rope and we got the signal to raise the bucket up—and it was my turn.

I swung out over the shaft with one foot in the bucket watching the rope stretch, shaking with fear and praying that it wouldn't part. The sounds on the surface receded as I dropped down, down, down; heard the drip of falling water, saw the wet rock face flashing by in the glow of my carbide lamp. Then the bucket struck a piece of shoring timber that was leaning out from the side. The rotten timber cracked apart like match-wood but not before tipping the bucket so that I was almost thrown out. I dropped the lamp, saw the spark of it falling through the darkness; then the flame went out and I clutched at the rope for dear life. The bucket spun violently across the shaft and I kicked myself off the other side. The light from the surface had faded to a tiny glow far above me and the darkness rushed in. With it came a vast, eerie silence. A sensation of falling silently through an emptiness without bottom or sides.

I seemed to go down forever, half paralysed with fear, through the empty, eerie darkness with water drumming off my miner's helmet and splashing off my shoulders. Then I saw the welcome sight of the old man's light flashing up at me and I tugged at the string so hard that I nearly took Joseph's hand off. The bucket swayed to a stop level with the old man standing on a wooden platform.

'You'll have to jump,' he said, holding his light on me. 'It's only a couple of feet. Be careful—the rock's crumbled beneath and this platform's the only thing left.' He stamped on the rotting wood with his boot. 'Seems strong enough to hold. Come on,' he said irritably, 'I haven't got all day.'

I clung to the rope a little bit longer, plucking up courage. Then I let go of it and leapt across the gap. The old man caught me as I landed. The platform tottered under our combined weights and with a groan of splintering timber it gave way and went crashing down the shaft. The old man and I leapt backwards and clawed at the rock for a grip. With great effort we hauled ourselves up on to the drive. The old man stood up and gingerly shone his light over where the platform had been. 'Jesus Christ,' he said softly. 'I thought it would hold.'

The bucket dangled tantalizingly fifteen feet away—below it lay emptiness and darkness. 'If you took a run could you jump that far?' the old man asked. I licked my dry lips and shook my head. I was trembling so badly with fear that I could hardly remain upright. The old man didn't seem to notice.

'All right,' he said, 'we'll climb up through the stopes and try from the station on the next level. Tell them to pull the bucket up.' But as he spoke there came a crack of parting timber and the slither of shifting rock farther up. Then shoring debris came crashing down the shaft. 'The blast must have weakened it,' the old man shouted. 'The whole shaft's going.' The thunder and vibration of the falling rock subsided. In the deafening silence that followed the old man shone his light out over the gap. The bucket was gone. We were trapped.

The silence of an empty mine, the complete lack of all identifiable background sounds that I'd grown used to on the surface, disorientated me. That and, without the aid of the old man's lamp, an all-enveloping darkness, so black, so dense, that I could not tell which direction I was facing, and had difficulty in keeping my balance.

'What are we going to do now?' I whispered, trying to control the panic that was rising within me.

'There's got to be an air shaft,' the old man answered confidently, 'otherwise Bismarck couldn't have ventilated his mine. We'll find it.' The underground was the old man's element and it held no fears for him. 'Seeing as we're here,' he added, 'we might as well have a look

144

around. I'd like to see the bottom if we can. It can't be more than a couple of levels farther down.'

He set off along the drive flashing his lamp to show the way. The air was warm and damp carrying the musty, acid smell of minerals oxidising in the rock that dried up my saliva and coated my mouth and throat. Within a few yards the humidity caused the sweat to pour off me and my clothes stuck wetly to my body. We followed a narrow gauge railway line, all twisted and rusted through, that ran along the floor past ore shutes, winch cables, de-railed coco pans— the debris of an abandoned mine lay everywhere.

The old man stopped and shone his light up through a hole in the roof. 'That's where they've been stoping out the reef,' he said. 'They leave a pillar about eleven feet deep to support the drive and take out the rest right up to the next level. I'd say this reef's running east to west and dipping at nearly sixty to sixty-five degrees to the vertical. That's good. I can't abide a flat reef,' he said with a proprietary air, 'it's difficult to work.'

He shone his light down. At my feet was a gaping hole where the rotten timber covering had fallen through into the stope below. I was standing on the lip and I'd been just about to step into it. I froze. 'Walk careful,' the old man said. 'It's empty in there.' He tossed in a stone and I heard it rattle down forever.

The old man walked on, flashing his light, watching the white quartz reef shining like marble amid the dark waste rock of the ceiling. Leading off from the main drive was a maze of secondary tunnels, their dark gaping mouths inviting you in like a spider's web a fly. 'It's a terrible thing to lose your way in a strange mine, boy,' the old man warned. 'So stay close. Even experienced miners have been known to go raving mad when they've been lost in the darkness for a while. If anything happens to me, remember there are three ways you can find your way out of a mine. First is follow the narrow gauge tracks. If there are no tracks, follow the water's flow. In a well-developed mine every drive is built on a slight incline and it'll lead you back to the shaft. And last—if for some reason there's no water, follow the air draught. A mine's got to be ventilated or they'd never clear the fumes out after a blast. Usually the main shaft with the hoist carries the up-draught. Then there's a down-draught shaft that's also used as an escape way at the other end of the mine. If you're still a moment you'll feel it blowing the stale air out. God knows where he's hidden it. But that's the way we'll go when we get out of here.'

I followed hard on the old man's heels. He had been looking for something and when he came to a hole with a rusted cable ladder-way

146

showing through, he stopped. 'That's it,' he said. 'That's the escape way. First we'll go down and have a look at the bottom. Then we'll go up again—it'll lead us to the air shaft. That is . . .' he flashed his light at my white face, 'unless you'd like to stay here and wait while I go down.'

There was no way that I was going to let him leave me alone without a light in the dark and the silence, so I followed him.

The ladder-way which led down through the stopes lay hard against the rock face and it was difficult for my fingers and toes to grip on the rungs. But the thought of falling made me hang on tightly, using up much more strength than I needed, and beads of sweat from the strain stood out on my forehead and ran into my eyes. Sometimes the roof and floor of the stopes pinched together so that I had to squeeze myself between massive shoulders of rock that seemed to be crushing down on me. And sometimes the stopes opened right up until I felt I was in a vast empty cavern carved out of the rock. My panting breath echoed and the old man's light, shining out through the empty space, faded into the darkness before it could find the sides.

We rested on a ledge mid-way between the levels, then carried on down, the old man leading the way. I was suffering from giddy spells and I followed him with my eyes closed, just feeling the way. Suddenly I felt the ladder

147

jerk as a weight left it, heard the bump of a body falling. The light disappeared. And then silence. The ladder must have rusted through below me and the old man stepped into space.

I froze on the ladder. My helmet had fallen over my face. I pressed myself against the rock, my feet and fingers wrapped around the rungs clinging for all I was worth. The old man had gone. I was left all alone in the darkness and the silence. I'd never been so terrified. Tears of anguish squeezed out from beneath my eyelids. This was the end. I was going to die here. I was sure of it. I couldn't climb the ladder again. I couldn't move.

'Hey you,' a harsh voice spoke, and a light shone in my face. 'Are you going to stay there all day?' I looked down. There was only a four-foot drop to the drive below and the old man had come back to find me. I let myself go, giddy with relief, and came up sheepishly beside him. 'Come on,' the old man said. 'This lamp will only last a few more hours.'

He let me rest for only a moment, then we lowered ourselves down into the next slope. Bismarck had been working in here before he abandoned his mine. The reef had been cut down in steps, leaving platforms for the men to work on, like an inverted pyramid. But towards the bottom the ladder stopped and the sides of reef funnelled down into a smooth-sided shaft where they used to shoot the ore down to the drive below.

The old man squatted on the edge of the lowest step shining his light at the band of white reef sandwiched in the rock. 'Will you look at this,' he said, and waited for me to scramble up beside him.

The reef was so rich in mineral that it sparkled in the light; from the green to blue to almost purple colours of copper pyrites to the harsher glint of iron pyrites. And when he chipped that away the very special glow from a vein of visible gold shone in the light. 'It's got to be running ounces to the ton,' the old man said beside himself with excitement. 'I've never seen it so rich! Dear God, boy, I've never seen a reef so rich!' He chipped a piece off. 'Hold that and tap it with your fingers,' he ordered.

I did so and felt the gold delling through the rock into the palm of my hand. The old man let out a yell of triumph that echoed round the empty mine. 'Bismarck, you old bastard. Can you hear me?' he shouted. 'I found your mine— I found your mine and it's rich, rich, rich! No wonder you tried so hard to hide it!'

He turned to me, a grin on his face, and his eyes staring wildly in the reflected light. 'I'll bet just seeing us here is sending him spinning cartwheels in hell,' the old man said happily. He set to work with his hammer chipping away samples of reef for assaying later. We filled our pockets with them until they weighed us down.

149

'Now can we get out of here?' I pleaded.

But the old man had the gold fever raging in him and he ignored me. 'We'll just try the bottom level,' he said. 'See if it's as rich. Then we'll go.' He shone his light down, but the beam disappeared into the darkness. There was no rope or ladder to support ourselves. 'It's not far,' the old man said. 'Just let yourself go and slide down on your backside.'

We followed each other tobogganning down the slope on the loose rubble. The old man went over the edge first. I heard a yell of warning, then a splash as he hit the water. I was going too fast to stop myself and I went over the edge after him. The water closed over my head. It was black and thick and blood-warm against my skin, and I felt myself sinking. My helmet slid down beside me and I grabbed at it. I thrashed with my arms and feet, but my boots were heavy and they weighed me down. 'Dear God,' I pleaded silently. 'After all this, don't let me drown.' I found a ledge and kicked myself off, swimming upwards, terrified that I'd miss the hole and come up trapped under the rock. I'd completely lost my sense of direction and I wouldn't have known which way to swim. My head broke the surface, my fingers found a grip and I hauled myself over the edge, the water falling off me like warm oil.

The old man, I thought suddenly. He couldn't swim! It was totally dark. There was not a ripple on the water, not a sound. I'd lost him and I was seized with panic. 'Where are you?' I shouted desperately with all the strength left in my lungs.

'I'm here,' a voice said grumpily beside me. 'You don't have to shout so loud.'

I nearly fainted with relief. 'Christ, I thought you were dead,' I said brokenly. 'How did you get out?'

'Kicked myself off the bottom, same as you. But it was a near thing and all that rock in my pocket didn't help. Have you got a match?' I reached into my pockets. The matches were sodden and the box crumbling. We sat silently in the darkness for a while getting our breath back. 'I should have known there'd be water here,' the old man said, disgusted with himself. 'With the amount coming through the mine I'm only surprised there's so little. Give me a light for my lamp and let's get going.'

'I can't,' I said weakly, shivering, ready to cry with frustration. 'The matches are wet. Oh Christ, why did we have to come down here?'

The old man crawled up to a drier spot and struck two rocks together until he produced a spark The carbide gas flared and the flame in the lamp lit his strong, battered face, making his eyes glow unnaturally. 'Come on, it's time we were getting out of here,' he said. 'The way I figure it is that we follow the ladders. They'll take us up to an escape way or the air shaft. We

151

should strike it somewhere on the top levels so there's quite a climb ahead of us.'

We scrambled up the funnel for the ladder. Every yard we made we slid back half in the rubble, tearing our fingers as we fought for holds in the rock. Then we started to climb. After two levels the ladder gave way to a single rusted cable that dangled over the nearly vertical face of the rock. We went up it like mountaineers, arm over arm, our boots scrambling for toe-holds on the face, dislodging stones that fell into the darkness below.

The old man went first, carrying the precious light. 'I've tied it on to my belt,' he said. 'If I fall, all you've got to do is find my body.' The cable was nearly rusted through in parts and fastened to the rock with pinions at thirty foot intervals. I let him get well ahead so that it wouldn't have to take too much weight.

The air was becoming stale and I was finding it difficult to breathe. The old man waited for me. 'I know,' he said worriedly. 'There should be a draught. But this cable's got to lead somewhere.' He went ahead, climbing up through the mine.

I reached a point where the space between the rock narrowed and the cable I was following came to a dead end. A little to one side and above me I could see the old man's light flashing, but couldn't figure out how he got there. He shone the beam down to show me. A few feet away the reef opened wide and it had been mined out leaving an empty cavern. Another cable was dangling there, hanging free of the side, well out of reach, with a sheer drop below.

'You're going to have to jump,' the old man shouted. 'It's not far.' I clung on to the cable, trying to pluck up the courage, my mind telling me that if I missed my grip I'd fall screaming into the darkness. 'Jump, damn you,' the old man yelled.

I let go and threw myself out. I caught hold of the cable, but the pinion higher up broke and I swung out into the darkness, spinning round and round. I hung on grimly with all that I had, burying my face in my arms. The old man steadied the cable. 'Come on,' he said, reaching down for me. 'You can make it.' There were more cables like that one. The courage was sapping out of me and the only thing that kept me going was the thought that we were reaching the top of the mine and the escape shaft couldn't be much farther.

The last and worst part of the climb was when the cable led over an overhanging spit of rock. My arms were aching, sweat blinded my eyes and my breath came in great sobbing gasps. I had to pull myself across with just the aid of my arms, leaving my legs kicking free, my fingers trying to grip as they were caught between the rock and the cable that was pressing down on them under my weight until they bled freely. Using the last of my strength I pulled myself up beside the old man. We were perched on a narrow outcrop of rock that jutted out over the vast empty cavern with a sheer drop just a few inches on either side. I sat there swaying, semi-conscious, with my lungs screaming for air and the blood pounding in my ears. The old man shone his light up on the roof. The escape-way was there all right, but it was blocked in solidly with concrete. He shone his beam around as far as it would focus. There was no other way out. 'It's a dead end,' he said. 'I'm sorry.'

The air was no good up there. It tasted acid and burnt our lungs. The old man was gasping too, his chest heaving. My whole body was shivering and my mind was blanking out. I felt the old man shaking me. 'We've got to go down,' he was yelling. 'The air's bad. We'll die up here.' I couldn't do it. I couldn't go down again. My nerve had cracked. I was beginning to freeze on that ledge, so scared I couldn't move.

The old man saw the panic taking control of me, saw my body growing rigid. He heaved me up and held me over the side by the scruff of my neck. Tears streamed down my face. I was tired and all my courage had gone. 'Leave me alone,' I whimpered. 'I can't go down again. Just leave me alone.'

'Catch hold of the cable,' the old man ordered ruthlessly. 'Boy, the only way you've got now is down. If you try to come up I'll stamp on your hands.'

I started slowly down, crying to myself, hating him, promising myself that if I got out of there alive I'd kill him for what he'd done to me. The old man followed close behind. 'Whatever you do, don't freeze,' he yelled. 'Just keep going, boy. You'll make it. God bless you boy,' he encouraged me. 'You've got spirit in you. I could love you for that. Keep going, damn you,' he swore at me, urging me on. We swung on the cables and scrabbled on the rock face for a grip. It was an endless nightmare of a journey. But somehow we reached the lower levels back into the good air.

The lamp was burning low. The old man put it out and we sat with our backs against the rock in the pitch black darkness. We were well and truly trapped and all we could look forward to now was a slow death unless one of us had the guts to end it all by throwing himself down a stope.

'How long have we been down here?' I asked.

'I don't know,' the old man answered. 'My watch is broken. Listen to me, boy,' he said huskily—the eternal optimist—'I'll admit you've had a rough start in mining, but then look at it this way. It's been good training for you and if we ever get out of here alive there's no mine dug that's going to scare you so bad again.' The old man waited for my answer, but all he got was silence. 'Get some rest, boy,' he said gruffly. 'I've got some thinking to do.'

I awoke to find that he had covered me with his shirt. 'You feeling better?' he asked, almost kindly. I had no idea how long I'd been asleep. My limbs were sore but my strength was coming back.

'Listen to me,' the old man said, 'and I'll give you my thinking out loud. When the main up-draught shaft was sealed, it blocked the airflow. The oxygen was cut off which is why the metal hasn't rusted too bad. But as soon as we opened it up, the draught started again. So we know there's another shaft somewhere, and it's a good one. Next, the air at the bottom of the mine is good but it hasn't reached the top yet.'

'I felt a breeze down by the water,' I said.

'That's it!' the old man replied excitedly. 'The water! I knew I'd figure it out. By rights the mine should be flooded by now. But the water's escaping somewhere and my guess is through the air shaft. Old Bismarck must have driven another shaft in from the bottom of the hill when he started going deep, probably along the old bed of an underground spring so that it drains the mine water as well. And if the air can get in, we can get out! You ready boy?' he asked. 'If we're going to move we've got to move now. There's not much light left in the lamp.'

He let a little water trickle into the carbide and shook the lamp. The gas hissed and he lit it

156

from a spark. We went down through the stopes on ladders and crawled along the level above the water. By this time the light was down to a feeble glow and I found myself on my hands and knees feeling in front of me for holes. The fear of dying was in me. I was tired and ready to give up. Only the instinct for survival kept me moving on through the darkness, the old man crawling in front of me, following the glimmer of his light.

We stopped before a sheer rock face at the end of the drive. The draught funnelled up through a hole at our side with a moaning, crying sound. It set the weak flame flickering and sent shadows dancing on the old man's face. 'Listen,' he said. 'Can you hear the water moving below?'

I heard a gurgling, sucking noise way down below me. There was a cable leading down through the hole. But I knew that if I followed it I wouldn't have the strength to come up again. The old man was in the same condition. 'We might as well,' he said, reading my mind. 'The light's nearly gone and it's our last chance.'

We climbed down the cable through a narrow well that must have been used as an ore pass. All the time we could hear the water swirling below and then it sounded quite close. The old man stopped. 'Empty your pockets,' he said. 'And take off your boots.' He did the same; then he leant out and dropped the lamp. We watched the sparks describe a clear arc. Then it hit the water and went out.

'You know I can't swim,' the old man said into the darkness. 'So if you see any light when we're down there, hold me up. But if you don't, let me drown. It'll be quicker that way.'

With that he let go of the cable and dropped. I followed and we hit the water one after the other. I went down, down, down, until I touched bottom and felt the force of the current carrying me along. I came up with my head clear of the rock and found the old man splashing beside me. I caught hold of his collar and held him up for there was a faint glow of light at the end of the tunnel.

The rock bed shelved upwards and we bumped over it. The light grew stronger. I was so weary that I had to fight to keep the old man's head above water. But the current swept us on and I could see the end of the tunnel with grass overhanging the edges. Then we were through it into the blinding sunlight, sliding down a rock waterfall into a pool below.

I lost hold of the old man as we hit the pool and went plunging down through the cool green water. But then I found him again and dragged him coughing and spluttering like a half-drowned rat to the bank. We lay there with the sun on our backs, gasping in the fresh, bush-scented air. Oh God—the sunlit world had never seemed so beautiful to me.

When he managed to gain enough breath the

old man turned to me. 'Did you keep any of those reef samples?' he asked. I nodded. 'I did too,' he said. 'No wonder we damn near drowned.'

He laid his samples out on the grass before him so that the sunlight caught the veins of gold. 'Boy,' he said in awe, 'you and I—we're rich men.'

CHAPTER FOURTEEN

WE climbed the hill as evening drew in, two weary, bedraggled figures. To our surprise the top was littered with men and equipment all working frantically to clear the shaft. Ace and Sam were there setting up generators and arc lamps so that work could continue through the night. So was McLeod, who had called out all his men and was directing rescue operations himself.

People who had never even known us had come from miles around to help. I was deeply touched by the concern of one miner for another in trouble. But the old man's face fell when he saw them. 'Keep those specimens of yours out of sight,' he muttered uncharitably. 'Don't let those vultures see them.'

Joseph was the first to recognize us and he came running over. 'What in the hell did you have to call them in for?' the old man said to him furiously. 'Now everyone knows where our mine is!'

Joseph was looking as though he had seen a couple of ghosts and relief flooded across his wizened old face. 'Oh my Mambo,' he said, 'what else could I do? I thought you were dead.'

A bucket was being winched up the shaft with a man in it. We heard him shout to McLeod. 'The rock's stopped moving and it's clear now down to a hundred and fifty feet. The drives are holding up all right, but I can't find any trace of them.'

The old man was horrified at someone going down our mine and he stamped over to McLeod in a rage. McLeod turned as he came up, surprise showing in his face. 'Well I'm damned,' he said, 'I thought you were dead for sure. I've got men looking for your bodies. How in the hell did you get out of there?'

'That's no concern of yours,' the old man said rudely.

The rest of the men on the surface gathered round us. I wanted to thank them but the old man cut me short. 'People,' he shouted, addressing the crowd, 'As you can see, me and my partner here are alive. I thank you all for coming to our help. We'll do the same for you one day. But you're on our claims and we don't want you here, so collect up your equipment and go.'

'For Christ's sake,' I interrupted him angrily. 'They were only trying to help.'

'The hell they were!' the old man muttered. 'They're after spying on us to see what we've found. And we haven't finished our pegging yet.'

The old man was right. Once the crowd knew we were safe their attitude changed.

'You old bastard,' Ace yelled, fairly dancing with rage. 'I know how you found this mine. It was the bladed rock I told you about, wasn't it? By rights Sam and me should be in for a cut.' The old man ignored him.

'Hey!' someone else shouted. 'Did you see the reef while you were down there? Was it as rich as they say?'

'None of your business,' the old man yelled back furiously, trying to protect his mine. 'Now get off my claims—all of you—or me and my partner here, we'll run you off.'

McLeod was the last to leave. He held the old man's eyes for a moment. 'You're still on my land,' he said. 'Now more than ever I want you off it.' With that he slammed the Land-Rover door and nodded to his driver to go.

The old man watched McLeod out of sight, then he turned to me. 'We'll rest up tonight,' he said. 'First light tomorrow we'll complete our pegging of the claims and head as fast as we can for the Mining Commissioner's office in Gwanda to register it. I don't trust

161

any of those bastards.'

★　　★　　★

We completed our pegging and hurried across the Gwanda hills, through the village and into the Mining Commissioner's office. 'Is he in?' the old man demanded of the woman behind the counter. Before she had time to answer he strode past her and hammered on the door.

The Mining Commissioner was a sandy-haired man in his thirties. His office was littered with mineral specimens and maps. Word of our discovery had already reached him. He cleared a space on his desk and studied our sketch plans that clearly identified the position of our block of claims, its beacons, the discovery peg at the head of the shaft, and the distance between the beacons and the north point in relation to the features on the ground.

I watched him worriedly. We had spent valuable time in trying to get our plan exactly right. But then he looked up and smiled, and I relaxed.

'Everything appears to be in order,' he said. 'I'm prepared to register your claim. The records of the mine were lost in a fire way back. I'm treating it as a new claim and you have the right to re-name it if you wish. Do you have a name in mind?'

The old man looked at me, then shook his

head. 'Keep it the same,' he said. 'Call it the Bismarck Mine. Bismarck would have liked that.'

For the first time we really felt safe. The mine was ours now. And I left the office in a glow of happiness. Joseph and Phillimon were waiting outside. We split equally the money we had. They went off in search of a beer drink. The old man and I headed straight for the pub for a celebration.

During the boom days the Mount Cazlet Hotel had earned a reputation for being one of the rip-roaringest pubs in the country. But in the quiet times that followed it had gone downhill. New owners had tried half-heartedly to modernize the hotel—and all they'd achieved was the destruction of most of its character. But to the old man the hard-drinking bar at its side was still a home away from home. And he pointed himself out to me in fading, yellowed photographs of the old-time miners that hung above the counter.

The news that the old man and I were in the bar and offering free liquor soon sped round the town, and within hours the place was packed. I was beginning to like miners as a breed. They came from every walk of life and they made good, wild company when they were gathered together. Tobacco smoke, the smell of liquor, the swell of laughter, filled the air. Someone had brought along an accordion and in response to

163

public demand the old man and I danced on the counter amid the bottles and glasses.

At closing time, in deference to the police, the landlord locked the doors—but the party carried on inside gathering steam. And I'd never seen the old man in so wild a mood. A toothless old-timer came up beside me. He must have been well into his eighties and he was throwing back liquor at an alarming rate.

'Have you known the old man long?' I asked, trying to find out something about him. The old-timer nodded. 'What's his real name?'

'I don't rightly know,' the old-timer answered. 'That's private with him. I heard that he came north to this country ahead of the law, aiming to get lost in the bush. And he's not keen to let anyone get to know him too well—except his old partner, name of Mouldy Duncan. You ever meet Mouldy?' I shook my head. 'He had a past, too,' the old timer said. 'His family were wealthy and I heard they paid him good money for a while to keep him out of England. They were always fighting. I remember he and the old man used to go weeks without speaking to each other. Then they'd go on a drunk and take this place apart.' The old-timer chuckled. 'Those were the good old days,' he said. 'I'm not talking ten, twenty years ago. That was yesterday. I'm talking long ago.'

'And the old man?' I asked, 'What was he running from?'

The old-timer shrugged his shoulders. 'It's just a story,' he said, 'but it goes that once he had a good farm somewhere down in South Africa. Married himself a very pretty girl and loved her like a drowning man loves life. He was happy as hell for a while until the time came for him to go off to the War in Europe. He got himself wounded there and taken prisoner. When he's tired, if you watch him careful, you'll see he still walks with a limp.

'He was away a long time and the girl got lonely on the farm. They say she went into Johannesburg and got in with a bad crowd. Ended up living with some wealthy man who was making a fortune out of the War.

'The old man was used to freedom and open country and he nearly went mad behind that wire. All he had to look forward to was her letters. After a while they grew less and less, then they stopped coming. He took it badly, tried to break out and get back to her. But they caught him and put him in a cage. When the War was over he went home to the farm. Found it empty with the equipment rusting in the lands and the house boarded up. The only person still waiting for him was his old African boss boy who'd grown up with him as a child.

'They went into Jo'burg and he found his woman living with the rich man. Some say he lost his mind and killed them both—others that he just beat them up. Anyway, it was something bad because he never went back to his farm. Instead he went north to the Rhodesian bush and lost himself, prospecting and living rough so that he'd always be on the move. But he could never out-run the pain of the girl leaving him or the feeling of that wire cage around him. Some men never can. And they say that when the memories get too bad, he heads for the nearest pub and goes on a drunk to try and blot them out. Then, when he's better, he wanders back to the bush and loses himself again.

'There's many stories told about him,' the old-timer said as he moved away to refill his glass. 'Most of them are a pack of lies. This one probably is too.'

The celebrations went on until the early hours, until few men were left standing. I went in search of the old man and found him lying unconscious with his back propped up against the bar. There was so little that I knew about him or about Joseph for that matter. I lifted his head, saw the tears in his face, and I thought of the story the old-timer had told me. But I couldn't be sure if the old man was sad or if it was just the brandy in him crying.

I walked outside. I needed the fresh air after the smoke-filled room. It had rained in the night. Puddles lay in the deserted street and the air was cool and still. In the grey dawn light I saw a shadowy figure detach itself from the wall and make its way towards me. It was Joseph, his

166

old gnarled limbs cramped with the cold of waiting. 'Baas,' he said quietly, 'is my Mambo still there?' I helped him take the old man home.

★   ★   ★

A few days later, while we were still in town purchasing the equipment we needed to re-open the mine, we received a message requesting us to report to the Mining Commissioner. We made our way worriedly to his office. The little room was crowded with men—Ace and Sam on one side, McLeod, van Tonder and his two sons, and a thin hawk-faced man, who turned out to be a high-priced lawyer, on the other. 'What is it?' the old man asked, sensing trouble. 'What are they doing here?'

'I'm afraid there's been an objection to your claim,' the Mining Commissioner replied. 'In fact, there's been two. I'll deal with the first one. I don't think it'll give us much trouble. These gentlemen,' he indicated Ace and Sam who were sitting uncomfortably on the edge of their chairs, 'have informed me that your pegs encroach upon their claims which are adjacent to yours. On these grounds they want me to upset your claim and throw it open again for pegging.'

The old man shot Ace a murderous look.

'However,' the Mining Commissioner continued, 'I have been out there to check and I find that their pegs do not accord with the diagram which was lodged with me. In fact, there's evidence of them being recently moved. So I find their objection groundless.'

'Now listen here,' Ace shouted angrily, starting up. But the old man pushed him back into his seat.

'One more word out of you,' he warned, 'and I'll knock you senseless.' He turned to the Commissioner. 'What's the next objection?' he asked.

'It's a more serious one,' the Commissioner replied worriedly. I had the feeling that he was on our side, though he was young and lacked experience in dealing with men like McLeod. 'It's a point of law that I haven't come across before,' he admitted. 'Perhaps you'd like to tell them, Mr McLeod?'

McLeod nodded to his lawyer. 'He'll speak for me,' he said. The hawk-faced man cleared his throat. He had a dry, precise manner of speech. 'I propose to state my client's case briefly,' he said, 'and reserve the rest of our argument, should the matter go further.'

I watched that lawyer at work, thinking that if any man could take our mine off us, he could. And my heart sank as he spoke.

'The law on this matter is quite clear,' the lawyer said. 'The discovery peg must be placed on the actual reef that is to be mined—or at least on some sample of that reef which appears on the surface—whereas these gentlemen have placed their peg on the top of the shaft over a particular reef that has long since been mined out.

'The first reef Bismarck found went down a hundred and forty feet. At that stage it gave out. But at a hundred and seventy feet and sixty feet to the north he found another much bigger reef running east to west. It is this reef that both parties intend to mine. My client has sunk a borehole on to the reef and if you care to go out to the site and inspect it you will see his discovery notice. We therefore contend that the peg at the top of the shaft has no standing in law and the claims must be awarded to my client.'

'What he's saying,' McLeod broke in, tired of the legal talk, 'is that I've got grounds to fight you through every court in the land. You haven't got the money to go that far. More than that, if I have to I'll get a High Court injunction to stop you doing any work on the claims while we're arguing the case. It could take years just to get it into court. And long before that your claims will have gone to forfeiture through your not being able to do any improvements on them. You've had it, either way, but I'll tell you what I'll do. Give in now and make it easy on yourselves. And I'll see to it that you don't lose by it.'

The old man had murder in him. So did I. No one was going to take our mine away from us just like that. The old man leaned over to McLeod. 'I'll see you in hell first,' he warned, red-eyed with rage. 'And if it comes down to who's got the money to buy the best lawyers, we've got Chinaman Lee backing us and he can match you dollar for dollar.'

'Gentlemen, gentlemen,' the Mining Commissioner pleaded, trying to prevent a fight from breaking out in his office. Neither of them paid any attention to him and he forced his way between them. 'The whole idea of my calling you together,' he said, 'was to see if we could settle this matter with reason.'

'I'm not talking anymore,' the old man replied furiously. 'I want a lawyer, too.'

'All right,' the Mining Commissioner said, 'but I'm still hoping for both your sakes that we can keep this out of court. We'll meet back here this evening. Will that suit you?' The old man nodded. 'That'll do,' he said grimly.

We got outside and I turned to him. 'For Christ's sake,' I said desperately. 'We don't even know a lawyer. How are we going to get one here by this evening?'

'I don't mean one of that sort,' the old man replied contemptuously. 'I mean Chinaman Lee. His family have been in mining all their lives, right from the time his father backed the old Sun Yet mine down by the Botswana border when no one else had the guts. He'll find a way to get us out of this.'

'Do not underestimate McLeod,' Chinaman Lee said to us in his little back room when he had heard us through. 'If anyone knows the finer points of mining, he does. You know that there was a time when the big companies had difficulty in moving their chrome, so they stockpiled it by the railway line. The law states that any mineral on or below the ground becomes the property of the man who owns the claim. McLeod watched them building up their stockpile and then he went and put a peg on the top of it. It cost the companies a fortune to settle with him out of court.

'However, in this case he is treading on thin ground and knows it. The lawyer was merely brought along in an attempt to scare you off. But if he fails McLeod will have several other cards up his sleeve.' The Chinaman thought for a moment. 'You say that van Tonder and his sons were there. Under the mining laws no claim is valid unless it is pegged between the hours of six a.m. and six p.m. We know they were set to watch you and I should imagine they could be called upon to swear that you put your notice up outside those hours. That would be enough to invalidate your claim.'

'I'm promising you,' the old man said angrily, 'we did it legal. I know that much of the law.'

171

He stood up from the table. 'You beat McLeod for us,' he said grimly, 'and you'll be doing him a favour, because if he goes so low as to get witnesses to lie for him, I'll kill him.'

Chinaman Lee rose to his feet. 'It is nearly time for the meeting,' he said. 'Come, we will talk on the way. I have a suggestion to put to you.'

McLeod was late. He had been to visit his wife who was seriously ill in the village hospital. They had been together for a long time and he was worried about her—which is probably why he accepted our proposition without thinking on it long enough.

He stamped into the room. 'You backing them?' he demanded of Lee before he sat down.

The Chinaman nodded. McLeod looked narrowly at the small, frail figure almost lost in the chair and he knew that he had a fight on his hands.

'I've been looking into this matter,' the Mining Commissioner said, calling the meeting to order, 'and it appears to me that you're both in the wrong.'

'That gives us a chance,' Ace said, still there though his case had been put aside.

I was all for throwing him out, but the old man nodded to me to be quiet. 'Speak to you a moment?' he said to the Mining Commissioner and took him aside.

A little while later they came back. 'I've had a

suggestion put to me,' the Commissioner said. 'It's most irregular, but nevertheless, if you agree to it it could save us all a great deal of time and trouble. The suggestion is simply this: at first light tomorrow morning I declare the claims open for pegging again. To make it fair you all set off on foot at my signal from a point two miles distant from the claim. The first one to reach the top and place his peg by the shaft becomes the rightful owner, by agreement between you all, of the Bismarck Mine.'

McLeod was instantly suspicious. But Chinaman Lee turned to him. 'You have as good a chance as the rest of them,' he said softly. 'And a case as complicated as this could cost us both a fortune in the courts.'

'I'm too old to run,' McLeod said. 'So are you,' he nodded to the old man.

'We'll each choose a runner to peg for us,' the old man said. 'I choose the boy here to run for me.'

'I've heard of this done once before,' McLeod said, warming to the idea, 'back in the old days. All right, I choose Conraad,' he pointed to one of van Tonder's sons, 'to run for me.'

'Sam,' Ace said excitedly pushing his brother forward, 'run your heart out!'

'I'm not sure that this is going to hold up in law,' the lawyer cut in worriedly.

'Just make out the agreement,' McLeod ordered. 'And keep it simple so that we can understand it. The first one to put his peg by the shaft gets thirty-one days clear to make his claims good and legal. And the others swear to keep out of his way for that time. We play it by the rules,' McLeod warned, sweeping his gaze across the men in the room. 'No one starts before the Mining Commissioner's signal at first light tomorrow. Agreed?'

'Agreed,' everyone swore solemnly and signed.

*   *   *

Chinaman Lee stayed at our camp that night. And he and the old man treated me like a prize fighter in training before a big fight. They had me running up and down outside the tent, skipping, doing knee bends and press-ups. They gave me a light supper, pummelled my muscles to loosen me up, then put me early to bed.

We left for the start line in the dark and reached there just as dawn was breaking. The old man kept me running on the spot while the Mining Commissioner looked at his watch. Ace was dressed like a regular trainer with a towel round his shoulders and he was making Sam run up and down. Sam was in no state for a run; his baggy trousers were tied up with string and he was tiring already, even though Ace kept slipping the odd shot of brandy to him to keep him going. Conraad was running barefoot, African style, and he just walked calmly and confidently around. I watched him anxiously. He looked superbly fit, with a lithe, muscular athlete's body—the sort of man who'd run an easy twelve miles along the boundary wire of the ranch before breakfast. I didn't think I stood a chance against him.

A crowd had gathered from the town at the start, and another stood with an umpire at the top of the hill. They cheered as we came up to the line. Joseph was there, grinning encouragement, but I noticed that Phillimon was missing. 'Where is he?' I asked.

'Don't you worry about him,' the old man said. 'You just run like the devil. And no matter what happens,' he warned 'no matter what you hear, you just keep running. Understand?' I nodded. I'd do my best, but there was no way that I was going to beat Conraad. He had been raised in the bush and he had all the style of a natural runner. I realized then why McLeod had agreed to our proposition so easily. The old man saw my concern and a twinkle appeared in his eye. 'Don't worry,' he said, 'I've attended to him,' and went back to mount the mule on which he would follow the race.

Ace pushed his contender to the starting line. Sam was so full of brandy by this time that his knees were buckling. But Ace wasn't about to give up hope. He slapped his brother's face and

175

pummelled his chest to keep him sober. 'Ready!' he shouted, holding Sam up.

The rim of the sun appeared clear of the horizon and the light flowed across the sky. Each runner gripped his peg. The Mining Commissioner raised his rifle, looked at his watch, then pulled the trigger. The report echoed in the hills. The crowd cheered madly and out of the corner of my eye I saw the old man getting tossed off his mule. 'Run, you bastard!' he shouted at me from where he lay sprawled in a heap on the ground. 'Run!'

Sam started with an amazing turn of speed and for a while he took the lead—though I'd swear he was running with his eyes closed, just burning alcohol. Conraad and I followed more cautiously. The route lay along the valley and then up the steep side of the hill. It was this, the last part that we both knew would break our hearts if we took it too fast.

After the first mile Sam dropped out, coughing up all the tobacco and brandy in him as though he was dying. And no matter how hard Ace kicked him when he eventually came up, he couldn't get him started again. Conraad and I carried on. He was increasing the pace now, jumping effortlessly over the rocks and across small dongas, his breathing still easy— and he was beginning to pull away from me.

By the time we came to a narrow gully he was well ahead and still increasing the pace. That man was fairly flying across the bush in long, loping easy strides. I struggled to keep up. I was torn by thorns, sweat was pouring off me and my breath was coming in great panting gasps. My mind was struggling to fight off the pain that was tearing at my lungs. But with the old man once more back on the mule and galloping up behind me, I didn't dare stop.

A rifle shot crashed out of nowhere. A bullet kicked up the earth just in front of Conraad and he threw himself down for cover. I was about to do the same when the old man's voice rang out behind me. 'Run, damn you. Run!' In a daze I kept on running, convinced that I'd be shot at any moment. I passed Conraad who was pinned down behind a boulder and every time his head showed over the top, a bullet ricochetted off the rock.

I started up the hill, the blood drumming in my ears and the darkness floating before my eyes, my heart beating so loud I could hear it. The crowd roared and I knew that Conraad had broken free and was coming after me. 'Go on,' I heard the old man yell. 'You've got him. Run!'

I staggered past the people who had come half way down the hill to meet me. 'He's behind you!' the old man yelled. 'Run!' But my legs were giving out. They would not hold me up anymore. I crawled up the last part of the hill on my hands and knees oblivious to the noise and excitement around me. With the last spark of energy I possessed I planted the peg in the ground by the shaft and passed out beside it.

The old man threw a bucket of water over me and brought me round. I saw his battered face beaming down at me. 'You won!' he shouted excitedly. 'God bless you, boy, you won.'

'With a little help from my friends,' I muttered, as I thought of the rifle shots.

The mischievous twinkle appeared again in the old man's eyes at the thought of his getting even with McLeod. 'Don't you worry about that boy,' he said warmly. 'It was our mine anyway.'

The crowd had gone off to search for the gunman but they found nothing. Ace appeared staggering along with Sam across his shoulders. 'It wasn't fair,' he shouted. 'The race should be run again.'

'It was run according to the rules,' the old man retorted. 'They didn't say anything about hazards on the way. Besides, no one rightly saw what happened in the gully. It affected my man just as much as McLeod's.'

McLeod stormed up. 'Where's that savage of yours?' he asked dangerously.

'There,' the old man pointed. 'Been there all the time. I've got witnesses to prove it.' Chinaman Lee and Joseph both nodded as Phillimon sauntered up innocently, but when he turned away from the crowd to face me, a broad grin broke out all over his fierce scarred face.

There was nothing McLeod could do.

'You've got your thirty-one days,' he said tiredly.

'There'll be no mistake in our pegging this time,' the old man replied. 'Now get off my claim. You too,' he said to Ace. 'Get the hell out of here. We've got work to do.'

CHAPTER FIFTEEN

I NEVER lost my fear of the underground, but in time I learned to control it. Joseph worked on the surface while the old man, Phillimon and I cleared the debris from the shaft. That done, we made a concrete collar to line the 'oxide cap', a zone where the water-table had percolated through the first hundred feet or so of rock, making it soft and unstable.

It was dirty, dangerous work, dangling from a bucket in a darkness lit only by the narrow beam of our lamps, fitting circular iron water storage tanks with their bottoms knocked out to act as shuttering for the concrete we poured in behind them. The water rained down on us making it difficult to grip. And sometimes the rock would slide in a shower of mud and stones, sending the bucket with you clinging on to it spinning madly in the darkness. And you'd hear the clatter of stones bouncing off the sides and plunging into the emptiness below.

Gradually we cleaned out the drives and stopes, ripping out all the old rotted equipment. Chinaman Lee heard of a small worker who was selling up and he bought his plant for us at rock-bottom prices. We put in new ladder-ways, laid new rails and brought down coco pans to run on them. Under the old man's directions we re-built the underground coffer dam that Bismarck had used to contain the spring and pumped water from the rest of the mine into it, letting it all flow out through the bottom of the hill.

The great ore stamps arrived in pieces with massive hard-wood supports and rusted iron bolts. The design hadn't changed in a century and a half of gold mining. And the old man who, like most small workers, could turn his hand to anything, cherished them and put the machinery together with a craftsman's hand. When he had finished we had a battery of five big stamps powered by a massive wood and iron flywheel.

But all the gold in the mine was just promises—of no use to us until we could get it out. And so far, all that we had done was to borrow money from Chinaman Lee at an alarming rate. We were amazed at the amount it cost to open a mine, and the burden of our mounting debt weighed us down until the old man and I decided to borrow no more until the mine began to produce. So we made do without electricity, using an antiquated boiler and steam engine instead to power the hoist, the stamps and the pumps.

We needed labour to help us underground and miners drifted in in ones and twos from across the hills—proud men, some of whom had worked the 'Golde' two miles deep on the South African mines. They set themselves apart from the others and wore their battered miners' helmets everywhere as a testimony of their courage.

At last the day came when all was ready and we had a mine capable of producing gold. The hammer boys went underground to drill in the stopes. When they were finished the old man, Phillimon and I went down to charge the holes with explosive. Everyone had cleared out of the mine and we were alone down there. It was like the first time all over again. The dark, the smell of the underground and the sound of trickling water. Our lights shone on the reef, gleaming with mineral amid the dark walls of rock, picking out the pattern of holes.

The old man had been teaching Phillimon and me, often impatiently, to become miners.

'One thing to remember when you're handling this stuff,' the old man added, 'is that the principal ingredient of gelignite is nitro-glycerine which, when it's old or hot is liable to exude from the cartridge. And then, if you go digging holes in it, you'll blow yourselves to kingdom come.

'Now insert the primer into the hole and push it gently down to the bottom with this wooden tamping stick. Then put in the rest of the charge, tamping each gelignite cartridge firmly so as to make good contact with the last. When you've done that, seal the opening with a wooden stake—a thick plug of mud will serve just as well—and it's ready for lighting.'

We charged holes in the three main stopes aiming to bring down the richest most accessible reef that Bismarck left behind. We were ready to light. The old man applied a match to his cheesa stick. It caught with a hiss of smoke, the orange flame glaring in the darkness. He reached up and touched the flame to the cut ends of the fuses. Immediately the gunpowder core took fire, the flame bubbling and spitting through the tar and white cotton binding, racing back towards the gelignite that had been tamped into the holes.

We made our way to the shaft, clambering into the swaying bucket that was waiting for us and the old man pressed the bell. It took a moment for the hoist operator on the surface to respond and we felt the snap of the third shock-wave sizzling through the rock. But before the blast could reach us and perhaps throw us out of the bucket the winch drum on the surface spun, winding in the steel cable. And the bucket sped us upwards, the walls of rock flashing by in our lights.

It took four hours for the fresh air to clear the mine. We stood watching the deadly yellow fumes from the explosive drift lazily over the lip of the shaft. Night came, bringing with it a warm wind that blew over the mine. The lamps on the headgear were turned on and the lasher boys went underground.

They worked in the stopes, sometimes bent over almost double in the confined space beneath the roof of rock, shooting ore down into the 'Cousin Jack' boxes with short-handled shovels and crowbars. From there the ore was fed into coco pans that waited below. Each lasher's task was to load twelve tons of ore in a shift. They worked half naked with their muscles rippling under skins that were shiny with sweat.

Another gang pushed the loaded coco pans, sending three-quarters of a ton of ore rattling along the narrow rails, their lights flashing in the darkness of the drive, their voices chanting, urging each other on under the strain. As they reached the shaft they grappled their coco pans on to the cable. The bell-boy at the station rang out the signal and the winch hoisted it to the surface. An empty coco pan was then pushed back, racing down the rails, the lasher boys singing now that the strain was gone.

After so many years of silence the old Bismarck mine came to life again. It was filled with noise and movement and the rhythm of working men. The lasher boys finished their shift and came up from the warmth of the underground, their breath steaming in the crispy cold air of dawn. By the head-gear they'd stand for a moment as the shadows receded, letting the rays of the rising sun warm their bodies; tired men, laughing quietly at a joke made by one of the hammer boys whose turn it was to go down. And the only time the mine was silent now was just before a blast.

We stockpiled ore. We should have stockpiled much more, but we could contain our impatience no longer. And we held a party to celebrate the 'dropping of the stamps'. Chinaman Lee was the guest of honour; and the old man laboriously carved all our names on the wooden crossbeam so that the occasion would be remembered.

The fires were stoked until the boiler lay under a cloud of smoke. The ancient engine trembled and wheezed, steam escaping from a hundred leaking joints. The old man pulled the lever, praying that his cherished machinery would work. The belt drive took up the slack and the massive flywheel turned, causing the great stamps to rise and fall like five inverted pistons.

The ore had already been passed through a primary crusher to reduce it to chips of a manageable size. From there it was fed through the mortar box of the stamps to fall beneath the

184

iron shoes—and the chips were pounded to a powder against the metal dies. Water was sprayed in and a muddy-coloured silt splashed through a fine mesh screen and flowed down a launder on to the James table.

The James table was built on springs and tilted slightly on one side with raised wooden riffles extending along its length. Another spray of water splashed the silt over the riffles, and as the table juddered to and fro on its springs the sand separated and washed over the edge. The heavier concentrates containing iron and other minerals separated farther up the table and were washed into a funnel and out to the cyanide tanks. Only the heaviest minerals remained at the top of the table, and as they were shaken along, a band of gold, about a quarter of an inch wide, appeared on the topmost riffle.

The old man put an arm around my shoulder, and the other around Chinaman Lee, and his eyes glowed as he watched the sparkling water-washed grains of gold dancing to the rhythm of the table. He had planned to make a speech on the occasion of the 'dropping of the stamps'—I knew because I'd heard him practising it. But now words failed him. He was mesmerized. He could only whisper as he gazed reverently down at the table. 'Will you look at that, boy. Will you just look at all that gold.'

Above the clatter of the stamps and the thudding of the James table came the sounds

185

from the miners' compound of a beer drink reaching full swing. We heard the beckoning call of their laughter, the throbbing of their drums. The old man raised his bottle and wordlessly blessed the mine. Then he led the way to the compound.

We all got very drunk and at some stage that night I was treated to the astonishing sight of the little Chinaman, a conservative to the core, with his arms flailing and his feet pounding, dancing beside the old man on the sand. And it was then that I began to understand the relationship that existed between those two. Chinaman Lee had been born behind the counter of his store, brought up all his life to bear responsibility. And now, with vast possessions to protect, and bound by a practical, cautious nature, he had no freedom to move, no possible way to break out. So he backed the old man's wild schemes. Because when the old man and his mule trekked over the hills, free as the wind, searching for that elusive reef of gold, a part of the Chinaman travelled with him.

In the morning Chinaman Lee was back to his conservative self again. 'You will be rich men in a few years' time if you listen to me,' he said, nursing a hangover while sitting across the table from us in the shack we'd built.

We had a good reef and a mine producing gold. We thought we were rich already. But when Chinaman Lee had finished listing our debts, and then the interest we owed on those debts, then the tax we could expect to pay on future earnings, and then allowed for depreciation and replacement of plant and machinery, and much more besides, both the old man and I felt poorer by far than when we had started out with just the dream.

'A mine must have a development programme,' Lee said. 'We must prove ore reserves and thereby prolong the life of the mine and increase its value. To find the cash to finance this we must increase the tonnage, produce more gold. We need more men, more modern machinery. But first we must have electricity.'

'Why go to all that trouble,' the old man asked, 'when we're doing all right as we are?' The old man was a true small worker/prospector and Lee knew that the technical and accounting intricacies of running a big mine would leave him completely out of his depth.

'We have to create a favourable cash flow,' Lee said. The old man thought he could understand that. 'All right,' he agreed unhappily.

At the end of that month an accountant arrived to put our books in order. The following month we grudgingly paid the Electricity Supply Commission an exorbitant sum of money and they brought their power lines to us on tall poles that spanned the empty miles of bush. Electricity, when it came, changed everything. The old fashioned, much-cherished machinery was ripped out. I saw the need to modernize and understood that the moves towards progress would repay us handsomely in the future. But the old man hated it and resisted change where he could.

He had made me the Mine Captain of the underground. 'Don't let the title go to your head,' he warned. 'I just gave it to you so that the miners would respect you and do your bidding. But you still don't know a damn thing about mining, so just do what Joseph and I tell you.'

I worked in the underground with the miners. They gave me a bad time in the beginning. But for every shift they worked, I worked half as much again. I drove myself and them hard for I wanted to impress the old man. And every month-end somehow we met, or exceeded, our call of tonnage.

The old man came underground with me to inspect the progress of the work. We climbed into a new drive that I was extending. And then I heard a sound that has haunted me ever since, for in it lay all the romance of mining in Rhodesia. A lone man chanting, his voice whispering along the dark, silent passages, seven hundred and fifty feet under the ground. Then a single grunt came from twenty throats as twenty massive hammers swung, and the ringing clash of the steel on the jumpers.

We drew near. The miners in the stopes were expecting us, saw our lights. Their rhythm speeded up and the chant changed. 'Boraku Capato' they sang in unison, and then the great belly grunt of 'Hew' as they struck. One carbine lamp flickered between two men and each man had a tobacco tin of water by his side from which the jumper boys wet their tongues and spat into the holes to keep the dust down.

'What are they saying?' I asked.

'Balls to you, Mine Captain,' the old man translated. 'Balls to you!'

At first I thought that I had pushed them too hard and I was paying the penalty. But then I saw them grinning at me from out of the darkness. They knew how desperately I had wanted to impress the old man. And they knew the work was done—he could not help but be impressed.

Phillimon flashed his light for silence and took the old man forward to the rock face. The old man checked every inch of that drive, looking for faults for thirty yards or more. But it was a beautiful bit of mining, clean and straight as a die. 'All right,' the old man admitted grudgingly. 'You've done a good job.' He knew how to make his praises seem sincere to the men and he flashed his light up to the stopes. 'All of you,' he growled and there was a proud feeling amongst the miners of a job well done.

We made our way back along the drive, the old man and I. And the chanting started up again, whispering after us along the passage in the darkness. 'And balls to you too, old man,' the miners chanted delightedly as they swung their heavy hammers, 'and balls to you, too.'

The old man stopped. 'You've done well, boy,' he said. 'They'll work for you now.' He cocked his head to listen better, then his face filled with sadness.

'Listen, boy,' he said, 'because that's probably the last time you'll ever hear it. I know the days when a man went down his mine with one foot in a bucket and a candle in his hand are gone now. And I'll never hear the chanting in the stopes again. But I loved that music—it was part of me—and now it's ending.'

Within the next two months the steam engine gave way to an electric motor of twice its horsepower and efficiency; the carbide lamps to battery-powered lights that didn't blow out. The miners were made to lay aside their great steel sledgehammers. And the frantic drilling racket of the more efficient compressed air-powered jack hammers replaced their chanting.

Mining engineers, surveyors and geologists swarmed over our mine. It got so we could hardly move underground for high-priced experts of one kind or another all advising us on what we should do next. In the space of a year the mine grew and grew. We were forced to employ more skilled men, electricians and fitters and a reduction engineer at the mill. They brought with them their wives who demanded better houses than the one we lived in ourselves. It was all getting too much for the old man.

April came, the best month in Rhodesia, according to him. A time of crisp early mornings and cool, cloudless days. A time when the rains were over and the bush was changing again from a lush, almost violent green, to the harsher burnt colours of Africa. The old man woke each dawn and sniffed the air. It was ideal trekking weather. I watched him grow more and more restless until a day came, when, without saying anything, he just hitched up the mule to the scotch-cart and went trekking. Joseph went with him and it was five months before I saw them again.

CHAPTER SIXTEEN

THE old man returned, wandering in from the bush with the glow of the late afternoon sun behind him.

'I missed you, boy,' he said to me. 'Damn me, but I missed you. Especially when I remembered how you could swim. There was this river pool,' he told me enthusiastically over a drink in the shack that night. 'I could have sworn I saw the glint of gold in the bottom. But it was so deep and I couldn't get at it. Joseph can't swim any more than I can. So I had this idea of tying a stone round him and dropping him over the side. I figured that when he hit the bottom he could grab a hatful of sand, cut the rope, and as he bobbed to the surface I'd be waiting there to catch him with a pole before he drifted away down stream.' The old man sadly shook his head. 'But Joseph wouldn't do it. You should have been there with me,' he accused. 'I missed you, damn it.'

I missed him too—it had been lonely without him. The old man found many changes. Phillimon had taken over my job in the underground and I was now running the mine. I had grown to love that mine and was proud of the changes I'd wrought. We were producing more gold than ever before. I worked the hardest hours of my life, but I felt a sense of achievement that made it all worthwhile. And I awoke each morning looking forward to the day—a far cry from my job at a desk in the city.

I tried to share my enthusiasm for the mine with the old man, tried to involve him and make him appreciate the sheer organizational skill that was required to hoist vast tonnages of ore out of the underground to feed into the mill. But the old man belittled my efforts. He had lost interest in the mine, felt neglected and resented my fascination with it. Now the mine was found and running smoothly, he was anxious to be on the move again, but he didn't want to go without me. Instead he was always trying to persuade me to go trekking with him in search of some hare-brained impossible dream. And each time I refused. I needed to be successful, if only so that word of it might one day reach Judith. And I thought sometimes of seeing her again.

Within three months of the old man's return a shiny black Mercedes Benz came bumping over the bad bush roads towards us. It climbed the hill and drove right in amongst the mine buildings, hooting at the old man to get out of the way as though the driver owned the place. An electrically-operated window wound down, and the old man leaned in to enquire what the hell the driver thought he was doing, he was hit by the chill blast of air-conditioned air.

'Get me the mine manager,' a cool, immaculately-suited executive ordered from behind the driver. Then impatiently, 'Don't just stand there, man—hurry!'

'I'm the owner,' the old man said mildly when he recovered from the shock. 'Will I do?'

Immediately the passenger door opened and the executive rushed eagerly around the car, hand outstretched to shake the old man's hand. 'I'm terribly sorry,' he said. 'Really, it's too bad that I wasn't properly briefed or I'd have recognized you immediately.' He looked

193

uneasily around and spotted the shack. 'Could we go inside?' he asked. 'There is a matter of some importance that I wish to discuss with you.'

'What is it?' the old man demanded, standing his ground. He could smell a big company man a mile away and he hated them for the way they drove the small workers off all the good mines.

'Really,' the executive stammered, 'it would be better inside.'

The old man didn't move. 'Just tell what you want,' he said.

'We'd like to buy your mine. We've sent you several letters outlining our proposals, but you've never replied,' the executive added hurriedly. He took a breath and squared his shoulders. 'We feel you should consider the merits in dealing with us...' Standing there shoe-deep in clinging dust he launched into his prepared speech. His city-white skin was frying in the sun, sweat poured off him.

The old man interrupted him. 'Get off my mine, you poncey little bugger.' He spoke quietly, but the way he said it had the executive hurrying for the safety of his car. Once inside the executive cautiously let down the window an inch.

'Does that mean,' he asked, 'that you have definitely decided not to sell your mine?'

'It means,' the old man growled, 'that I don't deal with the big companies.'

Two weeks later almost to the day three black Mercedes Benz came bumping over the bad bush roads towards us, the big saloon cars kicking up a trail of dust behind them that could be seen for miles. The old man watched their progress from the top of the hill. 'They've brought up reinforcements, boy,' he said grimly, looking forward to the encounter. 'Leave them to me—I'll settle them.'

The cars drew up outside the shack. A grey-haired man with a thin nervous face, climbed out. 'Mr Private,' he addressed the old man— and I was interested to see that they had done their homework this time—'I'm the local director of British Amalgamated Mining.' He turned to the clutch of junior executives, lawyers and accountants who were climbing out of the other cars and introduced them with a sweep of his hand. 'These are my assistants. Our information is that you have found a very rich reef. You may not be keen on selling, but every man has his price. And you'll find that we at Amalgamated don't haggle. We'll pay it. Now what will you sell for?'

The old man shrugged his shoulders. 'Two million dollars,' he said. And the local director of Amalgamated Mining rocked back on his heels.

'You're joking,' he said with a thin smile.

'I'm not,' the old man replied. 'You said every man's got his price. Mine's two million

195

dollars. Now are you going to pay it or not?'

'We'll need to discuss this with you,' the local director said patiently as though pacifying a madman. 'Can we come inside?'

'No,' the old man replied. 'You asked what I'd sell for and you have my answer. There's nothing to discuss.'

'At least grant us an option and let us send in exploration teams so that we can see what we're buying,' the director protested. 'That's reasonable, surely?'

The old man thought for a moment, then he went into the shack and returned with a tin of paint and a small brush. 'I want none of your men on my mine,' he said, 'but I'll grant you an option at two million dollars for one month.' He wrote the option out laboriously on the large whitewashed verandah pillars and signed it. 'There,' he said, 'that's legal under Rhodesian law. I can't be much fairer than that.'

The local director shook his head, bemused at the old man's method of doing business. 'I'll have to contact Head Office in London,' he muttered, and climbed back into his car.

Six weeks later the convoy returned and the local director climbed stiffly out of the passenger seat.

'We wondered if you have reconsidered your position,' he said to the old man who was waiting for him on the verandah.

'I have,' the old man replied triumphantly,

and moved aside. Behind him on the pillar the option figure for two million dollars had been painted out and a new figure of two million two hundred thousand dollars had been neatly written in. 'Your option expired. That's my price now,' the old man said. 'Your rivals have been sniffing around here. And my price goes up by that figure every month from now on.'

'Of course we'll never have to sell,' the old man assured me. 'No big mining company will pay that price sight unseen. They'd rather steal it from us. I'm just teaching them a lesson, that's all.' But the feeling of power was going to the old man's head. For the first time in his life he owned something that someone else badly wanted. He knew that he had the big companies over a barrel and rather than invite them into the shack he let them sweat bare-headed in the sun while they tried to argue with him.

The convoy returned twice more to our mine. The local director, obviously under great pressure from London, tried desperately to negotiate with the old man—but he got nowhere. If he could only have understood the small workers' hatred and suspicion of the big mining companies, he would never have tried in the first place.

On his last visit the local director admitted defeat. 'I won't be dealing with you again,' he said bitterly. 'In fact, I hope never to see you again. My Managing Director has decided to fly out from England—though I can't imagine why he wants this mine so badly, there are others.'

Nothing happened for some time; then a battered Land-Rover, belonging to one of Amalgamated Mining's prospecting teams, pitched up covered in dust from a long journey, and a tall, well-built man climbed out. He wore his tie loose, swung his jacket over his shoulder, and ambled towards us, turning every now and then to look over the mine and the positioning of the mill and headgear.

'Hello,' he said and held out his hand to the old man.

'You've been expecting me. My name's John Maitland. My friends call me Little John.' He reached into his jacket and brought out a bottle. 'Here, I brought this for you,' he said. He took out another bottle and smiled. 'This one's to drink myself.'

Before the old man knew what he was doing he had led the way inside the shack and we were seated round the table. The old man poured himself a tot.

'Martel brandy dregs,' he said, sipping the liquor appreciatively, 'harsh enough to burn the skin from your throat. The mining communities used to get hogsheads of the stuff sent out from France,' he explained to me. 'If you got hold of a bottle of the real dregs and tipped it up in the light you could see all manner of strange things swimming about in it like young crocs. You can't buy it here anymore, but I've never lost my taste for it. How did you know to bring this brandy?' the old man asked.

'I was a small worker once,' Maitland answered. 'After I finished with farming up in Mashonaland I went down a mine one foot in a bucket and a candle in my hand like the rest of you—I built British Amalgamated up from there. In fact, I'd heard of you and Mouldy Duncan,' he said to the old man, 'and that was long ago in the late 'thirties. Weren't you working down by Lonely Mine then?'

The old man nodded. 'That was us. We found no gold though, and we lived on the smell of an oil rag.'

'That reminds me,' Maitland said, leaning back, half his bottle gone already. 'Did you hear the story of old McConville who owned the New Jersey mine just below here—made a fortune out of it then he returned to Ireland to live high and lost the lot to the stock market crash and a woman. He returned to this country flat broke and he used to work his mine in a top hat and tails—claimed it was all he had left.'

'Hear of him,' the old man snorted, 'I knew him. I used to feed the bastard when he was down. But did you know that he later found the Great Abercorn and made another fortune?'

We had been warned that Maitland was a modern-day pirate in a business suit. A man of extraordinary ruthlessness and ambition. He had knifed in the back and stolen from countless people on the way to the top of the international mining empire he controlled. But we didn't see him in that light. We saw a big, good-looking man with great charm and a strong, open face, eyes wide apart with a steady lazy gaze. Dormant within him one could appreciate lay great authority and energy. But he was not a man to use his authority or energy needlessly and he was content now to enjoy our company, leaning back against the wall of the shack trading small worker stories with the old man. And the old man loved to tell the stories, for they conjured forth the ghosts of his long dead friends and eased the loneliness of age for a while.

'You must have heard about Tom Cameron, he was about your time,' the old man said, thoroughly mellowed now towards Maitland. 'Well, he prospected for fifty years and he never found a damn thing worth keeping. The time came when he got too old for the bush and a farmer took pity on him and let him live in a cottage near his homestead. Trouble was the farmer was a disaster too. His crops failed, cattle died—both of them damn near starved. Now Tom had brought with him his old boss boy. And so as not to offend the farmers with their free, backveld ways, he swore to murder the boss boy if he crapped anywhere but in the long drop provided.

'One evening the boss boy was on his way to the homestead with a message when he was caught short. Before he thought about what he was doing, he had dropped his pants and was squatting in the short grass. And while he was at it he picked up chips of rock and looked them over as prospectors are always doing. And damn me but he finds he's squatting over an exposed piece of quartz reef stiff with visible gold.

'The boss boy wasn't too keen to say anything because of the evidence he'd left behind. He left it until Tom Cameron and the farmer were on their last legs and the Land Bank was about to re-possess the farm. Then he showed Tom the reef.

'They managed between them to scrape up enough money to buy a tiny stamp. They didn't need any more machinery than that because the gravel was so rich all they had to do was mill it. And they made a fortune—or the farmer did. Tom was so amazed at his luck that he drank himself to death soon afterwards.'

The Martel brandy bottles were emptied early on in the evening and the old man and Maitland drank on with the local 'brandy' that tasted of flavoured cane spirit, but by that time it made no difference to them. Just before dawn the old man walked out on to the verandah to breathe in some fresh air after the fug that had built up in the shack. Maitland staggered out after him and leant against the pillar. It was November—the

201

early mornings were misty and held the soft scent of rain.

'I haven't been drunk under the table by anyone in a long time,' Maitland said ruefully. 'But then I'm not used to the local brew—do you distil it yourself?' He washed his face in a bucket and poured cold water over his head and neck. 'Now,' he said, 'how about selling me this mine? You know it's just tying you down.'

The old man showed him the option figure painted on the pillar.

'I heard about that,' Maitland said. 'I also heard how you treated my local director.' Suddenly he grinned. 'Still, it doesn't matter. He's only a bought man who earns a monthly salary—all he can understand is figures, not people.

'Now I'll tell you what I'll do. I'll make you both my partners. We'll form a special company to own this mine and we'll split the shares fifty-fifty down the middle. I'll pay you five hundred thousand dollars cash for my share.'

'The hell you will,' the old man interrupted him. 'You know my price.'

'Let me finish,' Maitland said. 'On top of the five hundred thousand dollars, I'll lend the company a minimum of two million dollars at a nominal rate of interest. That's about what I figure it'll cost to develop this into a big mine.'

Maitland turned to me. Somehow he appeared to have understood my blind faith in the mine and my desire to see it develop. 'At the moment we're just scratching the surface,' he said enthusiastically. 'My loan will go to buy new ball mills, the very latest equipment. We're wasting time working on the top of the hill. We must move everything down to the bottom and sink an incline shaft directly on to the reef. I haven't been underground, but I've talked to Government geologists who have. And they tell me that, properly handled, this mine is capable of producing thousands of tons of ore each month. I'm gambling that sooner or later the price of gold must go up. If it does the profits could be enormous.'

Dawn found us seated around the table eating breakfast. Neither the old man nor I were feeling too good, but Maitland's vitality was enormous. He had shaken off all signs of a night's drinking, his eyes were clear and his mind sharp.

'This is how it's going to work,' he said. 'We each appoint two directors to the board. You can be chairman, if you like,' he said to the old man, 'but there'll be no casting vote. And until my loan is repaid out of profits I want a management contract with the company empowering me to run the mine as I see fit. We are embarking on a great enterprise and you'll have to let me work with men of experience who know how to run a big modern mine. You may stay and work the mine under advice from my experts if you wish—or merely attend board meetings and run it from an executive level.'

The old man liked the sound of Chairman of the Board. Especially if he could keep the title and still be free to wander where he liked. For my part I liked the fifty per cent we would still hold—I didn't want to be parted completely from my mine.

'Look at it this way,' Maitland said, still thinking that he had to convince us. 'You'll get five hundred thousand dollars in cash. You'll get directors' fees and dividends every year. And your assets will increase by half the value of the mine that my loan of two million has gone to develop. I don't know the full extent of the reef yet, and rather than take a guess at what you're worth, I've found a way to give you a share of the profits and a share of the risks. I can't be fairer than that.'

'What about my miners already working here?' the old man asked gruffly.

'I'll give you my word,' Maitland replied sincerely. 'They'll be looked after. No man will lose his job. And I'll guarantee you something else. You'll make more money out of this mine with me in three or four years than you could ever have done if you had sold it outright to one of the other mining companies.'

'We'll need to talk this over,' the old man said as we walked Maitland to his Land-Rover. But anyone who knew the old man could tell that he was already committed.

*   *   *

We called in Chinaman Lee.

'Do not deal with Maitland,' the little Chinaman warned. 'He is too clever for you. That man will steal the mine from right under your noses.'

'But we'll still own fifty per cent of the shares,' I protested. 'We could block any move he made. Especially if you're with us to advise us.'

'I will not deal with Maitland,' the Chinaman said stubbornly. 'Neither should you. He is a crook.'

'Damn it, I've met the man!' the old man protested. 'I drank all night with him. You get to know a man then. He won't cheat us. He was a small worker once and he understands us.'

'He was never a small worker,' Chinaman Lee replied patiently. 'He just traded in small worker mines to get started—bought and sold the men who worked them. And remember, he grew rich but each of his partners went to the wall. Do you want to go the same way? You have a good mine. You are making money—not a lot, but that will come. Why grow greedy now?'

But once the old man had put his faith in someone nothing could shake him and he was ready now to defend Maitland to the end. 'I like the man,' he said. 'I trust him. And I know what you want, Lee,' he added, cruelly touching on the Chinaman's weak spot. 'Your father backed the Sun Yet Sen mine and it made him famous. You want the same from us. You want your name to be known through the Bismarck mine—not Maitland's.'

'If that is what you think,' the little Chinaman said deeply hurt, 'then you are both very foolish men.'

'I call a vote,' the old man interrupted him. 'I vote aye to selling the mine,' and he raised his hand. Reluctantly, more out of loyalty than conviction, I raised my hand to vote with the old man. Lee was out-voted. Before my eyes all the joy went out of the little Chinaman and he shrivelled back into his dry, wrinkled shell. He sold his shareholding to us—there was little else he could do.

I watched Chinaman Lee leave the mine with a sick feeling in the pit of my stomach. 'He was a good friend to us,' I said quietly to the old man, 'and we've just stabbed him in the back.'

'Balls,' the old man replied heatedly. 'It's our mine, not his, and we gave him a chance to come with us. What more can we do? Damn it, boy,' he said impatiently, 'we're involved in big business. There's decisions to make, deals to be done. I don't want you getting squeamish on me now.'

From the moment that he had met up with Maitland a change had begun working through the old man's character. He was besotted by the feeling of power that great wealth brought—and the urge to protect that wealth whatever the cost. The money fever was going to my head too.

We sat up in the shack late into that night laying our final plans. Then we sent Maitland a message accepting his offer, on condition that the cash payment was raised from five hundred thousand dollars to eight hundred thousand dollars. As the old man had predicted, Maitland accepted the increase without a quibble, and we were summoned to the capital to sign the contracts.

We put on our cleanest khaki clothes and went by road to Bulawayo, leaving Phillimon and Joseph to look after the mine. We spent that night in the famous old Grand Hotel—a Bulawayo landmark that was situated on the corner of Eighth Street near Rhodes' statue. We allowed servants to lay out our meagre possessions in vast bedrooms with creaking floorboards, and ornate tin ceilings. And feeling awkward and out of place, we gingerly tested for comfort the great old-fashioned single beds that dominated the centre of each palatial room like a throne.

That night we ate in the Victorian elegance of the first floor dining-room. The old man had demanded a table by the window, and he sat silently staring out of the window for most of the meal.

'Long ago,' he said to me suddenly, feeling the need to talk, 'I walked to this city from South Africa and spent a night huddled in that doorway across the street over there,' he pointed with his fork. 'It was a night as cold as only Matabeleland can get and I was half starved—so hungry I could have eaten my boots. I had known only pain and hunger for the past six years, and I was nearly driven out of my mind. I remember looking across the road up to these very windows and watching all the gracious people seated at their tables in the soft light—and I could taste the food they were stuffing into their mouths. I swore then that I'd sit at a table up here one day.' The old man was silent for a moment. 'I forgot about it when I met up with Mouldy Duncan and got used to the bush ways. But being here in all this luxury makes me realize what I've been missing—that I've been poor most of my life, boy. And now that I'm rich, I'm going to enjoy it.'

A sleek, twin-engined 'plane was waiting for us at the airport early the following morning. Apart from the two pilots there was just the old man and I alone in the cabin. And we travelled in style, reclining with a glass in hand on broad, sheepskin-covered seats. We were met, as we landed, by an official Amalgamated car and whisked into the capital. It was exhilarating to see Salisbury's modern city skyline appearing as it did, suddenly out of the bush. To be coming home in the back of a big black limousine, having left it on foot following a mule and cart!

The best suite had been reserved for us on the top floor of Meikles Hotel. And we wandered through the rooms, trying out all the gadgets and peering into cupboards. Everything was new and different after being so long in the bush. The old man threw himself down on a bed to rest before the meeting. 'Boy,' he said, happily wallowing in the luxury before he closed his eyes, 'didn't I tell you long ago that the best thing you could ever do was to become my partner?'

At the appointed time of the meeting we strolled across the park to a tall building that houses the Rhodesian office of the British Amalgamated Mining Company; we were ushered like visiting Royalty into an enormous board room that reeked of vast fortunes and power. We were left alone with the portraits of past directors staring grimly down at us. And in that time the cockiness went out of us and a nervousness and awe at our surroundings set in.

Suddenly the great double doors at the far end of the room were thrown open and the executives of the mining house filed in to their appointed places at the table. They were led by the local director. He was icily polite and his executives took their cue from him. The old man and I were subtly made to know that the tables were turned. We stood on their ground now, supplicants at their court.

The old man had the panicky feeling that he had made a mistake and was looking around for a means of escape when Maitland entered the room. A stir, like ripples racing out across a pool, emanated from his presence as he waved down the executives who had stiffened to attention from their seats. Maitland looked different on his home ground—immaculately dressed with not a hair out of place—so smooth as to be almost sinister. But he ignored his assistants who followed him thrusting forward papers for his attention and, brushing them aside, he made his way straight down the room towards us.

He was clearly delighted to see us. 'I've managed to find you a few more bottles of that brandy,' he said, to the old man. 'But I had a hell of a job—it seems they're not bottling it in Europe anymore.' All eyes in the room were watching us and we felt flattered by Maitland's attention. I could see the old man warming to him again, needing to be reassured that his judgment of Maitland was correct, especially after Chinaman Lee's warnings.

Gently, while still deep in conversation, Maitland steered us to our seats around the polished table and drew up a chair beside us. At his signal the local director set a sheaf of papers before us to sign. The close-typed pages would have taken half a day to read, especially the clauses concerning management contracts and loans. We both found ourselves wishing passionately that Chinaman Lee was there to advise us.

'Why all these papers?' the old man asked worriedly. 'Our agreement was simple, wasn't it?' he said hesitantly, floundering out of his depth. Some of the executives seated round the table snickered at the old man's remarks, making him feel ever more vulnerable.

'It has to be recorded legally,' Maitland explained patiently. Then he smiled, soothing our fears. 'I assure you, our agreement hasn't changed. Sign the paper,' he said, 'they're in order.'

The old man studied Maitland's face, remembering the man he had drunk under our table and who had won our confidence. 'We've gone this far with you,' the old man said quietly to him, 'we'll trust you now.' And we signed.

'Gentlemen,' Maitland said triumphantly to the executives gathered round the table. 'Meet our new partners.' The Press were called in to photograph Maitland surrounded by his executives shaking us each warmly by the hand and then presenting us with our cheque.

The ceremony over, we suddenly found ourselves alone on the steps of the building with

211

the traffic rushing by on the street below. The old man held up the cheque for me to see over his shoulder. We read the figures—eight hundred thousand dollars. 'Dear God, boy,' the old man breathed in wonder. 'Will you look at all those noughts.'

We walked across the road to the bank. I was embarrassed by the enormous amount on the cheque. And I went hesitantly up to a teller and asked to open an account. We were still dressed in our faded khaki bush clothes, not having had time to buy others, and the teller regarded us with deep suspicion.

'Bank rules require a mimimum deposit of fifty dollars before an account can be opened,' he said pompously and turned to serve another customer obviously believing that neither I nor the old man could raise a tenth of that amount between us. I could understand how we must have appeared to him. But before I could say anything the old man snatched the cheque out of my hand and slapped it down on the counter.

'Bugger opening an account with your bank, then,' he said, his eyes snapping angrily—'just cash this for us, will you?' The teller glanced casually at the amount of the cheque and nearly collapsed.

I returned to the hotel leaving the old man demanding cash—boxes of it—while the Bank Manager, Assistant Bank Manager, and Accountant all tried vainly to persuade him to come into an office and talk the matter over.

In the days that followed the old man caused havoc in the financial circles of the town. He saw himself as a financial genius like Maitland, but he distrusted all banks. He set out to revenge himself on them from the days when he and Mouldy Duncan had been thrown out of their tiny district branches for asking for a grub stake. And he no sooner placed our money with one bank long enough only for them to get the feel of it, as the old man put it, than he moved it all to another bank—then to another. Then the old man discovered the stock exchange and soon he had the very small, extremely conservative, share market in a turmoil. Fortunately, because no good judgment at all was involved, we made more money than we lost.

I left the old man to the stock exchange, the accounts and the company reports and took no interest in them. I wanted to see Judith again. I could feel her close to me in this town. She must have been aware that I was there for my picture had been in the papers.

I had planned my return carefully once I'd been sure that the old man and I were going to make it rich, rehearsing this first meeting over and over again on lonely nights at the mine. I chose a day when I knew that she would be at home. I paid great attention to my appearance and dressed carefully that morning in the most expensive clothes money could buy. I had hired

213

the longest, sleekest car I could find and employed a chauffeur to drive it. Every detail was important to me. If Judith, or more especially her mother, had wanted success then I would show them success.

The car turned into the driveway, its wheels crunching on the gravel. It was all as I had remembered it; the great old colonial homestead set amongst grounds that kept an army of gardeners at work, with Judith's paddocks and stables at the back. But for all its grandeur I sensed that the homestead was fading—as though not as cherished as before. The car drew up and the chauffeur leapt out and stood to attention by my door. I climbed the steps, hoping that my arrival was being watched from a window.

I rang the bell, heard it echo through the house, heard footsteps coming to answer it, and suddenly my confidence evaporated and my stomach knotted with fear. By the time the latch was lifted and the door began to open my planned speech was gone from my head and I knew hopelessly that when I saw Judith again I'd stammer before her like a fool. A servant stood enquiringly before me, not the old family retainer who had been my ally so often in the past, but a stranger. 'Mrs Stanislau,' I stammered, 'is she or her daughter in?'

Silently he ushered me through the hall into the living- room. I stood there bewildered, everything was different—the furniture changed, the carpets, the paintings— everything. There was nothing there I could recognize.

A middle-aged lady entered the room dressed in gardening clothes with a scarf around her hair. 'Can I help you?' she asked, her eyes regarding me with polite astonishment.

'Where's Mrs Stanislau?' I demanded. 'Doesn't she live here?'

'Mrs Stanislau and her husband sold the house and emigrated to South Africa some time ago,' the woman answered. 'They didn't like the political situation that is developing here.'

'And Judith?' I demanded wildly. 'Where's Judith?'

'That would be their daughter,' the woman said. 'I'm sorry, I never met her. I don't know where she is.'

I suppose all that time alone with only the old man for company had sent me a little bush mad. I had simply stopped the clock in my mind from counting time—forgetting that nearly four years had passed. I never doubted finding Judith at home with her mother when I called for that was the way I had planned it—not married and living with another man. I wanted so badly to believe that nothing had changed, that I had simply blanked out that part from my mind. But now, standing in this room with a strange woman watching me anxiously as though I were a madman, the sickening realization of my foolishness came flooding back—and with it all the bitter memories.

I drove back to town and changed out of my elegant clothes. There was no point in displaying my wealth any more—I had nothing to prove. And I walked the streets of Salisbury again as I had done that night years ago, sad and lonely and full of hurt. But this time I had lost more than the girl—I was trying to bury the dream of her which had sustained me through the achingly lonely times as well.

I ordered myself to think sensibly. I knew that you could never go back and expect to find what you once had. I cursed myself for having tried... If only I could have seen her again, perhaps I could have erased her from my memory. But walking alone in the empty streets she remained in my mind and I couldn't shake myself free of her.

I returned to the hotel in the early hours of the morning. The old man had waited up for me. I found him sitting in my room on the floor surrounded by company reports and calculations. His eyes searched my face and he understood.

'Boy,' he said, stretching himself, pretending that he had seen nothing. 'I'm tired of all this hotel luxury and of making money. The city's no good for people like us. Let's go home to our mine...'

CHAPTER SEVENTEEN

WHILE living in the city the old man and I had been made conscious for the first time of the changes that were taking place in Rhodesia. In the aftermath of British Prime Minister Macmillan's 'Winds of Change' speech directed at the white man in Africa, and the break-up of Federation, a tide of nationalism swept the country. By 1965 it had reached fever pitch. In a country where no one had bothered about politics, now people talked of nothing else. They felt Britain had cheated them of their lawful right to independence. The controlling white minority looked anxiously at the chaos of the Congo and the Africanization of the states to the north and, fearing the same thing would happen in Rhodesia, resolved to take independence unilaterally if necessary. Prime Minister Ian Smith shuttled back and forth to England, pleading his case, but nothing was resolved. I had been called into the Police Reserve and spent my days and nights patrolling an African tribal trust land. On November 11th, 1965, people in the cities, on isolated farms and mines, spent the day glued to their radios. At 1.15 p.m. the Prime Minister spoke to the nation and Rhodesia's Unilateral Declaration of Independence from Britain was declared.

The old man had cleaned his guns ready to take the war to the bush in the traditional Boer commando style. After a build-up of almost unbearable tension, nothing happened. The sky did not darken with British and American war planes, the African majority of some 4,000,000—to 250,000 whites—did not rise up and slaughter us all. Instead everything within the country became calm and peaceful. It took censorship and the blank spaces in the newspapers to make me believe that anything had in fact happened at all. Then one by one sanctions were applied and tiny, landlocked Rhodesia found herself involved in an economic war with the world.

There was no problem in selling gold, but as the country was changing, so was our mine and we found that it was not the same anymore. The big company men had taken over. As McLeod had predicted, great ugly slimes dumps and cyanide tanks to cope with the increased production now desecrated the skyline. An adit was being driven through to link up with the main shaft and a village was growing up at the bottom of the hill.

In accordance with the agreement we had signed with Maitland, though we still owned half the mine, another company, one of his, held full responsibility for the way in which it was run. And we found that the clauses of the contract hemmed us in—ensuring that we remained just figureheads with no power at all. We resented those big company men. It was like having strangers tramping through our home. And they barely tolerated us. As the tension between us grew worse, they tried to drive us out.

The first person the new mine captain picked on was Phillimon—and that was a bad mistake for Phillimon possessed a temper with a short fuse. Over the years his lanky frame had filled out and he was now big and savagely powerful. One morning the mine captain came up from the underground with his head split open and blood pouring down his face. He wanted to call the police and have Phillimon charged with attempted murder. Fortunately the old man and I were able to dissuade him by offering to throw him back down the shaft. But from then on matters got really bad and the big company men started to niggle away at us.

One of their bulldozer drivers took his machine right over a mark the old man had built in memory of Bismarck, the great steel tracks tearing up the flowers and the carefully-placed stones. The old man saw it all from the verandah of the shack and, speechless with rage, he dashed across the open ground, hauled the driver from his seat, and punched him bloody.

Our labour force was already fighting theirs in the compounds and it was getting dangerous to go underground. We tried to appeal to

Maitland, but he was never in the country. At first we thought that our messages weren't reaching him, but then we realized that he was just not going to reply. More and more we saw him quoted in the papers, attacking Rhodesia in order to protect his profits in Black Africa—and more and more he shamed us as our partner. We heard, but could never confirm, that we were being squeezed out on his instructions—but the old man never did want to believe that.

A meeting was called to settle the dispute before open war broke out. The old man was chairman, but a chairman without power— Maitland had seen to that. And in the end, for the good of the mine, the four of us sadly packed up and left.

We should have gone back to Chinaman Lee for advice, but we couldn't face him for being so right about Maitland. Instead we sent him his share of the extra money we made when we raised the stake from five to eight hundred thousand, and left it at that.

The rest of the money was burning a hole in our pockets. There seemed no sense in not spending it, so we headed into Bulawayo. We took a fine house in the suburbs, staffed it with servants, put the cart away in one of the garages, let the mule graze in the back garden, and went out on the town. We had been in the bush so long that we had no real concept of the value of money and spent it like water. In fact, money as cash was difficult to spend. Word of our shareholding in a rich mine and of Maitland as our partner had spread through the city. Everyone wanted to give us credit and seemed hurt if we offered cash. We lived a fine wild life, even keeping stables of race horses for a while. Bums, spongers, and all kinds of drifters filled our house There was gambling in one room and a party in another almost every night and the old man never went to bed sober. Our money even secured us an introduction to Bulawayo society, but that didn't suit the old man at all and he was soon back in his dirty old clothes, telling his stories to anyone who'd listen, and wandering the streets with pockets full of sweets for the children. The high life was exciting for a while, but then, as we didn't need each other any more, we started drifting apart.

Phillimon was the first to go. Each time he got drunk and offered to fight any man in the beerhall, the Police would throw him in gaol. Eventually he got fed up with them, took his money, bought a great black American car, and went home to his kraal where he claimed he intended to buy himself a fine herd of cattle and fat young wives and spend all day relaxing in the shade of a tree.

Then I grew restless. I would stand alone amid the crush and the music of a party, meeting many pretty girls, but none of them meant anything to me. I was still deeply scarred from the early days in the bush when my need for people my own age had been at its greatest. I had learnt—in order to keep my sanity—to bury my loneliness, so deep inside me that now I didn't need anyone. I walked alone from choice, never involved, never hurt—invulnerable. I saw this ability to live without people, without ties of any kind, as a source of great strength. But the truth was I measured every woman I met against Judith and found them wanting. She was the only woman I had ever really cared about. Perhaps she had left too deep a mark for me ever to erase it. I would not admit that. I told myself I was haunted by the need for another dream like the Bismarck mine, something to aim for, something to believe in, and it was dangerous just to let myself drift.

Soon I began to avoid the parties and the wild life. I pulled myself together and decided to buy a ranch, to work on land that I could cherish. I found a wide and beautiful block of grazing country in the Tuli area near the Botswana border, packed my bags and went to live out there. I tried to persuade the old man to come with me, but he was still fascinated by the city and stayed behind.

I was happy on the ranch for a while, working from sunrise to sunset and rattling around in a great big house. But as soon as the ranch was operating efficiently and I had time to relax, I found there was still something missing inside me—it took the form of a dull ache of longing. I grew restless and dissatisfied, bored of waiting for the grass to grow and watching the cattle grow fat. I told myself it wasn't the emptiness of the life I was leading, but the stimulation of the challenge of mining that I missed—the excitement before a blast, of not knowing what lay behind the next face of rock.

I went to town to see the old man. We met in the corner bar of the old Grand Hotel. The city life was doing him no good. His face was puffy from too much alcohol and he had put on weight from lack of exercise.

'You look terrible,' I said. 'Why don't you go back to the bush for a while? The hard life and fresh air would do you good.'

The old man shrugged his shoulders miserably, trying not to let me notice his cronies ordering rounds of drinks on his account.

'I tried to go prospecting a couple of times,' he said. 'Me and old Joseph used to hitch up the mule and head off some place. But it wasn't the same, the ants ate my food and the bugs bit me. Anyway, what's the point of looking over the next hill for a pot of gold when you've already got it in the bank? It's no fun anymore. How's it been with you?' he asked shrewdly.

'Pretty much the same,' I admitted.

'That's the trouble with a lot of money,' the old man grumbled. 'You work so hard to get it that you feel you've got to spend it. And it ties

223

you down like chains. But I'll tell you something, boy,' he admitted as we made our way up to the restaurant. 'Though I always used to claim that it was the looking that gave me pleasure, not the finding, money's changed me. I've grown accustomed to being rich. I'd find it hard to be poor again now.'

'In that case,' I said, 'we'd better go over all those bills you've been running up.'

'Can't we leave them for tonight?' the old man asked. 'I haven't seen you in a long time, boy. I'd like just to talk with you a while.'

We went up to the restaurant. The maitre d'hotel met us at the door and the rest of his waiters flocked around us.

'Anybody'd think we owned this place,' I muttered to the old man as they ushered us with great ceremony to our table.

'We do,' the old man muttered back.

'What?' I yelled, startled.

'We own it,' the old man admitted, not knowing whether to look pleased with himself or guilty. 'I bought it the other day.'

'But it must have cost a million,' I said.

'More,' the old man admitted. And when he saw my expression he busied himself with cleaning his knife and fork with his napkin.

It transpired that the old man had grown lonely in town by himself and he began to take his supper every night at the little table by the window of the hotel restaurant. The waiters pretended not to notice that he wore no tie or jacket and that he shovelled his food into his mouth with the flat of his knife. But then the owners employed a new manager in an effort to stop the old hotel from losing money—a new broom to sweep clean. One of the first things the manager did was to catch the old man in his dirty bush clothes heading for the restaurant— and he threw him out. The old man protested that he always ate his supper there, but it did him no good. As soon as the manager's back was turned the old man tried to sneak up to the restaurant where his supper was waiting. But he was caught, and this time the manager warned him that if he so much as saw the old man on the premises again he'd call the police.

The old man stood on the pavement opposite the hotel looking up at the warmly lit windows of the restaurant, his stomach rumbling from his missed supper and he brooded angrily a while. Then some of his old fire returned and he spent the remainder of the night tramping the town, waking up the shareholders of the private company that owned the hotel. By morning the hotel was his. The manager reported for duty at eight a.m. and found the old man waiting for him in the hotel lobby still dressed defiantly in his dirty old bush clothes. The manager called the police to have him thrown out and with savage delight the old man fired him on the spot.

I went to the bank the next morning to arrange for the payment that was due on the transfer of the hotel company shares. And this time the bank wasn't keen to advance us credit. The Grand Hotel had been built soon after the city was founded and with its ornate architecture, enormous rooms and polished wood furnishings, it was about as expensive to keep and as out of place as a dinosaur beside the more modern buildings that had sprung up around it. And if the hotel had been losing money before, it was sure to lose a fortune the way the old man wanted to run it. His cronies were already flocking into the bars, driving the regulars out, and they never paid for their drinks. I couldn't stand by and see the old man renege on a debt. In the end I had to mortgage my ranch and most of our remaining assets in order to raise the cash.

That afternoon I went through the old man's bills with my temperature rising. 'You've got to cut down on your spending,' I warned him. 'Between us we've still got some assets but we're running out of cash. And for God's sake, try and sell this hotel—even if you have to take a loss. We simply can't afford to keep it.'

'What about the mine?' the old man protested. 'We should be getting dividends from it soon.'

'We'll need that money badly to cover our debts until we can find someone fool enough to take that hotel off our hands,' I replied. 'Until then, don't spend anything.'

Reluctantly the old man agreed and I went back to my ranch.

★ ★ ★

Less than two months later the old man summoned me to town. 'Maitland's sneaked into the country without anyone knowing and he wants to see us,' he told me worriedly. 'And there's something else you should know,' he added hesitantly, watching my expression darken. 'I'm due in court tomorrow.'

The story gradually came out. Apparently one of his parties had got out of hand and the old man and his cronies, remembering a mad Australian by the name of Boomerang Smith who celebrated his striking it rich by bathing a barmaid called Blanche from the Grand in champagne, tried to do it again. But the days of Blanche were gone. And a more modern barmaid indignantly reported them to the police.

I accompanied the old man to court. He was charged with *crimen injuria* and though he tried to explain to the magistrate that they were only re-living the old days, he was given a heavy fine and a severe warning that he'd go to gaol if he ever tried it again. It was a chastened old man who left the Magistrates' Court for the meeting

227

with Maitland. 'The bloody country's changed,' he complained bitterly to me. 'They've got no guts. No one knows how to enjoy themselves anymore.'

The familiar black Mercedes was drawn up outside the hotel. Maitland was waiting impatiently inside it. 'Get in,' he said, 'we're going to the mine.'

'Trouble?' the old man asked.

'We've lost the reef,' Maitland replied. He flicked a switch and the windows rolled up. The car was air-conditioned and it was cool inside. The driver turned in the traffic and headed out of town for the bush.

'Impossible,' the old man said harshly. 'That reef was good.'

'It's been cut by a dolerite dyke,' Maitland replied. 'We had no warning that it was there—other than that the gold values have been dropping as we've been driving towards it. I didn't tell you before because I didn't want to worry you until it was absolutely necessary.'

'What's the dyke like?' the old man asked.

'It's massive,' Maitland replied. 'Some of the hardest rock that we've come across. We've sent diamond drills through it but the reef's disappeared on the other side and we can't find it. I assure you,' he added tiredly, 'we've tried. Read the geologists' report.'

He handed the old man a bulky file and turned his face to the window. I read the report

228

over the old man's shoulder. A dolerite dyke, some three hundred and eighty feet thick, sloping at a forty-five degree angle, had cut through the reef like a knife at the eighth level. They had drilled extensive patterns of test holes but there was no trace of the reef on the other side. And according to the geologists' report, the enormous pressures which occurred beneath the earth's crust when the dyke was formed would have disrupted the reef so badly that there was little chance of our ever finding it again. The old man was stunned and he sat silently through the rest of the journey.

The mine manager and the geologists were waiting for us on the surface by the shaft. We changed into overalls and hard hats and went down into the mine. It was a depressing sight. A well-run mine is clean and neatly ordered and it is run on the basis that for every ton of ore that is hauled to the surface you develop along the reef and block out a ton of ore to hold in reserve. But these men had obviously been instructed to work only for quick profit. They had ripped the guts out of our mine and left nothing in reserve. I could imagine their concern now that they had hit the dyke. The mills would be silent in a couple of weeks.

We stood before the dyke shining our lights on the dark expanse of foreign rock with no mineral of any sort glowing in it. And I could clearly see the holes in the rock face where they

229

had drilled through in search of the reef. I looked around for Red O'Connell. We had worked together when Maitland took over the mine and I trusted that man. O'Connell was a big, two-fisted Canadian geologist with flaming red hair, a bulbous nose and warts on his face who had fought and drunk his way through the Rhodesian mining scene for more years than anyone could remember. And whereas most geologists followed a cold and logical science, O'Connell had an almost magical touch—even with his brain half pickled in alcohol, he was said to be able to smell a reef of gold in the rock. The old man, who loathed all geologists on principle, respected him. 'That's the only one-handed geologist I've ever come across,' he once told me. 'At least he'll point to one direction and stick to it. For the rest of them, if you want advice, it's always "on the one hand the reef's down there, and on the other it could be in the opposite direction."' So in spite of the evidence from the test hole reports, I knew that O'Connell had been through dykes before and picked up the reef on the other side and I was ready to pin my faith on him.

'Where's O'Connell?' I asked. 'What does he think?'

'O'Connell doesn't work for us anymore,' Maitland said. 'He's finished now—too heavy in the bottle for us to trust him.'

I should have found that strange. Red

O'Connell had never really worked for the Company—he had always been Maitland's man, right from the start when he had saved Maitland's career. The story went that the company had lost the reef on one of the biggest gold mines they owned. The directors were for closing the mine down, but O'Connell swore that he could find the reef again. And Maitland, who was still an employee of the company at that stage, believed him. He persuaded the directors to give the go-ahead and a drive was sent out underground through thousands of feet of dead rock searching for the reef. Once every week the board of directors of the mining house would meet and one of them would say, 'Bugger O'Connell, this is costing us a fortune—close the mine down.' But Maitland persuaded the board to keep their nerve and they drove through nothing but barren waste, using up all the profits the mine had made and went into debt besides. Then O'Connell found it—a reef so rich that it seemed to glow amidst the rock. The company recouped the whole of their profits from the first blow of ore. The board of directors sent for O'Connell to congratulate him. His secretary tried his office, but he wasn't there. She went across the street to the corner bar and there she found him, slumped insensible across the counter. He had already had a private celebration. And in his absence, but in his honour, the board of directors formally changed the name of the mine to the Bloody O'Connell reef.

The mine was long worked out and O'Connell was old now and nearly an alcoholic. But his fame lingered on and drunk or not, he was still too good a geologist for Maitland to let him go just like that. I should have enquired further, but I had other things on my mind and I left it.

We went up to the surface. Maitland led us to an office. 'I've brought you here so that you could see for yourselves,' he said. 'Because I'm going to close the mine down and I have to call in your loan. I'm sorry, but I'm under great pressure from my partners in England. I took a gamble and failed and now my head's on the block. Your shares are ceded to cover an advance of more than 600,000 dollars that is still outstanding. Can you pay me within the next fourteen days?'

'Of course we can't,' I said. 'We haven't got all that much money in cash.' I thought fast. 'Couldn't we both go to the bank and raise a new loan on the mine? The money could be used to pay your company back and get you off the hook. And it would give us another chance. I'm sure that reef's still there somewhere behind that dyke.'

'I'll swear it's there,' the old man chipped in earnestly. 'We'll find it again if we just keep looking.'

We were pleading with Maitland. He knew it

and he turned us down flat. 'No bank's going to lend us a cent on a report like this,' he replied. 'And we'd have to show it to them or they'll call their own experts in. I'm sorry,' he said coldly, 'but there's nothing I can do. We had a rich mine for a while but it didn't last. We're both going to lose now. Gentlemen, if you can't pay, I'm going to have to take over your shares in the mine—I have to protect my shareholders. But if I can I'll leave the rest of your assets untouched. I don't want to hurt you any more than I have to. That's the best I can do.' He pushed a document towards us. 'Sign here.'

My head was spinning. Everything was happening too fast. The old man picked up a pen.

'No,' I said, 'wait a minute.'

'If you consult with a lawyer,' Maitland said quietly, 'he'll advise you that I'm being extremely gentle with you. Under the terms of the contract you signed with me, I could take everything you've got. You know that and we're wasting time. Sign here.'

'We'll think about it,' I said. I wasn't going to be hurried into signing any documents again.

'Sign,' the old man whispered to me, terrified of what Maitland could do to us. 'For Christ's sake, sign or we'll lose everything.'

I couldn't tell him in front of Maitland that if we lost our shareholding in the mine we were broke anyway. His bills and the Grand Hotel had seen to that. Maitland was watching me, the cold glare in his eyes pressuring me so that I couldn't think clearly. I pulled the old man out of his chair. 'Come on,' I said, 'let's get back to town. We'll give you our answer in forty-eight hours,' I said to Maitland over my shoulder.

I was silent all the way to Bulawayo. There was something worrying me. I had seen the dyke and read the report. But Maitland's offer to take over the majority of the loss himself just wasn't in character. What could he want with the shares of a useless mine? No amount of tax loss could be worth the opportunity of taking over our assets and recovering at least part of the money. There was no way that he could know that our properties were mortgaged to the hilt and without the promise of the profits from the mine we were insolvent. Or was there? His information system was second to none.

'Listen,' I said to the old man as I dropped him off at the hotel. 'I'm going to Salisbury to try and find Red O'Connell. Don't sign anything while I'm gone,' I warned. 'Don't even see Maitland or any of his men. And don't go and get drunk. You understand?' The old man nodded, but he was badly scared.

I found O'Connell in his usual place in the corner bar. He was only just sober enough to answer my questions.

'Yes, they fired me,' he said, 'because they falsified the geologists' reports and I wouldn't go along with it. But you'll never be able to prove that in a court of law. The dyke's there all right, but they've found the reef. Here,' he said, using a puddle of spilt beer on the counter to draw me a map, 'let me show you. Imagine hundreds of millions of years ago the earth's crust forming and the various rock strata cooling like coloured layers of treacle. One of those layers was a gold-bearing quartz reef running like this—' and he drew a sloping line. 'Then a mass of molten dolerite was forced up from the earth's core and it fractured the reef here.' He drew another line. 'Well, if you're lucky the reef will continue on the other side. But if you're not—and you've got to remember the pressures that were let loose at that time—then the reef would have been disrupted and it could be anywhere, even forced down into the bowels of the earth way beyond your reach. So the geologists were right when they came up with a negative report from their test holes and they advised that there was little chance of finding the reef again. But in this case—by some freak of nature—when the dyke broke through it buckled the reef back against itself. And just two hundred yards to the north of the dyke, starting on number seven level, there's a massive ore body—enough to run the mine for years. No one would have thought of looking for it there. And if you had taken the gamble and gone through the dyke you'd have gone right past it. Even the geologists don't know it's there—no one does. Except for Maitland, a few of his most trusted people and a diamond driller who, by sheer chance, drilled off course and found it. And Maitland paid him a lot of money to keep his mouth closed. He paid me well too. But to hell with it. I'm drinking myself to death just sitting here.'

'Do you know what he intends to do?' I asked.

O'Connell shook his head. 'I don't,' he said, 'but I'll venture a good guess. You and his other shareholders will lose all your money and the mine will close down. Then another company will take over—send drilling teams in. And would you believe it—they'll find the ore body. Maitland's name won't appear, but he'll own the mine. I promise you that. He's done it before.'

I got up to go. 'What am I?' Red O'Connell asked, his bloodshot eyes watching mine, expecting me to call him a bastard. But I knew that he was asking for his self-respect back—and I grinned at him.

'Drunk or sober, you're the best damn geologist in the business,' I answered.

'Thank you,' he said gravely. 'If you want any help, call on me.' And he turned back to his drink.

I spent the night in a hotel. Every hour on the hour I tried to contact the old man by telephone, but he wasn't in. I had people out looking but no one could find him. The receptionist at the Grand told me that Maitland had been trying to contact him as well. And I worried through the night, hoping like hell the old man had gone and locked himself away.

I caught the early morning 'plane back to Bulawayo and by this time I was seething with anger. I figured that Maitland had played us for a couple of fools right from the start. He must have been setting this theft up from the moment he sat round our table in the shack and won the old man over. The way he phrased the contracts. All that he had to do was to wait for the opportunity and then rob us legally in his cold-bloodedly efficient style. But I could still stop him. More than that, I had a plan to take the mine back from him.

The old man was waiting for me when I got back into the hotel. He looked worn out, grey with strain and fatigue, as though he had been up all night.

'Listen,' he said before I could speak. 'I've been with Maitland. He had lawyers and everything. And they told me to sign so I did.'

'You did what?' I shouted.

'Boy,' he said weakly, 'it was for the best. There was nothing else I could do. They had us over a barrel—we could have lost everything.'

One signature was enough. The old man held a Power of Attorney to sign company documents on my behalf. I had given it to him when I left

237

town to go ranching. And the agreement that he signed had been drawn by craftsmen—it was unbreakable.

Given the opportunity to sell off our assets, I could perhaps have saved something. But Maitland lost no time in announcing that the mine was closing and, to twist the knife in, he spread the word that we were hopelessly lacking in liquidity. Which was true—our income was insufficient to meet the mortgage repayments on the properties. I tramped the town in a desperate effort to save something of what we owned—begging the creditors to hold off—to give us time to put our affairs in order. But when they knew that we were in trouble they gathered like a flock of vultures flapping their wings over the spoils.

And in the end we lost everything. They left us broken and poorer, if that was possible, than when we started out.

CHAPTER EIGHTEEN

OUR friends turned their backs on us. The old man nearly went mad with resentment. He couldn't take the shame of the court proceedings that were instituted to liquidate our companies and he fled into the bush leaving me to wind things up.

I managed with great difficulty to find a job as a clerk in a big insurance office. I worked beneath callow eighteen year-olds for I had no business qualifications of any sort, and I earned just enough to survive on. From shame I shunned people entirely. I never spoke unless I absolutely had to, working silently at my desk all day, returning silently to a tiny room at night to sit on a narrow bed staring at the paint peeling above a cracked washbasin until it grew too dark to see.

I lived on a diet consisting mainly of breakfast cereal and, after paying the deposit and rent for the room, it was three months before I could afford to have the electricity connected. So my evenings were spent in the dark. And if I needed to read I waited until everyone else was asleep and used the light in the communal lavatory. Having tasted success and failed, I was swamped with bitterness, filled with a desperate emptiness of spirit that only grinding poverty can bring.

I lived in that manner for almost a year, then a letter from Chinaman Lee found me. It was a gentle, courteous letter from a very civilized man. He made no mention of the past, but rather let me know that he was still our friend, and he bade me find the old man and bring him with me to see him. I had nothing to lose. If I had lived in that cell-like room much longer there was a chance I would have shot myself. So

I threw up my job and went into the bush looking for the old man.

The old man and I had parted company amid angry words and bitter accusations. I had heard nothing from him in all the time I had been in the city and though I searched the usual haunts there was no sign of him—it was as though he had vanished from the face of the earth and I began to wonder if he was dead. Then word reached me that he had been seen down in the Gwanda area, and I set off after him.

It seemed that he had recently emerged from the solitude of the backveld and built himself a shack right on the very edge of the Bismarck mine property. But what really upset me was that people who'd met him claimed that he had completely lost his mind.

I took a bus and arrived in the Gwanda hills on the second night just as the moon was rising. I crossed McLeod's property on foot following the dusty road and then before me was the recently re-opened mine, working even harder than before. The sounds from the ball mills, the lights on the headgear, the winch cable winding up ore. It brought back so many memories— waves of nostalgia flooded through me, and I could understand how the old man had been drawn back.

I stopped a tired miner in his hard hat and boots who was going off duty and asked him if he knew where I could find the old man. As I

240

spoke there came a wailing cry, rising like no human sound, from the direction of the mine dumps. The cry tailed away and was immediately replaced by a burst of maniacal laughter which sent shivers running down my spine. The miner nodded in answer to my unspoken question. 'Oh, Mambo,' he warned, almost grey with fear, 'don't go near him, he's the devil.' And with that he hurried away.

I climbed up the steep side of the mine dump with the moon throwing shadows from the trees on the yellow sand. As I came over the tip on to the flat top I saw in the distance the figure of the old man leaping about, dancing and crying like a werewolf in the light of the moon. I came up silently behind him, but, warned by some animal instinct, the old man spun round, dropped on his knee and aimed his rifle at me.

For a moment I was sure I was dead. Then I saw his finger ease off the trigger. The old man lowered his gun. 'Boy?' he shouted, trying to see my face which was shadowed in the moonlight. 'Is that you, boy?' He dropped his rifle and came running across the sand towards me. 'Is that you, boy?' he cried, pathetically pleased to see me. 'Is that really you?' He caught me in his arms and hugged me and buried his face in my neck. 'I knew you'd come back, boy.' He put his arm around me and walked me back to his shack which was little more than a shanty made of wood and rusted corrugated iron. 'I haven't

241

got much to offer you, boy,' he said, trying to make amends, 'but you can have half of anything I've got.'

The old man was so poor that he didn't even have enough money to buy paraffin to fuel the lamp, so we sat on the dynamite wood boxes in the light of a guttering candle and we talked and talked, neither of us realizing how much we had missed each other. And in a little while it occurred to me that the old man was perfectly sane.

'What in the hell were you doing?' I asked him indignantly, 'dancing about up there?'

The old man chuckled and a cunning look came into his eye. 'Boy,' he said, 'no one's ever cheated me as bad as Maitland and got away with it. It drove me mad for a while, then I figured out a way to get even. First, I built this shack just off mine property and put stories about witchcraft about, and then on a full moon I dance up on those mine dumps there.' He looked pleased with himself. 'I've already got his labour force scared half to death. Soon they won't even be able to get them to go underground, much less get any work out of them. And one of these days Maitland's going to come here to find out why. And when he does I'll be waiting and I'm going to drill a bullet right between that bastard's eyes.' The old man raised his hand to forestall my protest. 'You haven't heard the best part,' he said proudly.

'The beauty of it is that no one's going to be able to touch me for it, because I'm going to have fifty and more witnesses, including his own men, who are going to have to swear that I'm as mad as a hatter. But, of course, as soon as Maitland's good and dead, boy, damn me if I don't get better! Now, what do you think of that?'

'Forget Maitland,' I said. 'He's not worth it.' I held up the letter. 'Chinaman Lee wants to see us.' But the old man was stubborn once he got an idea into his head. 'To tell you the truth, boy,' he said, regarding me sadly, 'I am half mad and I'm not going to feel better until I've killed that bastard Maitland.'

It took me the rest of the night to persuade him to come with me. Even so, he refused to leave immediately, and the following night the old man danced in the moonlight on the mine dumps, while Joseph, dressed in skulls and feathers, whirled through the miners' compounds. And between them they laid such a hideous curse upon that mine that the terror-struck miners walked out the next morning and refused to return to work again.

Invoking witchcraft on the superstitious African is a serious offence in Rhodesia and we left the area the next morning just ahead of the police. 'Well, it was the next best thing,' the old man said to me, still heartsore at not killing Maitland.

We trekked through the bush in the crystal-clear dawn, following the cart tracks, hearing the soft crunch of its wheels on the sand. It was good to be back together again. In a while even the old man's spirits returned, now that he had got his pride back. 'Maitland may have been better than me at business,' he said, 'but I know the African, and that mine's going to have trouble for the rest of its life.'

★   ★   ★

Chinaman Lee sat us down in his small back room and laid before us one of the best meals that either of us had seen in a long time. But the old man couldn't touch his food. Instead he cleared his throat nervously. 'Chinaman Lee,' he said, 'we owe you an apology.'

The little Chinaman stopped him before he could say any more. 'That is in the past,' he said softly. 'I have brought you here to discuss the future. But there is one thing I would like you to know before the subject is closed. I appreciated you sending me my share of the extra money.' He smiled at the old man, making him feel comfortable. 'Now eat,' the little Chinaman gestured impatiently, 'then to business.' And the old man and I fell to eating like ravenous wolves.

As soon as the plates were cleared the Chinaman began—his voice dry and precise as he hid behind the mask of a businessman again.

'I have had the misfortune to back a mine that has caused me nothing but anguish,' he said. 'It is called the Molvan and it lies on the Bembezi River north of Bulawayo above Eastnor.' He drew out the large scale sets of plans containing all the information on the mine and spread them on the table. 'As you can see, it has a flat reef dipping at less than thirty-five degrees and this reef has pinched out on the fifth level.' He marked the spot. 'The country rock is a talc schist and the eastern drives run under the Bembezi River. It is a wet and dangerous mine and the flat dipping reef makes it doubly difficult to work. My partners are convinced that there is no more gold to be won from this mine. But I believe that there is, if someone has the courage to follow the stringers of quartz just a little bit farther. You will note from the values recorded before that for a small mine it did quite well. I resent having lost a great deal of money to what is now only a hole in the ground. Thus I am prepared to offer you the mine and a limited amount of backing to get you started. All I want in return from you is my money back. You can pay it to me as a tribute on each ounce of gold you bring out—after that the mine is yours. I am offering you no favours,' Chinaman Lee said. 'If you do not find the reef, then we both lose. And the talc schist country rock can collapse without warning—several men have already been buried

245

alive in this mine. So think my offer over carefully and let me know what you decide tomorrow.'

I saw it as the badly-needed chance to start again and I was ready to take up the offer immediately. But the old man wasn't so sure. The journey across the bush had put him in the mood to go trekking again. 'Let's rather try our luck in the bewitched pools,' he said, 'there's a fortune waiting for us there.'

'We can't even cross the border now without getting shot at,' I replied. 'And I've heard that Frelimo have built a military base camp within ten miles of the pool—they're probably drawing their water from it.'

'There are other places we could try,' the old man said hopefully. But I shook my head. 'Boy,' the old man warned as we sat over the camp fire that night, 'the Bismarck mine was a find in a million. If we start again on this mine we'll sweat like mules just to make a living and that's the best we can hope for for the rest of our lives. We'll have lost our freedom. We'll end up just like everyone else.'

'I don't care,' I said desperately. 'Don't you see? I don't want to live on dreams any more—I know they can't last, and I'm scared of ending up a clerk in an office when I'm fifty-five or lying dead drunk in a gutter which is where I found you. Every man has a talent of some sort if he can only get the chance to use it. Mine's mining. I've spent all day studying the plans and I know that I can make a go of the place. But I understand how you feel—you can go your own way if you like.'

'Boy,' the old man said quietly, 'you've never worked in a mine like this one. Most rock talks to you—you hear it creaking and snapping and when you get to know it it'll always warn you before it goes. But not with talc schist. All you'll get there is a puff of dust in the dark and then it slides. If you're not careful, boy, that mine is going to bury you. It's holding the bones of better miners than you already.' The old man saw that he wasn't going to change my mind and he poked moodily at the fire. 'Tell you what I'll do,' he said at last. 'I'll come along with you to get you started, I reckon I owe you that.'

*   *   *

The Molvan mine was situated just over a hundred miles to the north of Bulawayo. It had been abandoned for a while and the equipment that remained on site was in a bad state of neglect. The old man and I built ourselves a shack and took stock of the mine. Finding the reef again was no problem. Following the stringers led us right to a small blow of ore and the reef, though small, was good from there. But I soon understood why the other miners had lost interest.

The mine lay in a small depression close to the banks of the dry river-bed and though no water showed on the surface, there must have been millions of gallons flowing beneath the sands, for much of it seeped down into the mine and then gushed from fissures in the rock deep underground. We kept the pumps working night and day and still we had to wade everywhere through drives inches deep in water. And we found it hard to get labour. Mainly because we couldn't afford to pay the wages and bonuses of the richer mines. But also because the reef was small with only a few degrees of dip so that the stopes were also narrow and claustrophobic and the miners had to lash down the ore while lying on their sides with their shoulders jammed between walls of rock and then crawl on their bellies through rubble and water. And every time we lit the blast the old man and I silently prayed that it wouldn't bring the whole mine down about our ears.

But for all that, there was gold in the reef— nowhere near the quantity we had found in the Bismarck, but enough to buy food and clothing and pay our account at the local store. And every ounce of gold that we freed from the rock brought us nearer to owning the mine.

I was determined not to fail. I feared more than death to go back to that cell-like room with the paint peeling above the washbasin and to feel again that emptiness inside me. So I worked with the sweat in my eyes, muscles aching, mind-numbing hours until I moved like a robot in a constant state of exhaustion—no longer feeling anything. And I'll say this for the old man, who usually ensured that he got the easy jobs: this time he got his shirt off and sweated alongside me—Joseph too. Both of them vainly cursing me for a fool.

'This is no way to live, boy,' the old man said bitterly one night after he had reeled back exhausted from his shift. 'I hurt so much all over that I might as well be dead.'

The months went by, but I didn't notice them for I was completely involved in the mine. Gradually, as our financial position improved, I let myself relax a little. It was then I most missed the company of people my own age. I started listening to the radio again. I lived in my mind and the music sparked dreams in me, brought me company. It became my link with the outside world.

Then one day a police unit camped near the mine. The patrol officer came over and we found that we knew each other. His name was Justin Cassells and we had grown friendly during my prosperous days in Bulawayo. Justin was a tall, rakishly elegant, likeable man whose primary concern was with the pursuit of women and the good life in the city—when he could get there. A Londoner who claimed that he couldn't sleep wihout the reassuring sounds of traffic passing beneath his windows, Justin constantly applied for town postings and became understandably frustrated when Police Headquarters posted him deeper and deeper into the Matabeleland bush.

I visited his camp and sat by his fire long into the evening talking over the old times. He told me that he had tickets for the South African Ballet Company who were coming to Bulawayo. More than that, he had a date with one of the dancers, a girl he had known long ago, and was looking forward to seeing her again. He offered me his spare ticket and said he would try to fix up a date for me with one of her friends. I had never been to a ballet and wasn't much interested in going. Justin glanced at me shrewdly. 'A man can grow a little bush-mad staying out here on his own too long. Look, I know it's a strange offer, but a night in town would do you good.' He tried to persuade me, but I turned his offer down.

It was late when I got up to go. I was walking home across the bush when I saw an aeroplane flying high overhead, its lights winking amongst the stars. I watched it—just a whisper in the night sky—heading north, thinking that by morning the 'plane would be in Europe. And it's strange what such a small thing can trigger off in your mind. I was filled with a longing to be on it, for suddenly I was lonely, very lonely, deep inside and I knew that I needed to be with

250

people for a while. I turned and walked back to Justin's camp. 'All right,' I called out from the darkness beyond his fire, 'I'll come with you.'

I made a mistake in telling the old man that I was going to the ballet. At first he questioned my sanity, then he jeered at me for the next two weeks. Bulawayo was an old-fashioned city where people were still expected to dress for any formal occasion, and the day came when I got out the faded old dinner jacket that I had borrowed from a nearby farmer, carefully cleaned and pressed it, and tried it on in front of the cracked mirror in the smoky gloom of the shack. The old man watched me from across the table. 'You're mad,' he said scornfully.

At this time we owned a battered old truck with its doors tied on with string. It broke down on me twice on the dirt road and by the time I reached Bulawayo I was covered in oil and dust, in a filthy temper and regretting that I had ever agreed to go to the ballet. Justin bought me a couple of drinks to calm me down. 'Don't worry,' he assured me, 'you'll enjoy it—it's an experience you shouldn't miss. God damn it, Patrick,' he said, annoyed by my lack of enthusiasm, 'don't you know that nothing ever happens in Bulawayo? The South African Ballet Company coming here has set the whole place astir. I had to fight like a madman to get tickets—every performance is fully booked.'

We joined the people who were making their

way across the park to an open-air amphitheatre where the ballet was to be staged. Bulawayo was a dust-bowl in October with the bush dry and lifeless, waiting for the rains. But the park was an oasis, cool and green with soft grass underfoot. And after the harsh existence on the mine, where I could afford no gentleness in my life, I found the setting disturbing, strangely haunting—the soft evening light, the borders of flowers, the graceful women in long evening dresses strolling with their escorts beneath the tall palm trees.

We were shown to our places towards the back of the amphitheatre. Below us the stage was a semi-circle with seats fanning out and upwards in steeply-tiered banks. As we waited I began to move about restlessly, cursing Justin for making me come, telling myself I was out of place here, dreading the long evening ahead. Then the conductor raised his baton and the ballet began.

Tall pine trees, a soft wind rustling their branches, formed a backdrop against the night sky. And under them on the stage the ballerinas danced beneath the stars. Within minutes I was leaning forward in my seat, my eyes fixed on the stage, completely caught up by the poetry, the beauty, the magic of it all. I couldn't understand the subtle intricacies of the ballet—I didn't try. All I knew was that it was the most graceful art I had ever seen. It filled my eyes and ears and

252

heart. My senses were already heightened by the perfumed scent of jasmine and moon flower which floated across the park. I hadn't realized how deeply I had yearned for something this gentle, this civilized, or how tired I was of the years of hard living and the rough company of men.

The music caught me, reaching deep inside me, filling the emptiness that had been there, and carried me with it. I knew extremes of emotion and the moods came flooding through me, breaking down the barriers I had built to protect myself against all feeling. Tears welled in my eyes. I tried to hold them back but felt them trickle down my face. The tears were not for the loneliness in myself, but for the beauty I saw. I was swept up by the magic of it all and couldn't take my eyes off the stage. The ballerinas were so perfect, so fragile, so far removed from the harshness of the life I knew. And, because of that, they were all the more beautiful to me—softer, more special like a flower found in the desert.

Interval came. The audience filed out to the bars. But I refused to leave. Eventually I was left alone in an empty row of the amphitheatre, not daring to move in case I broke the spell, praying that the night would last for ever.

The second act started. Justin leant over to me. 'I think that's your date,' he whispered, 'the one dancing second from the left at the back.' I stared and stared, but I could not make her out. Our seats were just too far from the stage and the girls who danced in the chorus appeared to me to be tiny sparks of colour where the spotlight touched their dresses.

'What's her name?' I whispered.

'I've forgotten,' Justin replied, 'but she's a stunner.'

'You sure she's my date?' I asked dubiously, for I was very unsure of myself and had the sinking feeling that I could prove a great disappointment to that girl. 'Does she know about me?'

'It's all been arranged,' Justin answered smoothly, and settled back in his seat.

The ballet ended in a chorus of encores and when the audience finally let them go, Justin hurried me over to the dancers' dressing-room. We didn't make it a moment too soon. Already a crowd of men had gathered, many of them had not even been to the ballet, but they were all hoping for dates with the girls. It was always like that in Bulawayo. There was a shortage of women in the town and the competition was fierce.

We literally fought our way through the crowd, arriving breathless and dishevelled at the door. Justin's date came out first, a pretty dark-haired girl called Mary. She looked me over anxiously and I could imagine the pressure that must have been brought to bear on her friend to persuade her to accept a blind date. I was nervously trying to hide the oil stains on my shirt when my date came through the door.

'Hello, Patrick,' Judith said, smiling at me. Both her smile and her voice were warm with pleasure and I felt my knees turn to jelly.

'Mary told me that you two knew each other,' Justin said, grinning like a lunatic. I wanted to curse him for not having warned me, but my mind was numb with shock. I should at least have kissed her, but instead, like a fool, I awkwardly shook her hand.

'That was a long time ago,' Judith said quietly, hiding her disappointment, and let him lead the way.

Fortunately Justin had insisted that we take his car to the park and leave my battered old truck behind. He was in fine form as we drove into town for a late supper, and the conversation flowed easily between the three of them. From my corner in the back seat there was silence. I was a different, stronger, man from the one Judith had known. But I had lost my confidence with women from being too long in the bush. And though there was so much I wanted to say and ask, the words would not come.

We had booked a table on the top floor nightclub of the hotel. The music was soft and I began to look forward to dancing with Judith. The years had improved her, brought kindness and character to her face. From a pretty, rather

255

spoilt, girl she had matured into a beautiful, sophisticated woman with poise and grace. I found myself still very attracted to her and at least when we danced I would not need words.

But soon after we arrived a group of men came in. They had been part of the crowd outside the dressing-room door. The night-club was one of the few places still open in Bulawayo at that hour. On the strength of a slight acquaintance with Justin, they gate-crashed our table. They were true city men who carried their clothes like peacocks, all smug and self-confident. We paid for the meal and the wine, but they soon monopolized our women. I envied the ease of their conversation and despised their practised arrogance, wondering if I had ever been like that. But they could also be good company and amusing and I knew that now, on their ground, I did not stand a chance against them.

The conversation turned to ballet. Judith broke free from one of the men who was pinning her down just long enough to ask me if I had liked it. I stammered that it was the most beautiful thing I had ever seen. She looked at me oddly for, despite her interest in dancing, she knew that I had never bothered with ballet before. The others laughed, and I relapsed into silence, feeling naïve for displaying my emotions so openly. They talked of other seasons and famous performers and as I couldn't follow them I remained silent.

All through the evening I sat at the table watching Judith dance with these men, watching them flirt with her, unable to compete for they handed her one to the other, effectively cutting me out. Though I no longer had any claim over her, she was my date and I felt possessive about her. Justin was in much the same state over Mary. Gradually the anger in me built up. And then I could stand it no longer. I might have been straight from the bush and I might have been short of words, but by Christ, I could fight when I needed to. And I was ready to splatter their polished faces all over the night-club walls. I leant over to Justin, my eyes growing cold and my muscles relaxing, steadying my breathing before I went berserk. 'You're a policeman,' I warned him, 'you'd better get out of here because I'm about to take those bastards apart.'

'No way,' Justin said, equally angry. 'I'm set to join in.' Just then Mary shook off her partner and returned to the table. She saw the look in our eyes and she understood. Her hand reached out and covered my clenched fist.

'Don't bother,' she said gently, 'we're leaving.'

Julith was staying in the hotel. I had only a short time as we went down in the lift to ask if I could see her again. I had hardly spoken to her throughout the evening and I was sure that one of the other men must already have made a date with her. But at least I could try. We stood silently by the door. There was so much of the past between us, so much we should have spoken of that night but left unsaid. Instead I muttered something about it having been a nice evening and hurried away.

I walked down the passage. In my mind was the bitter memory of the times I'd walked the streets of Salisbury trying to convince myself that one can never go back, trying to block her out of my mind. The lift was gone. As I waited I cursed myself for being a coward and suddenly I was desperate to be with her again. I ran back down the passage and knocked on her door. 'Can I see you again,' I said breathlessly when she opened it, 'tomorrow night?'

She could have made me sweat, but she didn't. She looked at me with her clear grey eyes and smiled. 'I'd love to,' she said simply, 'except this time let's go somewhere quiet. 'Phone me around three o'clock tomorrow.'

My heart sank. 'I can't,' I admitted weakly. 'I'm a miner. I'll be underground then.' I knew that miners created an impression in people's minds of dirty-faced men burrowing around in the dark, and I was afraid that it would put her off me. But it didn't.

'I know,' she said, her eyes twinkling. 'How else do you think I found you, you fool. Justin promised Mary faithfully that he'd bring you here in handcuffs if he had to. Come to the dressing-room when the performance is finished. I'll be there.'

CHAPTER NINETEEN

THE next evening found me back at the entrance to the amphitheatre frantically trying to buy a ticket to the performance from someone in the passing crowd. I had almost given up hope when a middle-aged man who was being dragged there unwillingly sold me his ticket and slipped quietly off to the bar, leaving me to sit next to his wife.

The seat was close to the stage and I watched Judith dance. I saw no one else. She was dancing for me. A gossamer figure of a girl who moved effortlessly to the music as though her feet were dancing on the notes. And there was an ethereal quality about her: a radiance that captivated me completely. I added up all that I could offer her: a shack on a mine, years of hard work for the promise of gold. I'd progressed little further from when she had first met me—except that I was my own man now.

As soon as the performance finished I hurried around to the dressing-room and elbowed my way through the other men who were waiting by the door. Judith came out. She looked for me in the crowd, smiled when she saw me. She walked over and took my arm. She made it appear a deeply personal gesture of belonging. I stood taller than the other men around me, felt a pride in her surge through me, felt my confidence returning.

We had supper in a small Italian restaurant and sat in a corner where we could be alone. 'You're a beautiful woman now, Judith,' I said softly. 'And you are even more beautiful when you dance.'

Judith shook her head. 'I'm still very much an amateur. One of the girls had to drop out at the last moment. I was offered her part and I jumped at the chance—I wanted to see Rhodesia again,' a smile touched her eyes, 'and maybe find out what happened to you. What have you been up to?'

I told her of the old man and the letters, of the bewitched pools and the mines and the words came tumbling out of me like a dam wall breaking. It's like that when you have been alone too long. You grow silent and introverted, and then when you meet someone you care about you can never stop talking.

It was late. We were the last people in the restaurant and the waiters were yawning. I suddenly realized that I had been monopolizing the conversation. I stopped and looked up guiltily. But she smiled and the warmth in her eyes told me that she had enjoyed the evening. I paid the bill, took her hand and walked her home through the sleeping city.

'What happened to your marriage?' I asked.

Judith made a face. 'It's over—a disaster of my own making. Thank God there were no children.' I wanted to ask her more, but she stopped me. 'Leave it at that, Patrick,' she warned. 'The past will make neither of us happy.'

I knew she was right and I let the questions go unasked. We were happy, deeply content just to be with each other, strolling slowly along the wide tree-lined streets on a hot October night, the petals of the jacaranda in bloom forming soft lilac carpets of colour underfoot. And now that there was no need for words, the silence between us was filled with warmth and peace.

We entered her hotel and, in the brightly lit foyer, the spell was broken and uncertainty returned. I collected her key from the night porter and walked over to the lift where she was waiting, searching for the words to ask her if she would see me again. After all, she was only in town for a short time and she might not have wanted to be monopolized by one man. She must have seen the concern in my face for she smiled at me and a twinkle of amusement appeared in her eyes. She reached out and shook my hand.

'I've had a lovely evening,' she said distantly. Then, before I could speak, she reached up and kissed me. 'Same time, same place tomorrow,' she whispered. The lift doors closed and she was gone.

★   ★   ★

I returned to the mine as dawn was breaking, changed into my working clothes and went underground. There was still a little time before my shift was due on duty, and I wound my way along the narrow drives to an old working which had been abandoned when the rock falls made it too dangerous to mine. It was an empty, silent place with the tracks and all the equipment removed. But it was here I used to come when I needed to think, a private place where I could be alone. I slithered down and sat with my back against the rock, switched out my light and let the darkness and the silence envelop me. My mind was full of the glow of Judith. I could feel her near me as though I had only to reach out through the darkness to touch her.

Gradually I came to realize that I still loved her, that I had loved her for a long time. I thought over again of what I could offer her in the way of a future and it did not amount to much. Then I threw off the doubts that had been plaguing me and took a grip of myself. Damn it, I had the strength now and the courage, and with her to back me I knew for certain that there was no challenge that we could not meet together, no heights we could not reach. Sure, we would start poor. But this mine was only our beginning—from here we would found a mining empire and leave it to our heirs. Why not? Other men had dreamed such dreams and they had built this country from bush in less than eighty years. If they could do it, why not me? If Judith would trust me, I would not disappoint her. Alone in the quiet of the underground I made up my mind then that I was going to marry her. And no matter what the odds or how hard the fight, I promised myself that I would make a good life for her.

There came a soft sound stealing through the mine like a distant finger tapping on the rock and I knew that the drilling gangs had started work. I climbed up the rusted ladder out of the old stopes and made my way back to work. Now that I had made up my mind there was still one major problem facing me—I had only a short while left to convince Judith. She was returning to South Africa with the ballet company in eleven days' time.

From then on each evening found me driving the rickety old truck to Bulawayo to see her. We were happy to be alone together, getting to know each other again, growing warmer in each other's company. Neither of us mentioned her leaving. We made no plans beyond the following day. And because of that each moment we could spend together became of vital importance.

I would stand at the entrance of the amphitheatre trying to buy a ticket to the performance, offering double the value and more. And on the occasions I failed to get one, I sat in the park and listened to the music and then collected her from outside the dressing-room door.

Friday evening came. Judith was leaving on the following Wednesday. 'Mary's giving a birthday party at the hotel tonight,' she said as she came from the dressing-room. 'It's just for a few friends.' We sat towards the top of a long table in the night-club. I listened idly to the chatter for as long as was polite and then I rose and led Judith on to the dance floor. The band were good, especially the African on the clarinet, and, though it was late, they weaved a mood for us.

At first I held Judith lightly, and her hands reached up unconsciously and smoothed beneath the lapels of my jacket. It was an old familiar gesture of hers that brought back memories of the way we once were. I touched her hair, lifting it from her face. Then my fingers gently traced the outline of her cheek bones, to the pulse spots behind her ears and then down her neck. She looked up and saw the hunger in my eyes and under the gentle pressure of my arms, she moved in closer, closer until she moulded her body into mine.

The wine flowed, the party grew noisy and

our food grew cold on the table. But we remained on the dance floor, a solitary couple swaying close together to the music in the shadows of a darkened room, oblivious to everything, conscious only of each other. We remained that way long after the band took a break, then reluctantly I brought her back to the table.

We joined in with the conversation, and when the band started again it was with a fast number and Justin was on his feet before me. 'Judith,' he said, his eyes twinkling wickedly at her, 'you're a gorgeous lady and after all I've done for you I reckon you owe me this dance.'

'Justin,' Judith replied lightly, 'you know I'll always be grateful.'

'Show me,' he challenged, and led her out on to the floor. Justin, fancying himself as a ladies' man, took a pride in dancing well and he urged her into the beat. Judith was wearing a simple summer dress that floated as she moved, her long sun-tanned legs flashing beneath, and she danced completely unselfconsciously, moving in such a sensuous rhythm to the music that every man at the table stared after her. Someone spoke, but I didn't notice, so completely absorbed was I by her. Suddenly I knew that I had had enough of people and I wanted to be alone with Judith. I caught her eyes, a silent, urgent signal snapped between us, and she nodded in reply.

I quietly left the table and waited for her by the exit. From there I watched Judith leave the dance floor and hurry to the top of the table, kiss Mary goodnight, then come to me, her eyes shining, still slightly breathless from the dance. There was an urgency about us then as we waited for the lift. When it came we were the only people in it and we stood facing each other, unable to take our eyes off one another—not speaking, not touching, just wanting each other. The lift stopped and we hurried down the endless corridor to her room. She opened the door and slipped inside. As I followed her and stood framed in the doorway, I heard the soft rustling sound of her dress falling to the floor.

In the shadows of the room I saw the brown and white contours of her body as she turned, completely naked, offering herself to me. She was beautiful. Every sense in my body was tingling unbearably. I felt as though I was burning up in a furnace. I closed the door and moved towards her.

My mouth was dry, my body aching with longing for her. She reached up, put her arms around my neck, her body pressing into mine, and kissed me—a long, deep kiss. I picked her up and carried her to bed. I kissed her eyes, her ears, her mouth, her neck. I touched each secret part of her. Lying in the warmth of each other's arms, we loved each other then with tenderness. And the physical act of love with the gentleness later and the giving did more than any words to wash the scars away.

I worked like an automaton through the days that followed, cat-napping when and where I could. I felt I didn't need sleep and I was filled to the very core of my being with happiness.

The old man had begun to miss my company in the evenings. He knew I was avoiding him and eventually, in order to talk to me, he had to follow me underground and corner me in one of the drives. 'Once,' he said, 'and I could have been mad enough to believe that you really went to a ballet. But six nights in a row and I know you've got to be lying! What are you up to? Is something troubling you, boy?' I told him about Judith and the old man's shoulders sagged. 'Listen, boy,' he said urgently. 'You're walking into a trap. Get out of it before she snares you. That woman nearly did for you before, remember? You don't want to go back there again.'

'I am back,' I said quietly. 'I love her and if she'll have me I'm going to marry her. Don't interfere with us this time,' I warned. 'Don't get in my way. And if she should write to me, make sure I get the letter.'

The old man saw the determination in my face. 'So that's the way it's going to be between us now?' he said quietly. I nodded.

He was silent for a while, thinking things over. 'You going to bring her to live out here?'

he asked. I nodded again.

'All right,' he said heavily. 'Let me know when she's coming and I'll get the shack cleaned up.' The old man and I knew each other so well that we could almost read each other's minds. I had expected anger, pleading, even blackmail. Anything, but surrender. It threw me completely off guard. I looked at him in amazement.

'You really mean that? You will make her welcome here?'

'I don't say I'm going to enjoy having a woman getting in the way round here,' the old man growled. 'But I will do my damnedest to give it a try. Here, eat this,' he said, pushing a roughly wrapped package across to me. 'I brought you some lunch. I figure you'll starve to death if you keep on the way you're going.'

The old man heaved himself tiredly to his feet and started down the drive. Then he turned. 'About those letters, boy,' he said. 'You were young then and I thought I was doing it for your own good. But now I reckon you're old enough to make your own decisions.' He thought for a moment, then nodded to himself. 'I reckon you are, Patrick,' he said softly.

Sunday came, our last Sunday together. We had only three days left. I packed a picnic lunch and a bottle of wine, and then I picked Judith up from outside her hotel and took her into the bush for the day. We drove along the dirt roads

268

of the Matopos National Park, following the route the old man and I had taken on foot when we crossed this region in search of the Bismarck mine. I took her deep into wild country, past herds of buffalo, sable, giraffe and wildebeest. She was a girl who had spent most of her time in the city and I wanted to show her as much as I could. I told her all I knew about the habits of each of the herds, the African folk-lore associated with the trees and shrubs and the wild birds, for I loved the bush. It held an endless fascination for me and I wanted to share it with her.

We left the truck parked under a tree and followed game spoor on foot, choosing one animal and tracking it, watching where it fed and where it rested. When the sun grew hot we picnicked by a waterhole and watched the game pass within a few feet of us on their way down to drink. The sun and the wine went to her head. Judith's eyes closed and she slept in the crook of my arm beneath the shade of a spreading waterboom tree. In the afternoon I woke her. She stretched in delicious contentment, testing each limb like a cat. Then she saw that the picnic basket was packed. 'Do we have to go back now?' she asked, disappointed.

I shook my head, grinning at her to hide my nervousness. 'The day is far from over yet. I'm taking you to my special place.'

I drove her some distance through an empty

269

land and parked the truck amongst wild and windswept kopjes—great towering citadels of rock. And above us, situated at the summit of the tallest kopje and guarded by massive sentinels of wind-eroded boulders that balanced one upon the other, lay the grave of Cecil Rhodes. I persuaded Judith to walk to the top. There was something vitally important I wanted to ask her and I had chosen the place and the setting with care.

As we climbed the narrow path I told her the tale of how Rhodes had called a great *indaba* amongst these rocks of all the *indunas*, or chiefs, of the Matabele nation, in an attempt to end the war between them and the white men. The Matabele, an off-shoot of the Zulu, were a proud and warlike people. Rhodes came out to meet them unarmed and alone except for an interpreter. And through sheer force of personality, he persuaded the *indunas* to stop the war and follow him.

When Rhodes died his body was carried up to the top of this kopje to a place he had named 'World's View', and as he was lowered into a grave hollowed out of the rock, the Matabele tribe, who had come quietly and lined the way, gave him the *Byatte*—the royal salute reserved for their kings. It was the highest honour a proud people could pay him.

We reached the top of the kopje in time to watch the sun set from his grave. 'Dear God,

Patrick,' Judith said in awe. 'I can understand now why he wanted to be buried here.' From the high point where Rhodes lay with the wind constantly crying across the barren rock you could see for fifty miles over some of the most searingly beautiful, harsh, rugged and untamed scenery in Africa. We sat up there alone and in love in the silence, moved by the beauty stretching way before us. A cool wind tugged at Judith's hair as she watched the rays from the dying sun touch the dark rock with gold. And above us an eagle soared, its harsh cry echoing out over the high places.

I reached out and touched Judith's hand. 'Will you marry me?' I asked. Alone in the underground I had planned a whole speech, but that was all that came out. Judith shook her head, but she did not tell me no. Instead she looked at me. Her face was radiant and her eyes shone. She was silent for a moment. I waited for her to speak. And then she told me there was another man. My heart turned to stone. I felt physically sick. Of course there was another man. He was waiting for her in Johannesburg. 'Then why me?' I said savagely.

'I wanted to see you again,' Judith replied. 'I couldn't get you out of my mind. I didn't mean it to go this far.' Suddenly she reached across and tried to kiss me, but I held her away, my fingers pressing fiercely into her arms. 'You fool!' she said, 'you crazy fool! Don't hurt so much. Can't you see I love you too? It's just that I'm so confused at the moment. I have to go back and see this man, find out how I really feel. It's only fair to him, and I have to be sure in myself.'

I should have respected her for her honesty. But I was confused myself and I hurt so much inside that I didn't try. No one could hurt me as badly as she could. I clamped a shutter down on my emotions and retreated into myself. It was like a light in me going out.

'Judith,' I said bitterly in a voice beyond caring, 'you're better off with him. All I could have offered you was a hard life on a small mine. But I give you this to think about when you are a housewife in Johannesburg—together we could have made a life, we could have created an empire, you and I, if we chose. We could have touched any star you wanted to reach. And those are not just dreams, Judith, like the ones you used to tease me about. Look at me, woman, and you will know I don't boast anymore.'

I led her in silence down to the truck and drove her back to her hotel. There she tried to speak. 'Will I see you again?' she said. I shook my head.

Monday, Tuesday, passed and I worked underground, cursing Judith, hating her, hurting so much, trying to get her out of my mind. Wednesday came. The day she was leaving. I knew the ballet company, together with all their props and equipment, were returning to South Africa by train, and I stayed underground, trying to concentrate on other things but a clock ticked away the hours in my brain until I could stand it no longer. I came bursting up from the mine and ran for the truck. If I drove like a madman I could still make the station before the train pulled out.

I arrived close to the last minute and found Judith on the platform. Most of the company were already on board and her friends were calling to her to hurry. We stood there, like islands in a surging sea of humanity, both of us ashen faced, hiding our emotions, strangers to each other. The guard was getting ready to blow his whistle. Unconsciously I reached out for her. She fell into my arms and we held each other so desperately that I could feel myself shaking. Judith's lips trembled and her eyes filled with tears. 'Patrick, if I call, will you come for me?' she asked brokenly.

'No,' I said harshly. 'I'm no lap dog to come when I'm called. I'll give you a fortnight to see that man and make up your mind. Then, two weeks from today, I'm going to take this same train down to South Africa. If you're waiting for me on the station in Johannesburg, then I'll know you're going to marry me. If you're not, I'll understand and then I won't embarrass you. I'll just catch the next train home.'

CHAPTER TWENTY

SEVEN days passed. Eight. Nine. Time dragged by so slowly. I could imagine Judith with the other man and I was consumed with jealousy. I lay awake in the shack at night staring at the walls, my stomach knotted with fear. And I had a recurring nightmare in which the train pulled into Johannesburg station and she was not there. A part of me needed her desperately, and a part of me hated the humbling effect of that need. The old man, who knew I was going, said and did nothing to stop me, but he subtly played on those fears.

On the eleventh day the old man and I went underground as usual. The mine was empty and silent—ready for the blast. We parted on the sixth level, he to light a series of rounds in the stopes at the end of that drive. I turned into a side tunnel to set off the blast in a raise that we were driving up to the next level. With the water gushing down it was a slippery, messy job and for that reason I preferred to do it myself.

The raise was shaped like a well and rose steeply up along the reef. I ducked under a ledge and then swung myself up on the narrow timbers that had been wedged against the rough rock walls at four foot intervals. I tapped each timber above me as I climbed, listening for the hollow sound that would warn if it was weak. A sound you soon learned to recognise, for if a timber gave under your weight there was a chance, as in this case, that you would fall sixty feet through the darkness to your death.

I went up fast, with practised ease, hardly concentrating. In my mind I was already at the railway station catching the train. Anything I did between now and then was just using up that time. I reached the top and scrambled on to the crosspiece of timber that made a crude platform for the drillers. There I leant my back against the rock, balancing myself as I carefully drew out my matches and cheesa stick.

Good mining practice dictates that for each blast you use a fresh stick. But, for reasons of economy, the one I was using had already been burnt three-quarters down. However, I wasn't too worried, for as the beam of my light fell on the pattern of fuses which dangled from their holes in the rock above me, I could tell that it should only take a minute or so to light them.

The old man had been working deeper in the mine than me, and he lit his blast first. I heard him shout on his way back to the shaft that his fuses were burning and it was understood that when I knew he was clear I would light mine and then join him at the bucket that was waiting to speed us to the surface. We were an experienced team now, and had done this many times before.

The cheesa stick sparked to life in my hand, the gunpowder, protected by its cladding, giving off a bright orange flame. I reached up, took hold of the first bunch of fuses, and started to light them. They went off with a hissing sound, oozing tar marking the path of the flame that was racing beneath the white cotton lining to ignite the explosive in the holes. I was less than half-way through my work when the cheesa stick suddenly flared and a blue flame took over from the orange, a warning that it had only a few seconds left to burn before it went out. Some of the powder must have shaken out into my pocket during the climb. I had been over-confident. It was criminally careless of me not to have checked it before I started.

I began to work frantically, my head wreathed in smoke given off from the burning fuses, my eyes watering from the acrid gunpowder fumes, cursing myself for not having brought another cheesa stick. It went out and I tried to continue lighting the remaining fuses with matches. But it was painfully slow. The water extinguished the matches and again and again I had to strike fresh ones. The seconds dragged by. The first fuses were now burning dangerously close to their holes. I realized that there was no possibility of my being able to light the whole round in time. And even if I did, the charges would go off unevenly, destroying the effect of the pattern. The only alternative left was to cut

276

the fuses and abandon the blast.

I was becoming enveloped by the thickening smoke that had been trapped by the dead end of the rise. I had been up there too long and was coughing and spluttering as I fumbled blindly in my pockets for my knife. Once a fuse is burning, the only way of stopping it is to cut in front of the flame. My knife was not in its usual pocket. For a moment I thought I had left it behind. By now my light could no longer penetrate the smoke and I couldn't see what I was doing. Then I found the knife and relief flooded through me. I tore the blade open and, as I did so, it slipped from my sweaty hands and I heard it fall. My heart dropped with it. I knew there was no way I could stop the blast from going off now. And my only chance of saving my life was to get out of that raise as fast as possible.

I ducked under the platform and swung myself on to the first timber support, my heart in my mouth, legs kicking out in the dark for a grip on the rung below. As soon as I found it I let myself go and made a grab for the next one, then again with the next one. The timbers were slimy and sodden with moisture. In my panic I went down too fast. I missed my grip, felt my hands slip and I fell, out of control. I hit more supports and they slowed my fall, but I couldn't hold on to them. And I crashed down through the dark, cannoning off the rock walls. Then I felt a jerk and a searing pain cut across my waist.

I found myself hanging, face down, over the raise with the back of my belt caught on a length of drill steel that had been driven into the rock like an upraised rung. My helmet had fallen off and was dangling below me, held on only by the light attached by a lead to the battery on my belt. The light was swinging, pointing downwards and there was no reflection. I kicked out wildly in the darkness, wriggling like a fish trying to get off a hook, trying to find some grip that would support my weight long enough to lever myself off the rung. But there was nothing I could do. I was stranded there with the fuses hissing angrily above me. The first ones must already have entered their holes. There came a series of sharp crashes as the rounds deeper in the mine went off, followed by a dull reverberating thunder that grew louder and louder. I knew that now I only had a few seconds left before my own blast went off; the full force of it funnelling down the narrow raise would smash me to pieces in its path.

My only chance was to let myself drop and hope that I would hit the bottom without breaking my legs, and then somehow crawl out of the direct line of the blast. And if I had not been too badly injured, there was a slim possibility that I could still make my way to the shaft before the fumes overcame me. My fingers scrabbled at the broad buckle of my belt, forcing it open. The flap came away under the weight of my body and tore through my fingers. My light fell first and I felt myself falling through the darkness after it.

My head struck one of the supports and I bounced off another. Though I was half stunned, I was instinctively grabbing at them, trying to slow myself down. It was like falling face down along the rungs of a ladder. I doubled over one of the supports on my stomach. It knocked all the breath out of me and then it gave way. But it slowed me down long enough to get a grip on the next one.

I was gagging with pain, crying for breath, my body bruised and hurting. But an instinct for self-preservation over-rode the pain and the panic and I made myself wait for a moment, regaining control. If I was crippled when I hit the bottom I would have to lie there waiting for the blast. I scrambled down again more slowly. My light was still shining where it lay on the bottom, the rubber protector having absorbed the shock of the fall. I used it to gauge the distance and figured that I was nearly low enough to jump. I was already dropping when above me there came the sharp crack of the first charges going off. My boots crashed on the bottom rock and I threw myself sideways, rolling out of the raise, desperately trying to hide under the protective roof of the drive. Then the blast hit me.

I must have passed out. When I regained consciousness I found I couldn't move. The lower half of my body was trapped under a pile of rock. I felt no pain at first, just numbness. The mine creaked with silence. It was pitch black and I knew that I was alone with no hope of help. The old man, if he had had the sense, would have gone up in the bucket when he heard the first blast.

The rock had stopped moving. The dust had settled and I knew what would be happening now. In my mind's eye I could see the thick yellow fumes from the explosive, like a swirling mist in the dark, being drawn through the mine to the shaft. And I was lying right in its path. Even if the old man made it to the surface to get help, the rescue teams would never reach me in time. If a man managed to escape a blast, often he was killed by the fumes. Time and again a bucket had been rushed to the surface only to find that the man inside was dead.

I lay with my face pressed against the cold, wet rock, waiting for death. I'd heard that the fumes brought death quickly and almost painlessly. You fell unconscious soon after you inhaled them. Your lungs started to weep and you drowned in the liquid. I thought about it without panic. I'd given it my best and now it was as though my mind had grown tired of the struggle and refused to function anymore.

Dimly I saw the light coming towards me and

heard the sound of running footsteps. Then the old man was kneeling beside me, running his hands over the exposed part of my body, checking to see what bones were broken. He began to tear away at the wood and rock that was pinning me down. I tried to tell him that he was a fool to have come back, that the fumes were almost on us. But at the same time I loved him deeply for coming.

The old man moved round behind me, grabbed me under the arms and, grunting with effort, dragged me out from under the rubble, swung my arm over his shoulder and started to run with me back down the drive. He was not strong enough to support me for any distance, and we stumbled and fell. Immediately he was at me like a terrier, dragging me, urging me up. I was dizzy with shock and pain, but the old man had brought me hope, made me realize how scared I was of dying down there in the dark, and somehow I kept going. I vaguely remember being flung into the bucket and the old man tumbling in on top of me. He rang the emergency signal and, because the hoist operator was good at his job, the bucket raced the fumes up the shaft. Then severe shock set in and I passed out again before we reached the surface.

When I regained consciousness I was lying on my back on my bed in the shack with the old man bending over me. I tried to move but I found that I was swathed from head to foot in bandages. Terrible thoughts crossed my mind. 'How bad am I?' I whispered.

The old man looked at me and I could read immediately from the expression in his face that he was wondering how much he could tell me without worsening the effects of the shock.

'Very bad,' the old man answered grimly at last. 'For God's sake, don't move. I think we've managed to stop the bleeding inside.'

'My legs,' I said weakly, badly scared. 'I can't move them. I can't move anything below my hips.'

The old man shrugged his shoulders sadly and said nothing, but his face told me all I needed to know. Oh my God, I thought desperately. I'm a cripple. And with that knowledge I went cold and dead inside. I became aware only of the pain that floated round the edges of my brain. 'Rest easy,' the old man said gently. 'You'll do yourself no good worrying. I've got the best doctor money can buy coming to see what he can do for you.' I passed out again.

When I opened my eyes the room was in darkness and a glimmer of starlight shone in through the window. I lay alone and broken on my narrow bed, not daring to move, scared half to death. The old man came in.

'Has the doctor come yet?' I asked.

He shook his head. 'Maybe tomorrow,' he

said. 'Get some sleep.'

'What day is it?' I said as he left the room.

'I don't rightly know,' the old man answered me gruffly. 'You know I don't keep track of days.' And with that he closed the door.

I lay there trying to work it out, but I had no idea how long I had lain unconscious. Then I heard a miner pass beneath my window and I called to him. The answer came back. It was the night of the thirteenth. I had lost a day and a half. The train left Bulawayo tomorrow at noon and there was no way I could be on it. Tears of despair squeezed from beneath my eyelids. Oh dear God, I'd come so close to Judith, and now I was going to lose her. What in the hell would she want with a cripple?

Dawn broke, full morning came. The hours ticked away. Then the door creaked open and Joseph entered the room. I knew that Joseph had as good a knowledge of anatomy as most doctors—it was probably he who had bandaged my legs in the first place. 'How bad am I, Joseph?' I asked, ready to plead. 'Tell me the truth.'

Joseph was loyal to the old man, but he could stand my despair no longer. 'Mambo,' he said quietly, 'there's nothing wrong with you. The wooden supports protected you from most of the rock. You were very, very lucky. Your head was a little hurt and you have a few cracked ribs. The rest of your body is just bad bruises and cuts from your fall—your legs are all right.'

'I'm what?' I said, sitting bolt upright. The effort strained my torn stomach muscles and I collapsed back, groaning.

'No broken bones,' Joseph confessed, unsympathetic to my pain. 'No bleeding inside. It's just that the old man didn't want you to catch the train. Look,' he said, lifting the sheet. A heavy piece of board had been bound tightly round my legs right up to my hips—no wonder I couldn't move them. Joseph took off the bandages. There were yards of them. It was like unwrapping a mummy. When he finished, I tottered from my bed.

'What time is it?' I asked.

'Just after half past ten,' Joseph replied. The wizened old African looked at me, reading my mind. 'If you hurry,' he said, 'you can still catch that train.'

'Help me,' I said urgently.

He reached for my suitcase and began throwing clothes into it while I dressed. I hobbled stiffly from the shack, hurrying as fast as my bruised body would let me, towards the waiting truck. The old man saw me. 'What in the hell are you doing?' he shouted. 'You're supposed to be in bed!'

'Look at me, you bastard,' I said furiously. 'No legs. You're witnessing a bloody miracle. Now get out of my way.' I made for the truck with the old man following me.

284

'I did it for your own good,' he bellowed. 'We're doing all right as we are. We don't want a woman here. She'll spoil everything. Patrick,' the old man said more softly, almost pleading, 'if she comes here, sooner or later it'll be the end of us as partners. You know it will.'

The driver moved over. I climbed into his seat and slammed the door, paying no attention to the old man. I got the truck started, put it into gear and took off with the wheels kicking up clouds of red dust. The old man lost his temper and chased after the truck, cursing me. 'You'll live to see that woman make a fool of you. She'll change everything—women always do.'

I could not push the vehicle along any faster than a snail's pace on the rough mine road, but in spite of that the old man couldn't catch me and in his frustration he stopped and threw rocks after the truck. One struck against my door. I stood on the brakes. 'Now you listen to me,' I yelled furiously at him. 'You promised you wouldn't interfere. You promised me that if I could bring her back you'd make her welcome. Now you keep that promise.' I started the truck rolling, then stood on the brakes again and leant out of the door as another thought occurred to me. 'And see that the shack's cleaned up by the time I get back,' I shouted. 'It's like a pigsty in there!'

I missed the train at Bulawayo, but I chased it

285

towards the Botswana border as far as Figtree and caught it from the tiny bush halt there. The train crossed the border later that afternoon, passing through a flat, arid land of scrub and thorn trees. I sat by the window in an empty compartment swaying to the beat of the wheels. Occasionally small herds of duiker, impala or kudu crossed my line of sight. And along the telephone lines that followed the track, each fiercely guarding his territory, perched black hawk kites, chanting goshawks and Warberg eagles.

The sunset seemed to fill the whole horizon of that empty land, its rays setting the dusty sky afire with searing colours. In the few moments that it lasted, it made the dry land beautiful beyond belief and I stared after it long after it had gone. I unhooked a wedding ring from where it hung on the safety chain around my neck. The gold felt weighty and warm in my hands and I polished the ring absent-mindedly. I had designed it myself from the small ball of gold that we had won from the bewitched pools and which the old man had given me for luck all those years ago. It had become my special talisman. I had carried it through the good times and the bad, and now I proposed to give it to Judith. If she would have it.

The dinner gong sounded the first and second sittings and an attendant came to make up my bunk. The train stopped at countless tiny halts through the night. I sat in the darkness, my body stiff and filled with pain. But it wasn't that which worried me, for I was hard and fit and I knew the sores were healing even as I sat there. It was the emptiness in the pit of my stomach, the fear eating deep inside me. Dear God, I'd never been so afraid. I had learned to control my emotions. I had gained in strength and confidence. But this girl, with her dark hair and grey eyes, had established herself so deep within me, had become so beloved by me, that if she was not on that station platform, then I knew that an important part of me was going to die.

The train pulled in to Mafeking at four-thirty in the morning and the South African Customs came on board. Then we travelled through the Transvaal arriving on the outskirts of Johannesburg in the afternoon. For an hour before we were due to arrive I had been standing by the window staring down the track.

At last the train rumbled slowly down the long, long platform. There were quite a few people to meet it and I stared with a steadily sinking heart at the unfamiliar faces as they passed. Then I saw, way down the platform, the distant figure of a waiting girl behind a barrier of moving trolleys. The last trolley passed and then I could see her more clearly. It was Judith. It was Judith! Dear God, it *was* Judith! Everything in me, the fear, the tension, the joy, exploded at the same time. I yelled out her name

287

at the top of my voice, then I swung off the long moving train and raced down the platform towards her, scattering people out of my way.

Judith did not hear me shout. She did not see me coming—she was trying hard not to stare too obviously into the windows of the passing compartments. Then she heard the sound of running footsteps coming up behind her and she turned, and she was in my arms and I was holding her up, whirling her around and around, refusing to let her down. My relief was overwhelming.

'Thank God,' I kept saying over and over again as I hugged her to me. 'Thank God you're here. I was afraid you wouldn't come.'

Judith was crying, her face wet with tears, pressed against mine. 'Oh you fool,' she said, half angrily and half as though her heart was breaking. 'If only you had let me explain, you would have known I'd be here. I've been meeting every train for the last three days in case I missed you.' I set her down and clutched at my side. 'What's the matter?' she asked.

'My ribs,' I replied, breathless with pain. I'd forgotten all about them.

We were married by special licence two days later in a Johannesburg registry office. Judith's mother refused to attend. She had lined up one of Johannesburg's wealthiest young men and she was scandalized that her daughter had dropped him to marry a miner—more so when she discovered that the miner was me.

I knew no one in Johannesburg and I waited nervously on the pavement outside the registry office at the appointed time. Judith arrived with a few of her friends and as I went to meet her the nervousness disappeared and a great warmth took its place, for Judith was radiant and beautiful to my eyes and her friends, though they had no special reason to care for me, showed me great kindness.

We went inside. I imagined a grim impersonal government department that married people as though licensing cars. Instead, the registrar came first to talk to us. He was an Afrikaner, his English was slow and his voice deep and his face strong and kind. Perhaps he could feel the warmth of love that was passing between Judith and me. Perhaps he was the kind of man who cared. When he discovered that I was from Rhodesia and alone in the city, he both mentally and emotionally put his arms around us, became totally involved with us. He led us into a pleasant room and, ignoring an official-looking table, he placed Judith in the path of sunlight that came streaming in through the window. He paused for a moment to survey his handiwork and then both he and I found ourselves regarding Judith in stunned awe. For standing there, framed in the sunlight and shadow, flowers in her long dark hair, and her ivory-coloured dress flowing softly from her, she was beautiful, simply beautiful. Her eyes shone, she radiated happiness as though it welled from her soul. There was an ethereal, translucent, timeless, perfect quality about her that left me breathless. The registrar and I stood rooted to the spot. It took the impatient coughing of one of the witnesses to get us moving and, regretfully, the registrar stood me beside her.

We had come expecting very little understanding. This was a matter between ourselves, and all we required from this place was the licence. But the registrar made a simple service memorable for us. He made us feel that that room was our cathedral, and in a way it was. At the end he managed to kiss Judith several times before we left the building and invited himself and his wife to the wedding supper we held that night in a small Italian restaurant in Hillbrow.

We left Johannesburg the next day for Rhodesia—I couldn't afford to spend more time away from the mine. Our honeymoon was spent crossing Botswana for twenty-four hours in the tiny compartment of a travel-stained, rust and biscuit-coloured Rhodesia Railways carriage. Its fittings were of wood painted with age-darkened varnish, a small Victorian-style washbasin tucked away in a corner with a smoky mirror above. The design seemed not to have changed at all since Cecil Rhodes dreamt of opening his rail route from the Cape to Cairo at the turn of the century. But we didn't mind.

I woke up at some time that night and lay with Judith in my arms, swaying peacefully to the rhythm of the train, listening to the steady beat of steel wheels on the track. The window blind had shaken loose and beyond it the bush glided by like a limitless sea drenched in white moonlight, the thorn trees and scrub throwing shadows like wave troughs. It was a night to stir your bones—a perfect night to be travelling. The old man would have loved it. To him it would have been a real trekking moon.

I lay still for a long time, watching and thinking. The old man and the trekking moon. That part of my life was over. But if I had been completely free before, then I'd never been really happy. And I was now. The emptiness that had always been with me, alone in the bush, was now filled.

The train stopped at a halt and a hyena's weird cackle came from close by our window. No matter how often I heard that sound, it still sent shivers down my spine. Judith lifted her head to it and I realized that she had been awake for some time. She kissed my chest. 'How are your ribs?' she asked. 'Do you have any pain?'

'No,' I answered. And it was true. I was so much at peace, so deeply contented, that my mind seemed to be floating free of my body beyond all reach of pain.

'I'll be a good wife to you,' Judith said

sleepily, speaking her subconscious thoughts. 'But I'm frightened of the bush. I love you, Patrick,' she added softly. 'I always have. I wanted you to know that.' She snuggled closer to me, feeling warm and secure within my arms, and as the train pulled away from the halt she fell asleep with her dark hair spilling over my shoulder.

The train pulled into Bulawayo the next day, and set us down with our baggage on the platform. I had sent Justin a telegram and he was there to meet us. 'So you got her!' he exclaimed delightedly as he threw his arms around Judith and kissed her. 'Well done, you lucky bastard.'

Justin's face fell, and he shot me an anxious look when he saw Judith's mound of expensive matching luggage and took in her fashionable white skirt and top, wondering if I had prepared this city girl for conditions on a mine. It took the two of us and two hulking great askari to carry her luggage to a police Land-Rover that had been backed into a prohibited unloading zone. Justin grew agitated at the curious stares from passers-by and urged us to hurry. There was a battered metal body box, used for the transportation of corpses, strapped to the roof. Fortunately it was empty. Justin lowered it and to Judith's dismay pushed some of her smaller cases inside. The rest he crammed into the back of the truck.

'I'm afraid you'll have to keep your head down until we're clear of the city,' he said to Judith. 'I'm supposed to be out on patrol looking for some poor sod who has hanged himself about a hundred and fifty miles from here. My member-in-charge will lock me up and throw the key away if he catches me in town. He knows I'm always trying to get back here.' Judith was crammed in with her luggage, and only when we were well clear of the city was she allowed to climb over the gun racks and join us in front.

The Land-Rover pulled off the tar on to the dirt road. Justin looked back in his mirror. 'I hate leaving the tar,' he said wistfully. 'As long as I'm close to a tarred road I at least feel I'm within reach of civilization. But when I'm on the bush tracks, miles from anywhere, I feel like bloody Livingstone. This life of isolation does me no good at all. I'm surprised you stood it all those years,' he said to me.

The old man saw the dust of our truck approaching and he was standing waiting for us on the verandah when we arrived. He helped Judith out of the truck and I looked on nervously while the two of them stood warily summing each other up.

'Come,' the old man said to Judith after a moment, 'let me show you around.' Gallantly, I thought, he offered her his arm and she took it. 'Not you,' he snarled at me as I followed. 'She's

293

probably had enough of you hanging on to her skirts. She can do without you for a while.' And with that he led her into the shack. 'Watch the floorboards,' I heard him warn as they went through the door, 'they're not very strong.'

Justin had been waiting for a chance to talk privately with me and he took me to one side. 'Listen,' he said. 'And don't repeat this. In Bulawayo last Saturday night a patrol car was cruising around and kept crossing the path of an old Ford Zephyr. Eventually, more out of boredom than anything else, they stopped it and questioned the passengers. There were four of them—young Africans—and in the boot were two Russian-made machine guns, capable of firing upwards of eight hundred rounds a minute, and two assault rifles. It turned out they were a terrorist cell that had just been activated, and their mission was to take out the crowds when they came out of the cinemas after the evening show. Can you imagine the carnage if they had opened up indiscriminately on a densely-packed crowd in the confined space of a cinema foyer? And that patrol car stopped them with only ten minutes to spare. They're not going to release the news because the bloody government is terrified of alarming the population. But trouble is brewing, Patrick. I don't know where they will strike next, but I want you to take care out here.'

Before I could ask him any questions, Judith

appeared, white-faced, from the shack with the old man following gloomily behind her. 'It's revolting. It's a pigsty in there!' she said angrily. 'How can anyone live in that squalor?'

'It's not that bad,' the old man protested defensively. He had, after all, had a hand in building that shack. 'I knew a man once. He lived with his wife on a small working in the open for nine months with no shelter at all other than the shade of a tree. Mind you,' the old man added sombrely, 'she left him when the rains came. Couldn't stand all that mud.'

The old man knew how to pick his stories. I glared a warning at him, but he shrugged his shoulders as if to say 'I told you so.' Judith was depressed, and as she looked around at the stark mine headgear and the shack that appeared as a desolate speck of civilization set in an empty, endless sea of bush, she looked ready to cry. Justin, the coward, climbed hastily into his Land-Rover and left. I put my arm consolingly around her. 'It's not that bad,' I said, leading her into the shack. 'We can make it livable for you. Just tell us what you want done.'

I had never really bothered with where I had lived before, but now that I saw it through Judith's eyes I realized that she had a point. The old man had made only a very half-hearted attempt to clean the place up. The shack consisted of four small rooms, all inter-linked with each other, a narrow, dark lean-to kitchen at the back with a few blackened pots, a wood-burning stove, and a tattered evil-smelling paraffin 'fridge. And the lavatory was a long-drop in a small wooden shed some forty yards down a path through the bush. The door to my bedroom would only partly open, and I found that Joseph had scrounged a second bed and pushed the two together. The room was so small that the door now opened on to a bedstead and we had to climb over a corner of that bed every time we wanted to get in and out. There was no space for her luggage and certainly not enough for a cupboard. What few clothes I owned I had always been content to hang over a wire stretched across the corner of the room. Judith looked around in despair, and I hurried her outside and offered to show her the mine.

In the evening she took the path to the long-drop. A young cobra had lived by that path for some time. He always slithered well clear whenever the old man or I passed, but now he had grown large and advancing age had made him cantankerous. That night, rather than leave his place on the warm sand, he rose up, hood stretched before Judith, and angrily disputed her passing. I heard Judith's startled yell then the sound of running footsteps on the gravel and she came bursting through the door of the shack white-faced and shaking with shock. 'There's a snake out there,' she gasped.

The old man nodded without looking up. 'Go

round him,' he said, 'he was here first.'

I had to kill the snake and dispose of its body before I could persuade Judith to leave the safety of our room. She named that path Snake Alley. For some days thereafter I had to escort her down the path each evening and stand guard beyond the lavatory door while from inside Judith claimed nervously that she was being watched by the glowing eyes of great hunting spiders and I had to keep reassuring her that they were harmless.

That night, the first in our own bed, Judith looked up from her pillow and saw the stars through a crack in the roof above her. And that was it. The last straw. There was no security in her own home, not even a roof that fitted properly. She could not take any more. She dissolved into tears and spent the night sobbing in my arms and there seemed no way I could comfort her.

The old man wisely said nothing in the morning but everyone on the mine knew that Judith was unhappy. She spent the second night in tears as well and this time, in desperation, I took her firmly by the shoulders and shook her. 'You're going to have to get used to it,' I said. 'This is the Rhodesian bush. It's your home now.'

Judith was shocked into silence. She lay still for some time, then she gained control of herself. 'Well, just because it's the bush there's no reason to live in squalor,' she said defiantly. 'I want this place cleaned up, and I want curtains for our window.' She told me for some time of the other things she wanted.

I fixed the roof over our room and cleared the corners of spiders. Joseph made a stab at cleaning up the shack, starting with the layers of filth in the kitchen, and some miners cut down the long grass on either side of the path leading to the long-drop. The old man would have nothing to do with our efforts.

In a bid to please us both Judith took over the cooking. She slaved all day amid blackened pans in the tiny smoke-dark kitchen, coaxing a spluttering wood-fuelled stove into life. Flushed and dishevelled, after a series of minor disasters, she brought our supper to the table. It was a little overcooked. I pretended not to notice and chatted about the day. But Judith watched with a sinking heart as the old man stared mournfully at his crispy, black-edged portion until all conversation died away, then he began to eat with the air of a man certain of being poisoned. After a few mouthfuls he pushed his plate aside and stepped down from the table. He threw himself into his armchair and waited impatiently for his coffee. Judith brought it nervously. The old man took a few sips, then he looked at her in exasperation. 'Well, it's hot,' he growled. 'But it's not coffee.' He got up and stalked angrily out of the room leaving Judith with her confidence completely shattered. I found an excuse to follow him and cornered him outside. 'Now you listen to me,' I began angrily.

But to my surprise the old man offered no opposition. 'I'm sorry,' he said contritely, cunningly dissipating my anger, 'but I just can't get used to having a woman around. I'll try and make it easier for her in the future.' Like a fool I believed him. I should have known that he had no intention of doing any such thing.

I held Judith tightly in bed that night and I tried to defend the old man. 'Judith,' I said, 'he was rough on me too. He's like that when you first meet him, but he'll ease up on you in a while—just be patient.'

'I'm not giving that old bastard a chance to ease up on me,' Judith answered indignantly.

Joseph was returned to the kitchen but Judith made herself mistress of the shack. She scrubbed and cleaned that place from top to bottom all day long. However, within half an hour of the old man's return from the mine in the evening the place was filthy again. He seemed to attract dirt—it followed him from room to room.

I tried to keep the peace but sharing the shack became a source of great friction between us. The old man claimed that the standard of cleanliness Judith insisted on was making life unbearable. Having to remember to remove his boots so as not to tramp dust, and not being allowed to knock his pipe ash out on the floor, made him miserable. There were no locks on any of the doors, and when Judith could no longer stand the old man's lived-in dirt and squalor, she entered his room and had Joseph wash the walls and floor and all his clothes. The old man took this as the final invasion of his privacy and in high dudgeon he moved out of the shack the next day. Defiantly he set up his tent by the stoep and trod his dust and knocked his ash out. Then Judith made him move his tent to the back behind the kitchen because she said she was going to start a garden and she didn't want him spoiling it. And the old man retreated before her, muttering fiercely.

CHAPTER TWENTY-ONE

THE trouble that Justin had predicted came shortly, but it started in the north-east of the country, not in Matabeleland. I had never really accepted the sense in declaring the Unilateral Declaration of Independence, but then I was English-born and my loyalties were divided. I felt there was no way 250,000 Whites could hope to indefintely control 4,000,000 Africans. Most Europeans realised this and the popular slogans in the days after UDI were, 'Advancement on Merit', 'Any man of any colour for any job as long as he is good enough to hold it'. That seemed fair and I could identify with the cause emotionally now for I had a stake in the country and every instinct I possessed urged me to protect it.

At UDI there had been an enormous fund of goodwill between all races. However, over a five-year period sanctions and isolation took their toll and the Whites retreated into a laager, leaving the rest of the populace outside. Urged on by politicians, their slogans changed from 'Advancement on Merit' to a cry of 'No Majority Rule in our Lifetime' and with that the seeds of civil war were sown.

The African Nationalists launched an offensive at the end of 1972 which brought attacks on European farms and 'Operation Hurricane' began. At first, because distance in Africa is still such a great barrier, no one in Matabeleland took much notice. Certainly on the mine we were not aware of developments—it was as though they were taking place in some far-off country. There had been flare-ups before that which had fizzled out, but this time the war intensified. The whole of the Chiweshe tribal trust land from the Zambezi Valley downwards became subverted. The security forces, already thinly stretched and under-equipped, began calling for volunteers to join the ranks of the reserves.

I was called up for service with the Police

Reserve. Judith and I were newly married and unsure of ourselves and there couldn't have been a worse time to leave her, stranded on a lonely mine with only the old man for company. 'Watch over Judith,' I said to the old man who waited for me by the mine shaft as I left very early one morning. 'Keep the peace between you until I get back. I trust you for that,' I said to him quietly.

'I'll keep out of her way,' the old man muttered and moved aside.

I passed the selection course to the Police Anti-Terrorist Unit known as PATU and joined a five-man stick comprising four European reservists and an African regular. We were sent to the north-east border for a month. The country was totally unprepared for war and in the early days we were poorly trained and hopelessly ill-equipped. Fortunately the enemy were no better off.

As soon as my stick returned from duty I handed in my kit and hitched out to the mine. I had found it hard to adjust to the 'hurry up and wait' of military discipline, and it was a good, free feeling to wear civilian clothes again and to feel the hot Matabele sun on my shoulders.

Judith was pleased to see me, but underneath she was unnaturally reserved and strained. The old man was still living in his tent outside the shack as though setting up a siege. They had made no effort to compromise and the antagonism between them was reaching crisis point. I was aware of tension in every direction I moved.

'It's either him or me,' Judith said that night after we made love and I held her in my arms. 'We can't both stay here, Patrick,' she warned, 'I can't take it any longer. You have to make the choice.' I had no choice. My loyalty lay with Judith—she was my wife, I'd brought her here. But I was still torn. 'Judith, it's not as easy as that,' I tried to explain. 'He's my partner. You can't just fire a partner. Don't you see, the mine, this shack, half of everything we have, is his.' Judith was silent. 'Look,' I said, 'I know this can't go on. I thought about it in the bush and I'll tell you what I'll do. I'll get a job in the city if you wish it. I could make a good life for us there or anywhere—there's little I can't do if I set my mind to it.'

'You'd die in a city, Patrick,' Judith said softly. 'You were never the type of man who could live there, and perhaps I wouldn't love you so much if you were. Will you promise me something?' she asked.

'What is it?'

'I want you to build me a house to live in. I want a proper house with proper windows and doors and a roof that fits,' she said defiantly. 'And I want a bathroom inside, and I want water for my garden. The old man can have this shack.'

'I'll build you a house,' I promised. 'You choose the site you want and we'll build it ourselves.'

'All right,' Judith said sleepily. She nestled down beside me and her eyes closed. I lay holding her, staring into the dark, filled with relief for I had been worried about coming back and finding her gone.

One evening a few days later I came upon the old man packing up his camp, and this time I knew that he was not just going trekking. He was going for good. He was old now and lonely and though it had to be this way it hurt me to see him leave. And in spite of myself I asked, 'Where are you going?'

'Places,' the old man replied and turned away from me. 'I told you I'd stay with you long enough to get you started, but now you are on your own.'

'Don't go trying your luck in those pools again,' I warned, thinking I knew what was in his mind, 'because they'll shoot you now, even before you cross the border.'

'I don't know where I'm going,' the old man said. 'I don't have to know. I'm free again. I can go where I like.'

I took his meaning. I was married with responsibilities, and he made me feel like I had broken faith. 'What about your share of the mine?' I asked.

'Keep it,' the old man said.

'I could send you money every month,' I offered, trying to find a way to keep in touch with him.

'I said keep it,' the old man snapped. 'I don't want it, I'll find another strike.'

'When are you leaving?' I asked softly.

'First light. Always did like an early start.' There was nothing more to be said between us.

I went into the shack but I couldn't sleep. I got up quietly so as not to disturb Judith, and went and sat on the verandah. I heard the door open softly and she came and joined me in her nightdress. 'He's leaving,' I said, filled with sadness.

'I know,' she replied. She laid her head on my shoulder to comfort me. 'We are two different parts of you,' Judith said. 'You can only keep one of us.' She was shivering. 'Let him go, Patrick,' she urged. 'Come to bed now.'

'I'll stay here a while longer,' I said. I sat up all night. I told myself that I wanted to be up in plenty of time to see the old man off in the morning and not let him just slip away. But the truth was I couldn't sleep, and at his place round the back of the shack I don't think the old man slept either.

I heard him stirring well before dawn. Joseph brought in Jezebel and hitched her to the cart. She was so old and bony and her belly so full of grass, that she sagged, bow-legged, between the shafts. None of them looked as though they

305

could go a mile. But I knew they could probably still walk the legs off me. Jezebel was as nasty as ever and they had difficulty in getting her started. I went with them a little way, just to see them safely on their journey. The old man had become such a part of me that it was difficult to leave him now. As we walked I was remembering that night we first met, the gaol cell and his stories of gold. There were so many bonds of the past that held us. The anger and the fights were forgotten. And now all that remained in my memory was the warmth of the good times and the times when we needed and relied on each other.

The old man was thinking the same thing. 'You remember that race with the pegs for the Bismarck mine?' he said. I remembered it well and started to laugh. He shook his head, laughing too. 'And McLeod's face when he realised how we won. Those were good times,' he said wistfully.

It was still dark, with a sky full of stars, and a faint glow of colour just showing on the eastern horizon. A fresh wind blew off the bush, chill in our faces, setting the blood tingling. I had forgotten how good it felt to be trekking again. Within a few minutes the rim of the sun came raging up above a limitless horizon of thorn and scrub, setting the sky alight, the red glare colouring our clothes and hair and faces, as though we were facing a fire at the edge of the world.

'Will you look at that,' the old man exclaimed appreciatively. 'Let me tell you something I know to be true,' the old man said as we trudged along. 'And I have seen all sides now. The joy of being a prospector is that you've always got hope. You are never wasting your time, because you're always looking. And you are never poor because over the next hill you know you are going to find that pot of gold, or over the next hill or maybe the next one. And while you're looking and hoping, you're living free and you're happy. But if you find that pot of gold and become rich, then you've got nothing more to look forward to, nothing to hope for, and you are no longer free because owning anything, especially money, or even people, brings worry and responsibility. It's like cutting your own wings and loading yourself in chains ... Leave her,' the old man said urgently. 'It's easy,' he said. 'Just keep walking, Patrick, don't look back. She'll get by without you. Women always can. There's this dried up river valley I've been thinking about. It's close to the old Sun Yet Sen Mine, and I've a feeling about that valley. There's rich gold there. I know there is. I can feel it in my bones.' He looked at me. The man was like a Pied Piper with a burning light that awoke old dreams of adventure and freedom in his eyes.

I looked behind me. I had not realized I had

walked for miles. The shack was just a tiny speck on the horizon. My feet would have taken me on, but I felt the presence of Judith there draw me back. I shook my head and I stopped.

'It's no, then,' the old man said sadly, understanding the strength of that draw.

'No,' I confirmed quietly.

'Well then,' he said and held out his hand, 'goodbye, boy. You were a good partner to me. Look after yourself. I loved you, you know that,' he said as he turned quickly away from me and kept walking.

'I loved you too,' I said softly, staring after him.

About a hundred yards down the track, he turned. 'Listen,' he shouted and pointed. 'I'll be camped in those hills tonight and I'll light a big fire, so if you change your mind you'll know where to find me.' I waved to show I had heard. That was the old man—he never gave up. I watched him and Joseph until they were tiny figures in the distance. Then I began the long walk back.

Judith met me at the door of the shack. She was white with relief. 'I was afraid you weren't coming back,' she said. We sat on the verandah after supper that night. And against the moonlit distant hills I could just make out the tiny beckoning spark of a campfire. Judith saw me watching it and I knew I couldn't hide my thoughts from her.

'He's old now,' I said, 'and I feel responsible for him. He was always scared of dying alone. He wanted someone to remember him, to give him a Christian burial.'

'That old bastard,' Judith said bitterly. 'I used to think he was the devil. He hates me. And he is never going to die, he's going to haunt us all our lives. I'll always be afraid that some day when my back is turned he'll come along again and fill your head with stories and take you away from me.'

'You're imagining things,' I said to her fondly.

But she shook her head. 'He's got some kind of power over you.'

'We were partners,' I said, unable to explain how much that meant. 'That was all.'

CHAPTER TWENTY-TWO

I MISSED the old man and was at first nervous of running the mine without him. Sanctions were biting. It was difficult to replace ageing machines or obtain spare parts of any description. Rhodesians generally pulled in their belts and worked harder. And what you could not buy in the way of machinery, you made out of bits. Every scrap heap became a second gold mine. It is amazing what human ingenuity can achieve when forced.

Judith kept the mine books, made up the wages and ordered supplies or scrounged spare parts by using her charm on the mining agents. She took a great interest in the African miners' welfare, and in the mornings before going to work I would be quietly advised to go easy on a certain lasher because his wife was giving trouble or his child was sick. She had an uncanny knack of knowing those things. I learned to accept her advice and the men worked better for it.

I worried that the work would be too much for her, that the bush life would get her down. But Judith blossomed. Not like a precious flower as I had always imagined her to be, but rather like a tall tree sending down roots that took a hold on life, and her branches encircled all that she loved. Through her we became popular in the district. People on the ranches and other mines asked us to visit. We would think nothing of a thirty-mile trip there and back in our beaten-up truck for a game of tennis, or driving a hundred miles and stay the night for a party. I never knew the people in the area were so sociable. It was like becoming a part of a very large family.

But the best times were those when we were alone together—the nights when, after the searing heat of the day, we would take our chairs outside the shack to a cooling breeze. Above us the vast sky blazed with stars and we would sit side by side at peace, relaxing from the work of the day. Or weekends, when we camped by the river and I taught her to fish.

Christmas came and the annual concert was held at the country club. As we had to make our own entertainment, this was a great occasion and people came to it from all over the district. The organisers were always looking for new talent to help with the show and Judith had been persuaded to dance. I stood at the back of the crowded hall watching the preceding acts. There were jugglers and comic sketches and singers, all drawn from the community and all very amateur, very hearty. The audience was a raucous, hard-living, hard-drinking bunch of ranchers and miners. I knew these men for the roughnecks they were and I was worried that they would not appreciate Judith's dancing. I became fiercely protective and when it was time for her to go on to the stage, I was ready to go for the throat of the first man who so much as coughed.

Judith had chosen a piece from some ballet that few people in this audience had ever heard of, but the music was haunting and her dancing was simple and very beautiful. No one moved through the whole piece, and they cheered her when she finished. My eyes shone with pride as I watched her from the back of the hall. I remembered her telling me to refer to her as a

311

dancer—ballerina was old-fashioned, she had said. But I didn't care. To me she was a ballerina, graceful, beautiful, dignified, fragile, all that I understood the name to imply. She came forward to take her bow and I nudged the man next to me to make sure he was clapping, for she was my Judith, my ballerina, and I was so very proud of her. Later she came to find me, still flushed with her success.

'Oh, Patrick,' she said, when she got me alone. 'I was never able to be a successful dancer, but I did enjoy that. It worked for them, didn't it? They liked it?' She looked so very eager, very vulnerable, as though the applause still rang in her ears. I thought of her giving up all that for the mine and I couldn't find the words at that time to tell her how much she meant to me, how proud I was of her, and I hugged her.

'You're my ballerina,' I said huskily. And she always was.

Whenever I was with a group of miners and Judith was not around, I would ask for news of the old man, but there was none. The old man had the knack of vanishing without trace. I worried about him.

★   ★   ★

The mine prospered. Early in the New Year, by scraping every penny together and spending

312

little on ourselves, we managed to save enough money to repay Chinaman Lee all that I owed him. At last I was free of debt and we even began to save a little. Judith had lived in the shack without protesting but now she wanted her house. Like any miner I tried to stall her for there was equipment needed to develop the mine on which I would rather have spent our savings. But she had my promise and she remained firm. We agreed it was to be a small cottage and we spent hours drawing up the plans. We chose a piece of land on a small rise overlooking the mine, and while Judith stood over me I spent the weekend marking out the foundations.

I had meant to pay overtime to some lashers and trammers to dig the foundations the following week-end and thereby not interfere with their work on the mine. But that Monday I discovered men missing from their posts underground. I found out where they were and stormed up to the surface to protest at their digging foundations when they should have been in the stopes. But I found Judith totally unrepentant. 'When you have wanted something as badly as I have this,' she said, 'you cherish every brick, and I will not stay another day longer in that shack than I have to.' She would rise before dawn each morning to complete her work and then spend all day until dusk at the site supervising the building.

The mine revolved around the house and not the other way round. She found men to make her bricks and weld metal into window and door frames. Skilled artisans went missing from their work and the mine production felt the strain. I was summoned in the evenings, dog-tired from the mine, to comment or advise on the following day's work and I limited my protests at the loss of my men because, when I did protest, as often as not I found myself being made to shutter a lintel or fix a truss.

At last the house was almost finished. I came up from the underground and found Judith sitting on a stone outside the front door, staring at the ground, lost in thought.

'What are you thinking?' I asked.

I had startled her and she laughed, pleased to see me. 'I've been planning the garden,' she said, and I noticed the stick in her hand and the marks where she had been drawing in the dust. 'Come,' she said happily, 'and I'll show you what I'm going to do.' She took me on a guided tour around a broken, barren piece of ground covered in cement and discarded bricks. But to her it was already watered and soft green, not too cluttered, but with splashes of colour from banks of flowers.

'This place means a lot to you, doesn't it?' I asked quietly.

'Patrick,' she tried earnestly to explain, for I had been feeling neglected of late, 'I'm a city

314

girl. I have never built anything before. This house is mine. I made it. I know each brick and I cherish it like I have cherished nothing except you in my life before.'

We moved in the following week-end. We could afford no new furniture and the little we did own Judith had scrounged second-hand. I carried it up the slope to the house and sweated under her directions, moving this here and that there, for most of the day. But when she was finished and I had time to appreciate it, I was amazed at what that woman had been able to achieve with virtually no money to spend. The empty house was now bright and clean and airy and somehow filled with the warmth of home.

I came out of the lavatory and pulled the chain so that she could hear it flush. 'I'll miss the long-drop,' I said. 'I used to enjoy the walk.' It was a bad joke meant only to make her smile at the end of an exhausting day. But she was not listening to me. She was sitting in the living-room just glowing with pleasure at the comforting walls of her home. I walked over and sat quietly beside her, her pleasure infecting me, filling me too with joy in our home.

★　　★　　★

I was standing with a small crowd of miners by the shaft one morning, waiting to go down in the bucket, when I saw a big man coming towards me with an ambling gait that betrayed great physical power. It was Phillimon. He was dressed in rags and looked half starved, but I would have recognised that walk anywhere. Phillimon ignored me completely. He made straight for the miners and they moved out of his way. Then he stood before my mine captain and without saying a word he reached out and took the distinctive coloured helmet off his head. The mine captain was about to protest violently, but then he thought better of it, for in Phillimon's starved, scarred face there was the mark of a hard and very dangerous man.

The miners watched Phillimon amble over to me with the helmet in his hands.

'I'll take the job,' Phillimon said and put on the helmet. Then he turned to the miners. He did not say anything to them. He did not need to. Like himself they were Matabele, they understood, and from that moment the stamp of his authority was upon them.

I took him to the store and issued him with a pair of overalls and gumboots. 'You've been living rough,' I observed, as he cast away his rags.

He shrugged his shoulders non-committally. 'It took me a while to find you,' he said.

'What happened to your money?'

'I lost it. And you?'

'The same.'

'And the old man?'

'He's gone trekking with Joseph. I'm married now,' I said defensively.

Phillimon allowed a brief smile to touch his eyes. 'I heard,' he said. 'Show me the mine.'

Later I took Phillimon up to meet Judith. I'd have thought all she would have seen in him was the wild man. But with a woman's instinct she recognized something deeper.

Phillimon moved into our old shack. He kept to himself and didn't mix. There was a harshness in him now—except when he was with Judith—a deep but controlled anger and a sadness that sometimes came into his eyes. I knew he had been through bad times and was still wounded inside. But he never spoke of it, and I didn't question him.

And as we worked together again I noticed a change in our relationship. Phillimon had started out as my house servant. And even in the days when he held my head above the water of the Bewitched Pool, there had always been a deference, no matter how slight, to me as the white man. Now there was none. He let me know, without pushing it, that he was my equal with no barrier between us. I had to respect him as such.

★   ★   ★

The reef faulted and at the same time I had to completely overhaul the stamps and machinery.

The loss of production, coupled with the cost of the house and new parts for the mill brought serious problems with our creditors. Phillimon struck ore at last and his lashers sent it racing up to the surface to the mill, I got the big flywheel turning and the stamps crushed the ore to a powder. From there it flowed along a launder to the James table. We gathered anxiously round the table that evening but no gold came, nor the next day. We could not understand it for samples from the reef showed very good values. By the third day I was nearly frantic with worry. I could not think where we were losing the gold. Then I started at the table where the gold should have been showing on the topmost riffle and worked my way back from there.

I found the gold still in the mill. I had set the dies too far back and it had been trapped in the mortar box. Judith heard me yelling excitedly for her and she appeared in the doorway of the house. It was just after dawn. Worn out with worry she had slept for a couple of hours. Then with her dressing gown flapping behind her and a metal mug in her hands, she raced down the slope to the mill. Together we scraped up the gold in the mortar box and found enough dust and small nuggets to fill that mug to the brim. Judith took the mug of coarse gold, just as it was, to the bank that morning with the news that we had found the reef. And that saved us. The bank met my cheques and the Electricity

Supply Commission received payment for their power.

I re-set the dies and a broad band of gold appeared between the topmost James table riffles. I had not been home for some time and Judith came down from the house that night to find me standing watching the gold dancing under the light. We were both worn out, relieved, shattered, elated—all those emotions at the same time, a feeling you can only share when you have gambled every single thing you have, and won. She still did not quite believe it. Her most pressing concern was to pay the storekeeper what we owed him.

'We're rich,' I assured her.

'Flat broke one day, rich the next. I'm not sure I can take much more of this mining,' she said. 'I should have married a farmer.'

'What happens if it doesn't rain?'

'Well then,' she reconsidered, 'a businessman.'

'You'd be bored stiff,' I said confidently.

Her eyes met mine and she smiled. 'You're an impossible dreamer,' she said. 'Come to bed.'

CHAPTER TWENTY-THREE

WE never saw a newspaper unless we went into town, but Judith and I used to listen to the news on the radio in the evenings. The country seemed to have learnt to handle sanctions, but I was growing anxious about the terror war that was slowly spreading like a cancer through Mashonaland. The danger at that time was still an implied rather than a real threat. But it made it difficult to know what to do next, which path to follow. Judith and I talked it over. Our roots were here, our miners relied on us. It seemed the only thing we could do was to continue our lives as normally as we could in the hope that the politicians would find a way to bring peace.

I was called up for military service. We knew this would happen more regularly now and prepared ourselves for it. Phillimon, as an African, was not subject to military service and he and Judith took over the running of the mine while I was away.

My stick gathered in Bulawayo. We were civilians drawn from very different walks of life, all with our minds still on problems at home and it took us a day to two to shake down. We were then sent to Mount Darwin and the changes I saw there made me sad. The farming communities in the north east were now entering their second year of war. There were no major battles, no crash of artillery, no rumble of tanks—just hit-and-run strikes by shadowy figures that appeared and then disappeared into the bush. The farm homesteads, once oases of cool shade and colour against the burnt red earth and scrub of Africa, were now surrounded by high wire fences that cut like scars across lawns and flowerbeds, and the once wide doorways and windows were now sandbagged. At sunset the gate was locked, alarms set, and the family went into laager. When they moved from room to room to avoid setting a pattern, their weapons went with them.

Life was harsh for the Africans too. The terrorists demanded their support against the farmers and killed them if they refused. Then the security forces punished them with long terms of imprisonment if they aided the terrorists. No one was safe anymore. The children waving from the side of the road, the easy-going ways of Rhodesia, the laughter—it was ending now. And that was the sad part of it for if there was one thing I loved about this country more than the bush, it was the warmth and generosity and goodwill of its people of all races.

When I came home to the mine I was quiet and reserved for the few days it took me to unwind. Judith had been worried about me and she was feeling the strain of trying to run the mine alone. The people of the district had rallied round, as they did now with all the women whose men were away, with offers of help and hospitality. Many of them felt that she should not have remained on the mine by herself. But Judith knew that she was needed there if the mine was to keep up production, and she put her trust in Phillimon to protect her. Even so, it had been very lonely for her without me.

★   ★   ★

We decided we needed a break from everything, to get away and be alone for a day. So we packed a picnic and found a shady spot under a tree by the river. It was a hot, drowsy Sunday. I lay back comfortably waiting for the kettle to boil and out of half-closed eyes watched Judith preparing our meal. I seemed to have been away for ages and I enjoyed watching her. I liked the shape of her breasts as they pressed against the thin material of her dress, the sweep of her long brown legs. Her face was shaded by a wide-brimmed straw hat and she looked fresh and cool and very beautiful to me. She knew immediately the thought that was growing in my head and she tossed me a sandwich instead. As I levered myself up on one arm to eat it, she asked seriously, 'What's it like in the north-eastern operational area?'

It was the first time she had really spoken about the war since I got back. I told her of the farm homesteads scarred by wire fences and sandbags, of the sadness and strain on the Africans' faces. I tried to describe the effects of the war and the evils that accompanied it on a society which had been completely non-violent for fifty years, of the drawing apart of the races and the suspicion and fear that was taking its place. And though the war was still confined to only a small corner of Rhodesia, it was spreading.

'Oh, dear God,' Judith breathed, badly shaken, when I had finished. She had had no idea, for the Government-controlled radio always underplayed the news. 'Is it really that bad?'

I shrugged gloomily. 'I think it is,' I said. 'But if you talk to the farmers in the operational area there's still an enormous air of optimism. They'll tell you the war is bound to end soon, and next year the rains will come on time, their crops will grow. Next year will be better!'

I looked up and caught Judith's eye and we grinned ruefully at each other. *Next Year Will Be Better* was the title of a beautifully-written book by a farmer's wife. The story caught the best of the Rhodesian character and the title summed up so succinctly all the stubborn courage and optimism and the prayers of the people in their struggle for survival in this land, that it had almost become the unofficial motto of the country. Now we were using it. We were Rhodesians and we were involved—our roots were in this country.

'I bumped into Justin while I was in Mount Darwin,' I said.

'Did you?' Judith asked, her interest quickening. 'Did he say anything about Mary?'

'They're engaged.'

'Oh, that's wonderful!' Judith said warmly, then a perplexed expression crossed her face. 'I wonder why I haven't heard about it from Mary?'

'She doesn't know yet,' I answered dryly. 'Justin only decided to ask her less than a week ago. He's worried about the strain his new job could have on a marriage.'

'What's he doing now?'

'He's in Ground Coverage. It's part of Special Branch. They make contact with informers and try to infiltrate terror gangs.'

'Is that dangerous?'

'I think so. While I was up there he told me a story. Do you want to hear it?'

Judith made a wry face. 'As long as it doesn't depress me any more.'

'Well,' I said, 'Justin told me this story drunk at about three o'clock in the morning in a base camp, so I don't know how true it is. Anyway, apparently in the early days of this war the terror gangs were made up of small units of

324

dedicated men—most of them were well-educated and truly believed in their cause. They returned to this country with the intention of attacking mainly strategic targets in order to force change, but none of the African tribesmen wanted to know their troubles. They received no food or help and so they were hunted down by our security forces quite easily.

'Justin claims that he was part of a unit that followed one gang right across the country, picking them off one by one. But the terrorists who could, still kept going and they only got the last one just outside the wire surrounding the oil refinery near Umtali—he'd been going to blow it up. Well, they took him alive. He was in fairly bad shape for the dogs had got him and chewed him up first, but they bandaged him up and put him in a cell to be interrogated next morning. Justin was delegated to go in and guard him in case he tried to commit suicide.

'Justin had been hunting that man for six weeks and suddenly there he was, sitting opposite him in the same cell. The way Justin tells it, they ignored each other for the first few hours and then, because it was going to be a long night and they had nothing else to do, somehow they started to talk. And they talked and talked all through that night. They talked about God and about justice and humanity and all the other bullshit things people talk about in the middle of the night and they found that they agreed with each other right the way down the line. And Justin was just about to say to the African, "Listen, what in the hell are we fighting for? What are you doing lying there all chewed up?" when the African said to him, "You say you believe in justice, but tell me, if the Blacks were marching on Salisbury, your capital city, and they were right—you knew the Black cause was absolutely right—on which side would you fight?" And Justin thought about it and he knew he didn't want to lie to that man because they had said too much to each other that night in the cell, and he said, "I'd fight for the Whites. Man, I'd have to—they're my family, my friends, they're my kind." The African nodded. And Justin said to him, "Tell me, if the Whites were marching on the African townships and they were right—you knew they were right—on which side would you fight?" And the African said, "Like you, I'd fight for my kind. I've talked with you all night, I've got so close I could touch you, and I know I could have loved you as my friend, white man. But don't you see, the war has started and no matter what we say to each other, in our hearts we have no choice, we must fight for our own kind. We're different now and we can never be together as a country until someone finds a way to end this war.'"

I was silent. 'Go on,' Judith said impatiently. 'What happened to him?'

'They hanged him for bringing weapons of

war into the country. He was due to die the day Justin told me the story. Justin was very cut up about it, that's why he got so drunk.'

'Well,' Judith said, 'the terrorist may have felt that way, but I don't think his leaders in the African Nationalist movements are going to settle for less than every single thing in this country. They'll take our mine, our home, and force us out like they have done in the rest of Black Africa. We have no choice but to fight against that.'

'I know, I know,' I answered tiredly. 'It's just that Justin's story made me hate what is happening to my country.'

'Do you think that the miners know about the war?' Judith asked. 'It's still such a long way away.'

'I'm sure they do,' I answered. 'They don't talk about it, but I can sense the fear in them when I come home in camouflage. I think you had better start being careful now when you go out alone.'

We had talked too seriously too long. The warmth seemed to have gone out of the day and we went home.

*   *   *

The rainy season was approaching and it was with relief that I turned my attention from the war to the mine. We had been having difficulty coping with the water that leaked in along the fault. In my absence Phillimon blocked off the drive ahead of the fault zone with three feet of reinforced concrete. This cut down considerably the amount of water entering the mine, but as an added precaution I invested in another big pump and serviced the ones I had.

The area of Matabeleland we were in normally experienced fourteen to eighteen inches of rain a year. That year we were hit by a series of freak storms. It rained for nine days without stopping. One night four inches of rain fell in seven hours. The pumps coped for the first two days. But on the third night I was summoned urgently from my bed. I stumbled from the house in the blinding rain, wading through what seemed like a sea of mud formed from the dust of many droughts. Around the lip of the shaft I had had to build a collar of sandbags to stop the mud from sliding down. I climbed into the swaying bucket with the thunder and lightning crashing above me and went underground.

As the bucket swooped down past glistening walls of water-wet rock there was silence again. At first I felt relief at descending into the warm womb of the earth away from the noise of the storm. Then I became aware of a different sound—that of rock talking and straining against unbearable pressures and the swelling roar of water rushing down the empty stopes.

The flickering lights from miners' lanterns greeted me as the bucket swayed to a halt at number six level and I climbed out on to the station. Below me was a forty-foot extension of the main shaft towards what would have been number seven level. We were using it as a sump to drain the water out of the mine and then pump it to the surface. But the water was beating the combined power of the pumps by inches each hour. The sump was full. Water, gleaming like black oil in the beam of the lights, was licking over the edges of the station. The miners would have to lift these pumps now or we would lose them.

I caught sight of the distinctive colour of Phillimon's mine captain's helmet and made my way over to him. He led me out of earshot of the miners. 'I think the bulkhead's going to go,' he said quietly. I followed him along the drive to the bulkhead. I reached out and put my hand against the wall of concrete. It was trembling, seeming to move, as the pressure built up behind it. The fault zone was entirely porous and it was acting like a giant pipe, leading the water straight down from the surface. The bulkhead was holding back thousands upon thousands of tons of water at a six hundred foot head of pressure. And it was weakening. If it gave way then a vast explosion of water would burst through the mine, sweeping away everything in its path. We took all the men we

329

could spare from moving the pumps and set them to work with heavy timbers to shore up the bulkhead.

The rain continued to fall and surface water found its way down through the sulphide zone, through any fault in the rock formation, any point of weakness, to come gushing out of fissures or old boreholes at the bottom of the mine, with a force that could tear the clothes off you. We plugged what we could. We blocked off what we couldn't, but it was a losing battle and inch by inch the water rose against the pumps.

The men under Phillimon were now working with water up to their chests, but they continued to try to hold up the bulkhead. The pressure found points of weakness where the concrete met the roof, and they were being blasted by fine jets of spray. Sparks began flashing as the switch boxes on six level burnt out. I could risk lives no longer. I decided to leave six level to the water and pull the men out. I counted the miners as they came up. One was missing—Phillimon. I had to go in and pull him off the bulkhead.

'It's not going to hold,' he shouted frantically.

'I know,' I answered. 'It's not your fault. You couldn't have expected conditions like this. Let's get out of here.'

We pulled back into the stopes between the fifth and six levels, and the battle to save the

330

mine continued. Water from the fault zone was working its way along the joints and fissures of the roof, or hanging wall as it's called, which was becoming waterlogged and unstable. Large slabs of rock, many tons in weight, were collapsing into the stopes and the water then gushed in through the opening joints. We supported the weak spots with timbers and when we ran out of wood I brought down concrete railway sleepers and we used those, anything to hold the hanging wall up and prevent the water breaking in from the fault.

I left Phillimon in the stopes and made my way up to five level station, to a scene of frenzied activity—men shouting, lights flashing, the roar of the pumps. A line was being lowered down the shaft to measure the rate of the rising water. A powerful spotlight followed the line as it snaked down some sixty yards. I heard a massive rumble and the whole mine shook for a moment as the bulkhead below gave way. Then a great column of boiling white water rushed up the shaft towards us. I thought for one horrifying moment that it was going to sweep us off five level, but it spread out through the stopes and fell back with a great sucking sound.

Water was now flooding into the mine, rising at too fast a rate for us to control. The situation seemed hopeless, but I wasn't ready to give up. I knew that the closer to the surface I took my pumps, the more efficient they would become and the pressure of water flooding into the mine would lessen. I decided to abandon five level and concentrate on saving four level. I sent word to Phillimon to pull his men out of the stopes.

A message came back that there had been an accident. I moved quickly a few feet back along the drive of five level and scrambled down through a hole in the floor pillar into the stopes. Forty feet below me, and some distance to my right, I saw a group of lights clustered together and I made for them, half falling, half sliding down through the rubble.

The miners parted to make room for me. A man was lying on his back on the floor. I knelt beside him and shone my light in his face. It was Phillimon. Both his legs were trapped. His men had been trying to wedge a prop beneath a slab of rock when suddenly the rock moved. Phillimon had been knocked down and the wooden wedges slipped over his legs. The pillar now lay at an angle, one end pinning Phillimon's legs, the other holding up the roof above him.

I cut away the material of his trousers. What I saw there turned my stomach. Both shin bones were broken cleanly just above the ankles and white bone shone in my light. Below that, trapped by the wedges, by the whole weight of rock bearing down, I knew his feet had been crushed to a bloody pulp. If we moved the wedges the prop would come down, and with it the rock. And the water was now only a few feet away.

I had to act quickly. My pocket knife wouldn't do. 'Get me an axe,' I ordered, white-faced, to the miners. 'And get me a stretcher with the first-aid box and bandages, lots of bandages.' His feet were going to have to come off. It was the only way. I couldn't move the wedges, I couldn't move the prop. I couldn't free him any other way and he would drown if I didn't hurry. I knew if I thought about it I would freeze. I wouldn't be able to do it, and I had to do it now, while he was still unconscious.

A miner came back with a small chopping axe. That would do. I didn't have to go through bone. I moved towards the wedges and a hand caught my arm, the fingers biting urgently into my flesh.

'Not my legs,' Phillimon said hoarsely. 'Don't cut off my legs.'

'It's the only thing I can do,' I said desperately, 'otherwise you will die.'

'Then let me die,' Phillimon said. 'But don't let me drown. Pull the roof down on top of me.'

The light caught his face and I knew clearly that he was serious. But I couldn't kill him. Not Phillimon. And now I couldn't take his legs off either. I dropped the axe and collapsed by his side. Phillimon tried to turn his head to see how much farther the water had risen.

'Don't let me drown,' he said quietly. 'You remember from our time in the Bewitched Pool,

I never liked water that much.'

'I won't let you drown,' I said.

'Good,' Phillimon answered and was silent.

I shone my light up at the slab of rock. It must have weighed twenty tons and it was loose, resting on a fine balance between the prop and the roof. I turned my light to the water. It was creeping up the slope towards us.

'Get me two more supports,' I said to the miners. 'And some wedges. Hurry!' To another I said, 'Gelignite and fuse.' If I had had cortex, I told myself, it would have been easy. With gelignite I would need a master's touch.

'How are my legs?' Phillimon asked. 'Are they badly damaged?'

I knew how I felt when I had asked the old man that very same question. Wanting the truth, but at the same time pleading inside for them to be all right. If I had told Phillimon the truth he would probably have pulled the prop down on himself. So I lied.

'You'll be all right,' I said, 'if I can get you out of here. Do you have much pain?'

'I feel it growing in me now,' Phillimon replied. He seemed almost to be reassured by the pain.

The miners came up with the extra props. 'What are you planning to do?' Phillimon asked.

'I'm going to try to support the rock at either end with these props,' I said. 'And then tap, just tap, the prop that is pinning you down out of the way with a small blast of gelignite. If I can set the blast just right so that it moves the prop without shattering the rock, then the rock will rest on the other two props long enough to get you out. What do you think?'

'I think it's the best chance I've got,' Phillimon answered quietly. I knew he was in great pain and I wished he would pass out.

He watched as we set the props and wedged them in place. Phillimon was an iron man exercising enormous self-discipline. But pain and fear and darkness and a phobia about drowning can weaken any man's self-control and he screamed when the water touched his face. He was lying head down from the prop across the angle of the dip. We had been working frantically and the water crept up unnoticed out of the darkness. He felt trapped, his nerve stretched like fine wire. In that moment he could have descended into madness. Instead, with both legs broken, I saw that man take control of his mind and impose his will upon it again. One of the miners held his head above the water while I went back to setting the half stick of gelignite that I was going to use as the charge. I knew I had but this one chance. And it had to be right. It had to work, for now I could not leave Phillimon. Someone would have to remain with him and hold his head above the water when the blast went off.

I packed the charge with mud and wet

sacking to concentrate the direction of the blast, and then I hung more wet sacking beneath it to try and protect Phillimon and myself. The water was lapping against Phillimon's body. He could feel his clothes grow wet and cold and taste the acid scum in his mouth.

'Hurry,' he said fearfully, 'hurry!'

I lit the fuse. It spluttered angrily into life, the yellow glare of gunpowder burning, the flame racing up through the cotton binding to the charge. I signalled the miners out of the way and took Phillimon's head in my arms. We were alone there, with just my light, the water rising and twenty tons of loose rock above us. 'Hold my head higher,' Phillimon complained, spitting water. I had been too intent on watching the fuse burn and I quickly raised him up. 'That's better,' he said. 'You shouldn't have stayed with me. You could have found some other way to prop me up.'

He needed to say that. But I could remember my own terror of waiting alone in the dark for the gas to come, and the feeling that was deeper than love which I experienced when the old man came back for me. There is a special terror of waiting for death, unprepared and alone in the dark. And I held him tightly, more for my sake than for his.

The fuse had disappeared behind the sacking. 'How much longer?'

'It's nearly there,' I said. I counted out aloud

to fill my head with words. 'Ten, nine, eight, seven . . .'

It blew at six. A sharp, clean crack that just tapped the prop away. It tottered and fell to one side. The roof ground and spat and came down an inch, then settled uneasily on the other supports. The miners dashed forward with long pinch bars and levered up the wedges. 'The old man taught you well,' Phillimon whispered, and passed out as we pulled him clear.

I set his legs in splints and strapped him tightly to the stretcher. He was a big man and it took three miners on either side to drag him out of the stopes. 'Take him to my wife,' I said, 'and tell her to get him to a doctor.' I saw the blood leaking out of his boots. 'And if he regains consciousness don't let him see his legs.'

At four level we slowed the rate of the water rising in the mine. But it wasn't enough. It must have been raining hard still on the surface and I knew then that I was going to lose my mine. All I could hope to do was to hold the water back long enough to try to salvage as much equipment as I could. The equipment was vital if I wanted any chance of ever starting again, for with sanctions and the country's chronic lack of foreign currency, I couldn't replace it.

I gave the order to start stripping the mine. It was like giving the order to abandon a ship that you loved and had built yourself. We assembled machinery at four level station ready to ship it

337

up to the surface. As the bucket drew level with the station a miner reached out and handed me a thermos flask and a box of sandwiches. I took them impatiently for I had no time to eat and turned to put them down. And then I had to smile to myself, for behind me was a whole row of flasks containing tea, coffee, soup, and boxes of sandwiches. If Judith couldn't actually help me underground, at least she was trying to make sure I was fed.

I thought that by now Judith would have been on her way into town with Phillimon. In fact she had him on a stretcher in the back of the truck. But they were stopped by the ford. Seven inches of rain had fallen that day and the whole of the broad dry river-bed was covered by a rising, swollen, roaring flood of dark water carrying tree trunks and rocks, anything, before it. Judith got out of the truck and set a stone on the slope to the ford. The water rose over it and she set down another one. The water rose over that and she knew this was no flash flood—it would take hours to subside. She went to check on Phillimon. As she did so, she glanced back at the mine lying in the small depression behind her. And in the fading light of that rain-soaked afternoon, lit by lightning flashes, she saw to her horror that the river, where it passed by the mine, had broken its banks. And a small wall of water, leaving a path behind it like a muddy brown snake uncoiling, was racing straight

338

towards the mine shaft. She was helpless. She could do nothing, not even give warning, merely watch as the bank of water and mud hit the collar of sandbags and swept them aside. Then the flood poured down the shaft in a solid torrent.

We had sent the bucket to the surface with two men and some equipment in it. They were passing two level when the water hit them, smashing the bucket against the side of the shaft, toppling it over. We heard the men scream as they fell through the darkness, their bodies hurtling past us amid the water, mud and sandbags. And then, protected by the drive, we felt the blast of cold spray-soaked air and heard a thunderous roar as the weight of water falling vertically four hundred and fifty feet shook the whole mine. The escape ladder-ways, compressed air pipes and electric cables were torn away from the sides of the shaft and fell. The lip of the shaft and the soft rock in the oxide zone began collapsing. The noise was vast and terrifying. All was panic and confusion. With the shaft gone and the mine filling below us, it was impossible to think clearly. I stood rooted to the spot for a few moments, then I moved away from the lip of the shaft, deeper into the mine.

The men followed me. I counted them. There were fifteen of us. We were in the new workings created by the fault. I knew now that our only way out of the mine was to go back into the old rabbit warren of tunnels and stopes mined seventy or so years ago but since abandoned and unsafe. The new part of the mine drew its air from those old workings, so there had to be a way to the surface. We climbed up through the stopes to three level. The rock still trembled, but it was quieter up there and you could hear yourself think. We took stock. Each man had grabbed what he thought would be of most use to him. Some carried rope, others picks or pinch bars. But we had all been underground continuously for twelve hours and more and our lights were beginning to fade. And where we were going the loss of lights would bring certain death. To conserve batteries I left one man in five with his light on. The others in his group had to follow him in the darkness.

We forced our way through a barricade of timber supports into the abandoned workings. The differences between the two areas was instantly apparent. The abandoned drive narrowed, the walls seeming to press down on us, and it was littered with rockfalls, scrapped machinery and other debris. In single file we made our way along that drive, away from the main shaft, being driven deeper and deeper into the mine, balancing across gaping chasms in the floor on narrow half-rotten planks, or skirting them, faces pressed against the rock, fingers and toes seeking holds. The drive-way dipped slightly. We followed it down and I felt the cold touch of water leak into my boots. The rising water had caught us up and it had come so quickly and so silently that my heart nearly stopped when I felt it. I waded on a few more paces, but there came a great boiling sound and white water appeared ahead and then a jagged timber support that had come free deep in the mine burst through the surface with terrific force and fell back almost hitting me. I had no way of telling how big the gap it had come through was, and few of my men could swim. I waded back and the men waited while I tried to think.

The reef that had opened this mine had pinched out just below this level. Thereafter they had found several smaller reefs and then along this drive the big roof that we were working on the other side of the mine. A maze of small drives and stopes, often finishing in deadends, led among the small pockets of reef. If we got lost amongst those I would never find my way out. I knew that I had to stay with this main drive for as long as I could.

We climbed up on to the roof of the drive. The roof was a series of rock pillars thirty-foot long with a six- to eight-foot gap in between which protected the drive. Above us, like an empty gap between two crusts of a sandwich, and dipping at sixty degrees, lay the worked-out stopes. We made our way by crawling along the pillars and jumping the gaps—until the water drove us off the pillars and we were forced to take to the stopes. There were no ropes or ladders. We came up with our backs and knees pressed against the slippery wet rock, one man leading with the rope and the others following. We climbed up over ledges of jutting rock, fingers bleeding, breath straining, legs kicking in space. And we huddled on narrow sills like wet moles in the darkness, fearful of sliding into the water that sucked and swirled below.

I took the men up and up, away from the water, through stopes where the timber supports split with noise like gunshots and the rock cracked and groaned and started collapsing. We reached what I thought must have been one level, a hundred feet below the surface. And there we got stuck in a dead-end stope. We were tired and bleeding and our lights were nearly gone. We had spent all this time trying to keep ahead of the water. Now we had to go down again and dive under it and try to find the other side.

I dived under a pillar about eight foot across and came up into the air on the other side. I went back for the men and roped them together in threes. To them the water had become an evil spirit, black and silent, always following us as though it had an appetite and was greedy for our lives. I had to pull them in and force them under the water and they dragged themselves up, half drowned, on the other side.

We climbed up again, not knowing where we were going, but always moving away from the water. We found a small drive and it led into a maze of twisting passages that I had dreaded being lost in. We could not go back so I chose a passage that led in the general direction that we wanted to go, and followed it. And then I felt an air draught, a tiny, chill current of blessed air that stirred along the dank passage and cooled the sweat on my face. The miners felt it too and suddenly those exhausted men were filled with a new spark of hope. The rising water was forcing air out of the mine and the draught, if only we could keep following it, would lead us to the surface.

Some way along the line of strike from the main shaft was a small open-cast surface working. It had been mined by the ancients in an earlier time when they sent slaves burrowing down tiny adits to work the gold reef as deep as their primitive tools would take them. We found the adit through which the air was escaping, but it was so narrow that only a child could have squeezed through. The smallest of the miners was chosen to go first. We formed a human ladder under him and he burrowed and scraped and wriggled and squirmed his way up to the surface. He lowered a rope for the next man and I waited with the water creeping over my boots as we widened the hole until all fifteen of my men had scrambled up to safety.

Judith knew that the old part of the mine had been developed under that open-cast working, and that the only hope of survival for the men trapped underground was to come up somewhere in there. She had been waiting on the surface half the night with the rest of the miners and their families nearly out of her mind with grief and worry. The hours had passed, the mine filled with water and still there was no sign of survivors. Judith had prayed and cursed and gradually lost hope, but still she stayed on. And then suddenly she saw me wriggle up out of that tiny adit covered from head to foot in mud and stumble towards her.

Judith's hair was plastered down with rain, her face was drawn and her eyes red. She was sick from fear and from willing me to survive and she looked worse than I did, but I was so exhausted that she had to hold me up. Her arms were around me and I was crying, the tears and the rain streaking the mud on my face. She had never seen me cry before—I had always been the strong one—but thirty hours trapped in the underground with no rest had finally beaten me. I had no more courage. I was completely broken.

'We've lost everything, Judith,' I choked. 'Two men, the mine, the pumps and equipment, everything. We've lost everything! There's nothing left.'

344

CHAPTER TWENTY-FOUR

JUDITH helped me back to the shack. She cleaned the mud off me and put me to bed and I lay there like a dead man. I had lost all will to continue. Within three days the rain eased, the river went down and the ambulance came for Phillimon. They wanted to take me too but Judith wouldn't let them. She refused to let me think I could give up.

She didn't understand the sheer impossibility of it all. I told her that we had no time, no wealth. And even if we had I could not find the strength to start all over again, to face the sheer bone-breaking hard work of re-opening a flooded mine.

Judith said help would come. I didn't believe her. But one morning as soon as the roads were dry enough to be passable, I heard the grinding roar of a heavy diesel truck climbing over the ford. By the time I reached the door a group of small workers from the neighbouring mines were busy off-loading an ancient twenty horse-power pump and motor. I knew every pump in the district was working flat out so God knows where they scrounged this relic from. 'We put it together from parts that we found,' one of the small workers said. 'It's not much but it works and you're welcome to use it.'

345

The other small workers continued offloading bits and pieces of equipment that they thought might come in useful. It never occurred to any of them that I could have considered giving up. 'If you need anything else,' they said as they climbed back into the truck, 'let us know.'

The farmers in the district found excuses to visit and after they left we would find a dozen eggs, or vegetables or chickens or milk, anything they could spare, upon the kitchen table. Even McLeod came to bury the feud between us. Harsh old McLeod—the years hadn't softened him. If anything he was leaner and harder than ever but he gave us a whole sheep carcass. 'She's got to eat,' he warned me seriously about Judith in his broad Scots accent. 'That way she'll keep up her strength.' His own wife was still very ill and he had talked about her a lot during his visit.

I had always been a loner, accustomed, with the old man's influence, to shunning society, and now I was terribly touched by the kindness and simple generosity of the people. It was as though the whole district had clubbed together to keep us going. And Judith's value to me became her unswerving faith, her consistency, never doubting.

She was able to infuse into people around her the trueness of her character, a warmth of belief, of bonding rather than push. She kept the African women together, the mine together, as a

346

family. I had the drive but she had the courageous spirit—the faith that gave me a greater strength than I would normally have had. It was then that I truly realised the contribution she made to our marriage. It wasn't just sympathy and cups of tea, but loyalty of a total kind. She made me believe in myself again and I loved her for it. And I went back to work.

With the help of my men I built a solid concrete collar around the top of the shaft. Then we cleared out the debris, lowered a corrugated iron frame, propped it into position with timbers and filled the sides with concrete. As this was setting we lowered the next corrugated iron former and repeated the operation. We reached the watertable at forty feet and lowered the pump to just above the water surface. Two of us went down in the bucket. One man's job was to hang out of the bucket and manually prime the foot valve. The other man held on to him to keep him from falling out and at the same time tried to keep the bucket from spinning because there were no guide ropes to hold it steady.

When at last all was ready I pulled the switch and the motor whined in the confined space. Then came a loud 'thump' as the pump started to lift water and I knew that the air lock had cleared and the foot valve was holding. The delivery column, made of steel piping as thick as a man's thigh, vibrated under the weight of the rising column of water and it surged up the shaft to the surface where it flowed down a canal designed to carry it away from the mine.

I spent that day and most of the night beside the pump trying to keep it from sucking in drift wood or from overheating. At the end of the first twenty-four hours I measured our progress. The water level was dropping at less than six inches a day, the pump was barely making an impression on the water that was still finding its way into the mine. Judith and I scoured the area and we managed to borrow a second fifteen horse-power pump. With both pumps working the water level started going down at two feet a day. As the water receded we concreted the shaft until we hit solid rock at eighty feet below the unstable oxide zone.

As soon as the pump operator heard the pitched whine of the pumps change in intensity or the volume of water alter at the surface he would go down to investigate. Half a dozen times a shift he would have to go down and 'nip' up the gland packing for if the packing worked loose and let air in then the column of water would drop and the foot valve would lose suction and the pump would stop. Then in the middle of the night there would be a voice at the door, and when I stumbled wearily from my bed to answer it, a man with a very sad expression on his face would say, 'Boss, Boss, *lo* pump *ena efele.*'

It was a phrase I learned to dread. I would struggle into my clothes and go out into the dark, hurrying to the shaft or the rising water would beat us and we had to get that pump going or lift it out of the way. Then dead-tired and grumbling and ready to kick the pump operator's arse, I'd hang from the bucket getting cold and soaked and covered in filth as I tried to prime the pump and get it started again. When at last it was working we would go up to my kitchen and drink some coffee and warm our hands over the fire together and that was all right. But then sometimes in order to please me and regain the previous level of water the pump operator would open the valves too far. The pumps would take on too many 'amphs' and burn out. I'd come down the shaft to the terrible acrid stench of burnt out electric motors. There was nothing to be done then but lift them out of the shaft and Judith would rush them into town to be fixed. I worked such long hours that I became a walking zombie. I grew so tired that I even dozed off in the bucket going down to the pumps. My men were exhausted too but I kept driving them on.

It took two months to clear that mine down to two level. The pumps and switch gear, tracks and cocopans were covered by slime and muck and rotting timber that had worked down through the old stopes. We laboriously uncoupled the pump motors from the flooded

349

station and together with the starting mechanism and switch gear raised them to the surface. Then we raised the cables and laid them out like greasy black snakes to dry in the sun all over the front lawn. The switch gear was painstakingly disassembled and the coils, broken contacts, springs, pawls—everything— was removed by hand, cleaned, filed, sandpapered, boiled in oil and then dried. Judith's kitchen was completely taken over and the sickly horrible smell of cooking machinery permeated through the whole house.

We spent nearly three months in really hard, twenty-four hours a day, non-stop work. And I came home from the mine one night to find Judith crying over the great pots of machinery that were bubbling on the stove. Her hair was oily, so were her clothes; her shoulders sagged with sheer exhaustion. Her fingers were raw, her face wan and drawn. She looked ill. I had been so involved with the mine and I'd been driving everyone so hard that I hadn't noticed how ill and exhausted she was looking, and I cursed myself for being so insensitive. I put my arms around her and made her rest against my shoulder, then gently I helped her into bed. I wet a warm cloth and sponged down her face and hands. 'Oh God, Judith,' I said, filled with remorse as I tended her. 'What have I done to you? Look at you—you were my ballerina and I've brought you from the city to this. How could I have let you work yourself into the ground. Oh God, Judith, I'm sorry.'

We'll leave here I decided. 'I'll get a job in town.' Judith reached out and touched my face and smiled at me. 'I love you Patrick,' she whispered. 'I believe in you and our mine. We'll come through.' I needed her to say that more than anything and I was so tired that I just collapsed beside her with my boots and clothes still dirty from the mine and we slept.

★   ★   ★

My call-up papers came. Judith could not pump out the mine on her own and we had less than three weeks to find a replacement for me while I was in the bush. We searched our area, but everyone who might have been suitable was already away or going on call-up soon. We were almost in despair, when I awoke one morning to the noise of a mule braying. I dashed outside to find the old man with Joseph behind him—they were setting up camp by our old shack. 'Well boy,' the old man said as he greeted me. 'I heard you were in trouble and I came as soon as I could.' He was grizzled and dirty and he reeked of brandy but God I was glad to see him.

The old man looked after the pumps while I was away. He also kept an eye on Judith for me but he refused to put one foot in our house or accept any hospitality from her. It was the same old state of siege, nothing had changed and the old man liked it that way—he wasn't going to let any woman near him.

I returned to find that he had re-established the sump and pumping station inside the mine, and pushed the water down as far as five level. I also noticed that he had spent a lot of money in buying new equipment that we badly needed but could not possibly afford. 'Look,' I said to him. 'I can't take your money. I can't pay it back.'

The old man was hurt. 'I'm just protecting my investment,' he said gruffly. 'This is still half my mine—or have you forgotten that?'

We used the money and the unexpected injection of capital went a long way towards saving the mine. 'You must have struck it rich somewhere,' I asked curiously, wondering how he got it. But the old man just shrugged.

I went into town to see Phillimon. He was lying in a long, high-ceilinged hospital ward. When he saw me he levered himself up and I took his outstretched hand. Around us were cries of pain and scurrying black nurses, and the place smelt of wound dressings and disinfectants. A bus had just hit a landmine on the dirt road to the reserve and there were beds squeezed into every nook and cranny and still more men lay on mattresses on the floor. I looked around at the needlessly maimed men and I wanted to retch. 'Bloody war,' I said bitterly.

But Phillimon had other things on his mind. He had lost one foot altogether. The other had been partially saved. He was experiencing a lot of pain and he had grown even more withdrawn and fierce. 'Get me out of here,' he said urgently. 'I can't stand this place. The cries of those men and the walls around me are driving me mad. I long to feel the sun on my shoulders again.'

The hospital authorities could do nothing more for Phillimon. The orderlies wheeled him out and I lifted him on to the truck. When we arrived at the mine he put his arms around my neck and I carried him up to his shack on my back. I knew he would be lonely there without family to look after him. He was my friend and I wanted to help him as much as I could. But Phillimon made me understand that as soon as he could be fitted with artificial limbs he would take over the underground again, and I encouraged him in this, for Phillimon was a proud man who would never accept charity, and the only way he would stay with me was if he could work. The mine carpenter made him up some crutches and he learned to hobble about on them. It cost him much pain and effort and whenever we passed by his shack we would hear him crashing and cursing as he collided with the furniture.

The old man and I worked on and re-plugged

the fissure on six level. We drilled deep into the side walls to accept the reinforcing—and this time we really made a job of it. Then we pumped out all the water—right down to the bottom of the mine.

Amid the rubble, timber and mud we found the remains of the two dead miners and lifted out their bodies for burial. The drums beat in the compound and the women ululated for two days as the miners grieved for the dead men according to their custom.

Then with the shaft re-claimed, the fissure blocked off and the equipment replaced, at last all the months of work were rewarded and the mine came to life again. Compressed air roared down the pipes to power the jack hammers at work in the stopes. Lashers, naked to the waist, loaded ore on to cocopans and chanting gangers, their lights flashing and their voices echoing down the drives, rattled cocopans along the rails to the station. There was a sound of pumps working, a whine of electric motors, a ring of steel and a whirr of hoists. All of it made up a much loved music to me, better than any other sound I'd heard. And then silence—complete silence before the blast.

As soon as enough ore was stockpiled on the surface to ensure a constant supply, the massive fly-wheel turned and the clack, de clack, de clack of the great iron stamps rang out over the silence of the bush. The powdered rock washed over the James table and a small band of gold, gleaming in the light, shuddered along the riffles. For Judith and I that meant that we had made it. We had come through the really bad times.

We sat on our verandah after supper that night listening to the sound of our mine working. And then Joseph and the old man appeared out of the dark swinging a lantern and singing off key. They staggered to a halt by the bottom step and the old man held up his brandy bottle. 'There's a party at my camp to celebrate. Women are not normally invited,' he said to Judith, 'but you can come.'

We collected Phillimon from his shack and gathered around the old man's camp fire. Judith was exhausted and she soon fell asleep but the four of us, together again, sat out beneath an enormous African night sky drinking and talking and telling stories of the old prospecting days. And the old man, full of brandy, felt warm towards us, as though we were his family, and he weaved stories into spells in his husky warm voice, in a way that made us care about him and want to be with him.

In the morning the old man packed up his camp and left. Judith was relieved to see him go. But I had hoped he'd stay for good. That night I found myself looking out over the bush to the distant line of hills searching for the tiny beckoning spark of his camp fire. But this time

355

he left no sign. And I was disappointed—not that I would have gone with him. But just hearing the old man's stories again awoke nostalgic memories of our trekking days. I remembered the times when the cart wheels rolled along dusty tracks amid a rippling sea of bush grass and the sun poured down on us like honey. We were free men then, without responsibility, just searching for dreams.

I noticed that a cool wind had sprung up and there was a bright moon rising for the old man and Joseph to follow. 'Don't worry,' Judith said bitterly, thinking of the old man's influence on me—'He'll be back.' But I worried about them out there in the bush with the terrorist war closing in.

*　　*　　*

I was called up for military service. My PATU stick was sent to an area aptly called the 'little Himalayas', on the Eastern border of Rhodesia. White rule in neighbouring Mozambique had collapsed and now the whole of that border had become hostile. We patrolled a rusted three-strand cattle fence which in those days was all that divided Rhodesia from Mozambique. The type of country came as a terrible shock to us Matabele, used as we were to the dry flat scrub land. It went straight up and down, from four thousand feet to over seven thousand feet and back again. And we walked and climbed. My God, did we walk, covering twenty miles and more a day. It was cold and raining and misty and miserable, and you knew you had been wet for a long time when mould grew on your camouflage.

Whenever I left Judith to go on military service, it was as though I entered a different world, became a different person. The first day on patrol in the bush I tried sub-consciously to keep clean. My weapon and pack felt awkward—I was very much a civilian in a camouflage uniform. The second day, after a night on the ground, tensing at every snapping twig, beard stubble growing and my pack straps wearing in, I moved more easily, more alert. The third and fourth day the thin veneer of civilization began to drop away and survival instincts took over. By the fifth day my camouflage was filthy and I smelt and I didn't care. And once, without even thinking about it I would have chosen to walk in the sunlit open, now I moved silently and kept to the shadows. And my senses responded immediately to danger and my eyes learned to pick out and define objects that normally would have remained hidden in the bush. My rifle barrel swung in line with my eyes and once I had wondered if I could ever actually kill anybody— now I knew I'd squeeze that trigger.

We had climbed all day and just before sunset

357

we waited on the high ground by a strip of cleared scrub that served as an emergency landing zone. An Allouette helicopter with the gunner's legs dangling over the side of the cabin came beating out of the red sky. It banked sharply overhead and then settled just long enough to offload supplies and for the gunner to pass a message on to our stick leader. Then the helicopter became airborne again, nose down and away hurrying home with the dark. The fleeting contact with something that was in touch with the outside world brought home a hollow gutted sense of isolation to the five of us who remained in the fading light by the landing zone. It only lasted a few seconds then Ian Anderson, our stick leader, signalled us to leave our positions of all-round defence and gather round him for a briefing.

Ian was a big bearlike man, older than the rest of us, with a deep kindness in him. He was an accountant but he should have been a farmer for he was independent and good with his hands and he loved the land.

The message passed on by the gunner was that a large gang of terrorists had crossed the border and were about to begin operating in our area. Headquarters ordered us to get on to their tracks and harass them. Our patrol area was just too vast and rugged for us to hope to make contact with them by chance. So Ian decided that we would ambush a path that was the only link between the two main villages.

We ate from our 'rat packs', buried the tins and then tramped on in single file through the night for we wanted to move into position under cover of darkness. I went ahead of the others following the shadowy figure of Joseph Mopofu. The only regular amongst us, he was a silent, dangerous man, good in the bush. He never laughed, he rarely smiled and he took this war very seriously—but then he had good reason to. Less than a year ago, while he was away on duty with us, the terrorists arrived at his home. They took his mother and father, his wife and three children. They herded them into a hut and set it alight and burned them alive.

We skirted the first village and heard the thin warning cry of its dogs, then we took up ambush positions some half a mile down the path. Ian, as stick leader, with two men squirmed carefully into the thick bush. On the path ahead of them lay an area marked out as the killing ground and they were to act as our central field of fire. Some way out on either flank lay the Scouts linked to the centre by a fine piece of string. We lay there not moving. The 'little Himalayas' had a hostile climate. The sun burned down and our tongues and lips cracked like parchment in the heat. Then at night it rained and we froze, shivering violently, trying to stop our teeth from chattering, trying to keep still. When we had to defecate we buried it beside us and lay in the mud just waiting, and waiting and watching. I was on the left flank lying a few feet farther down the path than the others and my job if the terrorists came that way, was to trigger the ambush. Nothing happened. I had only a narrow field of vision and nothing to occupy my mind other than the self-discipline of forcing myself to ignore the rain and the mud and the flies and the insect bites and lie still.

Gradually my mind grew blank. I became insensitive to the misery of my conditions and lay in a sort of comatose state functioning only by instinct. Many people passed us out of curfew hours not knowing we were there. Then very early in the morning of the third day a terrorist lead scout came noiselessly down the path. The man moved so silently that I hadn't realized he was there until he was almost on top of me.

The scout stopped, holding up his hand in silent warning to the men behind, telling them to wait. Then he went down on one knee, his eyes searching the path for footprints and then the bush on either side of the path noting everything from a broken twig to a bruised leaf. The scout was almost opposite me and though we had taken up our positions with the utmost care, that man had sensed something was wrong, he could smell danger. He was an older man than I, lean faced, dressed in ragged camouflage, with a high Arabic nose and thin lips and sunken cheeks, and he carried a lethal AKN rifle. Slowly, like a cobra, he turned his head and then he seemed to be staring straight at me. I didn't move, I didn't breathe, but I could hear my heart thudding and I began to sweat. In ambush we wore veils over our heads and shoulders to break our outline and I knew that my camouflage was effective—but not more than thirteen feet separated us and the scout with his cold staring eyes seemed to know I was there.

The terrorists behind him were tired. They had nearly reached the border and they grew restless as the seconds slowly ticked by. An impatient command from the group leader came up the line telling the scout to move on. But the scout didn't want to move—all his instincts were warning him and the others should have listened to him. But the command came again and grudgingly he rose off his knee and passed slowly through the killing ground. I watched him pass. There was a deadly quality in that man which chilled me to the marrow and I hoped Joseph Mopofu, who was on the other flank, would get him. The terrorist gangs normally moved in open order but they had bunched while waiting for the scout and when six of them at the same time were in the killing ground, I pulled the string.

Our combined FNs opened up on automatic fire. Adrenaline flowed through me as my rifle butt kicked against my shoulder. The deep bark of the high velocity shells came crashing off the mountain sides, and what those bullets struck, they shattered. An arm or a leg struck squarely on the bone could be completely ripped off. The six men on the killing ground fell, scythed down by the hail of bullets. Then we turned on the rest of the terrorists who were still stunned by the suddenness of the attack. Along the track to my left I saw a fleeing figure plunge wildly into the bush. I sent a burst after it and watched it fall, knocked down into the dust like a rag doll and in the heat of the moment I was filled with savage triumph. From my flank came answering fire. The distinctive high whiplash crack of their AKs followed by an RPD machine gun opening up at such a rapid rate that it sounded like canvas being ripped across. The terrorists were firing high, their bullets raked the trees above us and leaves, twigs and splinters of wood rained down about our heads. And then just as suddenly there was silence. The terrorists had pulled out, bombshelling, making for the border, leaving their wounded behind them.

There had been many unsuccessful ambushes before but this was my first real contact and it took me a while to stop shaking. My rifle barrel was hot and I was down to my last magazine. I came cautiously out of my hiding place in the bush. The others in my stick were doing the same thing. To our amazement not one of us had been hurt. We provided cover while Ian went forward and checked on the bodies of the terrorists. The six in the killing ground were dead. We found another one dead farther down the track and three wounded, one of them seriously, a lung shot judging by the bright colour of the blood.

I walked along the path to the figure that I'd shot. Even as I went up to it I had a feeling something was wrong. Then I saw outflung in the grass small hands not yet calloused by work, bare feet. A small fine-boned body almost lost in a blood soaked denim overall many sizes too large. It was a Majuba, a boy of ten or so, recruited by the terrorists to show them the way in strange country. The bullets had wreaked terrible damage; I'd almost blown that child away. To him it had all been a game but to me, retching beside him, the bewildered death mask forming on his face was going to be imprinted in my mind for the rest of my life. I knew this was part of war. I rationalized that if you picked up a gun you had to expect this. But at the same time I felt sick and ashamed and I hated the war and I hated myself.

'Did you see that lead scout?' someone said excitedly, coming up behind me. 'I thought he had you spotted.' As he spoke a shot rang out and Ian spun round clutching his head and fell. The scout had come back; I knew it was him even as I dived for cover. He was on high ground amongst some rocks. Before we could react and try to pin him down, and with chilling deliberacy in order to prevent us from obtaining information from them, he put a bullet into each of his own wounded men, and then he disappeared.

Joseph Mopofu went after him. Without thought of cover and sliding and scrabbling for holds he went straight up the side of that hill. The others followed Mopofu to try and give him support. I crawled over to Ian. He was still breathing but I could see what I thought looked like brain tissue through a hole in the top of his skull. I set up a drip, made up a litter for him and established radio communications with our base. A helicopter carried Ian out four hours later.

The others came back for me. Mopofu had managed to wound the scout and we followed up his blood spoor. We found him hiding in a thicket with his stomach half open, too weak from loss of blood to go farther.

We tried to get him out of the thicket but the scout was lying with a hand grenade pressed against his wound and he promised us that if we came closer he'd pull the pin. The sun grew hotter and hotter and we waited but he wouldn't pass out. Mopofu wanted to kill him. 'One shot,' he said savagely, 'only one shot and I'll blow him apart. I have the right. I know this man, he was from my village.' But the rest of us would not let him. We wanted information and we offered the scout bandages to staunch his bleeding and morphine for the pain. But the lean-faced man with his cold staring eyes lay still like a wounded animal in the thicket and would take nothing from us. For as long as he remained conscious we didn't dare go hear him for fear of his grenade. Night fell and we took it in turns to guard him. His breathing became shallow, occasionally we heard him grunt with pain or cry out softly. In the cold middle watches of the night he died having let himself bleed to death.

And that brought home the havoc of war to me. It wasn't the man but the manner of his death that affected me—that and the child I killed.

We went to see Ian in hospital as soon as we returned to base. Only then did we realize that he was a human vegetable, his brain damaged beyond all hope of recovery, unable to speak or move or cry. All he could do was breathe.

CHAPTER TWENTY-FIVE

I CAME home stiff and sore and spiritually exhausted. I peeled off my filthy camouflage uniform while Judith ran my bath, for this was now our special ritual of my home coming from the war. I shaved my matted beard and soaked away the ingrained dirt. Then I ran a fresh bath and she joined me in it and soaped the rest of me clean. I touched her, felt the softness of her body, the reassurance of her breasts. I rediscovered all over again the soft silky inner skin of her thighs, the feel of her hair, the lingering smell of her perfume. The warm water and her touch soothed me until gradually I relaxed and then we went to bed. We took a long time over making love, touching and kissing and valuing each part of each other; for without speaking out our dread, both of us were fearful of being permanently parted by the war, and we were desperately glad to be together again unharmed.

We lay after making love, warm within each other's arms and talked. And I told her what had happened, what it felt like in the ambush. I didn't speak about the child. I couldn't bring myself to tell her. I was too ashamed. I thought that I would never speak of the child again. I lay for a long time staring into the darkness and then I could not hold the shame within me any longer. And I made myself tell Judith exactly as it had happened. I whispered to her that I could not get the child's face out of my mind. There were children just like that in my mine compound who I had practically helped raise and who came running after me each morning as I went to work. That was the terrible curse of a civil war. You didn't just fight against the enemy, you fought your own people.

Judith understood. She didn't say anything stupid like, 'Well that's war,' she just held me tightly in her arms and made me feel her love for me. I had spent nearly five months of that year in the bush with no more than three weeks at home for every five weeks away. She said, 'We're both exhausted with this war and running the mine. We have to go away somewhere and think. We need to take a holiday.' she decided. 'Do you know how long we've been married now and never had a holiday? I've never even been to the cinema with my husband.' She nuzzled me and made me smile. She knew that all the pressures and tensions were tightening round my mind like twisting bands. She put her finger on my lips. 'Don't think about the war anymore,' she said. 'Leave it now and we'll talk it out when we're away from here.'

⋆   ⋆   ⋆

Phillimon was left to run the mine as best he could. For Judith took me far away from the pressure of the war and all our responsibilities. She took me right out of Rhodesia—down to the South African coast. Friends of her family had lent us their cottage at Plettenberg Bay. Beyond it was just a golden beach and then the Indian

Ocean.

At first it was strange to be away from home. There you lived under constant tension. In so small a community every radio broadcast could carry news of the death of a friend. But I relaxed by the sea. Dear God, the soul can grow so tired of war and peace can feel so good. Just the joy of walking without a rifle felt good to me, of not starting at shadows or being suspicious of strangers, of sleeping without a gun by my side in an unprotected cottage with the windows wide open to the sound of the surf. The discovering of what else was going on in the world and then little things like finding items in the shops that, with sanctions, I had almost forgotten existed, like Cadburys chocolate or good wine or whisky—or what the new models of motor cars looked like.

It was a time out of season. We had miles and miles of golden beaches almost to ourselves. I would run by the sea each day exercising my spiritually tired body on the soft sand, increasing the distance, getting myself physically fit. We were very happy then. Wine was cheap and we ate sea food. We walked through the rock pools to Robberg Point and camped in an isolated fishing shack. There on the farthermost rocks by the sea I fished the pounding surf while Judith searched among the pools for shells. That was the best time of all for me, eating the fish that I caught, in the light of candles stuck in bottles over a rough wood table. Judith and I, far from people, warm with each other.

We stayed there for two months and I felt strong again. Judith found me one day sitting on a rock watching the waves crashing down below me in a pounding white-framed surf. 'I never knew a man,' she said, seating herself beside me, 'who could love the sea or the bush so much.'

'It's the feeling of space that I love,' I replied. 'The bush in that it offers much the same as the sea. If ever you had grown up on a crowded little island you'd understand.'

Judith reached out, took my hand and held it against her cheek. 'Let's go home, Patrick,' she said.

I knew what she meant. This place was beautiful, but home was Rhodesia and all that we had there. I remembered a vast and empty land beneath the cold blue winter's sky and the dusty summer sunsets, the tall grass and trees—the wildness of it all and the smell of the bush in the dawn. There was no other place in the world that I loved so much and I was ready to go back.

★   ★   ★

We returned to Rhodesia that following week. The people of the district welcomed us back. Phillimon was especially glad to see us. 'Thank

God you've come,' he said feverishly. 'There are problems building up over obtaining spare parts for the mine that have got me tearing my hair out.'

One half of the country was trying to keep the economy going while the other half fought the war. The terrorists had begun making inroads into Matabeleland. The war had drawn much closer to our area in the short time that we had been away and I was called up almost as soon as I returned.

Judith and I, as did most of the Europeans in Rhodesia, saw ourselves as a thin white line, stretched across the southern end of the continent. The winds of change that had swept away colonial Africa, we believed, would stop here—they had to. The stories the white refugees from what was now Black Africa brought with them, of conditions in their former homes, of the total collapse of civil infrastructure brought about by sheer neglect, of hospitals that could no longer heal, for chaos amongst the staff and lack of medicine, of schools that could no longer teach for the purging of their teachers. 'Don't fool yourselves—there is no room for the white man in Black Africa' they warned. Men who cared for their country, who had a stake in it and objected to graft and corruption and incompetence of officials, were replaced by expatriate labour on three-year contracts, their salaries paid out of foreign aid handouts. Refugees from Mozambique and Angola swelled our ranks and the stories they brought with them of atrocities and chaos under African rule were told and retold and this stiffened our resolve. We felt that the Africans of our country couldn't be happy under those conditions, and that we were fighting not just for white man's privilege but for the whole of our society, and our homes.

I didn't see the men I worked with as my enemy but when I came back from the bush and changed out of camouflage and went underground, I began to realize that the African miners were frightened of me. It wasn't exaggerated respect for the 'Big Mambo', it was fear of me as 'Ma Soldier'. Even men I knew well from the old days were avoiding my eyes and sidling away from me.

I grew hurt by my isolation and spoke to Phillimon about it one evening over a beer in his house. 'What's wrong with them?' I complained. 'Don't they understand that I'm fighting for them as well?'

'Don't ask me,' Phillimon answered unsympathetically, 'I was fighting on the other side.' I thought for a moment that I misheard him, then as the full realization of what he said flooded in, my first instinct was to kill him.

My God! While I was off fighting I had been leaving a terrorist with my wife—and no doubt he had his own AK rifle stashed somewhere nearby. I should have known from the way he kept to himself and never went home. I should have realized that first time when he appeared ragged and half starved at the Molvan mine. The signs were there, it all fitted in. But I was too much of a fool to have seen them.

Those thoughts had taken less than a second to pass through my mind. Phillimon watched me tense, but he made no move to protect himself and he showed no fear.

I felt instinctive loathing for my enemy. Fury at the betrayal of a man I counted as my friend—bitterness—hurt—all of those. And then they gave way to pain and confusion in myself, as I realized that I was not going to touch him. For in this bloody war that had turned everything crazy, if Phillimon—who had saved my life and done so many things for me and I for him—was my enemy, then who was left for my friend.

'I wouldn't have let anyone touch Judith,' he said quietly, knowing what was of paramount importance to me.

I was silent for a while trying to make sense of it all. Then I said desperately, 'Phillimon, what in the hell's happened to us?'

Phillimon shrugged his shoulders, relieved in a way that it had come into the open. 'I don't know,' he said, tiredly. 'The war came. I'm black, you're white. We took different sides.'

'Are you still active?' I asked. I had to know.

'If I was would you turn me in?'

'I don't know. I'd have to find a way to stop you.'

'I'm not active,' Phillimon said. 'I deserted so I suppose I'm nothing now.'

'What happened?'

'It was a long time ago.' He shrugged. I could see that he didn't want to talk about it. Then something changed his mind. I think he wanted me to understand.

'When I made my money from the Bismarck mine,' he said, 'I thought a whole new world was going to open up for me. I'd seen the other side of life and I wanted out of my kraal, out of my grass hut. But I discovered that you whites owned everything, the businesses, the mines, the banks, the farms. Sure, your vision founded a modern country, sure, you educated us. But as we progressed, you wouldn't let us in. We kept nudging you and if you had moved over just a little bit at a time, none of this would have happened. But you wouldn't move. You wouldn't give up one thing so we had no alternative but to fight.'

He leaned across the table towards me—'I went to fight for the freedom of my people and I went with an anger burning in my belly. Trouble was I found that the people who were organizing us had no intention of letting us be free. The Russians and the Cubans were not training us for nothing. I made a friend in the training camp. He wasn't much good at fighting but he was a very bright guy and he was a thinker. He saw further than just the war against the whites, to the dangers of a civil war, black tribe against black. Every night the Communist Commissars used to give us political indoctrination lectures—and he used to ask them a whole lot of questions. He set too many of my people thinking, so one day they took him to the edge of camp, and they shot him, just like that. After that they shot anyone who openly disagreed with them and I realized what would happen to my country if these men took control of it. I waited until I came into Rhodesia. We were escorting the Senior Political Commissar of the camp who was going to indoctrinate the people in a new operational area. The Group Leader wasn't a bad guy so I didn't hurt him, but I cut the Political Commissar's throat before I left and then I just walked out of the war. They've been looking for me ever since because that was an important man to them and they won't give up until they've found me.'

'Our people will probably be looking for you too,' I said. 'We've been raiding your camps for the last few months and we've been picking up a lot of your records and other information. If you're that important to them your name could well be listed.'

The sides Phillimon and I had chosen no

longer divided us. To me first and foremost now he was a friend. 'I've got to get you out of the country,' I said, thinking aloud. 'I could hide you in the back of a truck and smuggle you across a border. How about Botswana?'

'I wouldn't last three weeks there,' Phillimon said. 'My people have listening posts up and down that border and so have yours. Besides, I'm tired of running. This is my country, this is my home.'

'The war is getting nearer,' I said. 'They'll be closing in on both sides. You haven't got much time left.'

'One way or another,' Phillimon answered, 'I know I'm going to die. I've had the nightmares, I've seen my death many times in my mind. It doesn't worry me any more.'

I wasn't ready to give up that easily. 'I don't suppose you'd use any of the information that you learned on the other side to help us, would you?' I asked. 'I could perhaps buy you a safe conduct from our side with that.'

Phillimon shook his head, as I knew he would. 'You know me better than that. Just because I'm not fighting anymore doesn't mean I'm on your side. Thanks for trying,' he said quietly, 'but leave it.' Then, as I got up to leave, he asked, 'What about Judith? As you say the war is growing closer, can't you move her into town?'

I shook my head. It was an old argument that

was being repeated between men and their wives all across our district. 'She flatly refuses to leave her home,' I said.

'If you can still trust me,' Phillimon said, 'I'll watch over Judith while you're away.'

I looked into Phillimon's harsh scarred face. The eyes were tired, resigned, beyond all reach of fear. But I knew how much he cared for Judith and that no man would harm her while he was still alive. 'I trust you,' I said. I told no one, not even Judith, I didn't think she would understand.

CHAPTER TWENTY-SIX

THE whites felt the hard times, but the war affected the African far more terribly. Schools closed, missions closed, food was scarce. They were moved from their traditional homes and placed behind the confining wire of protected villages. A bewildered tribesman watched his one son leave to join the terrorists and the other to join the security forces who were now eighty per cent black. It was no longer simply a war of black against white. Politicians were wrestling for power. Brother fought brother, cousin against cousin, tribe against tribe. Blood feuds grew. Civilians were blown up by landmines, or massacred by terrorists or shot as curfew breakers by the security forces. Every border surrounding the country had become hostile—except that with South Africa—and our casualty figures were mounting.

Against this increasingly desperate background we struck back by raiding deeper and deeper into foreign territory, trying to cut off the flood of terrorists before they could enter the country. We hit their base camps and lines of communications and blew up arsenals, depriving them of their Russian-supplied weapons. Always small groups of our men facing far larger numbers deep in enemy territory.

In places where once I wandered through the bush with the old man, now I sped overhead in a helicopter, clutching my weapon, chopping in low over the trees—or clung to the back of a lorry which kicked up clouds of dust as it raced towards a contact zone. Then sometimes amid all the fear and destruction and havoc of war I'd lift my head above the maelstrom and catch a glimpse of a bare-foot African herd boy driving his cattle towards a dusty sunset, his kraal of timeless little thatched huts tucked peacefully beneath a granite kopje. And encapsulated in that scene would be the memory of what the old Rhodesia was like and my heart would weep for the death of my country.

My stick was pulled back to a Ground Coverage base camp for redeployment. It was a hastily built ramshackle outpost surrounded by sandbags. In the centre of a dusty square a radio was playing forces' requests, a woman announcer reading out names. 'To Rifleman Johnny Munro, I hope you got the socks I sent you—we're all missing you here, love Mum and Dad. To Trooper Steinkamp RLI. Gee, but it's lonely without you Tim, missing you stacks, love from your fiancée Eileen.'

It was a hot, still day. Tired men in camouflage and men with only a towel around their waists who had been making their way to the showers began to gather round the radio just in case someone from home sent a message for them. There was a very popular song at that time—the words went. 'If I need you—I just close my eyes and I'm with you.' It was often requested and it made me think of Judith. The sandbags and the dusty square and the men gathered round the radio, the song carrying with it all their loneliness for home drifting out across the bush.

I looked into the faces of the men around me; some were less than eighteen years old, still bold eyed and anxious for action, others were men in their sixties who had already been through a world war and now they had sons of their own in the bush and women alone at home and their faces were sad for they had seen too much war.

Someone tapped me on the shoulder. 'You're wanted in the op's room.' I made my way to a

378

mortar-proof bunker. 'Telephone,' a special branch officer said glancing up from a map-strewn table and indicating a field telephone in the corner. 'It's your wife. God knows how she found you.'

Judith sounded very faint on the line but I could hear the joy in her voice when she realized that she had found me. 'Patrick,' she said. 'Oh darling, I'm so pleased—I had to tell you. I'm pregnant.' I was silent for a moment absorbing the information. 'Patrick,' she said anxiously, 'can you hear me? We're going to have a baby. I love you Patrick. Please come home safely.'

For security reasons I could not tell her how much longer I would be away. Her voice kept fading into the static of the telephone party line and so did mine. And I ended up driven half mad with frustration yelling, 'I love you, I love you, Judith,' as the line went dead.

My first instinct was to be jealous of anything that might come between me and Judith and perhaps change our way of life. Then gradually as the day wore on I got used to the idea of our having a child and the more I thought about it the more I was filled with a great sense of elation. I found some paper and a pencil and I sat in a patch of light thrown by the op's room doorway. 'Judith,' I said, 'I'm writing this letter to you because tonight I so badly want to talk to you and feel close to you and perhaps I'll never find the words so well again. In all the time

379

we've been together you have brought me great love, great warmth, great peace—and now a child.' I stopped there, I was so emotionally overwrought that I could think of nothing else to say so I ended with, 'I love you Judith, I really love you. Cherish our child until I can come home to you.'

★   ★   ★

The war came to our area just before Christmas. We had all been to the district's traditional children's party at the Country Club and a farmer driving back with his family was ambushed that night just beyond his farm entrance. A number of bullets struck the rear of the car. The farmer and his wife were unhurt but in the back seat his ten year old daughter, herself wounded in the thigh, cradled her dying young brother's head in her arms and said calmly, 'Drive quickly, Daddy. Mark's bleeding very badly.'

A back tyre had been shot to shreds. The farmer's wife fired back while he drove out of the ambush on a wheel rim. A quarter of a mile down the road, filled with fear in case the terrorists came after them, the farmer had to get out and change the wheel while his wife tried frantically to staunch her son's wounds. They drove on to the nearest village in search of a doctor but by the time they got there Mark was dead.

My stick was called out and I lay all Christmas night in ambush in a rain-filled ditch. But when it came to avenging the death of young Mark I welcomed the discomfort.

A few days later a nearby farm house was unsuccessfully attacked. Agric Alerts, radio devices linking each homestead with the local police station, were installed and the whole district went behind the wire. Judith and I had avoided it for as long as possible and now we too had to erect an eight-foot diamond mesh fence with barbed wire on the top around our home and another one around our African miners' compound. It cut through Judith's beautifully tended garden. She hated it for the eyesore it caused and fought with me when I made her level the ground behind so that we could have a clear field of fire at anyone creeping up to the fence.

The wire and the grenade screens fitted round our windows made us prisoners in our home and it separated us from our miners. In the mornings they would come to work from behind their fence and I from mine. The ritual of locking the gates at sunset, having made sure that no one was in the grounds, of putting on the security lights, of checking weapons and setting the alarms was a daily reminder of a war you had to live with in your home. And at first when the men were away the women would have to stay with neighbours in the district. Each night she would have to bundle up her children and take them somewhere different in order not to make too much of a burden of herself—or if several men were away from the same area then their families would spend the night in laager dossing on the floor of some fortified place, the women and the men too old for war, mounting guard over the children. But the women soon got tired of living like that and they rebelled and flatly refused to leave their own homes unless the police could prove that danger was imminent.

For all the fear and misery the war brought it also gathered the district closer together. There was a feeling of reliance in the community that had never been so strong before. Old enmities were healed, rifts forgotten. If a farmer was away his neighbour would help his wife gather in his crop and assist her in any way he could— the same went for the miners. The district was a community and the community had a close-knit identity and we cared for and protected one another.

In spite of being pregnant Judith joined the Police Reserve and she spent two nights a week working in the operations room of the local police station manning the radios. On a night when she was on duty a farm house at the other end of our district was attacked. I was pottering around our house doing odd jobs when suddenly the Agric Alert alarm went off and a woman whose voice I knew well shouted, 'We're under attack—oh my God, they're firing at us. We're under attack.'

I knew that in the police station a small red light under the farm homestead's name would be glowing on a board and Judith would be calling up the reserves. I heard Judith answer the woman and keeping her voice calm she began the list of action to take when under attack. 'Have you turned out your house lights?' she said. 'Have you secured your doors? Make sure your spare weapons and ammunition are with you and take up a safe position away from windows and doorways.' She said all this knowing that people can be so shocked that they remain almost frozen to the spot at the time of attack and have to be urged into responding. Whenever the woman replied I could hear the sound of her husband returning fire and Judith's voice constantly assuring her that help was coming, help was on its way, hold on, hold on. Return fire with everything you've got and hold on. Whoever was manning the radio was made to understand that this was the most important instruction they could deliver for alone in the dark in a farm homestead miles from a neighbour, surrounded by thirty or more terrorists, windows shattering, roof tiles crashing, bullets thudding into walls; the people under attack could sometimes react by feeling the most terrible sense of isolation and just give

383

up hope—and the reassurance they received on the radio gave them the courage to keep fighting.

The member-in-charge of the police station would be calling out PATU sticks closest to that farm house. I knew our stick would probably be held in reserve but the waiting for instructions and not being able to go in and help was driving me wild with frustration. I heard garbled exchanges on the radio from the other room as I changed into camouflage and packed up my kit in case we were summoned. By the time I returned to the radio I gathered that the woman's husband had been badly wounded and she was now returning fire alone. No one could interrupt on the Agric Alert—it was a matter between Judith and the woman and I waited helplessly by, hearing Judith telling the woman that the PATU sticks were nearly there. Hold on, hold on. Then the woman said calmly, 'They're in our yard, I can hear them. They're coming in.' She said it not in terror or desperation but rather with tired resignation. I could imagine her waiting now for the end with her wounded husband beside her and I turned away for I could not bear to hear anymore.

I was still kitted up and waiting to be called out when Judith returned in the early hours of the morning. 'Why didn't they call me out?' I asked in fierce frustration.

'They sent an army detachment after the

384

terrorists,' Judith answered tiredly. 'They need your stick to guard this end of the district.'

I saw that she had been crying and I held out my arms to her. She came into them and buried her head in my shoulder. 'Oh Patrick,' she said weeping, 'oh Patrick, did you hear it—it was horrible.'

'I heard,' I said as I held her. 'I heard.'

'Thank God there were just the two of them,' Judith sobbed, 'and that their children are still safely at school.'

I felt the gentle swell of Judith's stomach pressing against mine. I thought of our child forming within her and I wondered how much more of this type of living we could take. And then there was the added pressure of the telegrams sent by Judith's mother urging her to leave me and the mine—'if not for your sake then for your child's—my grandchild,' she blackmailed. And for once she was right—I knew that we were losing this war. 'I think you must go away from here, Judith,' I said gently. 'You must leave and stay with your mother for a while.' But Judith stubbornly shook her head.

I saw that dawn was breaking. I opened the french doors and we walked out into the garden and watched the sun rise. It was so very beautiful and peaceful there, the rays of light flowing over the rocks and trees touching the dew-filled flowers and tropical plants with colour, dispelling the gloom of the night. The birds began to sing for the break of the fresh day. And Judith seemed to take on new strength as she felt the warmth of the sun and walked with me in her garden.

'This is my place here with you,' she said. 'I built my home myself and I love every brick. They're never going to drive me out. My mother can't possibly understand. No one who has lived all their life in a city suburb and bought their houses from another man can understand what it feels like to clear your own land of scrub and rocks and plant it. Or find a gold reef and lose it and then find it again. The sheer cost of sweat and time and dedication—no man can understand that unless he has been a pioneer. And then when he has surrendered so much of his life to his land or his mine, the land owns him as much as he owns it. And that's how I feel about our mine and our home. Don't send me away,' Judith said. 'You know that if any one of us goes we leave a gap and weaken the resolve of the district. I feel that these are now my people, this is my country, my home. Don't try to send me away from you Patrick, because I won't leave.'

The district improved on their defences and life became peaceful for a while. But still there was the constant strain of always being on one's guard and never moving without a gun. I found the nights the longest to get through. I slept lightly for I was conscious of my role as

386

protector of Judith and my child. An unaccustomed sound, the different note in a dog's bark, a curtain stirring at the far end of the room as though a rifle muzzle was inching through it had me waking instantly from sleep in a cold sweat of fear, warnings whispering urgently in my mind that the terrorists were through the fence, past the sandbag blast walls—somebody was creeping into the room— and silently, scarcely breathing, while my eyes tried to pierce the darkness and my ears strained to identify the sound, I would edge away from Judith's sleeping form and my hand searched for the rifle that was always by my bed.

CHAPTER TWENTY-SEVEN

BY the end of that year events had reached such a critical stage that the politicians were forced to act and eventually the Prime Minister signed a settlement agreement with the three other leaders of the Internal Factions. The main provision of that agreement stipulated that the whites had to hand over power to the blacks by the 31st December of that year. So the era of white-ruled Rhodesia and the rebellion contained in the Unilateral Declaration of Independence was to end. Within the next year Rhodesia would be called Zimbabwe and change from a white-dominated country to a black-dominated country with all that the transition implied for the whites.

When the news of the settlement broke the effect was shattering. Some whites welcomed the settlement with relief, in the belief that the war would now end, the wounds would heal and that there would still be a future for the whites. Others saw the settlement as nothing less than a surrender. They saw no future for a white in a black-ruled country.

A meeting was held by the people of our district to discuss the settlement. It took place in the rambling, whitewashed mud brick and thatched Country Club which the community had built way back when the area was first pioneered, each man volunteering his labour so that in the days before travel was made easy, the families on their lonely, widely-spaced farms could have some place for special contact with their neighbours.

Someone made a bitter joke as Judith and I arrived. 'Next year Zimbabwe,' he said grimly twisting the catch phrase that had always summed up the optimism of Rhodesia through the defiant days of UDI.

We entered the big, cool, gumpole-raftered club hall. It was in here that our community's decisions were taken. And it was packed with open-necked, fiercely independent men and their families, many of them third and fourth generation Rhodesians.

A man stood up and gave Judith his seat. Beside her, sitting ramrod stiff with his wide brimmed bush hat on his knees, was old man van Staden. He was of typical pioneer stock, tall, lean and wiry and extremely fit for a man of his age. His hair was close-cropped on a bullet-like skull and his eyes were a light tan colour set into a hard, wrinkled leathery face.

Van Staden ranched close by our mine. A few months previously the terrorists had incited the tribesmen from the reserve to raid his cattle. They came in the night, rounded up his herds and drove them at full pelt down the dusty road. The cattle that broke their legs in the grids just lay where they fell, the rest disappeared into the reserve.

Van Staden could take being ambushed, and even having his homestead shot up. But he was an Afrikaner—a true Boer—and when they took his cattle he said enough! And he called in his three sons. They made coffee and biltong for the journey ahead. Then they saddled up their horses, gathered in their herdsmen to track, and rode knee to knee into the reserve. When they came to a kraal they made the headman provide them with fresh trackers so that their own men could rest. And in that way riding day and night they crossed the whole reserve. They rounded up every head of cattle that came their way— their own and the tribesmen's as well. And then they turned and rode right back through the reserve driving what was by now so vast a herd of cattle before them that the dust stretched to the horizon and darkened the sun. And such was the grim mask of fury on the face of the old Boer and the amazement his action caused to the tribesmen, the terrorists and the security forces that no one touched him. They just stood back and let him drive his cattle past.

Van Staden returned to his ranch and the tribesmen came to him and politely asked for their cattle back. A big *indaba* took place and van Staden kept all the cattle that were his and took compensation for the ones he had lost. When justice was done, in African fashion, he slaughtered oxen and made beer, and everyone departed well satisfied—except for the police who wanted to charge van Staden with cattle rustling.

The chairman tried to bring the meeting to order but the atmosphere in the club house was charged with emotion. Speaker after speaker rose and refused to acknowledge defeat. They were bewildered by the Prime Minister's actions in accepting such a settlement. The army was undefeated, they said, and still the most powerful in Central Africa. The farmers themselves who bore the brunt of the war felt undefeated. 'We can go on,' van Staden shouted waving his hat. 'Peoples, peoples,' he said appealing to us in halting English, 'we must go on—on our knees if necessary. But no surrender of what has taken us our lifetimes to build.'

Others, the more practical members of the community, explained that the economy was finished. Sanctions and a world trade recession had squeezed us dry and we could no longer support a war. The breaking strain was upon us. Besides, they argued, look at the proposals unemotionally. It was not surrender the Prime Minister offered, it was compromise. There was a future with safeguards and guarantees for the whites, if only we could make the settlement work.

But most of the men at that meeting were deeply suspicious of African rule. They argued that Rhodesia would go the way of many states to the north of us. An African elected government would last a year or two and then a military coup or a political despot would seize power. After that any agreement or guarantee was worthless. They feared for their lifetime's work, they feared for the future of their children. 'Don't give our country away,' they urged of us. 'Fight! And if we lose, then burn the land, destroy all that we built. Scorch the earth and fight our way out to South Africa— and then see if those African Nationalists who are so anxious to take over from us are willing to inherit the ashes.'

This was a very real threat from a people who would carry it out if desperate. All over the country, on farms, in cities and in various military units, there were men with skills enough and access to explosives who had sworn not to leave one power line, one dam wall standing. The mood of our district was fast turning that way when McLeod stood up. Old, lonely McLeod, with his wife dead and no children to inherit from him, he had nothing left to lose. He was the largest rancher in the district, a man of presence, of powerful personality. Whatever he said the people would listen, and they waited expectantly.

'I believe,' McLeod said, 'that when the desert is closing in, then the fertile land must remain in the hands of the people who will provide the most food, and not be divided amongst peasants who will scratch at the surface and lose the top soil to erosion. If a tree is cut down another must be planted. I believed that we were the pioneer race who developed this country and therefore we had a right to rule. But I realize now that from the very start we faced a choice. We could have refused to educate the African and therefore expect to continue to rule him—or we could educate and strive to eradicate disease, build hospitals and universities and then accept that by virtue of the African's greater numbers one day he would rule us.

'We of our own free will chose to educate—to put back what we took. And for that,' McLeod said simply, 'I am proud to be a Rhodesian and I always will be. So don't talk to me of scorched earth. Any fool can burn what another man has built. When the time was ripe for change we could not step aside. Now it is us that must end this war and accept the settlement. We have no other choice.

'And if, as we fear, this settlement should fail, and we should lose all that we have and be driven from this land, then know that those who come after us will walk on the roads we made, take water and power from the dams we constructed, till the land we cleared. History will claim that we made our mistakes but unlike such a race as the conquistadores of Peru, we did not come to destroy a civilization—we came to build on. And we did—and no matter what happens to us in the future,' McLeod said with the fierce pride of a man who had devoted his lifetime's work into turning barren rock and scrub into a ranch. 'That must be the epitaph of the white race in Rhodesia.'

An elderly lady with the formidable face of an English duchess, who had lost both her son and her grandson to the war, rose to join with McLeod and commanded the attention of the meeting. 'How can we have been fighting for a country that we intend to destroy?' she asked. 'If that were true then we have merely been fighting for our privilege as whites. And I don't believe that so many of us fought and died for that. If change must come,' she said, 'and it has, then we must accept it gracefully and with dignity. The future is not without hope. We have been offered a role to play under African rule. Don't whine like beaten children. Take the role of a minority whose skills are important to the well being of the country—and do it well. For in defeat, that and all that we have built, is our pride.'

It was the older generation who had used all their power and influence to most fiercely resist change. And now they led the way and swayed the meeting to accept the settlement.

Judith and I drove silently home from the club. 'Well, what do you think,' I asked. 'Will the settlement work?'

'You mean stop the fighting? I don't know. I don't think so, at least not for a long while. But it's the best chance we've got.'

'Judith, we're going to have to adjust to many changes. Do you want to leave here?'

'No.'

'Neither do I.'

'Well then,' Judith replied with great determination, 'we keep the mine going. We try to protect what we have and stay alive.' She caught my eye and smiled. 'And who knows,' she said, 'next year might be better.'

I glanced across at her and grinned for there was something incongruous about my very brave lady with her swelling tummy, her handbag and her sun hat, and an evil-looking sub-machine gun held ready on her lap. She was entering her seventh month of pregnancy. It seemed to suit her; she had never been so healthy and she radiated happiness as she sat there beside me.

CHAPTER TWENTY-EIGHT

WE locked the homestead gates, set the alarm and went to bed. Later that night I awoke in a cold sweat to an unfamiliar sound. The curtains flapping by the window—it wasn't that. The crack of the timber joists in the roof, not that. I thought I was just imagining things again. But there was something wrong—some unaccustomed sound had woken me. Then I heard the dogs snarling and the hairs on the nape of my neck began to prickle and rise up in fear. The sound changed. The dogs were now tearing and yelping and fighting amongst themselves as though someone was tossing them meat over the wire.

Judith stirred in her sleep, I put out my hand to quieten her. Then clutching my rifle I slipped out of bed and made my way across the room to the window. I carefully parted the curtain and looked out through the wire mesh of the antigrenade screens. Before me the grounds lay bathed in bright white moonlight, with patches of black shadow flung by the branches of the great garden shade trees reaching over portions of the wire.

The dogs were active to one side of the house beyond my line of sight. I gave a low whistle which they had been trained to obey—but not one answered. Then a small mongrel that I had grown fond of came staggering out of the shadows towards me. The dog was frothing at the mouth and racked by convulsions. It managed only a few more steps before it collapsed. I heard sounds of death moans and vomiting coming from my other dogs. The meat had been poisoned.

'Judith,' I called to her quietly but urgently, 'Judith, wake up.' I heard her stirring in the darkened room behind me, coming up out of sleep. 'Do you hear me, Judith? Get out of bed, keep down and go into the passage and press the alarm button on the Agric Alert. We're about to come under attack.'

Judith left her bed and quickly made her way to the passage. After she had gone I thought, 'My God what if the terrorists are already in the house.' I was about to go after her when the alarm from the trip wire on the fence went off.

I had lived with the fear of an attack for so long. Now it had come. I had to force myself to think clearly. I made my numb mind run through the precautions to take in event of attack. Ensure all outer doors and windows are locked. We had checked them before we went to bed and Judith would be checking them again now. Turn out all internal lights—make sure the homestead was completely in darkness—that was done. Turn on the boundary spot lights. They were designed to light up the fence and the patches of dark shadow beneath the trees. The switch was by my bed. I was about to activate it then I decided to leave the spot lights alone for the time being. The moon was bright enough for us to watch over most of the fence, and in the shadows where I thought people might hide, I had laid my own defences.

I stared through the grenade screens. At first everything appeared peaceful and serene. Then beyond the wire, in the clear light of the moon, I caught a glimpse of shadowy figures scrambling up and dropping over the wire into the grounds, dark shapes with sometimes just the glint of the moon on a rifle barrel as they flitted noiselessly from cover to cover.

I knew absolute terror as I watched disembodied ghost-like men advancing remorselessly on the homestead. I remained rooted to the spot, unable to move for a moment. Then I thought of what would happen to Judith if they got into the house and I raised my rifle, sought out a target and squeezed the trigger.

I heard a crash of breaking glass from the

next-door room and then a short ripping burst from Judith's light nine millimeter sub-machine gun joined with the deeper bark of my rifle. We brought down several men and their bodies lay sprawled on the grass, but the others kept coming on; and now there was a constant ripple of flashes as they returned our fire and bullets smashed the windows and smacked into the walls of our home.

I made myself wait. They were coming closer and closer, and still I made myself wait. They advanced right up to the house and I let them come on until they passed a small rock garden that I used as a marker. Then I stood up, reached for a cord that hung from the ceiling and pulled down hard on it. In the roof on specially reinforced beams and guarding each corner of the house, were forty four gallon petrol drums filled with concrete. Set securely in the concrete were two inch diameter cannons, charged with black powder and filled with nuts and bolts and screws and other rusted, jagged lumps of metal. The cord was attached to a mechanical trigger and when I pulled it, the home-made cannons went off. The noise was appalling. The whole house rocked under the force of the blasts but the effect was devastating. The metal shrapnel cut enormous swaths right through the garden and nothing remained upright in its path.

The few bleeding and wounded terrorists who

could regain their feet, fled.

Judith crawled into the bedroom. 'Did you see anything your side?' I asked.

'Nothing,' she answered breathlessly.

Before we could relax for even a moment we heard the harsh stammer of a machine gun coming from close by our room. A hail of bullets struck the window we were crouching under with such force that the whole frame simply caved inwards in an explosion of shattering glass and wood. The bullets went on, cutting through the air above our heads with a sound like ripping canvas, bullets thudding into the walls and ceiling above our bed showering our prostrate bodies with plaster, dust and debris.

The first assault had been a diversion. Another group must have slipped through the fence on our blind side and their machine gun had us pinned down in this one room so they could break through into the other rooms at leisure.

I wriggled across the bedroom on my belly. By the cord that had activated the roof-top cannon was an electrical circuit breaker. I had attached a local invention based on the claymore mine to the tree trunks. The wires to fire them ran from the circuit breaker under the ground. The whole contraption was powered by a twelve volt battery. I closed the circuit and the shadows below the trees were lit by flashes and a series of ear stunning blasts. At the same time I set off other mines that I had hidden about the grounds, and for a few moments the whole garden seemed to be lit up by flashes, and filled with the high pitched scream of ricocheting razor-sharp pieces of shrapnel.

The machine gun nest had been completely blown away. The terrorists caught within the grounds would have suffered heavy losses. But they would know that the roof-top cannons were not rechargeable—nor the mines replaceable, without exposing myself to their fire.

We broke open fresh ammunition from the gun cabinet and recharged our magazines. Judith went to answer the Agric Alert and while there was a lull in the firing, I took stock of our situation. The terrorists had been forced to withdraw temporarily. They could hold us prisoners here, and in time they would overrun the grounds. But as long as we could keep them out of our fortified homestead and provided help arrived before we were actually fighting from room to room we had a chance. A lot depended on their determination to kill us and the amount of fire power they possessed.

Judith crawled back from the radio and sat beside me with her back against the wall. 'Did they say how soon before they can get help to us?' I asked. Judith shook her head. From outside came sporadic bursts of firing, bullets smacking into the sandbag blast walls. They were just testing our reactions and we didn't bother to reply.

'Patrick,' Judith said quietly, 'I don't think we're going to get any help.'

'What makes you say that,'I asked trying to keep the alarm out of my voice. 'Did they tell you that on the radio?'

'No,' Judith said. 'They're saying all the usual things on the radio to keep our spirits up. But round about the time the Butler's farm got attacked, the army made a decision that if people are hit in very isolated places they are no longer going to risk losing several of their men and vehicles to a terrorist ambush. They have too few men left to risk those sort of casualties, and so the farmer is on his own until morning.'

'Do the other farmers know about this?' I asked aghast.

Judith shook her head. 'Only the wives who work in the police station and man the radios, otherwise it's top secret. They're afraid if the news gets out it'll damage moral.'

'Too right it will,' I agreed bitterly.

'In spite of those orders,' Judith said, 'the army will volunteer to go out as long as the terrain is reasonably easy for them to move over—but in our case . . .'

'In our case,' I finished the sentence for her, 'they would only have to look at a map to see they would have to cross the river at the ford and that's an ideal sight for an ambush. So we're on our own.'

'I think so,' Judith said. 'At least until morning—we can expect help to come then.' I put my arm around her and gave her a squeeze trying to give her the courage. But she didn't need it. Judith, my ballerina—who had lived all this time with me in the bush—had more courage than I did.

As we sat there, I became conscious of the distant sound of voices shouting, tractor engines and other machinery starting up, the sound of metal tearing and smashing against metal—and the noise was coming from the direction of the mine. The lights over the mill and the headgear were on and I could see that the terrorists had brought the night shift up from underground and herded the other men in from the compound. They were forcing them at gunpoint to smash and wreck and beat into shapeless hulks, with twelve pound hammers, every bit of machinery I possessed. And the tractors with buckets on the front for loading ore were pushing the wreckage down the mine shaft. The head-gear tottered and collapsed. I watched the mill being torn apart. I saw machinery that was virtually irreplaceable being tossed down the shaft. My own men, men who had worked day and night and risked their lives with me to save the mine from flooding, were destroying everything they had built with me. I was terribly hurt by their actions and yet I could not blame them—what could any man do with a gun at his back.

The flames spread from the ruptured fuel tanks and as I turned my face from the window Judith could see the hurt I felt. 'Thank God they haven't sent my miners to attack us yet,' I said. 'I couldn't bear to shoot my own men.'

I looked back to where the fire was blazing at the mine. 'Oh Judith,' I said. 'All that work, that sweat, the sacrifice—it's all been wasted.'

Sporadic bursts of firing still ripped into the sandbag blast walls or drilled holes through the roof to remind us that we had not been forgotten. I heard a broadcast over the Argric Alert calling us and I went to answer it. It was the member-in-charge of the police station. He was a man I liked and knew well, and it was good to hear his voice. He asked me for a position report which I gave him. Then I told him to stand by. Judith had followed me into the passage-way, she didn't like being left alone. 'Judith,' I said, 'if there really is no help coming and the terrorists launch a series of determined attacks, then we'll run out of ammunition and we'll be overrun. Without help we don't really stand a chance, you've seen how many of them there are out there. But if this was happening to one of my neighbours—you know I'd go to help him.'

'Yes,' Judith said.

'Well, would it be immoral or anything to tell the military to go to hell and ask our neighbours for help?'

Judith smiled at me and shook her head. 'No,' she said. 'Ask them.'

I got back on to the radio. The member-in-charge's name was Jack Connelly. 'Now listen to me Jack,' I said. 'I've got a wife and unborn child to protect and I want the truth from you. Is the army coming or not?'

I heard Jack pause, the years of discipline bidding him to obey orders, the knowledge that people fought better when they thought that they had a chance of survival, and the damage his answer could do to the moral of the district—but for all that Jack Connelly told the truth. 'No,' he said tiredly. 'You're on your own. How much longer can you last out? There's only three more hours till morning. We'll have help to you then I promise you.'

He and I both knew that we'd never make it till morning. 'Get off the air, Jack,' I said.

And then I began calling up my neighbours. I called up van Staden first. His wife was on radio watch but he must have been resting right beside her for he answered me in a moment. I told him that the army weren't coming and asked him for help. I knew that I was asking him to risk his own life and that of his family who he would be leaving unprotected, but he didn't hesitate for a moment. 'Ja,' he said, delighted to shake off the frustration of waiting and get into action. 'Hold on, I'm coming. I'll bring my sons and I'll get hold of our other neighbours. We'll leave our trucks on the road and trek to you across the bush. I know the way and besides I can see the light from the fire on your mine against the skyline. Remember we'll be coming in on foot so don't shoot us—and we'll fire a flare when we engage the terrs. Look for the flare. And hold on Patrick, hold on.'

I went back and sat by Judith. 'They're coming,' I said deeply relieved.

'What do we do now?' Judith asked.

'Well, we might as well remind them that we're not a soft target.' I had to force myself to my feet. The strain from being under fire was beginning to tell on us and we were both very tired. 'I'll go from window to window,' I said. 'When I give you the signal, switch on the outside spotlights covering that part of the grounds. Give me time enough to let off a couple of shots at anything that moves, then switch off fast before the terrorists can recover and shoot out the lights—okay?'

'I'm ready,' Judith said. I reached out and put my hand on her belly. 'How's our baby?'

'He's fine.' She smiled tiredly.

I crawled into position by the living-room window and signalled Judith to switch on the spotlights. She flicked the switch and nothing happened. She tried again with another switch. Nothing. They had cut the power. So someone out there was doing some thinking. I didn't like

405

that at all. The Agric Alert and the last of the mines were powered from a twelve volt battery. We had no other source of power.

Everything fell silent for a moment, then our ears caught a faint, vibrating hiss, which in seconds became a shrieking, tearing, screeching sound, and then the whole house rocked to an ear shattering explosion. More and more mortar shells rained down in close proximity to us. The terrorists had overshot at first but now they were finding our range. Judith and I clung terrified together in the passage beneath the Agric Alert. We felt helpless. There was nothing we could do. Shrapnel tore chunks out of the outside blast walls and the sand bags melted away. Time and again the whole house was rocked to its foundations. It seemed to be collapsing around us. White plaster dust sucked and swirled. The inside walls tottered. We heard bricks falling. Then the ceiling suddenly sagged as part of the roof collapsed above us.

I knew that the homestead could take little more of this kind of punishment, and that it was only a matter of time before we were either obliterated by a mortar or buried alive beneath the debris. I became filled with rage at our inability to respond and I crawled out of the passage with the hare-brained intention of going out alone and somehow silencing that mortar position. A large hole had been blown in the dining-room wall. I was crawling through it into the garden when suddenly I realized that I couldn't leave Judith behind. I came to my senses, turned and went back for her. As I did so I heard her scream.

Judith, all alone and huddled beneath the Agric Alert, trying to protect herself from the falling mortar, saw the handle of the door connecting the kitchen with the passage turn. The door joist had sagged pinning the door shut. The handle rattled as the unseen hand tried to force it open. The terrorists were in the house. Judith screamed and screamed and raised her gun and pointed it at the door with shaking hands. This had always been her final terror—when they came into the house. The person on the other side was throwing himself against the door now, smashing through the thin wood. Then the door burst open and a huge African with a brutally scarred face loomed in the passage.

Judith was half hypnotised with terror, her gun was raised, her finger squeezing on the trigger, and then suddenly she recognized the figure as Phillimon. He was carrying an AK rifle in his hands with a bloodied bayonet. 'You,' Judith said brokenly, 'not you. Don't tell me you're one of them.'

'No,' Phillimon said. He hobbled swiftly along the passage and crouched down beside her, pushing the muzzle of her gun aside. 'I'm not one of them. Are you all right? Where's

Patrick? I've got to get you out of here.'

I flung myself into the passage, rolling over and over and coming up on my elbows. I would have put a bullet straight into the black figure that was hunched over Judith but she screamed at me to stop.

'It's Phillimon,' she screamed. 'It's Phillimon.'

'Oh God,' I said weakly, 'oh thank God it's you.' Then I noticed his AK. He saw me looking at it and he laid it aside. 'I've got to get you out of here,' Phillimon said.

'There's help coming,' I replied.

He shook his head. 'It'll take too long. They're getting ready to overrun this place.'

'Who are these people?'

'They're a big detachment, crossed over from Zambia a couple of weeks ago. They've come to avenge one of your border raids. Now listen to me. The Land-Rover's in the garage with the keys in it. It's still all right—I've checked it out. I'll take over from you here and I'll draw their fire. You get Judith to that garage then you break through the doors and you drive like hell. They won't be expecting it—you've got a good chance.'

'What about you—where shall we wait for you?'

Phillimon glanced down at his crippled legs. 'I can't move very fast,' he said, 'but don't worry, when you're safely through that gate, I'll get away. I look the same as them in the dark remember. Now move, they'll be coming for you any minute.'

Phillimon covered us as far as the doorway. In the distance we could see the flames still licking around the charred remains of the mill. Phillimon saw the pain fill my face as I watched the flames. 'The men didn't want to do that,' he said quietly.

'I know,' I answered. Now that we had a chance of survival I didn't want to leave him.

'Goodbye, Phillimon,' Judith said quietly.

Phillimon's eyes smiled at her and for a moment his face was without the habitual creases of pain. He nodded goodbye and went back into the house.

I waited until I heard the steady crack of his rifle firing, then we dashed through the moonlight and shadows around the crumbling kitchen wall to the garage. I went in fast through the back door with Judith following me. There was no one in there but the roof was leaning over the mine-protected Land-Rover at a crazy angle. I forced open the driver's door, helped Judith inside and came in after her as she slid across. She cocked her weapon ready to fire out of the window as I started the engine, but I pushed her down. 'Stay on the floor,' I yelled. I put the Land-Rover into four wheeled drive, revved the engine and then let her go.

We crashed straight through the main garage

doors and careered wildly off across the lawns and flower beds. I pulled the Land-Rover around in a tight half circle and drove through the shadows thrown by the trees, spinning the vehicle this way and that to confuse the terrorists' aim. Then I put the accelerator down and headed straight for the main gates.

We struck the gates at thirty miles an hour. The steel chains and padlocks holding the wire mesh frames burst apart. The gates were flung open and we were through and racing down the road to safety. I took the bottom corner on two wheels heading for the river ford. The Land-Rover settled back on the road for only a moment and then there was the most almighty explosion. The terrorists had been expecting the security forces to arrive and they had land-mined the road. The Land-Rover's off-side front wheel was torn off the axle. The steering wheel was wrenched violently from my grasp and we plunged out of control off the road into the bush. The Land-Rover slewed sideways on and then it rolled over and over coming to a rest on its side.

'Judith,' I said, 'Judith.' But there was no reply. I dived back across the cab and found Judith, she was unconscious, crumpled against her door like a rag doll. I pulled her out as gently as I could. In the distance I heard the sound of men crashing through the bush, coming after us. I picked up Judith in my arms and staggered away from the wrecked Land-Rover. I was badly bruised and shaken and I couldn't go very far. I fought my way through some thick scrub and collapsed by the side of an anthill. The men were still plunging through the bush after us. Even now—in the darkness just before dawn—I knew that our trail would be easy to follow.

A green flare burst high in the sky and drifted down over our homestead signalling that van Staden and our neighbours had arrived. But they were too far away to be of any help to us. The sounds of pursuit were coming closer and closer. Judith and I were cornered, we had no other place to run to. I had lost my rifle, all I had left was a Webley .38 pistol. Judith was still unconscious. I fired four shots at the men advancing remorselessly at us through the bush, hoping to do as much damage as possible, then I placed the gun muzzle against her temple. I knew that it would be better this way—neither of us wanted to be taken alive. I was steeling myself to squeeze the trigger when the voice of one of my old miners said from the darkness close by, 'Mambo, Mambo don't shoot anymore. We've come to help you.'

'Who is it?' I shouted. 'Who's that?'

One by one my miners came out of the darkness. They had armed themselves with picks and shovels and lumps of wood. They had been unable to do anything before but now they

411

were ready to protect us from the terrorists if they could. I had prepared myself and Judith to die and now I was filled with gratitude to them.

The terrorists had taken many casualties and they broke off the attack and fled, with my neighbours, led by van Staden, harassing them all the way. The military arrived at daybreak and they radioed for an ambulance for Judith.

My miners made up a litter and helped me to carry her up to the road beyond the ford. Judith was barely conscious. I knew that there was something seriously wrong with her for she was experiencing a tremendous amount of pain. 'Oh Patrick,' she whispered to me, 'my neck, my arms, oh my neck, my arms. I feel so much pain in them.' I could find no limbs broken. She was having difficulty breathing. There was a small gash on her leg but she seemed to have no pain below her waist. We feared for our child but another terrible suspicion was forming in my mind. I prayed that she had just received a severe blow to her back coupled with shock, and I refused to let myself think any further.

CHAPTER TWENTY-NINE

DAYLIGHT revealed the full extent of the damage. The security forces moved into the area in strength. They set up a command post and the mine seemed filled with vehicles and men and shouted commands. A crack unit of troops was picking up the terrorist tracks and preparing for the follow up.

Phillimon's body was found in the wrecked house. When they brought me the news of his death, I felt only numbness. The sorrow, the pain would come later.

Judith and I waited forlornly by the side of the road for the ambulance to come, still stunned by the shock of the attack, our home and mine in ruins. Neighbours came to offer their help but I waved them away. I wanted no one near Judith. Time dragged by. I held her hand, tried to comfort her, to keep the sun off her face, the flies away.

Eventually an armoured and mine protected ambulance arrived and we set off over bumpy dirt roads to Gwelo Hospital. It was an old fashioned, double-storeyed, white-painted building on the outskirts of town.

We wheeled Judith into the Casualty Section and waited impatiently while someone went in search of the Duty Doctor. Eventually the

413

doctor arrived and I was excluded from the cubicle while he and a sister examined Judith.

I made myself wait quietly. After what seemed like an age Judith emerged on a trolley dressed in hospital clothes.

'There is serious spinal trauma, but I think there's no immediate danger to the life of your wife or child,' the doctor said reassuringly. 'I've given her something to ease the pain. She's being admitted to a single ward where we can keep an eye on her. We'll take X-rays and other tests when we've stabilized her condition.'

Judith's eyes were closed, an oxygen mask over her face. An orderly wheeled her along an empty high-ceilinged corridor. I took her hand to give her courage and walked beside her. Our footsteps echoed. I was conscious of the bitter disinfectant hospital smell. After the warmth of the sunlit morning it was like entering a tomb. We took the lift to the second floor and from there it was a short distance to a single, spartan, white-painted ward.

A sister and two nurses were waiting. They efficiently transferred Judith into the bed. I was ushered from the room. 'There's nothing more you can do here,' the sister said. 'Come back in visiting hours.' One of the nurses handed me a paper bag. 'Here, she said kindly, 'perhaps you'd like to have these cleaned.' I glanced into the room before the door closed on me. I could just make out the fragile, pale figure of my

Judith. She looked so helpless, so pathetic lost in a hospital bed. As I went down in the lift I opened the bag. Inside were her clothes. I carried them out of the hospital. After being so close, so dependent on each other, this was the first time I really felt separated from Judith and I hated it. I was filled with the fear of losing her.

I spent the afternoon with the police and then found myself a place to stay. I went back to see Judith that evening. She was on a drip and only semi-conscious. I sat by her bed and held her hand. She couldn't speak but she knew I was there and it reassured her.

Within two days Judith's condition stabilized enough for the hospital staff to begin tests. The resident surgical officer had taken over her case. He was a dapper, immaculately-dressed, slim built man who, due to the war and the shortage of staff, had stayed on well past retirement age. At first glance his approach was reserved, rather old fashioned. But what he lacked in modern medical knowledge he made up in experience and beneath that reserve lay great compassion for his patients.

He was studying Judith's X-rays as I entered his office and sat down. 'First results show that your wife has a fractured dislocation of the neck between the fifth and sixth cervical and a severely damaged spinal cord,' he said quietly. 'I do not think that she will ever walk again. However, she can have her baby. It has not been injured and there is a good chance of it being perfectly normal.'

I had guessed it would be bad, but I didn't believe that it would be that bad and I just sat there, stunned. 'Let me see now,' the doctor continued, trying to give me something to hope for. 'She is entering her seventh month. We can perform a Caesarian operation in her thirty-eighth week provided the baby remains well.'

'What about my wife? Will carrying the baby increase the danger to her.'

'Yes. There is always a risk of intercurrent diseases. We can only watch her and try to keep her in good health. If her condition deteriorates we can perform an immediate Caesarian with a fair chance that the child will survive.'

'If there is to be any choice between my wife or our child,' I said quietly, 'understand me, I want my wife.'

'Very soon now,' the doctor replied, 'we are going to have to tell your wife of the seriousness of her condition. At that time she will badly need something to live for, and the child may be all that she has. I do not believe that the risk outweighs the emotional value of that child.'

'Is there any hope at all for her recovery?' I asked.

The doctor thought about stalling me for a moment and then his professional honesty prevailed and he shook his head. 'As her state of shock recedes she may recover more use of her arms and her breathing may ease, but that's all. I don't believe she'll ever walk again. I'm sorry.'

As I stood outside his office door the full implication that Judith was paralysed with no hope of recovery hit me, and I started to shake. A wave of nausea swept through me and I barely made it to the lavatory.

I went back to the mine. Our neighbours and miners had salvaged what they could of our possessions and placed them in Phillimon's old shack which had been left undamaged. That night I wandered alone through the wreckage of our home, black with depression. I had some liquor with me. It was the first time since I'd heard the news that I'd been able to let myself go. Judith and I had faced many dangers together and the attack on the mine had always been half expected, but the sheer uselessness of it all was more than I could bear—and the nature of her injury was so final. I could re-open a mine, help rebuild a country, but I couldn't give Judith back her legs.

I felt so alone. 'God,' I screamed blind drunk at the night sky, 'why have you done this? I've tried so many times and each time I try again you find a way to kick me down. And now look what you've done to my Judith.'

I dried out through the next day and gathered my strength. Then an old miner who had been with me since the start, lead a deputation to see me. 'Mambo,' he said quietly, knowing I was

417

grieving, 'the terrorists have burnt our homes too. We have lost the mine and everything we have. What shall we do now? Do you want us to go away?'

The country was in such a precarious state that new work was almost impossible to find and without it they would starve. I knew clearly what Judith would want me to do. 'No,' I said to him, 'we have not lost everything. There is still gold in the ground. We'll clear the shaft and start again.' I made the old miner my mine captain and with the limited equipment that we could borrow we started again the laborious process of re-claiming the mine.

I returned to the hospital to find that an orthopaedic surgeon had put Judith into a spinal jacket which eased her pain; and soon afterwards our doctor told her the extent of her injuries. I visited Judith as he left. She was staring at the ceiling. She didn't have enough breath to cry properly but her eyes were streaming with tears. 'He told me that I would never walk again,' she whispered, as I came up beside her bed. 'He said that if I had the will to live he could build me up and he's sure that I'll have a fairly happy life, but I'll never walk again. Did you know that?' I nodded. 'Oh Patrick,' she whispered brokenly, 'I want to die.'

I couldn't hold her in my arms so I clung desperately to her hands trying to will her my strength. 'Judith,' I said, 'I love you and I need you and so does our child. No matter what happens to your legs, you'll always be my Judith, my Ballerina. I couldn't live without you—and our child. He told you, didn't he? We could still have our child.' Judith wasn't listening to me. She was just staring at the ceiling growing dead inside.

Visiting hours ended. I had protested in the past at being parted from Judith, but to no avail. This time when the sister came to switch out the main lights and kick me out, I flatly refused to budge. The sister summoned the matron who ruled the district hospital with a rod of iron. The matron left her rounds and came sweeping down the corridor, accustomed to her authority, she fixed me with a steely eye. 'I'm sorry,' she said firmly, 'but those are my rules.'

And unnerved by such a massive display of female authority, I left quietly. I stood outside the hospital and looked up at the glow of light in Judith's window. I remembered all the love and loyalty that she had given me. I could imagine how she was feeling now—so frightened and so alone—and that decided me. For a miner used to climbing around in the underground, the side of the building presented no problem. I swarmed up a drainpipe, side-stepped along a small ledge and climbed in through her window. I took Judith's hand and tried to will her my strength—tried to become so close, so much part of her, that I could take some of her pain and fear upon my shoulders, and make her feel that she was not alone.

The sister found me later that night and threw me out, but I just went straight up the side of the building and in through Judith's window again. The matron and the sister realized that they would have to nail that window shut if they wanted to keep me out and then I would probably break through the glass, so they ignored me.

Judith's parents arrived, her mother bringing with her the best neuro-surgeon in Southern Africa that money could buy. The great man dominated the hospital for a few days, but he could do nothing that would help. Judith's mother blamed me for this—she blamed me for the farm attack. She treated me like the murderer of her daughter. After doing as much damage as possible, she returned to South Africa, leaving Judith even more depressed.

The doctor and I cast around for a means to repair the damage. There were several war wounded in the hospital, most of them young men, and with a stroke of genius the doctor introduced them to Judith. They visited her whenever they could and they worked miracles for her. I noticed the change almost immediately. A special spirit grows in a hospital amongst the crippled and the badly maimed. They develop a sense of humour coupled with a complete lack of self-pity and they have imbued in them, as they struggle to be normal, a kind of fierce defiance against the fate that brought them their wounds.

I learned this one night as I sat by Judith's bed and heard the stealthy creek of wheels and limping footfalls coming down the corridor towards us. Judith smiled.

'My friends are coming,' she whispered. 'They want to meet you.' The door opened a crack and the first visitor, a good-looking blond-haired man, entered the room. He was on crutches—he had only one leg and his left hand was missing. I learned that he had been in the Military Engineers and he had left those limbs behind in a mine field. The next man was in a wheelchair and pushing him with most of his head still covered in bandages, was a blind man from my old unit. The last man in a wheelchair closed the door. He was a round-shaped, happy little fellow with two good hands but no legs at all. They gathered around the bed and from within their hospital dressing gowns they produced smuggled bottles of wine and fruit. They were bubbling with humour, brimful of laughter, and from that moment the party was on.

They wandered about the hospital, those men, known collectively as the sick, the lame and the blind, visiting patients who needed cheering up. They took a pride in being completely undisciplined. They fought running battles with the matron and her staff, delighting in having something to rebel against, and they seemed to adore Judith. Unlike the other patients, her permanent injuries made her one of them and so she was very special.

They taught me a lot about coping with Judith. Where I was concerned because she could not lift her head to drink, they teased her good-naturedly and fed her sips of wine through a straw. Judith responded—she didn't feel different with them and so she relaxed in their company. Watching her I felt a momentary twinge of jealousy for those men.

Judith had always had tremendous courage and it came through now. She cast off her depression and with it all self-pity. She seemed to gain enormously in inner strength. She learned to cope with her injury and she began to look forward to the future. We talked a lot about our child—planning for it gave us such great pleasure. It reached a stage where Judith accepted her injury much more easily than I did.

★   ★   ★

I still had not brought the mine back to producing gold and our capital was running out. The water had flooded the underground machinery and the mill had to be re-built. Equipment was almost impossible to obtain and the problems seemed to be almost insurmountable.

I realized that I was spending too much time away from the mine. So I worked a full day underground and then drove the round trip of a hundred and sixty miles to see Judith, arriving at the hospital late and tired. When the matron realized this, I found a thermos flask of steaming coffee left as though by chance near the window ledge in Judith's room and then a plate of sandwiches. No one said anything, but I realized that there was a human side to that matron after all.

Judith used to wait for my visits. She carried a complete picture of her garden in her head and she used to instruct me as to what areas needed watering and enquire into the progress of her plants. She also followed closely the progress of the mine. At first I made out that all was well and that we were bringing the mine back into production as planned, but she soon found me out.

'We're in trouble,' she said one night, sensing my worry. 'We're going broke, aren't we?'

I shrugged my shoulders, too tired to lie. 'Yes, we could go down,' I admitted. 'But I don't want you worrying about it. Judith', I reassured her earnestly, 'we've been broke before—we can always start again.'

Judith looked at me with tears of love in her eyes, and then she began to laugh. I had expected the opposite, then suddenly I understood her. We had made it almost to the top and been kicked all the way down. The country and the mines were in terrible trouble and she was in a hospital bed. All right, so we had reached bottom and now the only way was up again if we had the courage—and Judith had plenty of courage. She didn't give up. Things grew bad on the mine, but she kept me going.

The doctor warned us that in any event we would have to give up mining because Judith couldn't go into the bush again—she would always have to remain near doctors. We accepted that this would be the case at least for a while after she came out of hospital and we started planning what we would do. I had no business qualifications and anyway working for other people was out unless I was absolutely desperate. I had to find something I could make myself. I came up with various ideas which Judith rejected. I grew quite interested in plastics, and then I invented a revolutionary type of screw with an adjustable head. Very excitedly I presented my sketches to Judith and she laughed joyously—not at the design but at me—because in all the time she had known me I hadn't changed. I was totally convinced that that screw was going to make our fortunes.

'Oh Patrick,' she said warmly, 'I love it,' and she rested my hand against her cheek.

Strangely, at that time of greatest uncertainty,

we felt secure, more certain of a future together, whatever it might be, than ever before. We were happy, filled with the joy of our child which was due very soon and we endlessly made plans for it. Judith was worried about not being able to care for the baby properly when she left the hospital. 'I must be able to use my arms enough to wash it and hold it,' she would say determinedly. 'Patrick, I'm so looking forward to the baby—it's all I think about when things look black.'

The time arrived. I questioned the doctor about Judith's condition. We both knew the risks, but he felt they were acceptable and he prepared Judith for a Caesarian operation. I was waiting when they wheeled her out of the operating room.

'Oh Patrick,' she smiled, still drugged with anaesthetic but her face so filled with joy. 'Aren't I a clever girl? I've given you a beautiful child.'

They placed the baby beside Judith and left us alone. I looked at my son and then at my wife—both were safe. Tears of relief streamed down my face; I didn't make a sound but I couldn't stop them—I'd never been so happy.

Judith seemed to be recovering from the operation very well and then on the third day when I came to visit her I found the nursing staff fussing around her bed. 'You can't see her just yet,' the sister said. 'We're giving her oxygen.'

I waited for the doctor. I knew that he had grown fond of Judith and I trusted him. 'I think she has pneumonia,' the doctor said to me.

'Is that serious?'

'I don't know yet,' the doctor replied, but it was obvious to me that he was worried.

I sat outside Judith's door as long as I could. I had been warned of a post-operative risk, but I thought that she was past the dangerous time. The child had been delivered safely. Judith and I had come so far I couldn't believe anything could go wrong now. The nurses were busy outside Judith's room and it was obvious that they didn't want me to interfere. In the end they sent me home.

I returned the next day. Judith was sinking fast. Her lungs were just giving up the struggle. The doctor had remained with her nearly the whole time and I believe that he fought for her life as grimly as he knew how.

I watched helplessly the disciplined rush of nursing staff pass to and fro. Judith became unconscious and in the early hours of the morning she died.

The staff left me alone. I sat unmoving outside Judith's door hour after hour. I was beyond tears, beyond sorrow. My shoulders sagged for at last I was finally and totally defeated.

I heard footsteps coming down the corridor

towards me. I didn't look up. Wordlessly the matron placed my child in my arms and walked hurriedly on. I held it stiffly. I didn't want the child. I wanted my Judith. I looked down unwillingly at my tiny son and then I saw Judith clearly there in his face. So that was what she had left me—my remaining link with her. The baby cried, his face reflecting the triumph and the rage of his struggle to be born. I held him close to me. I began to rock him to soothe him . . . and my heart broke for love of my Judith.

EPILOGUE

I GLANCED across the high-ceilinged open plan office to the clock on the far wall. There were just a few minutes to go until five o'clock. The other clerks were surreptitiously glancing at the clock too, but none of them dared to pack up their papers before the buzzer sounded the end of the day. I knew that if I remained here, working amongst these sad drone-like men much longer, I'd lose my mind. And this time there was no phone to ring—no voice to say I love you.

I had returned to the city—right back to where I had started. I lived amongst the claustrophobic walls of a tiny one-bedroomed flat with the noise of traffic roaring past the windows. My life was routine—I had responsibilities now. In the mornings I took my small son to the creche, collecting him after work and on Sundays he and I played in the park.

Every month I sent what little money I could spare to the old man who had contacted me after Judith died. He and I had formulated a plan—tenuous dream of starting again—which provided me with enough hope to get me through each day and I felt myself not totally defeated.

The buzzer sounded. I rose from my desk and joined the crowds who were surging through the doors. I stood on the steps for a moment basking in the warmth of the late afternoon sunlight. And then suddenly my heart lifted for I saw a rusted, battered old lorry with mining equipment and supplies piled into the back. I could hardly believe it. There had been times when I thought he would never make it back. The lorry was parked in everyone's way, right in the midst of the car park. And there was the old man—wild looking as ever and brown from the sun and the wind, dressed in his bush hat and ragged prospecting clothes, waiting impatiently by the running board.

He waved his hat. 'I've found it,' he shouted excitedly when he spotted me—oblivious to the amazed glances he was getting from the passers-by. 'It's as fine a little reef as you could wish for,

428

Patrick, with gold enough to get us started. Come on,' he called impatiently to me, 'let's get going.'

I pushed my way through the crowd towards him, mentally shrugging off the office, the city and all the defeats. I felt a new lease of life begin tingling inside me. I knew that within a few hours we could be heading for the backveld. Tonight we would camp in the bush beneath a raging sky, with space to move and tomorrow was a dusty road to freedom. And I was filled with joy.

'We'll need to stop off and pick up my son,' I said breathlessly to the old man as I reached him.

'I've already got him,' the old man answered. When in town he acted as the boy's second father. He knew the trouble I was experiencing from my mother-in-law who had tried every means at her disposal to remove the child from my care. 'Don't worry,' he assured me. 'She'll never find us where we're going.'

The lorry, with the three of us in the front seat, ground slowly through the city traffic. The next day marked the third anniversary of the birth of Zimbabwe and workers were frantically engaged in putting the finishing touches to the flags and posters which lined the streets where the parade would take place. For the old man and I and many others the birth of Zimbabwe had meant the end of the Rhodesia we knew.

The death of the old dreams would bring the birth of new ones . . . perhaps.

The lorry left town for the open road, rattling and groaning as the ancient vehicle picked up speed.

'So it's agreed,' I said, looking to the future. 'If we can build a big enough stake out of this new reef, we go back and re-open the Bismarck mine.'

'Agreed,' the old man answered. He turned to the child perched on the seat between us. 'Where we're going,' he continued, 'you're sure to see elephants and perhaps rhinoceroses and hippopotamuses too.'

'Will we see lions?'

'Lions too,' he nodded.

When it came to telling a story there was no one to beat the old man. He could hypnotise you, make you feel the freedom of the warm sun on your shoulders, the smell of the bush in the dawn. 'You can't buy a dream, boy,' the old man said, 'you've got to go find one for yourself.' He grinned his wild magnetic grin. 'That's what we're doing.' And the little boy with Judith's eyes smiled up at him with excitement.

Photoset, printed and bound in Great Britain by REDWOOD BURN LIMITED, Trowbridge, Wiltshire